The Love Letter Ghost

Experience the Magic ~
Feel the Love

M.E. Saladino

The Love Letter Ghost

Copyright © 2022 by M.E. Saladino

All rights reserved

Published by Red Penguin Books

Bellerose Village, New York

Library of Congress Control Number: 2021922365

ISBN

Print 978-1-63777-175-4 / 978-1-63777-228-7 / 978-1-63777-229-4

Digital 978-1-63777-176-1

The Love Letter Ghost is a work of fiction. All incidents and dialogue between any historical figures are products of the author's imagination and are not to be construed as real or meant to depict true events. In all other respects, any resemblance to actual persons, living or dead, events, or locals is entirely coincidental.

This book is dedicated to my husband, Carmine, and to my late husband, Robert.
Both of these wonderful men contributed, each in his own special way, to make this book possible.

CONTENTS

Part One

Chapter One
The Break-Up

"The wedding is off!"

What?

Mac's brain went numb, and his heart felt like an over-chewed wad of gum in his chest. "What did you say?"

Angie's long red hair fell forward while staring down at her unfinished cocktail. Without lifting her gaze, she tucked the wayward locks behind her ear. "The wedding is off," she whispered as if a softer tone could possibly ease the pain those words inflicted on Mac.

"Wha—wha—what do you mean, the wedding is off?"

Slowly, Angie lifted tear-filled eyes. "I just can't marry you, that's all," she cried, springing from her seat.

Mac's arm shot across the table and grabbed Angie's wrist, knocking her glass to the floor. Diners at nearby tables gawked at them when it shattered on impact.

"Oh my God! I'm so sorry, Ang. C'mon, *please* sit down," he begged, releasing her.

Angie just stared at him. Her chin trembled, but she remained silent.

A busboy appeared with a dustpan and broom, and Mac tried to read Angie's face while he cleaned up the shards of crystal and what was left of her drink. *What is she hiding from me? What is she feeling? Sadness? Confusion? Fear?*

Sobbing now, Angie collapsed into her chair.

Mac wrapped his hands around her delicate fingers, gently stroking her palms, silently wishing she had slapped him—he could deal with that. Tears were a whole different matter.

"Aw, please don't cry, honey," he said and gave her his handkerchief.

Angie blew her nose. "I can't help it," she said between sniffles as she squeezed the handkerchief tightly in her hand.

"Then tell me what's going on. We're getting married in two months. How can you say the wedding is off? *Why* would you say that?"

"I can't explain. Not now."

"Oh, c'mon, angel face. What is it, baby? You know you can tell me anything." Mac brought her hands close to his lips, brushing them with tender kisses. "You know I love you."

Angie just shook her head.

With one hand under her chin, Mac turned her face toward him. "All right, then let's go back to my place and talk this over in private, okay? Don't worry, honey. We'll work this out together. Is that better?"

She just glanced sideways, avoiding his pleading eyes.

Mac felt like he was treading water after being pushed overboard in the dark. He wracked his brain trying to figure out why the woman he loved just called off their wedding; and if he didn't do something quick, he'd drown for sure.

"Omigod! Omigod! Omigod!"

Huh? Mac's head snapped up.

A bubbly teenager with hot pink hair sidled up to their table.

"Omigod! Omigod! Omigod!" she shrieked. "Is it you? Is it

really you? Are you like, you know, Conrad MacConnell, the writer?"

Here we go. The last thing I need tonight is an enthusiastic fan. "Yeah, that's me. Guilty as charged, but..."

The perky teen bobbed up and down like a cork on a fishing line. "Sweet! I mean, awesome—no, sweet!" Unable to contain herself, she waved her hand in front of her face like a southern belle with the vapors. "Omigod! Omigod! Omigod!"

Angie did a dramatic eye roll while she gushed.

"Could I, like, you know, have your autograph? I just read *Intrigue at the Inn.* It was *totally* the bomb, and I think you're *totally* hot."

"Well, thank you very much, miss; but I'm in the middle of something personal here."

Ignoring Mac's protests, she cuddled beside him, held up her phone, and smiled for a selfie. When the flash went off, Angie scooped up her handbag. "I have to go," she said and sprang from her seat.

Mac jumped up dashing after her. "No, Angie—wait!"

"Hey. What about my autograph?"

Mac caught up with Angie in two bounding steps. The heels of his shoes skidded on the wood floor when she did an abrupt about-face. "Mac, I'm only going to the ladies' room."

"Oh...I knew that," he said unconvincingly. "I was just—uh, stretching my legs."

Angie blew out a sigh, turned, and walked away.

Mac slapped his forehead with his palm. *What the hell's the matter with me? Women always go to the ladies' room, especially when they're upset. It's their sanctuary—a neutral zone. I should've known that.* With a helpless shrug, he shuffled back to their table where his over-excited fan waited.

"Look, miss. I'm very sorry, but this really isn't a very good time for autographs."

Her painted bottom lip stuck out so far, her feet were in its shadow.

"Why don't you give me your address? My secretary will mail you an autographed book."

"Oh, this will only take a minute," she said, pushing down the right side of her jeans. A tattoo of Mac's face stared back at him from her hip.

Holy shit!

Mac wasn't a man who blushed easily, but the sight of a shapely nymph dropping her pants in front of him lit a pilot light under his collar, and he loosened his tie with a quick tug. Snickers and laughter rippled through the restaurant when she handed him a felt-tipped marker and said, "Make it out to Candi, with an 'i'."

The heat under Mac's collar crept higher, burning his ears. He stared with disbelief at the marker in his hand and Candi's unblemished skin, except for the tattoo, of course. "Are you over eighteen?"

Candi reached over to the left side of her jeans. "Well, duh. Of course, I am, silly. See, it says my birthday is..."

Oh my God. Now she's taking off her clothes. "No! Stop! I believe you."

"I was just gonna show you my ID. It's in my pocket."

"Oh."

Mac aimed a glance toward the ladies' room door. No sign of Angie. Oh, what the hell. He wasn't going anywhere now, so he took a deep breath and scribbled something resembling his name under his unflattering image as beads of sweat sprouted on his forehead.

Satisfied, Candi zipped up her jeans. "Thanks! I'm gonna post this right now," she said, bouncing back to her table, as her thumbs danced over the keypad of her phone.

"Show's over, folks," Mac said to the amused diners like a

jaded detective and plopped down in his chair. Grabbing his napkin, he wiped the sweat from his brow and waited for Angie. Five minutes passed. Then ten. Mac was drumming his fingers on the table when the waiter brought their dinners.

"Is there anything else I can get for you, sir?" he asked.

"Yes. You can pack these meals in a box to go. My fiancée and I will be leaving as soon as she returns from the powder room."

"You mean that hot-looking babe in the smokin' black dress?"

Overcome by an unexpected surge of jealousy, Mac narrowed his eyes at the waiter. "Yeah. That's the one."

"She just left the restaurant."

"She what?" Mac flew out of his chair. "Out of my way!"

The waiter folded his arms across his chest. "Not until you pay your bill."

"Oh, for chrissake!" Mac grumbled as he tore into his wallet, threw a wad of cash on the table, and shoved the man aside.

"But your change..."

"Keep it!"

No one was laughing now as Mac charged through the busy dining room, bursting through the door in time to see Angie hop in the back of a yellow cab and watch it drive away. Breaking into a run for his car, Mac tumbled in, thrust the key in the ignition, and peeled out of the parking lot. Horns honked and tires screeched when he swerved into the next lane as he fumbled for his cell phone and dialed Angie's number.

"Hang up the phone and drive, asshole!" shouted an irate driver, flipping Mac the bird.

Usually quick tempered, Mac would have lashed out in return, but he wasn't aware of the insult or the offensive gesture as he jockeyed his SUV through traffic like a seasoned NASCAR driver vying for position.

"Will you tell that driver to stop!" he screamed when Angie picked up on her cell. "I just want to talk to you!"

"No! I called for a cab to take me home when I was in the ladies' room so I wouldn't *have* to talk to you."

"But, Ang..."

"There's nothing more to discuss, Mac. Now stop following me," she told him and disconnected. Then the cab accelerated, blasting through a yellow light, leaving Mac behind.

"I can't lose her now."

The wide tires on Mac's SUV screeched when he punched the gas pedal, tearing through the intersection like a slingshot as the light turned red. *Why is she doing this to me—I mean to us? Why? Why? Why?* A blaring siren and blue lights flashing in his rearview mirror jolted Mac out of his misery.

Overpowered by a nauseating sense of defeat, he slowed down, rolling to a stop into a Snappy Mart convenience store parking lot. The siren quit and the lights dimmed on the Nassau County cruiser that angled behind his SUV as he watched the cab *and* Angie disappear into the night like a rogue star down a black hole. Crunching footsteps approached seconds later. And as Mac lowered the driver's side window, all he could see in the dark was light from a parking lot lamp post reflected off a shiny chrome belt buckle.

"May I see your license and registration, please?" asked the burly officer.

"Sure, Constable." Mac produced the documents.

The patrolman chuckled under his breath, aiming the beam from his flashlight in Mac's face. "You can call me Officer Ritter."

Mac flinched from the sudden brightness. "Sure thing, Officer Ritter. What seems to be the problem?"

"Do you know how fast you were going, sir?"

"Uh...I don't know. As fast as the cab in front of me?"

Officer Ritter bent at the waist until he was at eye level with Mac. "Well, then, let me rephrase the question. Do you know how fast you were going when you were speeding *and* went through a red light?"

"Oh. Uh...no. Not exactly, but I can explain everything," stuttered Mac. "You see, my fiancée just broke our engagement and took off in that cab I was following. I was about to catch up with her when you pulled me over."

The officer's eyebrows shot up. Standing erect at his full intimidating height, an amused smirk spread across his face as he flipped open his ticket book. "Is that the best you can do? I usually get the my-wife-is-having-a-baby story."

"It's true! I swear, and she's getting away!"

"Maybe she doesn't *want* you to catch up with her. Ever think of that?"

Mac dropped his head against the steering wheel and moaned, "It's not fair. It's just not fair."

"I've got news for you, sir. Life's not fair," said Officer Ritter as he wrote a ticket. Mac winced when he ripped it out.

"That's it? Just one for speeding?" asked Mac, expecting a citation for both violations.

"Yeah, I'm in a generous mood tonight."

"Great. So are we done here?" asked Mac, stowing the ticket in his wallet. "Can I leave now?"

The officer slapped the ticket book closed. "No! Just stay where you are, sir. You're not out of the woods yet."

Turning on his heel, Officer Ritter strode back to his squad car. He returned ten minutes later and handed Mac his license and registration. "You check out okay, Mr. MacConnell, so why don't you go home and stay out of trouble."

"Works for me. I just need a few minutes to make an important call."

The officer threw Mac a threatening look. "Works for me, too, as long as you behave."

"Sure thing. No problem. Whatever you say," he replied, forcing a smile.

Officer Ritter arched one questioning brow and shook his head before lumbering back to the Nassau County cruiser. Stuffing his large frame behind the wheel, he cranked the engine, sending pebbles flying as he skidded out of the parking lot.

Mac let out a labored sigh, his breath visible in the crisp fall air like wispy puffs of smoke, as he pushed the door of his SUV open. Climbing out, he ran his fingers through his hair and over his face. *No use trying to catch up with the cab. Angie's probably home by now anyway. But it's getting late and if there's any chance of talking to her tonight, I have to act fast.* Whipping out his cell, he dialed her number again.

"Hello," Angie said, sounding listless and tired.

"Hi, baby. We have to talk. I'm coming over."

"Mac, no!"

"I have to. It's the only way I'll get any answers from you."

"Please, Mac. Don't make this more difficult than it has to be."

"But I don't get it, Ang. What the hell is going on? I must have done something. Just tell me what it is, and I'll never do it again, okay? Then we can forget this ever happened and get married just like we planned."

"It's not that simple," she said with a woeful sigh.

"Then talk to me! I'm going crazy here!" he shouted while walking around the empty lot. "My fiancée dumps me for no apparent reason, runs away, and I'm just supposed to accept that without an explanation?"

"I know it doesn't make much sense to you right now."

"You're damn right it doesn't!"

"I can't help that. The wedding is off! I need some time to myself, so don't call me anymore."

"But...but..."

The line went dead.

"I don't freakin' believe this!"

"Are you being okay, mister?"

Catching a whiff of curry and mulligatawny, Mac whirled around. A tall man with gaunt features stepped out of the shadows. The bulb from a singular lamp post illuminated him like a spotlight while his sandaled feet shuffled uncomfortably.

Mac glowered at him. "Who the hell are you?"

He regarded Mac from a safe distance with eyes as black as the hair that poked out from under his turban. "I am working at this Snappy Mart store."

"Well, I'm alright. I just got some bad news."

"So sorry to hear, mister, but you cannot stay here. This lot is for the Snappy Mart customers only."

"Fine. I'll take a pack of Juicy Fruit."

"Oh, you will have to buy more than that."

"Then forget about the gum, pal. I'll be out of here in a few minutes."

"That is okay with me." The clerk turned and scurried into the store.

Thwarted by Angie's refusal to talk, Mac began pacing erratically around the asphalt lot, his arms slashing the air as if dueling an imaginary foe as he ranted. "Shit like this only happens to characters in my novels. Not to me! Too bad I can't write myself out of this scene, or can I? What would one of my characters do? He'd man-up and try to call his girlfriend one last time before battering down her door, figuratively speaking of course."

Stopping short, Mac dialed Angie's number. No answer. It didn't even go to voicemail. Realizing her phone was turned off, he uttered a string of expletives that would make a longshoreman blush and hurled his phone aimlessly in frustration. It broke apart, bouncing off the glass window of the Snappy Mart.

"That's it! I'm going over there right now! I don't care how late it is!"

Mac gathered up the pieces and quickly reassembled his phone. The battery was low, but there was no time to charge it now. He dropped it in his pocket while heading for his SUV when a car flew into the lot and screeched to a halt. Mac shuddered at the ominous sound of crunching footsteps as the glow from a high-powered flashlight darted around like a beacon. He squinted when the beam settled on his face.

"Oh. It's you," said Officer Ritter. "I thought you'd be home by now."

Reaching for the driver's side door on his SUV, Mac said, "I was just on my way, actually."

"Well, don't leave yet. I got a report of a disturbance at this Snappy Mart, and I want to ask you a few questions."

Mac's arm dropped to his side. "Okay, shoot—I mean sure."

The officer shook his head. "Don't tempt me, Mr. MacConnell." He swept the lot again with the flashlight. "It seems pretty quiet here. Have you seen any suspicious activity in the past few minutes?"

Mac stuffed his hands in his pockets, rocking back on his heels. "Nope. Everything's just hunky-dory,"

"Hunky-dory? Who the hell says hunky-dory?"

"A-OK?"

Officer Ritter rolled his eyes.

"That is him, Officer! That is the man who is breaking into

my store!" yelled the excited clerk from the doorway. "Arrest him! Arrest him!"

"I'll handle this, Mr. Gupta. You can go now," said the officer, waving him inside.

"What's he talking about?" asked Mac.

"Mr. Gupta called in the report. According to him, a man was running around the parking lot like he was crazy. Said he threw a rock at the window—tried to break into his store."

Mac observed Mr. Gupta peeking around the cash register.

"Uh...that was probably me," he confessed, looking down at his shoes. "But I wasn't trying to rob him. And I didn't mean to hit the window with my cell phone either."

"What the hell is the matter with you? You scared the crap out of that man!"

"I guess you could say I let my emotions get the better of me." Mac turned and gave the frightened clerk a friendly wave. Mr. Gupta ducked behind the counter faster than a carnival game target.

Officer Ritter's brows knitted. His eyes narrowed to slits, staring accusingly at Mac. "Have you been drinking since I last saw you?"

"No! No!" Mac vowed. "Not yet anyway."

"This is no time to be a wise guy, Mr. MacConnell. Maybe I should arrest you. It'll make Mr. Gupta *very* happy."

Mac blanched. "Arrest me? You can't be serious." He could see the headlines now: *Famous murder mystery writer arrested for attempted convenience store robbery with a loaded cell phone.* "Couldn't I just tell him I'm sorry? I'll go home and never bother him again." Mac placed his right hand over his heart. "I promise."

"Good. There are real criminals on the streets, and I don't have time to babysit you all night just because you broke up with your girlfriend."

"Uh...for the record, Officer, *she* broke up with *me*."

The officer's nostrils flared. "I don't care if she broke up with the whole seventh fleet!" he roared as an unusual shade of crimson slowly spread across his face. "Just wait in your vehicle while I talk Mr. Gupta out of pressing charges. I hate paperwork," he mumbled and turned.

"But first, I have to see my fiancée," added Mac.

The heels of the officer's boots dug in the gravel when he spun around. "I don't think you heard me, Mr. MacConnell," he said, jabbing a finger in Mac's face. "Either you go home *now* and stay out of trouble, or you get a free night's stay compliments of the county. You decide."

"All right, all right. I'll go," groaned Mac, sliding behind the wheel of his car.

Chapter Two
The Morning After

A rumbling garbage truck roused Mac early the next morning. His eyelids felt weighted, and as he pried them open, thoughts of Angie and the worst evening of his life instantly replayed in his mind, along with the vague memory of a bottle of tequila.

Heads turned throughout the restaurant when Mac and Angie entered the crowded dining room the night before. There wasn't a female out of her training bra who didn't fall for Mac's liquid amber eyes and rugged masculinity, and their eyes devoured him as if he were a tasty treat on the dessert cart. He ignored their hungry stares but smiled inwardly when envious men ogled Angie muttering, "Lucky bastard," under their breaths.

Mac shook his head, remembering that a recording of Dean Martin crooned *That's Amore* as they followed the hostess to their table. How ironic a song about love preceded a new chapter in his life without it.

"I'll have another Cosmo," Angie told the hostess and stumbled.

Mac frowned as he caught her elbow. She had already chugged down two of the potent pink cocktails at the bar.

"Are you sure about that, honey?" he asked, easing her into her chair. "You know one's your limit."

Angie thumped her hand on the table rattling the silverware. "Damn skippy."

Mac's brows shot up. *Damn skippy?*

Turning to the hostess, he blew out a resigning sigh and said, "Please bring my fiancée another cocktail."

The hostess leaned forward, exposing ample cleavage above the neckline of her dress, as she placed two menus in front of Mac on the checkered tablecloth. "And what can I get for you, sir?" she asked, her eyes turning dark with a look suggesting more than a beverage.

"Uh...I'll *just* have a cola."

"I'll put your drink order in right away," she replied, unmoved by his rebuff.

Angie rolled her eyes.

Taking the seat facing Angie, Mac slid a menu to her past a wine bottle covered in candle wax drippings. "So, what'll it be tonight, Ang? Eggplant *parmesan* or linguini with..."

Mac blinked, watching in confused silence, as Angie unfolded her napkin, then crumpled it into a ball before finally spreading it flat over her lap. She rearranged the silverware three times before the waiter arrived with their drinks.

"Your Cosmopolitan, ma'am," he said, placing the wide martini glass on a cocktail napkin. "Your cola," he said to Mac and did the same. "Are you ready to order, sir?"

"Uh, yes," replied Mac. "We'll both have the linguini with white clam sauce."

"Excellent choice. Those clams were sleeping in the Great South Bay about an hour ago. They're so fresh we had to slap them," quipped the waiter, tucking the menus under his arm. "I'll be back in a moment with your bread."

Mac kept a wary eye on Angie. Her napkin was on the table again, and she was folding the piece of cloth like origami paper. *Is that a bird?*

"Is everything all right, sweetheart?" he asked, leaning forward.

Forgetting the napkin, Angie held up a shaky index finger while knocking back the Cosmo in one gulp. "Everything's peachy. Just peachy."

Mac's eyes widened when she slammed her empty glass on the table and wiped her mouth with the back of her hand. "Are you sure? You seem a little...jumpy."

"No, I'm fine, really."

He didn't believe that for a minute but decided to wait until after dinner to broach the subject again. "Well, in that case..."

"The wedding is off!"

In retrospect, Angie's behavior did seem a little odd. The eye rolls, chugging the Cosmos, the strange napkin folding, all out of character for his usually self-composed fiancée. Mac had attributed her behavior to a bad day at the office, never thinking she would utter the words that wrenched his heart from his chest like pages of a book ripped from their binding.

Swinging one leg at a time over the side of the mattress, Mac straightened, sitting upright, one creaky vertebra at a time. When his bare feet touched the cold wooden floor, a pathetic whimper was all he could muster as his insides shuddered like quivering gelatin.

"God, I feel like shit," he groaned.

Mac stood on shaky legs, almost tripping over his slacks and shirt lying on the floor beside the bed. "I'll never drink tequila again," he vowed, clutching his stomach. *Again? When did I ever drink tequila?*

Taking almost a full minute to steady himself, Mac staggered to the adjoining bathroom and flipped on the switch. Clamping his eyes shut against the sudden brightness, he planted his hands on either side of the sink and slowly lifted his head.

"Man, I look as bad as I feel," he sighed, squinting at his reflection in the mirror.

Dousing his stubbly cheeks with cold water sent a shiver through his body as he groped for a towel and dried his face. Clad in nothing but boxers, he pulled his robe from a hook on the bathroom door and headed to the kitchen for a much-needed cup of coffee, dragging the flannel garment behind him like a security blanket.

Mac made his way down the stairs with great care—or so he thought—unaware that his jacket was on the next riser. "Whoooa!" he cried as his feet flew out from under him. Unable to grip the handrail in his weakened condition, Mac's palms slid on the polished wood while bouncing down each step on the seat of his boxers. "Ow! Oof! Ow!" He stopped at the newel post, hanging onto the carved wooden finial like a high-rise window washer suspended on a faulty scaffold still clutching his robe.

The doorbell chimed.

What was that?

The fog in his brain began to lift. "Angie?" His heart raced.

Mac regained his footing and ran to the bay window in the living room. While shoving his arms into the sleeves of his robe, he tripped on one of his shoes, stubbed his toe, and fell over the coffee table. "Oof! Ow! Son of a...!"

The bell chimed again.

"I knew it! I knew she'd come back," he said face down, his voice muffled by the carpet.

Flushed with excitement now, he pulled himself up with newfound energy and limped to the window. Angie's car was parked at the curb, and a feeling of relief surged through his veins like a life-saving transfusion. *Everything's going to be all right now that she's back*, he thought, racing to the door.

"Oh, Angie, baby," he cried, throwing it open. "I'm so glad you're...Marie?"

"Sorry, Mac," said Angie's sister. "She's not here, it's just me."

Named after their paternal grandmother, Angelina Marie, in the order that they were born, the sisters shared no family resemblances, displayed no inherited physical features.

Movie star gorgeous with a chestnut-colored mane, Angie had dark brown eyes accented with long lashes most women would kill for. Tall and slim, she maintained her figure by eating just about anything she wanted. Marie's mousy brown hair did nothing for her nondescript features. To make matters worse, she stood a couple of inches shorter than Angie and gained weight if within a ten-mile radius of a piece of chocolate.

"Marie? What are you doing here?"

"God, Mac, you look like hell," she gasped.

"Forgive me if I'm not ready for my close-up, Mr. DeMille," he snapped. "My whole life got flushed down the toilet yesterday. Do you know what happened last night?"

Marie sighed. "Yeah, I heard."

"Then maybe you can tell me what's going on. Angie won't speak to me."

"I can't because I don't know anything either," said Marie, while rooting in her handbag. "All I know is that Angie insisted

I get here as soon as possible to give you this." She held a small, black velvet box in the palm of her hand.

"The ring?" Mac clutched the door for support. "She's giving back the ring?"

Until then, Mac had a glimmer of hope that Angie would come back to him. But returning the ring was final, like severing the last link that existed between them. The sudden reality tore him up inside, and he felt a lump in his throat the size of his Aunt Rita's bundt cake.

Marie shrugged helplessly.

Mac knew that ever since they were kids, Angie and Marie had each other's backs. But returning an engagement ring was way beyond the average childhood favor, and Marie looked as uncomfortable as a teenager confessing to wrecking the family car as she carried out her sisterly duty.

"Here, Mac. Take it," she urged, pushing the box toward him.

Hungry for information, Mac ignored her discomfort *and* the ring. "Did Angie give you a message for me?"

Marie shook her head.

"She *had* to say something."

"Sorry, Mac. This is it," said Marie, slapping the velvet box in his hand. "Gotta go." Then she hiked her bag on her shoulder and scurried to the car.

"Wait! Don't leave!"

Marie jerked the door open and hopped in. "Please start," she prayed, jamming the key in the ignition.

"Wait, Marie. I just want to know why."

Mac's woeful plea remained unheard and unanswered, drowned out by the roar of the car's engine. He dropped the small box in the pocket of his robe as Marie sped away, trailed by a cloud of black, smoky fumes. Her cell phone rang before she was halfway down the block.

"So how did it go?" asked Angie when Marie picked up.

"What do you think? It was a train wreck!"

"Thanks, Ree. I owe you big time."

"You're damn right you do!" said Marie, obviously shaken. "I don't care if you are my big sister. Next time you break up with a man, you're on your own. What if he started crying? I hate it when a man cries. What are you supposed to do? You can't put your arm around him and say, 'There, there it's okay, honey,' like he's a child. Oh, no. I had to get out of there before the waterworks started."

"I'm sorry you had to go through that, Ree. I mean it. I owe you."

"I'll get over it, although I can't say the same for Mac. That man is a mess. I still don't understand why you backed out. He's really a great guy."

"It's too complicated to explain over the phone. We'll talk when you get home."

Chapter Three
How I Met Your Mother

Mac achieved prosperity earlier than most with the deceiving ease and apparent grace of a ten-point Olympic dive, but karma had nothing to do with it. His successful writing career was attributed more to charisma, talent, and a network of connections rather than from benevolent acts performed in this lifetime, or any other. Add the morning jogs and weekly basketball games that kept Mac's lean, six-foot body toned and dangerously sexy to the equation, and he never spent a night alone unless he wanted to. However, all that changed when Angie entered his life. Mac fell for her hard and fast, like one of Wile E. Coyote's anvils pushed over a desert cliff.

They met on a cruise about a year earlier. Mac wanted a break from his hectic writing schedule; Angie won the cruise from the lottery. He needed to escape the grind of deadlines and revisions; Angie needed to escape after another failed relationship left her bitter and hurt. As far as she was concerned, men were ranked on the same level as maggots, oil sludge, and marauding hyenas, an opinion that didn't bode well for Mac when he literally bumped into her while reaching for the peel-and-eat shrimp on the Lido Deck buffet line.

"Excuse me," he said absently.

"Hey, quit pushing!" she squawked.

"Well, I wouldn't have to if you weren't so damn slow."

That flippant remark earned Mac a sample of hell's fury from a recently-scorned woman.

"Oh yeah?" said Angie, swinging around to face him. "Who do you think you are, buffet boy?"

"Buffet boy?"

Angie was about to tell him where he could stuff his shrimp cocktail when she lost her balance and stumbled. "Whoooooa, Nellie!" she cried, arms flailing, and fell backward onto the food-laden table.

Platters piled high with hors d'oeuvres, chips, and dips hit the floor with a crash, along with an anatomically correct ice sculpture of Michelangelo's *David*. The elaborate spread and the dismembered body of David splattered the carpet, walls, and a few unsuspecting passengers. When the food settled, Angie was sitting in an industrial-size bowl of coleslaw, hanging onto what was left of David's family jewels.

"Oh, my God! I'm so sorry," cried Mac, horrified at the calamity he unwittingly caused. He rushed over to help the mean-tempered, yet strangely appealing girl, but slipped on a deviled egg, landing headfirst in her lap.

"Help! He's trying to molest me!" Angie shouted. "Call 911! Call 911!"

"We're at sea, ma'am. Do you want me to call the captain?" asked the distraught purser, hastening to her side.

"I don't care who you call! Just get this pervert off of me!"

"Hey! Who the hell are you calling a per..."

That was as far as Mac got because his heart did backflips when he fixed his gaze on the hapless beauty draped in assorted appetizers. That, combined with the image of her holding a partially melted penis, was more than a normal man could take. He was instantly smitten. Angie took two seconds longer to ascend from the seductive depths of his topaz-colored eyes before she, too, was hopelessly besotted despite the fact—or maybe because—his head was unceremoniously positioned between her legs. Then with a devilish smile, Mac lifted his head, leaned forward and licked a blob of guacamole off the tip of her nose, and said, "I can see you've already had lunch, angel face. So why don't you meet me tonight at 8:00 in the main dining room for dinner."

"But, but," she stammered.

Mac held his finger over her quivering lips. "Shhh. Just say you'll be there."

Angie nodded obediently.

"Do you still want me to call the captain, ma'am?" The concerned purser asked again.

"No," she said to him, dreamily. "I'm okay. In fact, I've never been better."

Mac hadn't been waiting around for his special someone. He knew she'd show up sooner or later. And when he beheld the feisty, red-haired wildcat holding David's penis, the ice sculpture that is, there was no doubt in his mind she had arrived, and he was prepared to spend the rest of his life with her. What Mac wasn't prepared for was Angie's reaction when he told her his name over dinner that evening.

"Did you say, *Conrad* MacConnell?"

"Yeah, that's me," admitted Mac, misinterpreting her surprise. "I know it's a shock to find out I'm famous."

"No. I mean, is your name really Conrad?" she asked, giggling.

"Yeah, Conrad. What's so funny? You'd think I said my name was Bozo the Clown."

Angie dropped her salad fork and sat back in her chair. "Close enough," she teased. "The famous part doesn't bother me, but I can't go out with anyone named Conrad. In my neighborhood, I could get beat up just for admitting I know you. We have to come up with something else."

"Excuse me, sir," interrupted the waiter. "There are some ladies at the bar who would like to buy you a drink."

Angie glanced over as four women who could have been members of "Cougars R Us " leered unabashedly at the man sitting across from her.

"Please tell the ladies thank you, but my date and I have already ordered wine," replied Mac, and waved to the disappointed foursome when his message was delivered just to be polite.

"Who are they?" Angie asked, sounding a little jealous.

"Just some fans," replied Mac casually.

"Does that happen a lot?"

"No. Not often, ," he lied. "As I said, they're just fans. I don't get personally involved."

The waiter returned with a bottle of Merlot and Mac watched Angie glance toward the women again then back at him as their glasses were filled. She pressed her lips together and a soft "hmmm..." in her throat told him she wasn't buying his flimsy explanation. Even he had to admit his response wasn't very convincing. Truth is, there was a time when he would have joined those women at the bar or any other place they had in mind. But those days were over now that he met Angie.

"So, what name do you suggest if you can't stand Conrad?" he asked to change the subject.

"I don't know," she replied, grasping the crystal stem of her glass. "You're the writer. What does your family call you?"

A few seconds ticked by while Mac buttered a piece of

bread. With his eyes cast down, as if studying the crumbs on the tablecloth, he said, "Connie."

This time, Angie made no attempt to suppress her laughter.

"Connie? You've got to be kidding!" she howled. "That's even worse. It's a miracle you're not in therapy!"

Mac leaned back, folded his arms across his chest, and said with a playful snicker, "Well, I'll just have to remember that next time I feel the urge to strangle somebody."

Full of mischief a moment ago, Angie's eyes softened. She became pensive as she took a sip of her wine. "I've got it!" she cried.

Her sudden outburst startled him and he spilled wine on his shirt. "Got what?" he asked while blotting the red stain with his napkin.

"Your last name is MacConnell, right?"

"Yeah, so...?"

"Don't you see? I'll just call you Mac."

Although touted as a cruise to nowhere, for Mac and Angie that couldn't have been further from the truth. After dinner that night, they went somewhere, and often—to each other's cabins—drawn together like ferrous objects caught in a sexual magnetic field.

The depths of Mac's feelings for Angie were sudden and intense. That he could care so much for another human being took him completely by surprise. Equally astonished were his family and friends when he announced their engagement a few months later.

"Are you sure?" asked his bewildered parents.

"Yes," Mac answered with confidence. "I've never been so sure of anything before in my life."

Chapter Four
Margaret and Salvatore

The American dream became a reality for Angie's parents when Margaret and Salvatore Russo purchased a home in a quaint middle-class hamlet. Conceived shortly after WWII to provide affordable housing for returning GIs and their families, the community was first developed on the potato fields of Long Island. The houses in each section were identical, but as finances improved and families grew, so began the deviation from the basic floor plan. Garages and second-floor dormers were added, kitchens expanded, and bathrooms remodeled. Now, each house had its own personality, all but the Russo residence. It remained true to the original design except for the finished attic (a third bedroom for Margaret and Sal) and a garage. Angie and Marie still lived in the small house with their parents.

For Marie, it was an economic necessity. Having held several jobs over the years from cashier to telemarketer, she was currently unemployed. Angie worked at a local newspaper, *The Island Post*. She had planned on moving out after being promoted to assistant copy editor, but when Mac proposed, she decided to stay. How could she leave and deny her mother the bragging rights of having a daughter who lived at home until she married? Too bad that coveted privilege would now be wrested from her mother like soldier's stripes ripped off a uniform in disgrace.

Their blue-collar neighborhood was populated with families from diverse nationalities. The Russos were proud of their Italian heritage, and Sal believed that customs and traditions held a family together. On that issue he was unopposed, except for his old-fashioned notion that women didn't need a college education.

"You'll get married and have babies," he said to Angie one day while relaxing in his recliner. "Then your husband will take care of you."

Angie looked up from the latest issue of *Cosmopolitan* and tossed it on the floor beside her chair. "So, what's that supposed to mean?" she asked, although she'd heard it all before.

"So why go to college?" said her father. "Hey, Margaret, where's the clicker?"

Margaret Russo breezed into the living room and dug between the sofa cushions. "Your father's right, dear," she said, handing the remote to Sal.

"But what if I don't get married?"

As if on cue, Margaret fainted. The vinyl-covered sofa made a *whoosh* sound when she fell on it, alternating between making the sign of the cross and other hand gestures meant to ward off evil spirits and bad luck. It was obvious that she had faked it, but the family went along with her harmless ruse for attention. Besides, she was the only one who liked the blackberry brandy that never failed to revive her.

Sal jumped from the recliner and grabbed the bottle of brandy from the china cabinet. "See what you've done with your crazy ideas?" he said to Angie while pouring his wife a glass of the sweet liquor.

Angie moved across the living room and sat on the edge of the sofa beside her mother. "But Dad, it's not that I don't want to get married. It might not happen, that's all," she said, patting her mother's hand.

Margaret managed to sit up and accept the cordial from her husband. She downed it in one gulp, placed the empty glass on the coffee table, and said, "You know, Angela, you're just like your grandfather. We never know what to expect from him either. It must be the red hair you got from your father's side of the family," she added as if that explained everything.

Sal unconsciously touched his bald spot. "You can leave my father out of this."

"Well, he does get into quite a bit of mischief especially since Mom passed, may she rest in peace." Margaret stated flatly. "And you must admit, Angela, you can be a little high-strung and unpredictable at times like your grandfather."

Sal reached for the newspaper after lowering himself wearily in his recliner. "Just be glad he's living at the Almost Heaven Retirement Home and not here," he reminded his wife.

Margaret nodded, making a hasty sign of the cross. "Now, Angela. Don't ever think like that again. Of course, you'll get married."

"Well, she's not getting any younger, you know," her father shot back.

"Give me a break, Dad! Twenty-four's not that old. I don't even hear my clock ticking yet."

"Well, age doesn't matter anyway, Angela," her mother said philosophically. "You're never too young or too old to get married. The important thing is to find the right man who will love and take care of you. Look at your cousin, Evelyn."

Angie shot a questioning look at her mother. "What about her?"

"She married young, her husband adores her, and they have two beautiful children."

Angie leaped from the sofa, faced her mother, and said, "Ma, Evie got married at seventeen because she was pregnant."

"No, Angela. Don't you remember?" Margaret pointed to a framed photograph of an infant hanging on the wall. "Her baby was born premature."

Angie rolled her eyes until they almost disappeared into her head. "I can't believe you said that. Evie was showing when she walked down the aisle."

"She's family, dear. The baby was premature. Let's just leave it at that."

Angie plopped down on the sofa with her arms crossed. "Okay—fine—whatever."

What about Sister Lucia Immacolata?" her mother continued. "She married when she was almost forty."

"This has nothing to do with your sister," piped Sal. "She was a nun, for chrissake!"

Margaret made another fervent sign of the cross. "Don't blaspheme, dear."

"Ma, Aunt Lucy's not a nun anymore. Why do you keep calling her Sister? It's not like she's a retired general."

"Because she served God for almost twenty years," replied Margaret piously. "She deserves a little respect."

Sal threw the newspaper on the floor. "Respect? Not after she and her husband bought those Harleys. What the hell's the matter with them? They look ridiculous riding around on those motorcycles. Must be some sort of mid-life crisis."

"And I've been worried about my sister ever since," said Margaret. "Last week she called to tell me she got a tattoo on her..."

"Stop it! That's enough!" cried Angie. "I don't want to hear any more!"

~

One hour after leaving Mac stuttering on his doorstep, Marie rounded the corner of Dogwood Lane. Angie waited inside her parent's Cape Cod-style home, positioned by the front window with a box of Kleenex hugged close to her body like a life preserver. Every few minutes, she'd push the curtain aside, scanning the street as she mopped up her tears with a wad of tissues. "She should be home by now," Angie muttered as Marie screeched to a stop in front of the house.

The front door burst open, and Marie sprinted past Angie heading straight to the kitchen with a white bakery bag cradled in her arms like a linebacker running for a touchdown. When Angie caught up with her, the coffee was brewing, and Marie had already finished her first doughnut. Angie sighed and dropped the box of tissues on the small, round table. It was a warm and cozy kitchen despite the outdated appliances, worn linoleum, and Formica countertops—unlike the mood the sisters were in now.

Angie yanked a tissue from the box and blew her nose. "What took you so long, Ree? Mac's house is only a half-hour away."

"I had to make an important stop," replied Marie between swallows.

"Stop where?"

"You made me go to Mac's house so early I didn't have time for breakfast," she whined. "So I stopped at Sweet n' Crispy on the way home."

"Sweet n' Crispy is *not* on the way home."

"I know that. The Doughnut Depot *is*, and that's where I

was going. But they were closed so I went to Sweet n' Crispy anyway," explained Marie, grabbing another doughnut covered in white powdery sugar. She took a bite and sneezed. "*Ah, Achoo!*"

"God bless you."

Angie felt a little guilty about being angry with Marie and handed her a tissue, waving it like a white flag of truce. After all, she did her a big favor. Marie accepted it with a sheepish grin and wiped a powdered sugar mustache from her upper lip.

The coffee was ready now and Angie filled their cups, the hot liquid soothing their frazzled nerves like a balm. They sipped it in silence until the sweet aroma of doughnuts reached Angie's senses. She helped herself to a glazed cruller.

"Try the chocolate cream-filled," suggested Marie. "It's better than a cruller."

"You think?" she asked before taking a bite. "I thought jelly doughnuts were your favorite?"

"That was last week. Now I'm into cream-filled."

"Good morning, girls," said their mother.

Margaret had floated into the kitchen, unnoticed, and poured a cup of coffee. "It's so nice to see you together. Please keep your voices down. It's Saturday, and your father is sleeping in. Isn't it a lovely day?" she said, still talking, as her slippered feet shuffled down the hall.

Marie stood, peering through the open doorway, tearing herself away from a week's worth of cholesterol. "Boy, Ma sure is in a good mood."

"Yeah, I guess you could say that," Angie agreed.

"I wonder why? You'd think she'd be upset about..."

Thinking for a moment, Marie's brows knitted together then shot up. "Ma doesn't know you broke your engagement?"

Angie stirred her cup to a froth, shaking her head without meeting her sister's questioning gaze.

"You mean, you haven't told her?"

"Shhh," warned Angie. "She'll hear you."

"Well, maybe she *should* hear me. When do you plan to tell Ma and Dad that you're not getting married?"

"I don't know, maybe.... never?"

Marie sank into her chair and waved her arm back and forth like a sluggish windshield wiper. "Oooh no. I'm not going through that again. I returned the ring. The rest is up to you."

Angie covered her face with her hands. "I know, I know. I'll tell them," she moaned.

"So, how do you think the folks will take it?"

"Well, Ma loves Mac. This will probably break her heart," began Angie, dropping her hands to the table. Dad was happy I found a husband to take care of me. Getting the son he never had was a bonus. I'm afraid I'm going to burst both their bubbles. Just promise me you won't say anything. I'll tell them...eventually."

"All right. I'll keep your secret," agreed Marie. "But don't drag this out too long because keeping a secret makes me nervous, and you know what happens when I get nervous."

"You eat?"

"Like a high school football team at an all-you-can-eat buffet," said Marie "And I don't think there are enough dough-nuts in the world to keep me quiet for more than a day or two."

Chapter Five
The Pawn Shop

Marie took off in a cloud of exhaust, leaving Mac alone and speechless. The neighborhood was quiet on a Saturday—no one rushing to work, no parents chauffeuring their kids to school. Only the distant droning of landscaper's lawnmowers broke the lazy silence as he stood in the open doorway of his house.

Mac had purchased the two-story Dutch colonial a year before he booked the cruise that changed his life. It was a stately home built in the early 1950s with three bedrooms, two baths, and a detached, two-car garage. When he and Angie became engaged, he suggested selling and buying one that they could select together. Angie rejected the idea. She thought it was perfect.

"I can see our kids playing on the lawn," she'd say with her eyes closed, envisioning their idyllic family. "There's a pool and swing set in the backyard, too."

Mac didn't have the heart to tell her that in his neighborhood front lawns were just for show and kids spent the summer at camp.

A gardener cut and trimmed Mac's yard, so he never paid

attention to his or the other manicured lawns that lined his street. Now that he did, the lush landscaping reminded him of how neat and orderly his life had been prior to Angie's shocking announcement over dinner the night before. Another wave of nausea assaulted his gut when he relived that awful moment in his mind.

Emotionally exhausted, hungover, and in desperate need of caffeine, Mac shuffled into the house and plodded to the kitchen. His cell phone sat on the counter. *That's odd. I usually put my phone on charge before I go to bed.* "I must have been in worse shape than I thought last night," he muttered, recalling his clothes scattered about the house.

After connecting his phone to the charger, Mac scoured the pantry for his favorite brew. He owned every type of coffee maker known to man, but they were all useless without actual coffee. "Angie and I were supposed to go shopping today," he moaned when he realized he was out.

Glancing at his running shoes by the back door, his stomach turned again. Forgoing his morning run was a no-brainer. However, forgoing large amounts of caffeine was not an acceptable option. So he trudged upstairs to get dressed before venturing out for his daily fix.

Once in his room, Mac took the velvet box holding Angie's engagement ring out of the pocket of his robe. He recalled the day they picked it out as he placed it in the top drawer of his dresser.

A successful author could afford a large gem, and Mac had insisted on a brilliant three-karat solitaire flanked by glittering baguettes. Hesitant to be so extravagant, Angie selected a plain setting with a smaller, yet elegant diamond.

"She'll wear this again," he vowed, closing the drawer.

Shoving suits and sports jackets aside in his closet, Mac pulled out a tee-shirt, jeans, and sweatshirt. He dressed, stepped into sneakers, and slipped the hooded sweatshirt over his head. Returning to the kitchen, he grabbed his partially-charged cell phone and headed for the garage.

After keying in the combination, the wide garage door rolled up on its tracks revealing a late model SUV and a 1956 Ford Thunderbird. The classic peacock blue T-Bird had a detachable fiberglass roof, circular porthole windows, and a rear-mounted spare tire. Mac babied the vintage sports car like a spoiled child, only driving it on the weekends; and despite his queasy stomach, a smile spread across his face when he climbed in and turned the key. The engine kicked over on the first try. He smiled again and backed out onto the driveway, allowing the motor to idle while the garage door clattered down. Intending to stop at the nearest Brew Bucks for coffee, he eased onto the road.

Unexpected roadwork three blocks from Mac's house detoured him through an unfamiliar part of town. He followed the signs left, right, and left again until the car jolted, shaking him in his seat. Assuming he had driven over a deep pothole at first, his murder-mystery writer's intuition kicked in and he thought...*or over a body?*

Without thinking, Mac slammed on the brakes, slinging the car in park. He jumped out and dropped to the ground to check under the low chassis. No pothole or body, but the front left tire was definitely flat. It resembled a clock in a Salvatore Dali painting, looking melted and deflated like his ego. Mac straightened and kicked the tire in frustration leaving a scuff mark on the spotless vintage whitewall.

"Man, I don't freakin' believe this! What the hell is wrong with me?"

Using the sleeve of his sweatshirt, he quickly removed the black mark returning his baby to pristine condition, then dialed the Auto Club on his cell phone. A cheerful female voice answered after the first ring.

"Thank you for calling the Auto Club. How may I help with your problem today?"

That's just great—a happy person. The last thing I need right now is a nice, happy person.

"What makes you think I have a problem?" he asked brusquely.

"You just called the Auto Club, sir. Or did you mean to call your AA sponsor instead?"

"My what? Oh, I get it," he said, leaning against the car. "Okay, I'm sorry I snapped at you. I'm having a really crappy day."

"I understand. It's never a good day when you call us. How may I help you?"

"I'm a little embarrassed. This never happened to me before."

"What has never happened before? You being rude to a total stranger or calling the Auto Club?"

"I guess I deserved that," he grumbled.

"There's a first time for everything, sir."

Mac imagined the person behind the voice on the phone. Probably hasn't had a date in years and lives alone with three cats, two Great Danes, and a Cockatoo named Marquis de Sade.

"Well, I'm not usually like this," he explained. "But I'm under a lot of stress right now. Can we start over please?"

"Sure," she replied, still as sweet as sugar. "Everyone deserves a second chance."

Mac took a deep breath, massaged the space between his brows, and said, "I...have...a...flat...tire."

"That happens a lot. It's what we're here for. Just give me your location, and I'll have someone there in 30 minutes."

"I'd love to, but I'm not actually sure where I am."

"Are you sure you don't want your AA sponsor?"

"Listen, sunshine. I know they're a great bunch of people, but that's not the kind of problem I'm having at the moment."

"Just trying to be helpful, sir."

"Well, you can help by telling me where I am."

"Certainly, sir," she said unperturbed. "First look around. Are there any landmarks you recognize?"

"No. Nothing looks familiar," he lied without checking.

"Are you sure?"

Mac let out an impatient sigh, did a slow turn, and stopped. "Wait. I'm in front of a small business. It's a shop called Take It or Leave It Pawn."

"Is there a number on the building?"

"Yeah. Thirteen hundred," he said, craning his neck.

"Good. Are there any street names that you can see?"

Mac shaded his eyes with his hand. "It's hard to tell from here, but I think I'm on Des Tiny Road."

"Did you say Destiny Road?"

He paused for a beat. "Yeah, I guess I did."

"What about a cross street?"

"That one is easier to see," he told her. "It's Future Street."

"Okay, so you're at the crossroads of Future and Destiny. Just sit tight. We'll have you up and running in no time."

I'm at the crossroads of Future and Destiny. How weird is that?

"Thanks," he said and disconnected.

A powerful blast of frigid air prompted Mac to turn his back against the biting cold, spinning him around. When the wind suddenly stopped, he was facing the pawnshop. At that precise moment, the "Closed" sign in the pawnshop window turned over to "Open." *What a break. I'll wait inside the shop until the Auto Club gets here.*

Mac grasped the worn, brass knob on the door and turned. Bells attached to the aged, wooden portal jingled merrily, drowning out the eerie squeal of the rusty hinges when he nudged it open. The wide unfinished floorboards seemed to groan in protest when he stepped in, and his nose wrinkled, suppressing a sneeze, at the musty smell of old things. Street grime covered the front window preventing sunlight from penetrating the glass, and Mac strained his eyes to see. Bare incandescent bulbs dripping from the tin ceiling like stalactites barely illuminated the space; and when his eyes adjusted to the semi-darkness, he gasped, "Oh my God."

Shelves occupied every inch of the walls that were barely discernible in the murk from counters obscured by mounds of dusty items. Antique dolls sat as still as sentinels amid vintage clothing hanging on sagging racks beside tables set with china, silverware, and crystal that seemed to be waiting for dinner guests that would never arrive. Jewelry on display sparkled despite the low light. Mac forgot his troubles as he roamed the aisles, entranced by the treasure trove in the unique shop. Every item he found on the crowded shelves produced a happy thought or fond memory from his childhood. These unexpected, nostalgic feelings took him totally by surprise and he smiled, blissfully submerged in his past.

What an odd sensation.

Mac's mood turned serious when he spotted a dusty, old manual typewriter. Reflecting on his own profession, he imagined the daunting task of writing a novel with it, or with just pen and ink.

If it weren't for a computer, I don't think I would have become a writer.

The realization humbled him, stirring up the unexpected feeling of inadequacy.

Desperate to exchange his depressing mood for the

comforting emotions he experienced before, Mac turned sharply to peruse the aisles again and ran into a massive object that knocked him to the floor.

"Who? What the hell?"

"Don't you fret none. I'll help ya," said a deep voice.

Two muscular arms hoisted Mac effortlessly, placing him gently on his feet. A hand as big as a catcher's mitt dusted him off and straightened his clothing. And for the second time that day, he leaned his neck back to see something.

It was a man, although Mac had serious doubts that he was actually human. He must have been seven feet tall; and suddenly, the entire shop didn't seem big enough for the two of them. Mac's first instinct was to get as far away as possible from the giant, but his feelings were quickly assuaged when the stranger introduced himself.

"Howdy! The name's Otis, Otis Bean Pickett, like the fence," he said, offering his baseball-glove-sized hand. "My friends jest call me O.B. Pleased to meet ya."

Mac extended his hand, watching in amusement and disbelief as his normal-sized appendage all but disappeared in the other man's grasp.

"Nice to meet you, O.B. I'm Mac." Surprisingly, O.B. shook hands as gently as he had lifted him from the floor. "I didn't hurt you when I ran into you, did I?"

"No, sir. It takes a lot more than that to ruffle ole O.B.'s feathers. I'm jest fine."

O.B.'s shoulder-length hair was graying at the temples, and Mac estimated his age to be between forty-five and fifty. He wore blue jeans rolled up at the bottom and pointy-toed, lizard-skin cowboy boots. Around the neck of his western-style shirt hung a leather bolo tie with an enormous turquoise stone set in hand-tooled sterling silver.

"You're not from around here, are you, big guy?" asked Mac.

With his thumbs hooked into the pockets of his jeans, O.B. lifted his chin proudly. "No, sir. I hail from Amarillo, Texas."

Well, that figures, thought Mac. *They say everything's bigger in Texas.* In fact, O.B. Pickett was one big cliché: the embodiment of every western story ever written and seemed as out of place as most of the merchandise in the quirky shop. The only thing missing was a ten-gallon hat.

Mac picked up a perfect Rubik's cube from a nearby table. "So, how'd you end up on Long Island?"

O.B.'s eyes darkened, his shoulders slumped, and with sadness in his voice said, "After my daddy passed, Lord rest his soul, my mama took up with the gentleman that owned this here store while he was doin' business in Texas. He courted her faster than a hound dog picks up fleas; and before I knew what was goin' on, they was hitched and moved up to New York City. They're both gone, too, Lord rest their souls. But my step-daddy had no kin of his own, so he left the store and everything in it to me."

"That was nice of him," said Mac, rotating the squares, hopelessly ruining the solved puzzle.

"Yes, sir, it sure was. But I'm as uncomfortable here in the big city as a June bug in July."

"Hey, man, that's too bad. I feel for you, pal. Really, I do," began Mac, brushing him off. "But I have a problem. You see my car is out front with a flat and the Auto Club won't be here for at least half an hour. Mind if I look around while I wait?"

O.B. snatched the cube from Mac, solved the puzzle in three moves, and put it back on the shelf. "No, sir. That won't bother me none. In fact, I'd be happier than buzzards at road-kill if ya did."

Mac's eyes widened and his jaw dropped. "How'd you...?" he asked with a nervous laugh.

"How'd I what?"

"Uh, never mind."

"Well, I'll jest be moseying along," O.B. said, patting Mac on the shoulder. "I got a pile of work on my desk, and I'm fixin' to do it. Holler if you need me."

Strange, thought Mac. The old floorboards were inexplicably quiet as the big Texan turned and lumbered to his office.

Mac's attention quickly returned to the contents of the peculiar pawnshop. With so much to see in the haunting, yet familiar place, all sense of time slipped away. He turned abruptly when he spied a GI Joe on a shelf and POOF! O.B. seemed to appear in his path out of thin air.

"What the hell! Where did you come from this time?" Mac yelled, shaking his head to clear the cobwebs that *must* be there.

"Sorry, pardner. I didn't mean to rile ya none. I guess I do that sometimes without meanin' to. My mama always taught me to walk softly. You see, she didn't want me scaring the tar out of folks, you know, being so big and all."

"That's all right, big guy. Don't give it a second thought. I'm okay."

"Good. Then I got somethin' to show ya. C'mon this way."

Mac followed O.B. to a long display case in the back of the pawnshop near O.B.'s office. It had a glass top scratched from years of use where small, expensive items were kept under lock and key. Stepping behind it, O.B. motioned for Mac to look inside.

"Do ya see anything ya take a likin' to?" he asked, with a knowing smile.

Mac glanced at his watch. Feigning interest, he scanned the

contents of the case. "All I see are just some old coins and jewelry."

"Look again," O.B. urged, stroking the large turquoise stone in his bolo tie.

Mac's vision blurred instantly. *What the...?* He struggled to focus, but everything around him went fuzzy until his gaze was drawn to the only thing he could see clearly—an antique fountain pen. Mac rubbed his eyes. "Hey, I didn't see that before."

Passing his hand over the turquoise stone a second time, O.B. said, "It's a beauty, ain't it?"

As inexplicably as Mac's vision had blurred a moment ago, it cleared up the same way, leaving him confused by what had just occurred. Reluctant to admit to something as unmanly as a dizzy spell, Mac ignored the episode. "I've never seen anything like it. Is that silver?"

"Yes, sir. It sure is. Sterling silver, I reckon. Here, I'll take it out so you can get a better look at it." O.B. pulled an old church key from his pocket, unlocked the case, and placed the pen on Mac's upturned palm.

The old-world craftsmanship of the fountain pen was clearly evident even to Mac's untrained eye. And despite being tarnished from age, he was able to see faint markings on the darkened silver. Feeling unusually warm in his cool hand, Mac regarded the antique like it was a rare archeological find. "It's more like a work of art than an ordinary fountain pen."

"Well, folks really set a store on writin' instruments back then," O.B. told him. "It made 'em proud as a peacock to own a pen like this. Do ya know it's over 100 years old?"

Mac didn't answer because the extraordinary object held him mesmerized. He had never seen the pen before in his life, yet it seemed oddly familiar though he couldn't explain why.

A chuckle rumbled in O.B.'s throat as he observed the younger man's fascination.

Mac separated the cap from the barrel. "Where's the tip?" he asked.

"It's called a nib, son. Turn the bottom. It'll come up."

Mac did as instructed. A 14K gold nib appeared.

"Folks don't take the time to write letters no more," said O.B. sadly. "They's all fired-up and busy-like these days with no time for the niceties in life. They say writin' is a lost art. Who needs to write letters when ya have email and that dad-burn texting? I'm sorry to say they might be onto somethin'. Now the folks who collect pens like this one here, they fix 'em up like they're good as new and actually write with them. I hear tell that's what makes 'em more valuable."

Though old-fashioned, the pen is special, thought Mac. With a slim body and smooth form, it's a classic beauty. Something a person keeps for a lifetime. *Just like I intend to keep Angie close to my heart and by my side for life.*

"That's it!" Mac cried startling O.B. "I'll take it!"

"Dontcha want to know how much?" he teased.

"I don't care. I just want the pen."

"All right. That'll be five hundred dollars."

Mac's eyes widened. "Are you kidding?"

When O.B. saw Mac hesitate he said, "Cause you're such a nice guy, I'll give it to ya for three hundred. I'll even throw in a bottle of ink and some of that fancy writin' paper."

Oh, what the hell. Mac knew he could afford it and whipped out his credit card. Women shop all the time to feel better, and he certainly needed to feel better today.

O.B. grinned as he swiped the plastic and gave it back to Mac. "You won't be sorry, son," he said, placing the pen in a leather case. "It'll become a family heirloom. Somethin' you'll hand down to your young'uns. Don't ever part with it."

"Hey, man, chill out. It's only a pen."

O.B. handed Mac the bag with the pen, ink, and paper. "I know. Jest remember what I said."

The bells on the door clanged when the mechanic from the Auto Club breezed in.

"Anybody here need a flat fixed?" he shouted.

"Yeah, man. That's me." Mac turned to O.B. "Hey, thanks for the company, big guy. I won't forget you." Anxious to be on his way, Mac ran out of the shop without looking back.

"No sir," O.B. said when the door slammed shut. "You sure won't."

It didn't take long to change the tire. When the job was done, Mac gave the mechanic his Auto Club ID card and leaned forward to read the man's name sewn in his overalls. "Thanks, uh...Slick?"

"Yeah, my buddies at the garage pinned that on me," he explained, wiping the grime off his hands with a rag. "It's an automotive thing. Y'know, slick, like in motor oil?"

"Oh, sure. I get it," said Mac, remembering how he got his own moniker.

After completing the necessary paperwork, Slick returned Mac's ID card.

"Well, it was my pleasure to help you, Mr. MacConnell," he said, admiring the vintage T-Bird. "I don't get to see cars like this one too often."

Mac settled in the front seat. "Let's hope you won't see it again for a while. No offense," he added.

Slick packed up his tools and loaded them in the tow truck. "None taken, pal. You just take good care of her."

"Who? Angie?" asked Mac through the open window, somewhat befuddled.

How does he know about Angie? Does he know what happened?

"Angie?" asked Slick, approaching the car. "Angie," he

repeated slowly, saying the name again as if listening to a finely-tuned engine. "I might've picked something different myself, but if that's what you want to call your car, mister, that's as good a name as any I guess."

He's talking about the car, bonehead. Get a grip!

"I will," promised Mac, steering the T-Bird from the curb.

Chapter Six
Mommy Dearest

Mac arrived home without incident, feeling better physically. His tequila hangover had subsided, along with the need for coffee that had forced him out that morning. Emotionally, however, he was still a basket case. Parking his T-Bird in the driveway, Mac thought about the strange encounter with O.B. Pickett and the unusual shop. It was only a temporary distraction, leaving him even more confused about being dumped, as he climbed out of the car and moped up his front walk.

"Angie?" he called expectantly as he opened the door. She had a key to the house, and Mac hoped to see her there, laughing at him, because he actually took what she said seriously. "Of course, she's not here you moron," he grumbled and plodded into the kitchen to sulk.

Glancing at his phone, Mac noticed five new voicemail messages. He was about to listen to them when his stomach growled. So, he tossed his phone and pawnshop purchase on the granite counter, pulled a bowl and a box of cornflakes out of the cupboard, and sniffed what was left of a gallon of milk from the refrigerator before pouring it over his cereal. Mac ate while leaning against the counter and set the bowl in the sink when he was done. Then he grabbed his phone and keyed in his voicemail password.

Message number one. "Conrad, why aren't you home? What's going on? I want an answer now!"

"Oh, man, it's my mother," he groaned. "Sounds like she knows something's up."

The casters squeaked as Mac pulled up a kitchen chair, slumped down on the vinyl seat, and waited for the second message. It was his mother again, this time with a vengeance. He shuddered as her shrill voice seemed to reach through the speaker like a hand and grab him around the throat.

"Don't ignore me, Connie!" she shrieked. "I can tell when something's wrong. A mother knows these things. I called Angela and she didn't answer either. I demand that you call me!"

Mac got along with his mother even though she was a little bossy. That is if you consider a drill sergeant a little bossy. He had enjoyed a happy and pampered childhood, but even as a youngster, Mac could see that although his father was the master of the corporate boardroom, he wore the skirt in the family, so to speak. Despite the surrender of his manhood at home, his dad seemed content with his life.

After listening to his mother rant, Mac knew that a normal conversation with her seemed unlikely, and it was better to let her calm down before returning her call. Casually tossing his phone aside on the counter, he leaned back with his eyes closed, trying to think of a plausible story to tell her, when the phone rang.

"Please don't let it be my mother," he prayed, reaching for the phone.

Where the hell is it? I had it just a minute ago.

He jumped up, ignoring the clattering of the chair as he listened for the ring tone which seemed to come from the bag on the counter. Mac pounced on it and shoved it aside, exposing his phone that had slipped underneath, as the paper sack slid down the smooth counter like a mug of beer down a polished bar. Mac cursed under his breath and scooped up the phone as the pen, ink, and paper spilled out across the floor. "Hey man," he said after checking the caller ID.

"Hey yourself! What's up, dude?"

It was his buddy, Carrick DiNapoli.

Maureen DiNapoli, nee Flanagan, christened her son Carrick (which means rock in Gaelic) so he wouldn't forget his Irish roots. Everyone just called him Rick. Friends since high school, he and Mac met for an informal game of basketball on Saturday mornings—every Saturday, that is, until now.

"Hey, Rick. How's it going?"

"I'm great, man, but what happened to you?"

"What are you talking about?"

"You didn't show up this morning, that's what. Did that girl of yours keep you in bed all morning? Yeah, that's gotta be it. You were too tired to play," said Rick, laughing at his own bad joke.

Oh, man! I can't believe I forgot about the basketball game.

"The other guys were really ticked off that you did a no-show," continued Rick. "But some kid at the park wanted in so we let him play in your place. The little dude was good. I'd be worried if I were you."

"Yeah, well, something unexpected happened last night," said Mac in a guarded tone.

"Sounds serious. You weren't abducted by aliens, were you?" asked Rick, still joking.

"No, nothing that extraordinary," said Mac, pacing aimlessly around the kitchen as he spoke.

"I know! You're really a double agent and your cover's been blown. You can count on me, man. I'll help you. You need fake ID or phony fingerprints?"

"Come on, Rick. Quit kidding around."

"Sorry, dude. So, what happened?"

Usually reticent when it came to discussing personal issues with his friends, Mac hesitated but decided it was time to face reality. "Okay, but you have to keep this to yourself," he said and stopped pacing. "You can't tell anybody."

"My lips are sealed," promised Rick. "You know, like the time my little brother crazy glued my mouth while I was sleeping. Remember that? I had to suck on cotton balls soaked with nail polish remover. Man, that stuff was nasty."

Mac couldn't help but smile at the thought. "I remember, but this is serious."

"So was the crazy glue."

"I mean it, Rick!"

"Chill, dude. I got you covered. You'd have to use the Vulcan Mind Meld to get any information out of me."

That did it. Rick was a devout Trekkie and to him, the Vulcan Mind Meld was akin to the doctor's Hippocratic Oath. Neither one was taken lightly. Mac dropped into a chair, took a deep breath, and said, "Angie broke our engagement."

"No way!"

"Yeah way," he said mournfully. "She gave back the ring this morning. Actually, her sister Marie brought it over. I haven't seen or spoken to Angie since she dumped me over dinner last night. I don't have a clue why she did it."

"Brutal, man."

"Tell me about it. Then she snuck out of the restaurant and

took off in a cab. I even got a speeding ticket when I went after her."

"You know, I always liked Angie's sister," Rick said as if he didn't hear what Mac just told him. "She's no Marilyn Monroe, but there's something about her that's totally cool. Yeah, maybe you could give me her number."

"Go online and look it up yourself," said Mac and tapped the phone with his finger. "Helloooo? I thought we were talking about me?"

"Oh. Sorry, man. My bad. So what are you gonna do?"

Mac leaned back and stared at the ceiling. "I don't know. So far I drank a bottle of Tequila and bought a pen."

"Sounds like a plan to me," said Rick with approval. "Except for the pen part. You did say pen, like something you write with?"

"Yeah. I don't know why, but a big Texan at a pawn shop sort of talked me into buying it."

"What big Texan and what pawn shop?"

Mac rubbed the back of his neck. "It's a long story, Rick. I'll fill you in when I see you. Remember, don't tell anyone that Angie broke up with me."

"No problemo. Later dude," he said and disconnected.

The next two messages were from his mother, and Mac winced as her voice became louder and more hysterical with each recording. The last one was from his father, begging Mac to call because he couldn't take any more of his wife's foul mood.

"Poor Dad," he said, as he keyed in his mother's number on his cell. He regretted making the call as soon as he heard her voice.

"Well, it's about time you called your mother! I've been worried sick all morning."

"Give him a break, Liz!" his father shouted in the background. "He's thirty years old, for God's sake. Cut the umbilical cord already!"

"A mother never stops worrying about her child!" she yelled back. "Don't listen to your father," she said to Mac in a conspiring tone. "He doesn't understand the bond between us."

My mother—the original drama queen.

"So you might as well tell me," she said, getting down to business.

"Tell you what?" he asked, speaking for the first time.

"You know. Whatever it is you're keeping from me."

Unprepared for an interrogation, Mac stood with his feet spread apart, bracing himself as he spoke, refusing to be cowed by her. "Mother, I don't know what you're talking about."

"You most certainly do, Connie."

When Mac was a youngster, his mother would tell him to stick out his tongue whenever she thought he was lying, claiming she could see the lie there as plain as day. He fell for it every time and confessed. It wasn't until he thought of looking in the mirror that he realized she had tricked him. She still knew when he was lying though. There must be some credence to this mother-child bond thing after all.

"Everything's fine, Mother," he told her. "I'm a big boy now. I can take care of myself."

"I'm sure that's true, Connie," she agreed. "So please tell me why Angela canceled your wedding reception."

Holy shit! Angie didn't waste any time.

"Your Aunt Rita finally sent in her response, and I called the club this morning to add her to the guest list," his mother informed him." You can imagine my embarrassment when they asked me why I was adding a name to a canceled reservation."

Mac remained tense as he circled the kitchen table. "That was probably just a mistake. I think Angie called to confirm the menu. They must have misunderstood."

"That's what I thought," she agreed. "A simple misunderstanding."

How the hell do I get out of this without arousing my mother's suspicions? Handled properly, this could work to my advantage until I can talk to Angie.

"You know, Mother," began Mac with caution. "We can afford the country club, but Angie and I didn't feel comfortable having the reception there anyway. So why don't we just leave things the way they are and book someplace else?"

"Nonsense!" she cried. "Why would you even suggest such a thing? You know we have all our parties at the club. Lucky for us they hadn't re-booked the date, so I reserved it again just like before."

The creases in Mac's brow softened as he unclenched his jaw. "Thanks, Mom," he said, relieved that she accepted his lame explanation. He was also amazed that he just lied to her, and she didn't suspect a thing. "I have to go now. I'll call you tomorrow."

"Good. *Then* you can tell me the truth," she said tersely and hung up.

Mac disconnected and shoved his phone in his pocket.

Everything was happening much too fast. How could Angie cancel the wedding *and* the reception without even talking to him? Those decisions should've involved them both, like the two keys required when launching a missile. It was his life, too, and he had every right to know why she broke their engagement. She owed him that much or at least a chance to talk her out of it. Problem was, Angie had cut off all communication. Even with modern technology at his disposal, he felt isolated and alone.

The conversation with his mother left Mac despondent and stressed. He plopped down in a kitchen chair to wallow in self-pity when he heard an unfamiliar scraping sound. *What the...?*

Beneath one of the casters lay the antique fountain pen. "Oh, man. It isn't bad enough that I spent $300.00 on an old pen. Now I just trashed the damn thing!" Snatching it up with the other items that had scattered on the kitchen floor, Mac dashed to the counter to see the extent of the damage under the bright fluorescent lights.

The case was slightly dented, but the pen seemed unharmed. Thankfully, the bottle of ink wasn't broken. Relieved to see his investment intact, Mac dug in the kitchen junk drawer for the silver polishing cloth Angie had bought and proceeded to remove the dull oxidation from the antique pen. The results were startling. Once tarnished almost black, the intricate silver filigree overlay sparkled in contrast with the hard, black rubber barrel. Mac's efforts also exposed several markings. "Looks like dates," he mused.

Taken over by curiosity, Mac collected the pen, ink, and paper and went into his office. Pulling a magnifying glass from his desk drawer, he inspected the faint markings. Once magnified, he was able to see the words: *SPARTAN FOUNTAIN PEN* imprinted around the bottom edge of the cap and *STERLING PAT SEPT*.27.00 on the pocket clip.

"That date has to be 1900," he said in awe. "What do you know? O.B. was right. It's over 100 years old."

Moving to the flat end at the bottom of the black rubber barrel, Mac was able to see numbers, like a code: *19F #100 M.* That intrigued him the most, making a mental note to Google them later. Further up slightly on the black barrel were thin lines he mistook for scratches until the magnifying glass revealed: *PATD AUG, 4,1900, SPARTAN FOUNTAIN PEN N.Y.*

Mac took careful notes of all the markings, and just when he thought he'd seen everything, he discovered another inscription. Etched in the silver was a name followed by a city and state—presumably, the owner's home.

How the hell did I miss that?

Until then it was just a pen, an inanimate object. Now it was a Spartan fountain pen that had an owner, a person with a history who lived over 100 years ago. And his name was Edwin Alexander Sullivan.

Part Two

Chapter Seven
Gloucester, Massachusetts
1904

At the turn of the century, Gloucester, Massachusetts was a thriving New England harbor. On any given day, the wharf pulsed with the activities of a major seaport, the air wafting with scents of saltwater, rotting food, and unwashed bodies. Since colonial days, Gloucester's economy was based on the sea; and its citizens still relied on the vast, unpredictable ocean for their livelihood.

Merchants depended on the sea for the delivery of their goods from ships that sailed its rough waters. Commercial fishermen plied their trade in its hostile environment, harvesting cod, mackerel, herring, and halibut. And when homesick sailors returned with their wages, so profited the ladies of the night.

Even the poorest among them could afford to receive mail. Women, hungry for news from a husband, son, or brother, met ships daily only to shed bitter tears after receiving a letter, sometimes months old, telling of a loved one's death. While in the background, almost on a subliminal level, droned the never-ending creaking and groaning of the ship's masts and riggings, the beating heart of Gloucester.

Edwin Alexander Sullivan was born on May 20, 1888, in Gloucester, the only child of Irish immigrants, Bridget and Eddie Sullivan. With her husband at sea for long stretches of time, Bridget's widowed father moved in with the small family to help raise his grandson. Consequently, the boy wasn't close to his father and preferred to be called Alex—rather than Eddie, like his father—using his name as a tool to detach himself from a man he barely knew. To Alex, the name Eddie evoked the image of a slacker or a failure, and Alex had dreams of a different life—one far from the docks of Gloucester. A life that would earn him wealth and something money couldn't buy, respect. No one respected Eddie Sullivan.

Alex's childhood memories of his father were of a kind, loving man before life at sea altered him. It was as if the high ocean waves curled over Eddie in a briny cocoon, transforming him into a roughneck sailor prone to alcohol-induced violence in their wake. When sober, his blue eyes sparkled. A few tankards of ale turned them gray and menacing like the churning skies of an impending storm before unleashing its fury. Bridget Sullivan shielded her son during those drunken tirades, taking the blows herself before Alex's grandfather intervened. Then, banished from the house, Eddie would stumble back to his ship not to be seen again for months.

Surprisingly, Eddie always left a portion of his earnings with his wife. A frugal woman, Bridget managed to stretch the modest funds until his next turbulent visit. Life was difficult for the Sullivans. Alex knew he wanted more.

Like most boys his age, Alex quit school to help support his family. And on a typical morning, he elbowed his way past stevedores and fishmongers crowding the busy harbor in search of work, first approaching a man wearing a white apron in front of the General Store.

Alex removed his cap. "Good day to you, Mr. Nolan."

"Good mornin', Alex me boy!" he said, adjusting the garters on his shirtsleeves.

Sean Nolan grabbed a broom and began sweeping the wooden walkway in quick rhythmic motions. "And how's your sainted mother?" he asked, without missing a beat.

"She's grand, sir. Thank you for askin'," replied Alex wiping the perspiration from his brow with the back of his hand. "Are you needin' any help today?"

Mr. Nolan stopped sweeping. "No, lad. But I'm expecting a delivery tomorrow. Come back in the mornin'. I'll have a job for you then."

"That I'll do, sir," Alex said, replacing his cap. "That I'll do."

It had rained just before dawn, and the streets were already churned into a quagmire by horses' hoofs, booted feet, and wagon wheels. Alex jumped between the muddy puddles on his way to the wharf where Captain Samuel Pierce hailed him from the bow of his ship.

"Hellooo, Alex!"

Alex waved his arm in long arcs. "Ahoy, Captain."

"Aah you lookin' fah wahk, boy?"

"Yes, sir, Captain. What'll you have me do?"

Captain Pierce squinted into the sun. "I'll need a strong back to unload this aftahnoon. Come back latah. You can staht then."

It wasn't long before the gangly boy developed into a muscular young man from lifting large bales and heavy crates of cargo. Alex enjoyed the physical work but yearned to escape the drudgery of the docks and a seafaring life. Despite his dreams and willingness to work, he saw no way out until an unforeseen event plucked him from obscurity. Then, like a ship blown off course, his life took a new and uncertain direction.

The schooner, *Indigo Sky*, was readied to depart on the

next high tide for a cod-fishing trip off the Western Bank of Nova Scotia. Scheduled to be at sea for two months, Alex's father, Eddie, signed with the crew. The two-masted vessel set sail in fair weather from Gloucester. Two days later it ran aground at White Point, broke up, and sank. All hands went down except three lucky sailors. Of the three, two managed to swim ashore. The third was Eddie Sullivan. At first, he kept up with the younger men as they swam for their lives, but years of alcohol abuse had taken a toll on his body. He fell behind in the frigid water, never to be seen again.

Bridget Sullivan accepted the news of her husband's death with mixed emotions, adjusting quickly to life without Eddie. She received a small widow's pension; and ironically, thanks to Eddie, had a steady income. That, combined with what she earned from taking in wash, enabled Bridget to live a decent life.

For Alex, his father's death meant freedom. His mother no longer depended on him for support, and it was time to fulfill his dream, leaving home at sixteen years old. Severing all ties with his father, he also changed his name. From that day forward, he was known as Alexander Sullivan. The year was 1904.

Alex left Gloucester with no destination in mind, wandering south, simply because the first farmer to pick him up traveled in that direction. During the first days of his journey, he walked, hitched rides on wagons, or hopped in boxcars. If a wagon carried produce, the sympathetic farmer let Alex take what he could carry, and he lived on fresh fruit and raw vegetables for days. If the wagon or train car carried livestock, he took only a musky scent as malodorous as the animals with which he commuted. On one occasion, Alex even rode in an automobile. Fascinated with the two-passenger roadster, he bombarded the driver with endless questions as they bounced along the rutted, unpaved roadway. When it broke down, Alex discovered he possessed a natural mechanical instinct, assisting the driver with repairs en route. He could hardly contain his enthusiasm, imagining a future with the wonderful machines.

After giving his mother most of his wages from working the docks in Gloucester, Alex had squirreled away the rest. Unsure of the length of his journey, he slept in barns and outbuildings rather than spend his savings on lodging, leaving at dawn before anyone discovered his presence. Sometimes the animals made a ruckus, alerting the family that an intruder had taken refuge in their hayloft or stall. Then the sound of a shotgun was all he heard in the distance as he ran from the place.

Three weeks passed. Without realizing it, Alex had wandered inland, away from the coast, and was growing weary of his solitary adventure. So when his last ride ended in the small town of Peabody, Massachusetts, midway between Gloucester and Boston, he decided to stay.

Alex secured accommodations in a dilapidated, three-story boarding house located in the heart of town. The room he rented had sparse yet serviceable furnishings with a kitchen alcove consisting of a wood-burning stove, one shelf for his meager possessions, and a tub for bathing. He shared a water closet at the end of the hall with three other families. The entire run-down structure creaked and moaned like the ships in Gloucester harbor. In a strange way, that reminded him of home, his only comfort.

Alex had attended classes for a short time in Gloucester's one-room schoolhouse. Never a good student, he could barely read and write. Now, as he inquired around town for a job, any job, it became clear to Alex that sheer physical strength was not enough to succeed. He needed an education to achieve his goal of earning wealth and respect.

Two weeks later and still unemployed, Alex's landlady told him that the Peabody private school needed a custodian. His savings had dwindled to almost nothing so he jumped at the opportunity. The good woman even washed and ironed his clothes for the interview. Her boy would have been the same age, had he lived.

Alex was hired.

The following day, he walked to the two-story, brick school-house. A harried-looking woman dropped a stack of papers on a cluttered desk as he strolled into the vestibule. She was petite, clad in a plain black hobble skirt and white shirtwaist blouse. Tired lines on her face and a frost of gray at her temples suggested she was past her prime. Smoothing back her pinned-up hair, she straightened her bowed spine and asked, "May I help you?"

Alex removed his cap. Sandy brown locks fell in front of his hazel eyes. "Yes, ma'am. I'm to start work today."

"Are you the new custodian?"

"Yes, ma'am. That's me."

Sharp green eyes evaluated Alex with a discerning gaze. "Good. There's plenty that needs fixing around here. The last custodian we had was worthless. Did more harm than good."

Alex pushed the hair from his brow. "I'll do a good job, ma'am. I promise."

"I hope you're right," she said and chuckled. "The principal is a hard man to work for. Believe me, I know. I'm Miss. Lipton, his secretary."

"Pleasure to meet you, ma'am."

Miss Lipton's face brightened, bestowing Alex with a friendly but brief smile. "Well, don't keep him waiting. He's expecting you. His office is over there."

Taking a seat behind her desk, Miss Lipton flicked a hand over her left shoulder in the direction of two oak doors. *Broom Closet* was painted on one in bold black lettering. *Jeremiah Bass, Principal, Peabody Academy*, was embossed in kind on the other.

Alex didn't move.

"What are you waiting for?" she asked impatiently. "Do you want the job or not?"

"Uh...uh..." he sputtered, unable to move.

Miss Lipton pressed her palms flat on her desk, pushed up, and grumbled, "I don't have all day, young man." Stomping over to where Alex stood, she shoved him in front of the doors. "Don't be nervous. Just knock."

Alex ended up dead center—favoring neither the left nor right door and froze. Only his eyes moved, darting between the painted letters on the dark wood panels. They meant nothing to him, just squiggly lines and circles. How could he tell Miss. Lipton he couldn't read?

"Do I have to do everything around here? *This* is the principal's office," she said, stabbing the incomprehensible characters on the door to Alex's right with an ink-stained index finger. "See? It says Jeremiah Bass, Principal."

Alex heaved a tremendous sigh of relief. *God's help is nearer than the door. That's what me mam always said.* His mother's words never held more truth than at that moment. "Thank you, ma'am," he said, taking one step over.

Miss Lipton returned to her desk. "Good luck. I think you're going to need it."

Alex wiped the dust off his shoes on the back of his pant legs and knocked on the principal's door.

A pithy voice barked, "Enter!"

The word "Enter," uttered more like a command than an invitation, gave Alex pause. He recalled another one of his mother's Irish proverbs. *Your feet will bring you where your heart is.* Right now, his heart wanted to work, so he pushed apprehension aside and opened the door. His shoes scraped the floorboards as he walked in, heralding his presence.

Principal Bass looked up from his desk regarding Alex through hard, ice-blue eyes. "And you are?"

Alex twisted his cap in his hands. "Alexander Sullivan, sir, the new custodian."

Without preamble, the principal rose from his chair. "Then come with me, boyo," he snapped.

Jeremiah Bass walked with long, determined strides, breezing past Alex as he exited his office. Alex had no choice but to do as he was told and follow.

"Broom closet, coal furnace, classrooms..." Principal Bass ticked off each location. Quickening his pace to keep up, Alex studied his new employer as he marched down the hall.

Short-cropped gray hair contrasted sharply with the older man's thick handlebar mustache and unruly eyebrows. He wore an outdated, well-worn suit and despite the frayed collar and cuffs, looked down on Alex through pince-nez spectacles that rested on his long, aristocratic nose.

"Clean the classrooms every day," he continued as they made their way around the building. "Wait until the students have gone home, then erase the blackboard, empty the trash, and mop the floors. I will give you general maintenance assignments as they arise."

"Yes, sir."

"And remember," said Principal Bass, turning abruptly to face Alex. "*Never* under any circumstances are you to speak to the students. It's imperative that you remain apart in order to do your work properly. If you have a problem, come directly to me."

Initially, the underlying meaning of the principal's veiled

instructions wounded Alex's pride. The implication that he was not fit to speak to anyone above him socially infuriated him. But no one would talk to a lowly custodian anyway, and Alex realized he shouldn't be offended. Besides, this job was just a stepping-stone, although he had no idea where his next step would be.

For the first time in his life, Alex worked indoors during the bleak months of New England's bitter-cold winters. But with frigid temperatures approaching, he faced another dilemma. Although employed, he barely earned enough to cover his living expenses; and Alex had to choose between buying gloves or food. So every day he boiled two potatoes and held them, still hot, in his pockets. They warmed his hands on those raw, chilling mornings until he got to work where he then ate the cooled tubers for breakfast.

Alex received verbal assignments daily from Principal Bass. "Fix the broken shelves in the library, lad. Plug the leak in the roof before it rains. Nail down that loose floorboard in the hall."

Though exhausted at the end of the day, Alex looked forward to cleaning the classrooms because he had discovered his next step. He found a way to obtain a free education.

He wasn't supposed to begin cleaning the classrooms until lessons ended but slipped in early to do his chores anyway. In those last few minutes before the students were dismissed, Alex listened to every word the teachers said, absorbing all the knowledge he could while he swept and mopped. When the students left, he studied the chalkboard, teaching himself to read before erasing it, then emptied the trash, his most valuable resource. Not only did he find actual work to review, but he also used the clean sides of the discarded paper for his self-assigned homework. Although not an actual pupil, and with a different grade and subject taught in each room, Alex gained the knowledge and skills necessary for his new life.

On the last day of school, a group of students strolled leisurely toward Alex while he mopped the hall. Accustomed to being ignored, he stepped aside. Then, for the first time, one member of the group—a young girl—looked at him. She smiled, said hello, giggled, and continued down the hall without looking back. Alex was stunned, too shocked to move or respond. No one had ever shown him a bit of kindness before. Leaning on the handle of the mop, he watched her disappear down the corridor like a brilliant sunset sinking below the horizon. She was only a child. He didn't even know her name. But her innocent smile and sweet laughter became a treasured memory he'd always keep close to his heart.

Chapter Eight
Jonathan Cromwell
1905

One year after arriving in Peabody, Massachusetts, Alex Sullivan quit his custodian job at the private school. Through ingenuity and determination, he had managed to educate himself, landing a clerk's position at the Peabody Savings and Loan Company. The new job demanded long hours for the paltry wage it provided; but Alex endured the tedious work, knowing it was the next step of his journey towards the affluent future he envisioned.

Although Alex dressed the part of a clerk, he remained in his small room at the boarding house. Except for rent and food, he saved his wages to build a home for his mother. He wrote often, encouraging her to join him in his adopted hometown, but she always refused. Even when his grandfather passed away, Bridget Sullivan chose to stay in Gloucester.

While walking to work one morning, the sound of hammers pounding nails and the clamor of falling lumber startled him. He turned in time to see a large wooden sign fall from a scaffold to the unpaved road. Seconds later, a middle-aged man wearing a tailored suit and bowler hat burst through the door of the building below and charged into the resulting cloud of dust.

"You up there!" he yelled," to the men on the scaffold. "I can't afford to replace that sign so hang it right!"

"Yes, sir. Yes, sir, Mr. Cromwell," the workers replied. "It won't happen again."

"See that it doesn't if you want to get paid!" he warned, brushing the powdery film off his suit coat.

"Are you ready, boys?" the foreman shouted. "One, two, three!" Grunting and sweating, the crew pulled hard on the ropes until the sign was finally in place.

Alex shaded his eyes with his hand from the other side of the road. "Cromwell Power Automobile Company," he read. The name reminded him of another automobile and the journey that brought him to Peabody. He never lost his enthusiasm for the newfangled machines and strode over to speak to the man instead of continuing on his way to work. "Excuse me, sir, are you the owner of the Cromwell Automobile Company?"

"Yes, I am," replied the man, turning to face Alex. "I'm Jonathan Cromwell. And you, sir?"

"My name is Alexander Sullivan."

As they shook hands formally, Alex noticed a spark flicker in Jonathan Cromwell's inquisitive eyes. The spark spread to a grin that flashed across his face followed by a hearty slap on Alex's back.

"Egad! Look at you, boy!" he exclaimed.

Startled at first, Alex's stunned expression broke into a similar grin of recognition. "Of course!" How could I forget?" he cried, pumping Cromwell's arm. "You gave me a ride in your automobile almost a year ago."

"Yes, lad!" confirmed Jonathan. "I was astounded by your ability to repair the automobile's faulty engine. Now it seems fate has brought us together again."

"Mr. Cromwell," interrupted the foreman on the scaffold. "Has the job been done to your liking?"

Jonathan shielded his eyes from the sun with his hat, inspecting the placement of the sign bearing his name, as the sun peeked over the treetops.

"It is satisfactory, my good man," he called back. "Quite satisfactory." Turning again to Alex he said, "Please, come inside. Let me show you around."

After a brief tour, they withdrew to Jonathan's makeshift office—the air already hot and humid in the small room despite the early hour. Jonathan removed his coat, hung it on the back of his chair, and sat behind a crude desk made with a sheet of plywood supported by two sawhorses. Alex perched tentatively on an overturned crate.

"The secret to the Power Automobile, my young friend, is an auxiliary electric motor," began Jonathan, resting his folded hands on the unfinished wood. "I have liquidated all my assets, investing every penny of capital in this new venture."

"But will people buy such an automobile?" asked Alex, concerned for his friend's financial well-being.

"Of course, they will," he stated emphatically. "It is the future."

Jonathan Cromwell continued to explain his business plan to Alex with enthusiasm, confident the public would purchase his product in droves. And when he offered Alex a job on the spot, he accepted, instantly caught up in the older man's fervor. What choice did he have? By this time, he was late for work and as good as fired anyway.

March 1908. The Cromwell Machine Company prospered, aided by Alex's natural mechanical aptitude. He excelled in his new career, contributing talent and manpower to help build the fledgling company's first five automobiles. Jonathan saw great potential in Alex with high expectations for the young man he now looked upon as a son. When Alex proposed that instead of cars they manufacture a line of heavy-duty trucks for their new shipping business, Jonathan knew it was time to offer him a partnership.

To commemorate the occasion, Jonathan presented Alex with a sterling silver fountain pen made by the Spartan Pen Company of New York City. It was the most valuable thing Alex had ever owned, though not in monetary terms. The pen's value symbolized prosperity, a reflection of his personal success. To be in possession of such a fine writing instrument indicated his worth as a man.

"My father gave me a fountain pen when I was about your age, and I wanted to do the same for you."

Although overcome with emotion and pride, a shadow passed over Alex's face when he read the inscription etched on the silver cap.

Edwin Alexander Sullivan, Peabody, Massachusetts.

"Jonathan, my friend. You know I don't use that name anymore."

"I'm aware of that, dear boy," he said with a reassuring hand on Alex's shoulder, "but that's who you are. Everything that's happened in your life with that name has shaped you into the man you are today. No matter how successful you become, you must never forget that."

Alex accepted the well-intentioned gift yet marveled at the paradox of his life. Instead of the ships he despised and a life at sea he had struggled to escape, he was now transporting goods on dry land with his own fleet of trucks.

∾

June 28, 1914. A Bosnian-Serb student had assassinated Archduke Ferdinand of Austria in Sarajevo, Bosnia. The disturbing news arrived from Europe on the front pages of American newspapers; and within weeks, most European countries were engaged in World War I. To maintain peace and avoid U.S. involvement in the conflict, President Woodrow Wilson initiated a policy of isolationism.

Reports arrived daily of failed diplomacy, resulting in bloody rebellions and invasions while the U.S. remained in a neutral stance. As more countries were drawn in, Alex and Jonathan grew frustrated with their inability to take part in the growing conflict. So they took action the only way they could by becoming the major supplier of ambulances and trucks for the United States Army. Orders and money poured in. The Cromwell Automobile Company grew from its original building and small garage to three sprawling factories encompassing ten acres of land outside of town. Alex now supervised their sixty-five employees and production from his private office, working around the clock to meet manufacturing and shipping deadlines.

Despite the carnage overseas, day-to-day life in Peabody remained quite civilized. Citizens went to work, attended church services, and observed life's milestones with dances and parties. One such occasion was a debutante ball celebrating the coming out in society of Miss Winifred Cornelia Armstrong. Jonathan, a mature, wealthy bachelor, received an invitation.

It was not in Jonathan Cromwell's nature to dwell on the past. He rarely reflected on his own life, having few regrets. One that did haunt him was that he never married. Work always came before love, and he could see that Alex—wealthy and single at twenty-six—was heading down the same solitary path. He encouraged Alex to go to the ball in his place, knowing it was the perfect opportunity for him to meet an eligible young lady. Besides, he was fifty-nine years old and tired easily. He would never be able to keep up on the dance floor.

～

On September 14, 1914, the night of Miss Armstrong's coming-out party, Alex regarded his image in the entry-hall mirror of his new home. He had tried to persuade his mother to live with him in the modest house, but Bridget Sullivan was true to her word and remained in Gloucester. Except for the household staff, Alex lived alone.

"What do you think?" he asked Jamie, his butler. "Will I pass for a gentleman?"

"Oh yes, Mr. Sullivan. You're lookin' grand tonight, sir. Just grand."

Alex was elegantly dressed in a black suit, vest, and a one-button cutaway frock coat sporting lapels faced in satin. Under the vest, he wore a white shirt with French cuffs. Around his neck, a crisp white collar and a black bow tie.

"Put silk on a goat, and it's still a goat. That's what my mam always said," replied Alex in an Irish brogue. "But thank you, Jamie. The suit does fit me well."

"When should I expect you to return tonight, sir?" Jamie asked, brushing the shoulders of Alex's coat.

"Early, I hope. If it were up to me, I wouldn't go at all."

"You don't want to be disappointing Mr. Cromwell now, sir. It means a lot to him that you go."

"I know. He's done so much for me: I had to accept the invitation. Actually, I suspect he wants me to find a bride."

Jamie held up Alex's overcoat while he slipped his arms in. "And what's wrong with that, young sir?" he asked, handing Alex his hat and cane.

"Nothing, I guess," admitted Alex. "But that's a dream I can't afford now—not with a war going on. I have a responsibility to Jonathan and the business."

"The future's not set. There is no fate but what we make for ourselves," recited Jamie. "That's what *my* mam always said."

Unaccustomed to society functions, Alex pulled at the tight collar of his formal clothes feeling claustrophobic. *If the party is anything like the suit I'm wearing, it is bound to be an uncomfortable evening,* he thought, stepping onto his front porch. Once outside, Alex inhaled deeply, relishing the brisk night air. With his anxiety somewhat relieved, he declined his car, deciding to walk the short distance to the Armstrong residence.

"Wish me luck, Jamie," he said, descending the porch steps.

"May the strength of three be with thee tonight, sir!"

Alex turned to Jamie and tipped his hat.

Jonathan had given him a short course in social etiquette the day before. Alex reviewed his lessons as he trudged along like a condemned man to the gallows, hoping only to get through the evening without making a fool of himself. Fifteen minutes later, Alex arrived at the Armstrong mansion that even from the outside, boasted wealth, prosperity, and power.

Ablaze with lights, the opulent three-story brick home was bursting with music, laughter, and the high-pitched tinkling of sterling silverware on lead crystal and fine china. Alex stood under the columned portico, envying the guests he spied through the front window looking as comfortable in their finery as they were in their own skin. Then the large, polished oak door opened suddenly, and sounds of the lively affair washed over him like champagne from an uncorked bottle.

White Italian marble in the wide foyer, buffed to a high gloss for the occasion, glistened beneath his feet as he took an apprehensive step over the threshold. Above, a brilliant chandelier suspended from the ten-foot ceiling poured light on the bejeweled guests below who sparkled as if coated with a phosphorescent substance.

A liveried footman appeared at Alex's left. "Good evening, sir," he said, bowing slightly, taking Alex's hat, coat, and cane. Another footman waited at his right. "Come this way please, sir," he said, ushering Alex towards the receiving line and his hosts, Mr. and Mrs. Armstrong.

"Welcome! Welcome to our home," greeted Cornelius Armstrong with a firm handshake. "Thank you for coming, my good man."

"On the contrary, sir. The gratitude is all mine," responded Alex as rehearsed, grateful to Jonathan for his new manners.

Henrietta Armstrong stood beside her husband in a gown bedecked as elegantly as her splendid home and extended a white-gloved hand to Alex. "How good of you to come, sir," she said, appraising his expensive attire. "Winifred will be so honored to meet you."

For a moment, Alex had no idea who Winifred was until he remembered the girl's name on the invitation. It occurred to him as he left the receiving line that if she needed a party like this to meet a suitor, she must be homely and decided to avoid her if possible.

A servant balancing a silver tray laden with crystal stemware offered Alex champagne. Another proffered an assortment of sumptuous hors d'oeuvres. He declined both and ventured toward the massive ballroom.

Four dazzling chandeliers illuminated the resplendent room highlighting hand-carved molding on the walls that framed floor-to-ceiling windows draped in royal blue velvet.

Matching sconces twinkled on either side of the large Palladian windows, thrown open to let in the sweet scent from Mrs. Armstrong's prized rose garden. Alex's gaze wandered to the sweeping mahogany staircase flanked by two enormous potted ferns atop Grecian-style pedestals while one hundred guests whirled around the gleaming wood floor.

Although expected to dance with the unmarried young ladies, Alex preferred to remain invisible nevertheless during the first dance—a lively Foxtrot. Then the orchestra ceased playing, and a hush of anticipation fell over the room. It didn't take long for him to discover why. At the top of the wide, grand staircase stood Miss Winifred Cornelia Armstrong with a small-gloved hand on her proud papa's arm.

The epitome of an Edwardian debutante, Miss Armstrong wore a Parisian gown of layered, white chiffon over a rich, white satin under-dress. Her modest, scoop-necked bodice, dripping with pink satin roses, matched the trim on the gown's train, equipped with a wrist holder to facilitate dancing. Tiny glass beads and glittering rhinestones accented the short-capped sleeves and belt circling her waspish waist.

White Egret plumes bobbed in Miss Armstrong's raven black hair when she turned to face her father and Alex gaped unabashedly. The image he had of a homely girl vanished as her lovely chiffon gown made her appear more like an angel coming to earth on a cloud rather than a mere mortal alighting an ordinary flight of stairs.

When she completed her descent, Mrs. Armstrong took over, presenting her daughter to the older, and probably wealthier men first. Alex felt a twinge of resentment, realizing his low status on the list of prospective husbands. Then his pulse quickened, all negative thoughts suddenly purged from his mind, as he was introduced.

"Mr. Sullivan," began Winifred's mother. "May I present my daughter, Miss Winifred Armstrong."

Overwhelmed by her presence, Alex gazed into her dazzling blue eyes, shimmering against a luminous complexion as smooth as a cultured pearl.

"How do you do?" said Winifred politely.

"How do you do? It's a pleasure to meet you, Miss Armstrong," responded Alex. "Would you please be so kind as to add my name to your dance card?"

Winifred smiled. "Yes, Mr. Sullivan. It would be my honor," she replied, letting out a nervous giggle. "I will save the next waltz for you."

Then a sudden realization hit Alex like a blow to the head. The school—a hall filled with students—a passing girl with a sweet smile—that melodious laugh.

Impossible!

He fought to remain calm, his heart pounding in his chest.

I don't believe it! It can't be true!

Alex never dreamed he would see her again, yet here she was, years later—a well-bred young lady, Winifred Armstrong.

If he felt claustrophobic before, he was suffocating now. *What if she remembers me as a former custodian? I'll be shamed in public. Exposed as a fraud.*

Alex's first instinct was to flee, but there was no way he could leave. Not with her so close. Winifred was just a child when she touched his heart. Now, as a young woman, he helplessly surrendered it. *But would she have me if she knew the truth?*

Before Alex could profess his devotion, the next suitor on Winifred's dance card appeared, whisking her away. It pained him to see her in the arms of another, and he clenched his teeth as they danced. *Forget about the past. I'm as good as any man here.*

After what seemed like an eternity, the orchestra played the introduction to the waltz. Alex strode resolutely across the ballroom to claim his dance, and his destiny.

Timid at first, he held Winifred gently as they moved among the other couples, afraid she might break, afraid he'll wake from this wonderful dream. But the rhythmic one-two-three beats of the Viennese waltz urged him on, and the world around them melted away as they glided on the parquet floor. Winifred never looked up once.

When the music stopped, Alex released her. Bowing formally, he straightened and said, "My deepest gratitude, Miss Armstrong, for the pleasure of the dance."

Winifred remained silent.

Alex panicked, assuming her silence meant rejection or that he had unwittingly committed a social faux-pas, insulted her, or worse yet, stepped on her silk dancing shoes. "Miss Armstrong, please forgive me if..."

"I remember you, Mr. Sullivan," she said, cutting him off mid-sentence.

Dear God, she knows.

Smiling now, Winifred gazed into his eyes. "You may speak to my father."

Alex called on Mr. Armstrong the very next day. This time, he took his car and wore a new suit, eager to impress.

"Wait for me, Thomas," he said to his driver, stepping onto the sidewalk in front of the Armstrong mansion. "If all goes well, I should be out in a few minutes."

"Good luck, sir," Thomas said.

Alex scrambled up the granite steps. He rang the bell, tapping his foot while he waited. *Calm down. Don't show how nervous you are. And for God's sake don't say anything stupid.* He smoothed down his hair, checked his pocket watch, and was about to ring the bell again when a butler opened the door. He was of medium height, dressed in a dark blue suit that hung on his body like laundry on a clothesline. The few gray hairs left on his head were combed back neatly above bushy eyebrows that hooded his cloudy brown eyes.

"I'm here to see Mr. Armstrong," Alex told him.

"Eh?" he said, cupping his hand behind his ear.

Alex leaned forward. "I *said* I'm here to see Mr. Armstrong."

The veteran servant stared blankly at first, processing the information before his eyes lit up. "Oh, yes. Mr. Armstrong. And whom should I say is calling, sir?"

"Alexander Sullivan. Here's my card."

The butler accepted Alex's formal calling card, squinting as he brought it up to his nose.

"Please come in, Mr. Bumblelman."

"That's Sullivan, with an S."

"Sullivan? No, sir, my name is Jeffrey."

Alex let out an exasperated sigh. "No. *I'm* Alexander Sullivan."

"Of course, you are," said Jeffrey. "That's what it says on your calling card and a very nice one it is, sir."

Despite his jittery stomach, Alex smiled at the nearsighted, absent-minded butler as he stepped into the foyer. Jeffrey hobbled over to a table against the wall and placed Alex's card in a sterling silver tray. His heart sank when he saw how many cards it contained, indicating how many suitors had arrived before him.

"This way, sir. Mr. Armstrong will be with you shortly," said Jeffrey, directing Alex toward the library.

"I hope he delivers messages better than he reads," Alex muttered as Jeffrey shuffled down the hall.

The well-appointed library smelled of cigar smoke, dusty leather-bound books, and money—lots of it. Volume upon volume filled the ceiling-to-floor shelves, and Alex gaped at the variety of subjects and titles. He was leafing through a first edition of *Huckleberry Finn* when Mr. Armstrong appeared.

"I see you appreciate the written word, Mr. Sullivan," he boomed from the doorway. "It's reassuring to know that we have something in common, besides a profound affection for my daughter."

"Why, uh, uh, yes—of course, sir," Alex stuttered, taken aback by the man's bold, yet accurate statement.

"Now let me see what tome piqued your interest," Armstrong inquired, crossing the room in three long strides. "Well chosen. It's an amusing tale by an unconventional humorist. Please, be seated," he said, placing the book on his desk.

A quick scan of the library revealed a single, unoccupied chair. Alex was reluctant to take it, but Mr. Armstrong insisted. He figured it was a calculated strategy to make one feel intimidated—a ploy that was working. His cheek twitched as the commanding man towered over him.

"Samuel Clemens was a remarkable individual." Mr. Armstrong removed a cigar from the humidor on his desk. "I had the privilege of hearing him speak about a year before his death at a dinner given for Andrew Carnegie in New York City."

"And I'm certain it was a lovely evening, sir," Alex blurted out, unable to contain his emotions, while Armstrong reminisced. "But I came to ask your permission to call on your daughter."

For five agonizing seconds, Cornelius Armstrong just stared

at Alex. Then he threw his head back, letting out a loud, hearty guffaw.

Feeling mortified, Alex was certain that any chance he had of seeing Miss. Armstrong had been snuffed out like one of the older man's cigars.

Mr. Armstrong continued to laugh; unnerving Alex so much that he jumped from his chair, convinced his impertinence had earned him immediate rejection. "Please forgive me, sir, for taking up your valuable time," he said hastily. "I'll be on my way."

"Stay, young man," said Mr. Armstrong with a firm hand on his shoulder. "You give in too easily. For your sake, I hope you change your ways while courting my daughter."

Alex's face had turned a sickly pallor. But his frown of misunderstanding instantly switched to wide-eyed astonishment, his lips moving silently, unable to form coherent words as his complexion returned to a normal hue.

"Don't look so surprised, Mr. Sullivan."

"I don't understand," he said slowly, still not fully comprehending. "After my rude behavior, you still accept me?"

"Yes, well, I'll forgive that and attribute your conduct to love-sick nerves."

"But—but—the other cards," sputtered Alex. "Surely there is someone you and Mrs. Armstrong find more suitable for your daughter."

"Maybe," he admitted. "But you are the one she chose."

Unlike his mother, Alex had always doubted the existence of miracles, relying on dogged persistence and hard work to make his way in life. But at that moment, he was certain that a miraculous phenomenon had just occurred. After a silent prayer of thanks, he cleared his throat and asked, "Then when may I call on Miss Winifred, sir?"

Mr. Armstrong lit his cigar, studying the fumes as if the

answer to Alex's question was written in the ribbons of smoke. "Although my wife and I presented our daughter at a traditional ball last night," he began, "she was reared to be independent with a mind of her own. So why don't you ask *her* for permission to call? A letter would be most acceptable."

"Thank you, thank you, sir," said Alex, hastening from the library, then quickly returning to shake Mr. Armstrong's hand. "I'm very sorry, sir. Thank you, thank you," Alex repeated, pumping his arm, and rushed out again.

"Ah, young love," sighed Mr. Armstrong.

Minutes later, Alex burst through his front door. "Jamie! Jamie! Hurry, come here now!" He threw his hat and coat at the walnut hall tree and missed.

Up to his elbows in suds from the kitchen sink, Jamie appeared in the foyer wearing an apron, dripping water on the polished wood floor. "What is it, sir?" he asked wide-eyed.

"I'll be working for the rest of the morning," Alex said tersely. "I don't want to be interrupted for any reason. Do you understand?"

"Why, yes—yes, sir," replied the flustered servant. "Excuse me for askin', but is there anything wrong, Mr. Sullivan?"

"Wrong, you say? Good God, no!" Alex told him, with a jubilant slap on his back. "Nothing is wrong. In fact, nothing will ever be wrong again!" he added, closing the doors to his study.

Jamie shrugged, sighing as he hung up Alex's coat and hat. Then a flicker of comprehension flashed across his face, and he smiled a knowing smile as if he were just told a wonderful secret.

Alone in his study, Alex sat at his mahogany desk to write the most important letter of his life with his Spartan fountain pen, the special gift from Jonathan Cromwell. And as the nib caressed a sheet of monogrammed stationery, he declared his heart's desire in words he dared not speak aloud.

September 15, 1914

    My Dear Miss Armstrong,

    I have had a hundred images of you in my mind every hour since our first meeting. Your grace and beauty have overwhelmed my adoring, yet undeserving soul. My heart leapt with joy when we were introduced last night. I daresay, my feet barely touched the dance floor as we waltzed, already bonded in spirit, if not yet by matrimony. I will always be reminded of that glorious moment and be forever grateful.

    I pray, dear lady, that I may have your permission to call on you at a time of your convenience.

    The hours will pass slowly, tormenting this writer, as your favorable response is anticipated.

    Your servant,

    Alexander Sullivan

Chapter Nine
Winifred and Alex

Winifred Armstrong and Alex Sullivan were engaged the Christmas of 1914 with her parents' enthusiastic blessing. Her mother was ecstatic over the match with a successful businessman, secure in the knowledge that her daughter would be taken care of. All Winnie's father needed to know was that his daughter was happy. Although one year away, the Armstrong household revved up to high gear with everyone from the chauffeur to the upstairs maid occupied with wedding plans.

Alex wrote his mother with the news of his impending marriage, and she answered with the best wedding gift she could possibly give him. Bridget Sullivan would attend his wedding and move to Peabody. Alex couldn't believe he had finally achieved his goal. He had money to take care of his mother and had earned respect as a businessman and prominent citizen. Now he was marrying the woman he loved.

During their engagement, the young couple tried to spend every minute together; but Winnie's mother called her away frequently for shopping trips, gown fittings, menu, and flower selections. Alex endured the necessary separations knowing that after it was all over, Winnie would be his wife.

To fill the hours without her, Alex turned to his work. The business continued to prosper as the demand for vehicles overseas increased. He also began building a home for his bride. Designed in the neoclassical style, it would be equipped with modern amenities like indoor plumbing, electricity, and a telephone. It promised to be the grandest mansion in town. Jonathan, on the other hand, spent less time in the office.

"Don't worry about me," Jonathan said when Alex voiced concern for his friend's health. "I'm your best man. I wouldn't miss your wedding for the world."

September 1915. Cooler temperatures arrived, releasing summer's brutal grip on the northeastern states. At the same time much further south, a tropical storm formed over Cuba. Unbeknownst to the people of New England, trouble was brewing and heading their way.

At first, the storm skirted the southeastern seaboard, producing only slightly higher than normal winds and tides. However, once it moved over the Atlantic, the winds continued to intensify, fueled by the warm water. No longer a tropical storm, the newly-formed hurricane suddenly increased in speed and barreled north.

Residents along the northeastern coast were advised to move to higher ground. But the hardy folk of New England saw no cause for alarm and ignored the warning, relying solely on their views of the horizon to detect foul weather. Meanwhile, the hurricane strengthened.

On September 7, 1915, the storm that would become known as the Massachusetts Hurricane made landfall just after midnight. It had grazed the north fork of Long Island before unexpectedly turning west and slamming into northern Massachusetts.

Unaware of the killer storm's fury, the sleeping citizens of Gloucester were jolted awake, their homes pelted with blinding rain and powerful gale force winds, launching debris through the air like deadly shrapnel. Many of the boats and larger fishing vessels, torn from their moorings by the rising water, crashed into buildings, propelled by ferocious waves that uplifted docks and washed away piers. The relentless assault continued for approximately one hour before the eye, with its deceptive calm, reached Gloucester. Residents, mistakenly thinking all danger had passed, ventured out. This decision, for some, proved fatal.

The second half of the killer hurricane produced even stronger winds that, combined with the high tide, created a massive storm surge packing thirty-foot waves. In the dreadful darkness, people scrambled, fighting for their lives, as a wall of water rose up like a snarling grizzly with menacing claws held high.

The unrelenting pounding of the gigantic waves flattened the town, killing many instantly. Most died in their own homes, crushed under the rubble. In minutes, the town was completely flooded, washing helpless residents out to sea, their screams unheard over the roar of the mighty hurricane's wrath. Bridget Sullivan was among those doomed souls. Her last thoughts were of her son, Alex, as she felt the violent pull of the sea dragging her away from her home and all she loved.

After the hurricane passed, the remaining townspeople surveyed the destruction. Not one building remained standing, all reduced to piles of bricks and mortar. Boats wrenched from piers and moorings were found piled up on dry land, blocks from the harbor, like children's toys gathered after a bath.

Bodies lay strewn about the streets. Rescue efforts began immediately, but few were found alive. The hope of finding more
survivors dwindled with each passing day.

Further inland, south of Gloucester, Peabody suffered
substantial damage due to torrential rain and wind but was
spared the flooding, and no lives were lost. When news of the
destruction in Gloucester reached Alex, he feared for his mother's life. The following week, *The Peabody Gazette* printed a list
of casualties. Winnie was with Alex when he read: Bridget
Sullivan missing, presumed dead. She held him as he wept, his
shoulders gently quaking.

Alex wept for his mother—for the hard life she had
endured. He wept for the life he wanted to give her—a life
she'd never have the chance to enjoy. But mostly, he wept
because, despite his success and wealth, he couldn't save her.

Just about every resident in Peabody felt the effects of the
storm. Clean-up began quickly, with neighbor helping neighbor
to rebuild their town. Many lost family members in Gloucester
and memorial services were held for the victims. Weeks later,
the death toll for New England would exceed 500.

Winnie stood in her bedroom before a full-length cheval
mirror, clad in a fine linen chemise, silk stockings, and lace-
trimmed drawers. She fidgeted, feeling more like a life-sized
doll than a living person as her maid, Darcy, buttoned her into
a succession of uncomfortable, yet compulsory, undergarments.
Henrietta Armstrong supervised from a silk brocade wingback
chair.

"Do be still, Winifred," she scolded.

"Yes, Mama," replied Winnie dutifully, unable to contain
her excitement on her wedding day.

Darcy wrapped a silk taffeta corset around Winnie's already slender body. "Now take a deep breath, Miss Winifred." Darcy tugged on the laces in the back, then eased off slightly. "I'll leave your corset a wee bit loose, Miss, so you can breathe," she whispered in Winnie's ear. "I don't want you faintin' before you can say 'I do.'"

Both girls giggled, garnering a suspicious glare from Winnie's mother.

"What could possibly be so amusing?" she asked, her voice threatening.

Darcy bowed her head slightly. "Nothing, ma'am," she replied.

"Then please hurry. We mustn't be late."

Accustomed to being dressed, Winnie held her arms up as Darcy slipped a fine linen camisole over her head. Next, she helped Winnie step into a hand-embroidered petticoat before tying the ribbons around her cinched waist. Finally, the young maid guided Winnie into her elegant wedding gown and white satin high-heeled shoes.

Satisfied with her daughter's appearance, Henrietta said, "You may go now, Darcy."

"Yes, ma'am." The maid curtsied and hastened from the room.

Winnie's mother suppressed a grunt as she heaved her tightly-corseted body from the wingback chair. Her taffeta gown rustled as she glided across the hand-knotted Persian rug to face her daughter squarely. Clasping Winnie's hands in her own bejeweled fingers, Henrietta gazed soberly into her eyes.

"You are about to become a married woman, Winifred, and you know that you must submit to your husband." Henrietta paused, staring silently into space. Her powdered complexion paled briefly as if recalling an unpleasant memory before she continued. "It is a woman's lot in life and something that we all must endure, the only reward being motherhood." It was a solemn, almost foreboding statement, expressed much like a warning that something dreadful was about to occur.

Winnie wanted to have children, but her mother painted a confusing and rather gloomy image of that particular aspect of married life. She was innocent, not stupid, and knew there had to be some connection between the sexes for a woman to become pregnant. It was the actual mechanics of that union that she was unaware of. Henrietta's expression remained mournful as she draped Winnie's white lace veil over her beautifully coiffed head. Despite her joy that day, Winnie felt a pang of sorrow, sharing in what she imagined was her mother's sadness at being separated from her for the first time while she and Alex went on their honeymoon trip.

"Don't worry, Mama," Winnie said to comfort her. "I'll only be gone a few weeks."

Henrietta nodded, forcing a weak smile. "I know, dear. I know."

After the nuptials, a lavish reception was held in the same ballroom where Winnie made her debut as a young girl. Her life changed forever the instant she and Alex exchanged their wedding vows. Now, she was a married woman with many new responsibilities. That thought weighed heavily on her mind as Alex signed their names in the guest register of the Peabody Hotel. He reserved the honeymoon suite for their wedding night and had the sitting room decorated for Christmas.

The sweet scent of freshly-cut pine boughs hanging on the carved wooden mantel greeted the newlyweds as Alex carried Winnie over the threshold of the spacious suite. Bright red berries peeked out through holly bunting draped above every window and doorway in the room, and a roaring fire created welcoming warmth. Alex placed Winnie gently on her feet beside a ten-foot blue spruce ablaze with glittering candles, decorated with colorful glass balls and ribbons. She clapped her hands in delight, overwhelmed by his thoughtfulness. But when the door to the suite closed, Winnie felt an unexpected stab of panic, as her mother's parting words echoed in her ears.

Darcy had arrived at the hotel earlier that day to unpack her mistress's expansive trousseau. Alex booked a private Pullman car, and Darcy would accompany the couple on their honeymoon trip to Niagara Falls. She helped Winnie shed her coat and hung it in the wardrobe.

"I've finished with the unpacking, sir," she told Alex. "Is there anything else you'll be needin'?"

Alex lit a cigar. "No, thank you. That will be all for tonight."

Darcy's eyes shifted to Winnie, begging an unspoken question.

"Yes, Darcy," said Winnie. "You may go."

"Well, then goodnight, sir." She curtsied. "Good night, Miss—I'm sorry, I mean, Mrs. Sullivan," she stammered and scurried to the servant's quarters in the hotel.

Despite the crackling fire, Winnie shivered from a sudden chill. She sat on the sofa adjacent to the hearth kneading her hands above flickering flames that jumped and fluttered like the butterflies in her stomach.

"How stupid of me," said Alex when he noticed, rushing to her side. "Please forgive me, my dear. You must be cold and exhausted."

"I am a little tired," she confessed.

Alex cradled her hands gently in his, exhaling a warm breath over them. Winnie shuddered as an unfamiliar tingling sensation radiated throughout her body. Alex's ardent lips brushed the insides of her wrists with tender kisses as he gazed lovingly in her eyes with a longing that reached the very depths of his soul. Winnie trembled as another thrilling wave washed over her, and she returned Alex's gaze with eyes expressing her love for him, bearing witness to newfound emotions.

"Would you care to retire for the evening, my dear?"

"Why yes," she replied with a demure blush.

Alex remained in the sitting room while she prepared for her wedding night. Winnie found her white peignoir spread out on the four-poster bed. Smoothing her fingers over the delicate lace, she wondered why her mother had fussed so much over the design and material of something she was just going to sleep in. With Darcy dismissed for the night, it took longer than expected to undress without help, and Alex tapped gently on the door just as she slipped the gown over her head.

"May I enter, my dear?"

Like a frightened child during a thunderstorm, Winnie jumped into the large bed, pulling the blankets up to her chin. "Yes, Alex," she answered tentatively. "Come in."

Alex opened the door slowly, stepped into the room, and paused. Winnie noticed a shadow of concern pass over his face before he went into the adjoining bathroom to change into his nightclothes. When he emerged several minutes later, she could not conceal her fear and horror.

Winnie's parents had always shielded her from the unpleasant aspects of life, and education for young girls by the standards of the day didn't include biology or any mention of the male and female anatomy. Consequently, Winnie had no knowledge of men other than their function as husband and provider. Now her mind raced as she remembered her mother's grim words of advice, sending her into a panic. She thought she might faint. Unable to move or speak, Winnie just stared. She didn't see Alex look down at the natural result of his desire. She was too frightened to notice his expression of love and compassion for his innocent young bride.

"Goodnight, Winnie," he said abruptly and left the room.

Relief washed over Winnie in calming waves. She relaxed, not realizing she had backed up against the mahogany headboard, almost completely covered by the heavy quilts. Wrapped in a sanctuary of bed linens, she felt ashamed of her reaction. Alex never hurt her, always treating her like a delicate flower. There was no reason to fear him before, or now, as her husband. Sliding down from the high four-poster bed, Winnie padded barefoot to the door, pushing it slightly ajar. Through the small gap, she saw Alex curled up on the sofa, alone on his wedding night. Tears filled her eyes and her heart swelled with love. And as the new feelings of desire mingled with an intense longing to be near him, she whispered, "Alex. Come to bed, dear."

The wedding of Miss Winifred Cornelia Armstrong and Mr. Alexander Sullivan took place at four o'clock on December 24, 1915, in St. John's Episcopal Church.

The sanctuary was decorated for the Christmas holiday, with a profusion of red and white poinsettias in addition to evergreen bunting that was draped over the altar railings and pews.

Given away in marriage by her father, the bride was stunning in a Paris-made gown of white satin, trimmed in white fur about the bodice, sleeves, and six-foot train. Miss Armstrong carried a bouquet of red roses and wore a three-karat heart-shaped ruby pendant surrounded by sparkling diamonds, a wedding gift from the groom.

The maid of honor was the bride's cousin, Miss Aurelia Fowler, who wore a forest green velvet gown trimmed in white satin.

The bridegroom carried a gold pocket watch—a wedding gift from the bride. His friend and business partner, Jonathan Cromwell, acted as best man.

A private reception followed at the Armstrong residence after the ceremony.

Winnie read the wedding announcement in the society section several times before cutting it out and pasting it in the scrapbook she began when she and Alex were engaged. It was the happiest time of her life, a whirlwind of parties and planning overshadowed only by the tragic death of Alex's mother. Winnie wanted to remember every moment, nonetheless.

The newlyweds moved in with Winnie's parents after returning from their honeymoon until the construction of their mansion was completed. Alex sat next to his bride in the Armstrong's sun-drenched morning room reading the business section of the newspaper while Winnie sipped coffee from a bone china cup. Winnie's initial fears about marriage had vanished. And through love and trust, the couple's intimate relationship was satisfying in every respect. She almost pitied her mother, who meant well, with her rather ominous advice on her wedding day.

One year later, the Sullivans moved into their new home. The building surpassed the Armstrong residence in size and grandeur, but its elegant design was refined and esthetically pleasing, nonetheless. Now, the only thing missing was a baby. After suffering two miscarriages early in her pregnancies, Winnie's doctors discouraged the couple from trying again, but she could not be dissuaded. She desperately wanted to give Alex a child.

April 6, 1917. President Woodrow Wilson called for war on Germany, entering the United States in World War I. America had a small army, and men volunteered by the thousands to participate in the fighting. All, it seemed, except Jonathan, who was too old to enlist, and Alex, who felt he could do more good on the home front by supplying trucks and ambulance vehicles for the war. Besides, he would never leave Winnie.

Ironically, the war in Europe made Alex wealthy beyond expectation. And now that his mansion was complete, he financed the construction of a home for widows and orphans in Gloucester, to be named after his mother as a memorial in her honor. Another large sum was donated to the school in Peabody where he and Winnie first met. No one understood his generosity to the institution. Only he and Winnie knew what evoked such benevolence.

Despite the escalating hostilities overseas, the Sullivans planned to celebrate the coming new year of 1918 with a gala event equaled in lavish pageantry only by their own wedding reception two years earlier. Totally immersed in the preparations, Winnie managed every detail of the elaborate celebration. When her healthy luminescent skin suddenly turned pale, Alex insisted that she rest and let the servants take over. But she refused all help, knowing the reason for her pallid complexion.

Winnie consulted with her doctors but decided to wait two months past the critical first month before telling Alex she was pregnant again. Estimating her delivery date to be sometime in August, the concerned physicians insisted on monitoring

Winnie closely through another risky pregnancy. Because of her history of miscarriages, she agreed.

On the night of their New Year's party when the clock struck twelve, Winnie gave Alex the happy news. Thrilled and frightened at the same time, he held her gently in his arms, oblivious to the revelry around them, silently praying that this time would be different.

The severe nausea of morning sickness plagued Winnie daily, confining her to bed. Only able to keep down crackers and water, she lost weight, becoming weak and frail. Fearing for her life, Alex hired a private nurse and doctor to care for his wife twenty-four hours a day. Winnie gladly endured it all, knowing that as long as she felt sick, she still carried her baby. Weeks passed with no relief until she climbed out of bed one morning with unexpected energy. Although wobbly on her feet at first, she surprised everyone by eating a hearty breakfast, then proceeded to supervise the nursery renovations.

Winnie's strength returned as she continued to gain weight, and her doctors were pleased with her progress. Not even the war overseas could dampen the young couple's joy. Curiously, one small item of news appearing on page five of the *Peabody Gazette* should have been a cause for concern but was passed over by most of the world.

March 11, 1918. An Army private stationed in Fort Riley, Kansas, reported to the camp hospital with symptoms of sore throat, fever, and headache. Illnesses often spread rapidly in the close quarters of military camps, so when over 100 soldiers came down with the same unexplainable symptoms the same day, officials remained unconcerned. The number increased to 500 at the end of that week.

By July, hundreds of cases were being reported daily among the military population, and health officials in Philadelphia issued a bulletin referencing what was dubbed the

"Spanish" Influenza." Although newsworthy, no alerts or warnings were issued to civilians.

For the Sullivans, those months passed easily as the time for their baby's arrival drew near. Then on a hot, humid night, Winnie went into labor. She gave birth the following day, August 19, 1918, to a healthy girl. The proud parents named her Victoria Bridget Sullivan. It was an easy delivery for Winnie—surprising after experiencing so many complications before—making this child even more precious.

Rather than calling by phone, Alex sent a messenger to personally deliver the news of his daughter's birth to Jonathan Cromwell, his business partner and friend. Jonathan's health had been declining of late, and he had gradually surrendered his responsibilities to Alex. Jonathan no longer went to the office, and Alex hoped the happy news would brighten his spirits. But when the somber-looking messenger returned thirty minutes later, he knew something dreadful had occurred.

Earlier that day, Jonathan's housekeeper had heard him call out, and the good woman rushed to his aid, finding him slumped over his desk. She summoned his doctor immediately, but it was too late. A brief post-mortem examination determined that Jonathan had suffered a massive heart attack that had killed him instantly. Although the knowledge that he hadn't suffered was somewhat of a comfort to Alex, the pain of losing his trusted friend and mentor so abruptly, like his mother, was difficult to bear.

With no next of kin, Alex made all the arrangements for his elaborate funeral, and Peabody residents turned out en masse to pay their respects. The following week, Jonathan's attorneys executed the terms of his will, and Alex was overwhelmed by his dear friend's generosity. Jonathan had left his entire estate to Alex, and he was now the sole owner of The Cromwell Power Automobile Company.

~

When The Bridget Sullivan Widows and Orphans Home was completed, the Gloucester Chamber of Commerce invited Alex to speak at the memorial service. It was too soon after giving birth for Winnie and Victoria to make the journey with him, so he traveled alone. Before leaving, Alex met with his attorney to amend his will.

The current document stated that upon his death, Winnie would receive everything: the house, business, and any other properties he owned or managed. That remained the same. Alex added that in the event of Winnie's death, the estate would pass to Victoria, her interests held and managed in trust until reaching her majority. Satisfied that his affairs were in order, he kissed his wife and daughter goodbye.

Receiving a hero's welcome at the place of his birth, Alex was greeted at the train station like a campaigning politician. The mayor of Gloucester gave Alex a key to the city, then personally escorted him to a covered pavilion facing the widows and orphans home he built. Grateful applause that exploded after Alex's heartfelt speech during the dedication was followed by a reverent silence when he unveiled a monument in the front garden. Alex's heart knotted in his chest at the bas-relief image of his mother carved in the stone. His last official duty was to place a wreath at another stone monument —an obelisk in the town square, bearing the names of Gloucester's citizens lost in the New England Hurricane of 1915.

Exhausted from his journey and the emotional events of the day, Alex chose to return to his hotel rather than take part in the festivities planned for that evening, but not before one last walk to the harbor. Fully aware of the dangers of the wharf, especially at night, he was drawn to the place, nonetheless. And as the weathered planks of the deserted wharf creaked eerily under his feet, his chest swelled with pride thinking of how far he had come from where he toiled as a youth.

"Can you spare a few coins for an old sailor, sir?"

Startled, Alex froze in his tracks and gripped his cane like a club. "Who's there?"

"I don't need much. Just enough for a little whiskey to get these old bones through the night," replied a gravelly voice between lung-rattling coughs.

"Who are you?" cried Alex, indignation now replacing alarm. "I demand you show yourself!"

An ominous silence enveloped the wharf while murky saltwater slapped against the pier's wood pilings. With adrenaline pumping, Alex prepared to defend himself. "Come out, I say!"

A barrel fell over, and a black cat skittered across his path. Then a figure emerged from the inky shadows, one ragged limb at a time—a man so dark and dirty that if he hadn't opened his mouth to speak, Alex wouldn't have known the location of his head. "A few pennies will do," he wheezed, holding out a gnarled hand.

Despite his loathing for anything related to the sea, Alex felt pity for the old salt. *That could've been me.* Reaching in his pocket, he threw a couple of dollars in the unfortunate fellow's direction.

"God bless you, sir," he croaked, crawling across the splintered wood to retrieve the coins. "God bless you and your family."

Suddenly, the sound of the old man's grating voice catapulted Alex back in time. "No. No," he muttered as once buried, painful memories were forcibly exhumed.

Impossible! He's dead—drowned years ago. It can't be him.

But there was no mistake of the beggar's identity, and Alex wrestled with emotions ranging from disgust to an intense desire for revenge at the unbelievable sight of his father, Eddie Sullivan.

Although Eddie had been separated from the surviving crew members of the ill-fated *Indigo Sky* and presumed dead, he had miraculously made it to shore alone, exhausted and disoriented. Days later, when news of the sinking schooner appeared in the newspaper with him listed as dead, Eddie decided to stay that way. He spent the next years of his life wandering, begging, and drinking his way up and down the coast of Massachusetts, occasionally serving onboard a ship under an assumed name. Mostly, he remained in a drunken stupor, only recently finding his way back to Gloucester.

It's not fair! It just isn't fair that he lives and my mother is dead!

Alex fought the urge to kill Eddie himself, but relented, throwing a few more coins at his pitiful father instead. Eddie gathered them up, not knowing the reason for his good luck. "Thank you, sir. God bless you."

That's all he'll ever get from me.

Scurrying away like a water rat, Eddie disappeared into the gloomy darkness, never recognizing his own son.

September 5, 1918. On the day of his departure from Gloucester, Alex rose early, having breakfast alone in the hotel dining room. Anxious to return home to his family, he read the morning newspaper while checking out.

"Was everything to your satisfaction during your stay with us, sir," asked the front desk clerk. "Sir?"

"Oh, yes. Everything was fine," Alex replied absently, his eyes fixed on news that blared on the front page much like the way Joshua's horn trumpeted before the walls of Jericho fell.

In the article, the acting Surgeon General of the Army described horrifying symptoms and deadly results of the Spanish Influenza he witnessed at a nearby army camp in Boston. He reported that 200 men died in a single day, with more falling ill at a rapid rate. The Massachusetts Department of Health had issued an alert that an epidemic was underway, with the prophetic warning that unless precautions were taken; the virus would spread quickly to the civilian population, possibly affecting thousands. Although alarmed by the prediction, there was no way Alex could have been prepared for the deadly flu that now posed a threat to the entire nation and the world.

Chapter Ten

"I Opened the Window and In Flew Enza."

Colorful fall foliage and cooler temperatures returned as expected in the autumn of 1918. The previous year's "typical flu" reappeared, as well, but with a stronger, more powerful strain. At first, the disease was confined to military personnel and prison populations. But when three civilian residents of Boston dropped dead in early September, city officials were taken by surprise, totally unprepared for the enormity and scope of the virus that killed them. The flu had extended its deadly reach beyond the boundaries of army camps in a grisly campaign of terror.

By the first week of September 1918, Boston lost more than 1,000 citizens. It wasn't long before similar reports arrived from New York, Chicago, and Philadelphia as the Spanish Flu gripped the United States in a death-like hold. Newspapers across the nation described the symptoms of the deadly flu in frightening, graphic detail.

Those infected who were strong and in good health in the morning were so weak they could not walk by noon of the same day. Sufferers endured excruciating aches and pains throughout their entire bodies, feeling as if beaten with a bat. High fevers, often reaching 105 degrees, were common, accompanied by bouts of delirium, as ordinary, inanimate objects became horrifying images in the minds of the sick. As the virus ravaged their bodies, the faces of those stricken took on a bluish color. A relentless cough brought up bloodstained sputum.

The eventual cause of death was a fierce type of pneumonia. The victim's lungs quickly filled with bloody, foamy fluid rendering them gasping and unable to breathe. They eventually suffocated in their own secretions, bleeding from the nose, ears, and mouth. Most lingered, suffering for days, while others died within hours of feeling ill.

Peabody spiraled into a state of emergency. All public gatherings were canceled, schools and businesses closed, church services suspended, and funerals limited to fifteen minutes. Due to a shortage of morticians and gravediggers, the dead were buried in mass graves, some without coffins, which had become scarce and virtually unavailable.

Alex decided to take his family to a cottage in the White Mountains of New Hampshire. Hopefully, far from the crowded cities, they might escape the horrible infection. He planned to leave the next day, making hasty arrangements to communicate with his secretary by telephone and courier. When he left the house that morning to secure his office, Alex gave Winnie strict instructions.

"Do *not* for any reason, go out today," he told her sternly. "In fact, it would be better if you and Victoria stayed in your rooms until I return. Remember, you must both wear your masks at all times. Never take them off!"

Winnie just nodded.

The entire household staff worked feverishly to complete the monumental task of closing the mansion on short notice, leaving Winnie to pack her personal belongings alone. With baby Victoria safely in her bassinet wearing a tiny mask, the frightened young mother donned hers, preparing for the family's departure. The back doorbell rang, but Winnie ignored it, assuming the servants would respond, and Victoria began to cry.

"Hush, sweetie," Winnie murmured, lifting her from the bassinet.

The ringing escalated to frantic banging so Winnie wrapped Victoria in a blanket and hurried down the back stairs to answer the door herself. With the crying child balanced on her hip, she swung the servant's entrance door open with her free hand. A messenger boy waited on the other side.

"I have a special delivery for Mr. Sullivan, ma'am," he said, removing his cap.

Several locks of Winnie's black tresses had broken free of their hairpins.

"I'm Mrs. Sullivan," she said, smoothing them back in place. "I'll accept that for my husband."

"Yes, ma'am," replied the boy, holding out a clipboard and a pencil. "Sign here, please."

Victoria wriggled in her arms as she took the pencil and scribbled her name.

"Do you need any help, ma'am?"

"No thank you. I can manage," she replied as Victoria let out a piercing scream.

"Are you sure, ma'am?" he pressed. "I'm the oldest of six and pretty good with the little ones."

"No, I'm fine, really," she insisted as she returned the pencil and accepted the parcel, cradling it in her other free arm.

Then the infant's small hand became entangled in Winnie's mask and pulled it off her face. With one arm clutching her baby and the other still holding the parcel, Winnie's eyes widened in alarm as the messenger released a blusterous sneeze—a sneeze that in normal circumstances was no reason for concern. But the enormity of what had just occurred left Winnie frozen with fear, and she held her breath, silently praying for protection from the deadly virus. Oblivious to her distress, the boy wiped his nose on his sleeve, slapped his cap on his head and said, "Good day to you, ma'am."

Winnie stood, transfixed, as he tucked the clipboard under his arm, hopped on his bicycle, and pedaled away. Finally regaining her composure, she slammed the door shut and let the package drop to the floor. *It was only off for a moment,* she thought, as she repositioned her mask.

Alex arrived home at 2:30 that afternoon. The housekeeper, Nora, greeted him at the door.

"Good afternoon, sir," she said, taking his hat, coat, and gloves.

"Good afternoon, Nora. Where is Mrs. Sullivan?"

She handed Alex his mail. "Upstairs with the wee one, sir, tending to her packing."

"Thank you, Nora. That will be all until dinner."

"Yes, sir," she replied and scuttled to the kitchen.

"Winnie, dear! I'm home," called Alex, leaning on the balustrade. When she didn't answer, he casually climbed the stairs while flipping through his mail. "Winnie, is that any way to greet your loving husband?"

Silence.

A dreadful thought found its way, unbidden, into his mind.

"Winnie?" he called again as a stab of panic pierced his heart.

Filled now with terror, Alex's heart pounded like a sledgehammer in his chest with unspeakable fear. Fear that mounted with each step as he flew up the long staircase.

"Winnie, answer me!" he cried, coming to a sudden halt at the open door to their bedroom.

"Winnie?" he whispered. "Honey?"

Despite the bright afternoon light, the room felt oppressively dark and heavy. Unable to comprehend the grim scene before him, Alex stood frozen in place, seeing his beloved Winnie lying motionless on the bed. Fully clothed and still wearing her mask, Alex felt himself sinking into a dark abyss as he approached her lifeless form. Breathing became difficult as a morbid gloom grabbed him by the throat and squeezed. Lower and lower, descending helplessly into the awful darkness, he knelt beside the bed.

With a trembling hand, Alex removed her mask. "Winnie?" he whimpered. "Wake up, honey. Please wake up."

Only a trickle of blood at the corner of her mouth marred the peaceful expression on Winnie's lovely face. Alex's chin quivered as he caressed her ice-cold cheek, and an all-consuming pain exploded in his heart when the terrifying realization slowly penetrated his consciousness.

"No! Nooo!" he shouted, refusing to accept the unthinkable. "No. Oh, God no. Please, God. Not my Winnie!"

Alex gathered her lifeless body in his arms. Her arms and head fell, limp, as he held her close. Weeping softly, at first, like a mewling kitten, he collapsed helplessly into visceral, racking sobs.

"Mr. Sullivan!" cried Nora, from downstairs. "What is it, sir?"

"Go away! Leave us alone!" he wailed, dissolving into an agonizing flood of tears. "Don't leave me, Winnie. Please don't leave me," he begged, rocking back and forth, keening in unfathomable grief. "I love you. I can't live without you." Then suddenly, Alex heard another sound in the room, other than his own mournful weeping – the innocent gurgle and coo of his infant daughter.

"Victoria? Oh, my Lord, Victoria. You're alive!"

Winnie's body was interred within hours of her death. Her parents cared for Victoria while Alex sank to the deepest depths of mourning, refusing to eat or receive the many calls of condolences. Weeks later he experienced an epiphany.

He could do nothing to fight the deadly flu that took his dear wife, but he was able to help his country defeat the Germans; and rather than facilitate more killing, Alex volunteered for the Red Cross Ambulance Corps. Leaving Victoria in his in-laws' capable hands, he shipped out the following week with hundreds of young soldiers. But when the troops embarked from Boston harbor, no one knew they all carried a weapon far more powerful than in any military arsenal as they unwittingly transported the deadly Spanish Flu overseas.

Because of his mechanical background, Alex was appointed to supervise maintenance and repairs of the Red Cross fleet of vehicles, ironically, the very ones he and Jonathan had manufactured. However, when he reported for duty in Italy, he was assigned as an ambulance driver instead. He accepted the orders with phlegmatic indifference. Nothing mattered now that Winnie was gone.

October 8, 1918. Alex and another volunteer received orders to deliver medical supplies to a field hospital behind enemy lines.

They were on their way in minutes to complete the urgent mission, wasting no time for small talk or introductions.

Alex scanned the bombed and burning terrain for danger from the front seat while the young driver prudently took secondary roads, taking advantage of the natural cover provided by trees and brush. At one point, they were forced to drive across an open expanse. That's when they heard a sound neither would ever forget—the dreaded high-pitched whistle of a mortar shell. It was like hearing a gun cocked at your head—a sound that meant only one thing. Death was imminent. Panic, alarm, and a heart-pumping adrenaline rush took over.

"Look out! Take cover!" screamed Alex.

But there was no time to run, nowhere to hide. A deafening blast threw Alex from the vehicle, and his driver lay beside the ambulance with a gravely wounded leg.

The resourceful volunteer quickly assessed the situation using his belt as a tourniquet to staunch the bleeding. Several feet away, Alex lay unconscious, exposed to enemy fire. Despite his own serious injury, the brave young man reached Alex, dragging him out of harm's way, taking refuge under the wrecked ambulance. Hours later, both men were rescued and taken to a hospital in Milan where they received treatment. Miraculously, Alex only suffered a concussion with numerous cuts and scrapes and received a new assignment the following week. Before leaving, he made inquiries at the hospital as to the whereabouts of the man who had saved his life. An orderly directed him to a room where several nurses hovered around a patient; a mesh of cables and pulleys suspended the injured man's leg above crisp white sheets. Although appearing annoyed, Alex could see he thoroughly enjoyed the attention as one nurse fluffed his pillow while another tucked in his blanket.

"Hello," said Alex, stepping into the room. "Remember me?"

"Yeah. I remember," he said and chuckled. "How could I forget?"

Alex's gaze took in the stark white room. "Nice place."

"It's okay. Too bad I had to get blown up to enjoy it," he said, waving the nurses away.

"Well, it looks like you're in good hands," said Alex.

"One of the spoils of war, I guess," he said as a roguish grin flashed on his face. "It's not so bad though, considering the alternative."

He means death, thought Alex. *Funny, I would have preferred it.* "Uh, right. That's what I wanted to talk to you about. I never got the chance to thank you for saving my life."

The battlefield is the great leveler. Rich or poor, educated or illiterate—all men become equal the moment they're faced with the decision to kill or be killed. The moment when men are forced to perform acts to defend themselves and their comrades in arms. And though a life was saved on the battlefield, the young man made light of his heroic actions.

"Don't mention it. You would have done the same. Just think. You gave me my ticket home, so I guess we're even."

Alex shrugged. "So, how's your leg? It looks serious."

"It hurts like hell," he said with a grimace at a sudden stab of pain. "They pulled out a lot of shrapnel. I'll probably be here a while before I can get back to the States."

"Where're you from anyway?"

"Oak Park, Illinois. How 'bout yourself?"

"Peabody, Massachusetts."

"When do you think *you'll* be heading home?"

"I don't know, but it doesn't matter when," replied Alex. "In fact, I don't think I ever want to go home again."

"Uh, sure, pal," he said with furrowed brows at Alex's unusual declaration. "Thanks for stopping by."

"Yeah, I should get moving," said Alex, glancing at the clock. "I have new orders, and my train leaves in an hour."

"Uh...you know, I never did get your name in all the excitement."

"I'm Alexander Sullivan. And you?"

"Hemingway, Ernest Hemingway."

They shook hands, knowing they'd never meet again.

October 11, 1918. A shortage of volunteers forced Alex to drive solo on his next assignment, and he traveled for several desolate miles through clouds of white smoke, pungent with the odor of gunpowder. *Yea, though I walk through the valley of the shadow of death, I will fear no evil for thou art with me. Psalm 23.* His mother had read that bible verse to him many times, and Alex recited it to himself as the ambulance bounced along the rutted road to the field hospital. A crude map indicated he was approaching his destination; and as the engine sputtered, an ominous feeling in the pit of his stomach gripped him in warning. Slowing cautiously, Alex felt relieved when he arrived safely; but his heart sank when the ambulance finally ground to a halt. The field hospital was destroyed.

Alex ran through the still-smoldering wreckage to the burned, twisted bodies of the brave men and women who had been fighting to save lives. Their children will grow up without fathers and mothers. Parents will grieve over their untimely deaths. No one saved them. His body shook uncontrollably at the carnage, overcome with the futility of war—sick of the fighting, sick of senseless dying, sick of life without Winnie. Exhausted and weary of trying to stay alive, Alex fell to the ground, unable to feel even sadness. Then, his head snapped up when he heard it—the shrill harbinger of death. This time,

Alex made no attempt to run, fully aware the familiar whine of the mortar heralded his own grisly demise.

The first shell hit the ambulance, and it exploded into a fireball igniting what was left of the hospital, incinerating the dead in a horrific funeral pyre. The intense heat of the raging inferno surrounded Alex instantly, and breathing became impossible as the suffocating smoke and sheer terror stole the very breath from his body. Licks of flames crept closer, closer, tempting him to join them in their orgy of death. What was that smell—his own burning flesh? With his spirit finally broken, Alex surrendered, accepting his fate, never hearing the high-pitched peal of the second mortar as the hell-like blaze thundered in his ears.

When Alex opened his eyes, the fire had gone out. A misty haze replaced the turbid smoke, and it was quiet—too quiet. Alone and still wearing his uniform, Alex examined his body. Surprisingly, he was unharmed. *Well, my mother always said God watches over drunks, little children, and the Irish.* In the distance, a light beckoned. He walked toward it, hoping to find his way out of the fog. That's when Alex realized he wasn't alone.

A parade of humanity filed past him—apparitions of men, women, and children of all races, ages, and nationalities. Although confused, Alex remained calm as the somber procession shuffled along, disappearing one by one into the light. He watched the marching procession for what could have been hours, days, or years until a familiar voice called out.

"Oh, me darlin' boy!"

Alex spun around, his gaze darting, searching. "Mam? Where are you?"

"Over here, Alex. Over here."

"But I don't see you."

"Here I am," said Bridget Sullivan, stepping out of the fog. Half shadow, half silvery substance, her image flickered at first before condensing to appear in solid form. Mother and son ran to each other, and Alex's solemn eyes asked the dreaded question at their bittersweet reunion.

"Yes, son," she said gently. "It's true. I always knew we'd be together again, only not so soon."

"Then where's Grandad? Why isn't he with you?"

"We all go to our special place when we die, Alex," she explained. "He's happy again with your grandmother. I came to help you find your special place, then I'll be goin' too."

"But what *happened* to me? I don't remember anything after arriving at the bombed hospital."

Bridget waved her arm in a slow arc without reply, and a vision in the clouds appeared chronicling the last minutes of Alex's life like a film in a flickering kinetoscope. He gasped when the ambulance exploded, shielded his eyes at the blinding flash from the second shell, and cringed at his broken form, lying in the smoke and ashes. Feeling like millions of invisible needles pricking his skin, the needles seemed to grow as he watched, feeling more like knives mercilessly slashing his body.

Reaching out to his mother like a child seeking comfort from the excruciating pain, Alex recoiled in horror at the sight of his scorched hands and shriveled skin. A layer of black ash clung to his charred, blood-soaked uniform, shreds of metal stuck to what was left of his body, and he shuddered as the odor of death and decay assaulted his nostrils.

"The last bomb did you in, son," she told him, somberly.

The shocking truth hit Alex like another explosion. His mind reeled as he wrestled with the reality of his fate—the possibility of spending eternity mangled and in pain. He held out his burned and bloodied hands, pleading. "But what's to become of me now?"

"Go to your good wife," said his mother. "She'll know what to do."

"Winnie? Is she here?"

"Yes, Alex. She's expecting you."

"No!" he cried, hiding his shattered face. "I can't let her see me like this. I'm a monster!"

"You must go to your wife, son," she repeated, her image fading with every word. "Go to her. Go to her..."

"Mam, don't leave. Please, stay with me!"

Desperate for every second with his mother, Alex stumbled about, following her thinning wraithlike figure and waning voice.

"I'm sorry I couldn't save you, Mam. I love you."

"I know, son. The love we shared in life is the only thing that matters now. That love is eternal. It never dies," she said finally, melting into the clouds.

Losing his mother again was as unbearable as the pain that returned, leaving Alex engulfed again in a sickly miasma, miserable and alone. This must be hell—a punishment justly meted for not saving his mother, for not being with Jonathan when he needed his friend, and for leaving Winnie alone, unprotected, the day she died. Yes, this is what he deserved.

Then he heard a soft voice.

"I've been waiting for you, my darling."

"Winnie?"

"Yes, Alex. It's me."

"Winnie. Where are you?" He whirled around blindly. "I can't see you."

"I'm right here, Alex."

Nothing more than a glittering mist at first, Winnie's nebulous image seemed to condense like morning dew; and Alex gazed upon his beloved, dressed in the white gown she wore the night of her debutante ball.

"No!" cried Alex, turning away. "I'm hideous."

"Don't be afraid to look at me, my love. I know what happened. I'm here to help you."

Alex lifted his head slowly. "You can help me?"

"Yes, my darling," said Winnie, gazing at him with the same sweet smile that touched his heart many years ago. She opened her arms to embrace him, and shafts of pure white light poured from the palms of her hands. Cowering at the awesome sight, Alex stood transfixed, unable to move.

"There's nothing to be afraid of anymore," she said. "Now that you're with me, nothing will ever hurt you again."

Without warning, a howling wind blew up, shrieking like eons of suffering, tormented souls. Alex cringed as it whipped the heavy fog around him like the funnel cloud of a tornado. Pressing his hands over his ears, he screamed in the eye of the spectral storm. "Winnie! Help me! Help me!"

"Nothing will hurt you," echoed Winnie's voice. "Nothing will hurt you."

Then, Alex watched spellbound as the fierce wind bent the straight beams of light causing them to curl, engulfing him in a radiant coil. Terrified, he flinched as fiery streaks spiraled over his former body, methodically sloughing off his tattered uniform and charred skin. Around and around the beams moved, washing away all physical and emotional suffering. Finally, the wind receded and the cleansing rays dimmed, leaving Alex transformed into a young man donning the very suit he wore the night of Winnie's debutante ball. His body and soul healed through the power of Winnie's undying love.

"Come to me, my darling husband," she said. "I've been waiting for you."

Alex hesitated, afraid to touch her. Afraid that if he did, she would disappear and leave him again.

"There's no need to worry," she told him, reading his thoughts. "There is no pain or sadness here. There are no tears in heaven—only love and happiness. We'll never be separated again."

Filled with rapturous joy and peace, Alex gathered Winnie in his arms. "I'll love you forever," he whispered, holding her close.

And as the angels sang, Winnie and Alex danced to the heavenly music together again, partners for all eternity.

The Red Cross sent notice of Alex's death to the only family he had left—a house already in mourning where the Spanish Flu had claimed two more victims: Winnie's parents. Baby Victoria, only a few months old, had survived with no next of kin.

Liquidation of the Sullivan estate took place immediately. Proceeds from the sale paid back taxes and various loans Alex had secured to fund new business ventures with nothing left for Victoria. Once an heiress to a family fortune, she became a ward of the state. To make matters worse, a fire ravaged the Peabody Town Hall destroying thousands of legal documents, birth certificates included, leaving Victoria and countless other orphans without an identity.

Fortunately, a kind and loving couple adopted the nameless infant. She thrived in their care, eventually marrying and living a happy life, unaware of her family that perished during the war and the Spanish Flu pandemic. Her well-meaning adoptive parents kept the true circumstances of her birth a secret—her past lost, along with the Spartan pen.

November 9, 1918, Kaiser Wilhelm II abdicated. The Armistice took effect at the eleventh hour on the eleventh day of the eleventh month of 1918. The Great War ended just four weeks after Alex's death.

Peace had been restored, but the flu raged on, leaving more victims in its wake until June of 1920 when the pandemic that killed an estimated 675,000 Americans and 50 million people worldwide left as mysteriously as it had arrived.

Part Three

Chapter Eleven
Gramps

An empty box of tissues sat on the Russo's kitchen table. Feeling calmer now, Angie tossed it in the trash—her tears spent after breaking her engagement with Mac the night before. The bag of doughnuts from the Doughnut Depot remained on the table in front of Marie.

"What are you going to do now that you're not getting married, Ang?" she asked, eyeing the white paper bag.

Angie plodded over to the coffee pot on the counter. Her back was turned, but her ears perked up at the telltale sound of crinkling paper as she filled her cup. "Well, for starters, I called the country club while you were at Mac's returning the ring," she said and whipped around, plucking the bag of doughnuts from Marie's sugar-craving grasp.

"Aw, c'mon, Ang," she begged with outstretched arms. "Give 'em back."

Angie held the grease-stained bag beyond her reach. "You don't have to eat all of them now, Ree. Save some for tomorrow."

"They don't taste the same the next day," she insisted. "You gotta eat them when they're fresh."

Angie returned to her chair with a full cup of coffee and dropped the bag in her lap. "Instead of the next day, think of the next month they'll be your hips."

"Oh, I don't mind," said Marie, patting her Rubenesque thighs. "I like to think of them as good friends that just stay awhile."

"I'll remind you of that next time we shop for jeans."

"So what was so bad about calling the country club?" asked Marie, ignoring her well-intentioned warning. "They should've been grateful that you gave them enough notice to re-book the date."

Angie grimaced as if tasting something bitter, took a deep breath, and said, "I had to speak to Bianca Lombardi."

Marie gestured with her finger down her throat like she was gagging.

"That about sums up my feelings, too," said Angie, folding her arms across her chest.

"Sorry I asked. I forgot she's the banquet coordinator at the country club."

"That doesn't matter. I'd hate her if she were the Sunday school teacher," said Angie through gritted teeth. "Bianca's been out to get me *and* every boyfriend I ever had since the panty incident."

When they were in the fourth grade, Bianca told Angie an erroneous version of the facts of life, convincing Angie that a boy could make her pregnant just by touching her. From that moment on, Angie lived in fear of becoming an unwed mother from an accidental bump in the hall. She managed to avoid all male contact until David Gershowitz rammed into her during a co-ed volleyball tournament. Only Bianca knew why Angie screamed and collapsed on the court before the entire student body. To make matters worse, David scored the winning point. Bianca and Angie got along like Al Capone and the IRS ever since.

"That was so cool when you swiped Bianca's lace panties during gym class to get even," said Marie with sisterly pride.

Angie placed her elbows on the table, resting her chin in her hands. "Do you remember the look on Bianca's face when she found them dangling on the cafeteria bulletin board between the weekly lunch menu and the honor roll list?"

"Yeah, I do," said Marie, leaning back in her chair. "And I remember Dad's face, too, when Mr. Lombardi showed up at the house. I never knew the vein on Dad's head could bulge like that without exploding."

"I'll never forget that day as long as I live. It was a Monday."

"Yeah, Monday," echoed Marie with a grin.

Angie raised her cup to her lips and took a sip. "I hate to admit it, but I was kinda jealous that Bianca had panties with the days of the week embroidered on them. I always wanted those."

"Her family owns Lombardi Motors. It's the biggest car dealership in town," said Marie with a wry face. "They could afford to spoil her with fancy underwear."

"All I know is she deserved that and more," snarled Angie, banging her fist on the table. "Did you know Bianca even made a pass at Mac when we booked the wedding? It was like I wasn't even there! She only pulled that stunt once, but I don't trust her as far as I can spit."

"You don't spit, Ang."

"Exactly."

"The country club was a nice place," said Marie, changing the subject. "You were lucky to get it."

"I never really felt comfortable having the reception there, but Mac's mother insisted."

"Speaking of mothers, do you think Ma ever bought the story that you were on business trips all those weekends you stayed at Mac's?"

"If she didn't, she'll never admit it," said Angie. "You know Ma. When it comes to the family, we can do no wrong."

"Yeah. One of us could be standing over a dead body with the smoking gun in our hand. She'd say someone else pulled the trigger."

Angie left the bag of doughnuts on her chair and collected their empty coffee cups. "Well, I might as well get this over with," she sighed while loading them in the dishwasher.

"You mean you're going to break the news to Ma and Dad now?" asked Marie, rising. "Do you think it's a good time?"

Angie dried her hand with a dishtowel, draped it over the oven door handle, and said, "Do you think there's *ever* going to be a good time?"

"Good point," said Marie burrowing in her handbag. She came up with Angie's keyring. "So, you might as well take your car keys just in case you have to confess and run."

Angie shoved the key chain in the pocket of her jeans.

"I'll go with you, Ang, when you tell the folks," offered Marie. "You know, for moral support."

Angie gave her a hug. "Thanks, Ree."

"Now can I have the doughnuts?"

The doorbell rang a second later. Muffled voices got Marie's attention, and she sniffed the air like a bloodhound. "What's that smell?"

"I think it's a cigar. You know, the ones Dad calls Italian stinkers." Then they both smiled because that only meant one thing—Grandpa Nick.

Angie and Marie rushed into the living room but held back when they found their parents engaged in a serious conversation with a severe-looking woman dressed in a business suit and sensible, unattractive low heels. She had a briefcase slung over her shoulder and a manila envelope held against her chest like it contained top-secret information. In the open doorway stood their grandfather, Nick Russo, with a suitcase at his side and a smoldering cigar in his hand. The woman gave her business card to Sal Russo who read it and threw a disapproving scowl at his father. Gramps stamped out the cigar on the stoop.

"Who's the suit?" Marie whispered to Angie.

"I don't know, but it doesn't look good. I haven't seen the vein on Dad's head bulge like that since the panty incident."

"This is way worse," Marie whispered back. "The vein on the other side of his head is bulging, too."

Nick Russo had moved into a retirement home after his wife died two years ago. Problem was, at eighty years old he showed no signs of slowing down. Usually, his harmless antics just annoyed people. This time he may have gone too far.

"Nice to meet you, Miss Kevetcher. This is my wife, Margaret," began Sal. "And you might as well come in. I know you're there," he added shouting over his shoulder.

The sisters stepped into the living room.

"And these are our daughters, Angela and Marie."

"Pleasure to meet you all," she replied with a polite nod.

"Miss Kevetcher is from the Almost Heaven Retirement Home where Pop lives," Sal explained to his wife, pressing the business card in her hand.

Margaret read the card, furrowed her brow, and asked, "Miss Kevetcher, why is my father-in-law here and not at the home?"

"I'm very sorry, Mrs. Russo," she said in a patronizing tone." There have been some serious complaints lodged against him. As the director of the Almost Heaven community, I have an obligation to provide a safe environment for our residents."

"What kind of complaints?" asked Sal.

Miss Kevetcher glanced at Angie and Marie. "I'd rather not embarrass your family with the details, Mr. Russo."

"He's an old man, what could he possibly do? Does he snore too loud? Did he leave the toilet seat up?"

"That sort of problem we can deal with," Miss Kevetcher told him.

"What then?" he asked again.

"May I speak to you in private, Mr. Russo?"

Sal nodded wearily and led Miss Kevetcher into the kitchen. When they were gone, Gramps made his entrance.

"Angelina! Marie! Come to your grandpa!" he said, with his arms opened wide.

They ran to him just like when they were children, laughing when he pulled two quarters from their ears.

"Gramps, we're not babies anymore. We know how you do that now," said Angie.

"I guess I gotta get some new material, huh?"

"No, just make it a twenty instead of a quarter," joked Marie.

Meanwhile, Margaret had brought in Gramps' suitcase, closed the front door, and languished on the sofa with a faraway look in her eyes. Angie noticed her lips silently moving as she twisted her hands in her lap. She knew her mother believed in a litany of saints that were ready, willing, and able to help with a hopeless case or cure a serious illness. Although Gramps showing up unannounced on their doorstep wasn't exactly hopeless, it was definitely a situation that warranted divine intervention, and Angie wondered which saint her mother was praying to now.

Ten minutes later, Miss Kevetcher stood in the kitchen, gathered her files from the table, and shook Sal's hand. "So, you see, Mr. Russo, I have no choice."

"I know, I know," said Sal, bobbing his head. "Neither do I."

Margaret sprang from the sofa when they entered the living room, giving her husband a questioning look. Sal held up his hand, signaling her to wait, and walked Miss Kevetcher to the door.

"I'm very sorry, Mrs. Russo," she said to Margaret on her way out. "There was nothing I could do."

Sal closed the door behind her, and four sets of eyes shifted accusingly to Gramps.

"What?" he asked with an innocent look.

"What? Is that all you have to say for yourself?" asked his son.

Gramps sat on the sofa and picked up a magazine. "So, we find another place. I don't like the food there anyway."

Margaret tugged on her husband's sleeve. "Sal, dear, what did that woman mean by complaints? Why did she apologize? Why is your father still here?"

"Pop, there was nothing wrong with the food!" roared Sal, too agitated to hear his wife's questions. "Almost Heaven is rated one of the best retirement homes in the area."

"That's what *you* think." The magazine slipped from Gramps' fingers when he stood and faced his son. "You wanna know *why* they call it Almost Heaven? It's because after you move in, you're about this close to shakin' hands with St. Peter," he said with his thumb and forefinger held close together. "*Capisce?*"

"Oh my God."

"And that bunch of *gavones* couldn't wait for us old folks to get there either," he continued. "When my *paesano* Carlo passed, may he rest in peace, his bed wasn't even cold before someone new moved in. It's a senior puppy mill, in-out, badabing badaboom."

Sal threw his hands in the air. "So what do you suggest we do now?"

"We look for another home," replied Gramps with a dismissive wave.

"Oh, you think it's that simple?" demanded Sal as he paced around the room. "You've earned quite a reputation. You keep this up, there won't be a retirement home on Long Island that will accept you."

"Ehh, they make too much out of nothin'," replied Gramps, easing into the recliner.

"I still don't understand why he's here," said Margaret, sounding more confused than before. "Will somebody *please* tell me what this is all about?"

Sal whipped around. "I'll tell you. My father got kicked out of his retirement home again!"

Margaret sank into the nearest chair. "That's the third one in two years," she moaned.

"I'll get the brandy," said Angie.

"No, I'm fine, Angela. Just tell me what happened."

"It was nothin'. Just a little misunderstanding," explained Gramps.

"Pop, the ladies at the home did *not* misunderstand! They knew exactly what you said! You asked them if they wanted to get laid!"

A collective gasp seemed to suck all the air out of the room.

Margaret jumped from the sofa. "Holy Mary, Mother of God!" she prayed, her arm almost a blur from crossing herself over and over.

Angie scooted over and grabbed her mother's arm. "Ma, you can stop that now. I think God got the message."

"That's a new low, even for you, Pop," said Sal, glaring down at his father.

"I'm an old man. I was bored," he explained with his hands

spread apart. "Can't a guy have a little fun?"

"Fun? Those women aren't interested in that kind of fun," Sal told him. "You scared them half to death. They were afraid you were going to attack them in their beds at night."

For a moment, Gramps looked proud of himself. "I still got it, eh? They really thought I'd do it?"

"Apparently so, because that's what got you kicked out."

"It's just as well," said Gramps. "That wasn't the place for me. I need a home where the women aren't afraid of a man with a little lead in his pencil. But they had nothin' to worry about. All I got left is a stub anyway."

Without warning, Margaret's eyes rolled back in her head, her knees buckled, and she fell back on the sofa like a sack of potatoes. Sal flew to her side. "Angie, *now* you can get the brandy. But this time, leave the bottle."

"I'm much better now, dear," Margaret said after polishing off the rest of the blackberry liqueur.

"You still look a little pale, honey," observed Sal fussing over her. "Would you like to lie down for a while?"

"Yes, dear. Maybe I should. I think I'm getting a headache."

Gramps had commandeered the remote and made himself comfortable in front of the TV during Margaret's fainting spell. In all the commotion, no one noticed that he lit a cigar. Each puff he took on the Italian stogie sent a smoke ring above his head like a halo. Crooked, but a halo just the same.

"Pop, can you behave yourself for a few minutes while I take care of Margaret. She's not feeling well."

Gramps blew out another halo. "Yeah, sure, sure."

"What's that smell, dear?" asked Margaret.

"And put out that damn cigar!"

Twenty minutes later, Sal joined Angie and Marie at the kitchen table.

"Where's your grandfather?" he asked.

"Still watching TV," said Angie. "He wanted to know if we get X-rated movies."

Sal just rolled his eyes and dropped his head on the table.

"Is Ma going to be alright?" asked Marie, shaking his arm. "I never saw her faint for real before."

"Your mother is fine," he said, sitting up slowly. "She just drank enough brandy to put her out for the rest of the day."

"So, if Ma's going to be okay, Dad, what's the matter?" asked Angie. "You look really stressed out."

"Girls, I need your help."

"That's a switch," said Marie.

"Yeah," agreed Angie. "What could we possibly do for you?"

"Take your grandfather out for a while. When your mother gets up, we'll need some privacy to discuss the situation."

"What's to discuss? All you have to do is find another retirement home. I'll help you," offered Angie.

Sal rested his elbows on the kitchen table and rubbed his eyes. "I didn't have the heart to tell your mother the whole story. You see, your grandfather is in a bit of a financial bind, as well."

"He's retired. What kind of financial problems could he have?" asked Angie.

"Plenty. They have computers at the home. He lost most of his pension gambling online."

"Doesn't he have Social Security?" asked Marie.

"Yeah, but it's not enough to pay his expenses. He may have to live with us after all. So please keep him out of the house while your mother and I sort this out."

"Well, don't look at me," said Marie. "I've got a date."

Angie and her father blinked twice and stared blankly at Marie.

"Jeez, you don't have to look so surprised," she said, sounding hurt.

"Sorry, sis. Who's the lucky guy?"

"Mac's friend, Rick DiNapoli."

"Doesn't he own that movie memorabilia store, Real to Reel?" asked her father.

"Yeah, that's the one."

"No offense, Ree," said Angie. "But Rick's known you for a while. Why the sudden interest?"

"Beats me," she said with a shrug. "All I know is that it's Saturday night, and *I've* got a date!"

"What about his *Star Trek* obsession?" asked Angie.

"Don't forget *Superman, Star Wars,* and classic movies," added Marie.

"Well, do you think you can handle all that superhero sci-fi stuff?"

"Sure, I can, as long as he doesn't ask me to do anything kinky while pretending to be on the Enterprise. And I won't dress up like Lieutenant Uhura. I'd have to draw the line at the skimpy outfit. You know red's not my color. Though I wouldn't mind wearing that tricked-out Bluetooth thingy in my ear."

"That was way too much information, Marie," said her father, rubbing his temples.

"Sorry, Dad. Well, I gotta get ready for my date," she said as she rose from the table.

"But that's not until tonight," said Angie.

Marie turned and checked the clock on the wall next to a picture of the Last Supper. "You're right. I better get started. *Ciao* for now."

"So, I guess it's all up to you, Angie."

"What am *I* supposed to do with Gramps?"

"Take him to bingo. Your mother is in no condition to go out tonight. He can play in her place."

"Isn't it a little early to go to bingo?"

"Are you kidding? Those old biddies, your mother excluded, of course, get there two hours early to reserve their lucky seats. You can get Gramps settled in your room before you leave.

"My room? Where am I supposed to sleep?"

"On the pull-out bed in Marie's room. It won't be for long. You'll be moving out after the wedding anyway."

Angie did a mental *gulp*.

Sal pulled a twenty out of his wallet. "Here, take him out for pizza before you go to bingo."

The idea has merit, thought Angie. She'd be a good daughter by doing a huge favor for her parents. At the same time, she could put off breaking the news to them of her broken engagement for another day. A boring night of church bingo was just what she needed to get her head on straight.

"Sure, Dad. I'll take him," said Angie, accepting the cash. "Gramps will be fine with me."

Sal kissed her on the cheek, "Thanks. I knew I could count on you."

The TV was on when Angie ambled into the living room. Gramps had nodded off in her father's recliner with the remote in one hand, a smoldering cigar dangling from the other. "Ugh, wrestling," she grumbled, glancing at the screen.

"Leave me alone. Get your mitts offa me!" Gramps cried suddenly, thrashing in his sleep. The cigar slipped from his grasp and Angie caught it before it hit the carpet.

"Wake up, Gramps," she urged, shaking him.

"What do you mean, I can't cook in my room...what fire? I don't hear no smoke alarm."

"Come on, Gramps. Wake up. It's me, Angelina."

"My Angelina?" he asked in a far-away voice.

"No. Your granddaughter, Angelina."

Gramps sat up slowly and rubbed his eyes. "Oh. Then why'd you wake me up? Did somebody die?"

Angie slouched on the sofa. "No, Gramps. You were talking in your sleep. You sounded pretty upset, too."

"What'd I say?"

"Something about a fire in your room."

Gramps grimaced as if in pain. "Forget you heard that." Shifting in the recliner, he looked over his shoulder. "Hey, where'd everybody go?"

"Ma has a headache, and Marie has a date. It's just you and me tonight."

"So what are we gonna do?" asked Gramps, rubbing his arthritic hands together in anticipation.

"Nothing too exciting," Angie said, rising from the sofa. "How do you feel about bingo?"

"It's not Las Vegas, but beggars can't be choosers, right?" asked Gramps and switched off the TV with the remote. "When do we leave?"

Angie grabbed his suitcase. "Later. First, we'll get you moved in."

Gramps trailed Angie down the hall. His mouth opened, and then closed, when she stopped at the bathroom to flush his cigar down the toilet.

"How long do you think I'll have to sleep here, Angelina?" he asked when they entered her room.

"Until we figure out what to do with you, Gramps," she replied, heaving his suitcase on the bed.

"Well, you're getting married soon, right? I'll just stay here," he said, waltzing across the floor with an imaginary partner. "I can't wait to dance at your wedding."

"Well, I wouldn't get out my dancing shoes right away if I

were you."

"What? You're not gettin' married?"

Even as a child, Angie could never keep a secret from her grandpa.

"No, I'm not," she said, plopping down on the bed. "And Mom and Dad don't know yet. I'm waiting for the right time to tell them. So please don't say anything."

Gramps stopped dancing. "What happened? Did he cheat on you? Did he hurt you? If he did, I know people. You just tell your grandpa. Don't worry about a thing. It'll look like an accident."

Still an imposing figure despite his age, Angie had the alarming thought that her grandfather could do exactly what he suggested. "No! No! Gramps," she cried. "It's nothing like that."

"So what happened?"

"I don't want to talk about it right now," she said. "Just promise me you won't do or say anything until I tell Mom and Dad myself, okay?"

"Yeah, sure," he promised, sounding disappointed. "What about Marie? She know?"

"Yeah. Now you're both sworn to secrecy."

Gramps smiled, happy to be in the loop as a conspirator with his granddaughters. "All right. I'll do what I can. But remember, Angelina, I'm an old man and I forget sometimes."

"Yeah. That's what I'm afraid of."

A few hours later, Angie and Gramps were buckled in her 1999 Mustang GT. Purchased at a time when her hormones were out of whack, Angie allowed herself to be persuaded by an aggressive salesman at Lombardi Motors.

"It's a classic!" he had said. "The 35th Anniversary Limited Edition!"

So, against her non-hormone-affected judgment, Angie bought the hot-looking auto. After all, it was red. A decision she soon regretted. The car ran when it felt like it and occasionally bucked like the wild horse it was named for—the high-gloss exterior obscuring its true condition of an old stallion that had seen better days and was put out to pasture. Apparently, today wasn't one of them.

The engine backfired twice when Angie tried to start it. Then it sputtered as if sparking its last plug and died. Grumbling under her breath, she yanked the key from the ignition. "I guess we'll have to take Dad's car, Gramps. Meet me over by the Caddy while I get the keys," she said, jutting her chin toward the driveway.

Gramps eased out of the front seat and stepped onto the curb. "*That's* your father's car?" he asked, glancing in the direction she indicated.

Angie climbed out and slammed the door. "Yeah. Whose did you think it was?" she asked matter-of-factly.

"I...I don't know," he said, shrugging his shoulders. "Marie's?"

"No. It's Dad's."

Gramps braced himself against the Mustang's front fender. "But it's pink!" he cried, pointing to the vehicle parked on the concrete drive.

"Of course, it is. All Tammy Kay cars are pink."

"*Aspett*," said Gramps with his hand up. "Your father, *my son*, drives that?"

Angie hiked her handbag on her shoulder and sauntered beside him. "Yeah. Dad got a heck of a deal from Val Kaminski who used to live next door."

"I remember Valentino," said Gramps, distracted for a

moment. "Didn't he play baseball with the rest of the boys in the neighborhood?"

"He did, but back then no one noticed he cared more about his hair and the cut of his uniform than about who was rounding third. Anyway, after high school, he came out, moved out, and became a Tammy Kay consultant. He did wonders with the products, too. Val could take ten years off with just the right foundation and eye shadow."

Gramps' brow furrowed. "If he did so good, why sell the car?"

"Because the business tanked when the economy went south along with his clientele. Dad just happened to be in the right place at the right time when he needed to unload the car."

"But Angelina, it's pink!" he cried again, unable to come to terms with such a flagrant breach of the Italian male code of ethics.

Angie strolled up the driveway. "I know. Cool, isn't it?" she asked and patted the hood.

"*Madonna mia,*" Gramps moaned, shaking his head. "I don't know. It just don't feel right!"

It was obvious that Gramps was totally out of his comfort zone. Angie waited while his mind grappled with the new revelations. Funny, the news about Val Kaminski didn't seem to upset him as much as his son driving a pink Cadillac.

"C'mon, Gramps," she said, trying to tempt him. "It has soft leather seats."

Gramps approached the vehicle as if it were a ticking bomb about to explode. "What about my image? If somebody I know sees me in a pink car, I'll be ruined."

"Don't worry," Angie said, putting a consoling arm around his shoulder. "It'll be dark soon and once you're inside, you'll forget about the color."

Gramps wrinkled his nose as he mused. "All right," he

finally agreed, somewhat mollified. "If it's okay with your father, it's okay with me."

"Great. Wait here. I'll be right back."

"Sure, sure. Where am I gonna go anyway?"

When Angie returned with the keys five minutes later, Gramps was gone. She panicked until spotting him across the street with her widowed neighbor, Mrs. Esposito.

Bernice Esposito had lived alone ever since her husband took a one-way trip to the big, designated smoking area in the sky after inhaling enough tar to pave the parking lot at The Nassau Coliseum. A petite woman with dyed black hair, she slathered on red lipstick to match the bright-colored muumuus she wore every day. Bernice had lively brown eyes and would have been considered pleasant-looking if she didn't have a purple birthmark on her forehead in the shape of Italy. And if that wasn't bad enough, she had a mole right about where Rome should be that looked back at you like a third eye. Mrs. Esposito's dog, Tiny, sidled up beside Angie as she moseyed up her front walk.

The product of an accidental union between a purebred mini-Labradoodle and a mutt of unknown lineage, Tiny weighed ten pounds soaking wet but compensated for his size with a junkyard dog attitude. He greeted Angie by sticking his nose in her crotch and growled when she shoved him aside.

Gramps and Bernice swayed on a squeaky metal swing on her front porch like two teenagers on their first date; and as Angie mounted the steps, Tiny scampered beside his mistress on short, stubby legs.

"Hi, Mrs. Esposito." Angie stared at her shoes, avoiding the mole.

"Hello, Angela," responded Bernice, her eyes glued on Gramps. "I had no idea you had a grandfather who was such an interesting man. It was so nice of him to pay me a visit."

"Oh my God," she groaned.

Tiny bared his teeth and barked as if offended by her remark.

"What did you say, Angela?" asked Bernice.

"I said, 'Oh that's odd.' I really thought you two knew each other."

"Oh, no. And I hope Nicky doesn't make himself a stranger now that we've met," she said, placing her hand on Gramps' knobby knee.

Angie rolled her eyes.

"Well, it was really nice to see you again, Mrs. Esposito," she said, glancing at her watch. "But it's getting late, and we should be going. Right, Gramps?"

"Yeah, sure, Angelina."

Gramps' knees cracked as he hoisted himself from the swing. Then he turned and kissed Bernice's liver-spotted hand like a gallant knight. "Farewell, dear lady. Till we meet again," he said sweetly. She blushed all the way up to her gray roots. Angie bit her tongue.

"Well, goodbye, Mrs. Esposito," she said, taking hold of Gramps' arm.

"Goodbye, Nicky," called Bernice, waving, as Angie ushered her grandfather across the street.

"Gramps, you can't disappear on me like that," she scolded when they neared the pink Caddy in the driveway.

"I'm sorry, Angelina, but Bernice looked so lonely."

Angie stopped short. "Bernice?" she asked wide-eyed. "You're on a first-name basis already? You didn't ask her if she wanted to...you know, did you?"

"Nah. She's not my type."

Angie narrowed her eyes at him for a second. "It's the mole, isn't it?"

Gramps shuddered. "Yeah, it's the mole."

Chapter Twelve
Writer's Block

The afternoon sun cast shadows over Mac's desk like long, delicate fingers searching for a misplaced item. He had just discovered the markings on the Spartan pen and pondered their significance in the fading light.

"Edwin Alexander Sullivan, Peabody, Massachusetts," he said in wonder. "But Mr. Sullivan will have to wait. After 100 years, a few more days won't matter." Although curious about the inscription, Mac set the pen aside and dialed Angie's number on his cell phone. He lost track of how many times he had already called or how many messages he left since she snuck out of the restaurant Friday night. Was it thirty, forty or even fifty?

"Damn it! Not only is she a hot-blooded redhead but a stubborn one, too!" he grumbled when she didn't answer. So, he booted up his computer and sent her another desperate e-mail. He was running out of options.

A heavy sigh released some of Mac's tension as he leaned back in his leather desk chair and rubbed his eyes like a magic lamp, hoping a genie would appear and grant him three wishes.

All three would be for his heart's desire, Angie. But when he opened them there was no genie, just the Spartan pen on his desk where he left it. Strange, it seemed to be staring at him.

Staring?

"Why don't I just write to her?" he said, astonished that he didn't think of it before. "I'm an author for chrissake. I should be able to compose a damn good letter."

Spurred into action, Mac swiveled in his chair, pulling a clean sheet of paper from the bottom drawer of his desk. Frowning in concentration, he picked up a ballpoint pen and wrote, *Dear Angie, I love you.*

Now what? he thought, looking at the few words on the page. She already knows that, or does she? Is it possible Angie thinks I don't love her anymore? True, we haven't spent that much time together because of the wedding plans, but that's not my fault. Frankly, I don't understand the obsession women have with weddings. It's just *one* day. The marriage is every day *after* we say, "I do." That's what I'm looking forward to. I wouldn't care if we had the ceremony on Main Street with a parking meter for my best man as long as we were married. What else can I say to her in a letter that will make a difference?

The page looked sterile—absent of words, void of the love he felt for Angie—daring him in its blankness to continue. Mac rubbed his chin and tossed the cheap pen across his desk. "Writer's block? How the hell can I have writer's block when I'm writing a freakin' love letter," he whined as he crumbled the unfinished draft into a ball and missed when he threw it at the trashcan. "God, I'm pathetic," he moaned as he reached over to pick up the discarded letter.

What's this?

A plain envelope addressed simply to *Mac* in an unfamiliar hand rested against the trash can as if carefully placed there.

Bending over to retrieve it, he suddenly felt dizzy. With his head spinning, Mac held onto the edge of his desk as the sensation increased. When he finally managed to grasp the baffling envelope, the dizziness instantly vanished, only to be replaced by a more terrifying sensation. Somehow, Mac knew he wasn't alone. And as he read the short note, an icy chill ran up his spine.

Mac,
>   Write what you know but do it with love.
>   Your friend,
>   O.B. Pickett

Mac tried to shrug off the creepy feeling. "Must be the tequila," he mumbled. But how did the note get in his house? O.B. must have slipped it in the bag while he was fumbling with his credit card at the pawnshop. Even if that were true, how did it end up in his office, and what the hell was O.B. trying to tell him? Despite his quandary, Mac smiled at the memory of his strange encounter with the gentle giant from Texas. When he did, an image of the Spartan flashed in his mind, and a crazy notion occurred to him. *The big guy made a good point about writing with a fountain pen. It cost me three hundred dollars; I might as well write an old-fashioned love letter to Angie with an old-fashioned fountain pen.*

"Paper, pen, ink," Mac said, ticking off each item that was in the bag from the pawn shop in preparation. "Eyedropper?" O.B. had included a glass eyedropper with his purchase. "What am I supposed to do with this?"

For most of his adult life, Mac used a computer to write and send emails. He made calls and texted on his cell phone, rarely using a pen to communicate his thoughts on paper, let alone with a fountain pen. The thought of writing a letter with the Spartan was intimidating. The puzzling eyedropper didn't help either. Mac figured it had something to do with the ink, but he didn't know how to fill the vintage pen.

Refusing to give up, he Googled *Spartan fountain pens* on his computer. In seconds, websites crowded the screen dedicated to antique fountain pen collecting, history, and operation. Bookmarking several sites for later, Mac opened one with filling instructions, found a link to Spartan ink, and clicked on it. Leaning closer to the monitor, he scrolled through more filling methods than he needed or even knew existed. Lever, plunger, snorkel, and touchdown just to name a few. Scrolling further down the page, he found the eyedropper method and smiled.

To fill, hold the pen cap end up, and unscrew the cap. The nib should already be retracted inside the barrel, allowing ink to be introduced through the open barrel with an eyedropper.

"Sounds easy enough," said Mac reaching for the ink. The bottle opened easily, and Mac filled the Spartan as instructed using the eyedropper. He quickly regretted his cocky attitude because when he began to write, the black ink flooded the white paper like a maritime oil spill over pristine waters.

"What the hell did I do wrong?"

Mac yanked a fistful of tissues from a box Angie had left on his desk. The eerie sensation that someone else was in his office returned as he wiped up the mess. Only now, he imagined he heard someone laughing. Unnerved, Mac quickly twisted in his chair, his eyes darting around the room, the sound of his heart thumping in his ears. No one was there. He was definitely alone. *Must be one of Rick's practical jokes*, thought Mac as his heart rate returned to normal. *He still has a key to my house and probably set up the laugh track when I was at the pawnshop.*

"That's it. That *has* to be it." Convinced that Rick was responsible, he glanced back at the computer screen.

Once filled, the safety should not be capped or uncapped unless held upright otherwise the ink will pour out of the open barrel. Always remember to retract the nib before replacing the cap!

"Now you tell me," he groaned.

After successfully filling the Spartan, Mac placed it in the open leather case. Although he'd polished the sterling silver pen earlier, the filigree seemed to glow now. It almost looked happy, if that were possible.

"Get real, MacConnell," he said, chastising himself for the foolish thought.

Mac reached for another clean sheet of recycled paper but decided to make use of the more formal stationery O.B. had given him. It just seemed appropriate. And when he gingerly picked up the antique pen, the haunting presence returned. But instead of being frightened, Mac was surrounded by a comforting peace he hadn't felt since Angie made a quick exit from the restaurant, and his life, the night before.

"Well, here goes nothing."

The Spartan fit comfortably, perfectly balanced in Mac's hand. The writer's block he experienced a moment ago was suddenly gone. Then, without being fully aware of his actions, he composed a love letter to Angie.

Mac wrote quickly, not pausing or even thinking. It was as if another hand guided the Spartan as it looped and curled across the page. Faster and faster, the words burst from the sparkling gold nib, scratching the paper, gaining momentum like floodwaters down a mountainside. Then, just as abruptly as he began, Mac stopped writing and slumped back in his chair. The Spartan fell from his grasp, and a contented sigh breezed through the room. The bright silver turned dull again, and it lay on his desk looking like an ordinary fountain pen once more.

Minutes ticked by before Mac was able to think clearly enough to read the letter, first in awe, then in utter disbelief.

To My Dearest Angelina,

It is with a broken heart that I have pen in hand today.

Although a gentlewoman, my love, you possess the unrealized power to reduce me to a quaking mass of humanity with a mere look or word. It is in such a condition that I implore you to respond quickly to my numerous requests to call.

My love for you has never wavered. It is still strong and true, as I hope yours is for me.

With devotion forever,

Conrad

Mac sprang to his feet, knocking over his desk chair. "No way! No freakin' way!"

The letter was beautiful but not just the contents. Somehow, he'd managed to draft the letter in calligraphy script, with dramatic flourishes reminiscent of the early 1900s Edwardian era.

I know Rick had nothing to do with this. But how the hell did I?

The only script Mac ever wrote came from a drop-down font menu on his computer. He couldn't write calligraphy any more than he could paint the Mona Lisa, but the letter was proof that he did.

Mac pinched himself. "Ow!"

He glanced at the time and date on his computer. Still Saturday. Nothing had changed.

If Rick were here, he'd say he was in a parallel universe or had traveled back in time. Although that sounded crazy, Mac almost preferred those explanations, because to suggest that he actually wrote the letter was incomprehensible. A whirlwind of contradictions swirled in his head as he read the letter again.

First of all, I call her Angie, not Angelina. Second, all that flowery speech is not my style. The sentiments are true, but will she buy the language? And since when do I sign my name Conrad? I can't give her this. She'll laugh in my face!

"But it's a chance I have to take," said Mac, more determined than ever. "I'll even buy flowers and deliver this to Angie tonight. There isn't a woman on the planet who can resist a mushy love letter, especially one delivered by a man with his heart on his sleeve and a bouquet of flowers in his hand."

Energized with a sudden surge of excitement, Mac bounded up the stairs and rummaged through his closet, selecting a jacket, shirt, and tie. He was showered, shaved, and dressed, ready to go, when a thought stopped him dead in his tracks. It was an incredible, unbelievable possibility, almost too fantastic to consider. Yet he couldn't get it out of his mind.

Was it the Spartan?

∽

A half-hour later, Mac drove down Angie's street, rolling to a stop a block from her house. He spotted her Mustang parked at the curb. Sitting behind the wheel of his T-Bird, he watched the sky shift from pink to orange to purple like a canvas splashed with a series of pigment-suffused brushes. When the colors receded below the horizon, Mac remembered the poem, *Red sky at night, sailor's delight.* He hoped that was a good omen. Or was it: *Red sky at night, sailor take flight?* Either way, he knew this wasn't going to be easy. Angie could be tenacious as a pit bull, and given the present circumstances, it's possible she might slam the door in his face. What really put the fear of God in him was her father.

Sal Russo wasn't a tall man. He just gave the impression of a towering figure oozing with inherent, unquestioned authority. Mac had been accepted into the family but knew if he screwed up or hurt Angie in any way, he'd be up a creek without a paddle. Actually, *in* the creek, drowning, would be more like it by the time Sal was done with him. The two men got along fine, so Mac never worried about incurring Sal's wrath until that moment. If Mr. Russo answered the door, he had to be prepared for the worst from his future father-in-law, who surely knew of the broken engagement by now. "Time to rock and roll."

Mac climbed out of his car clutching the letter and flowers when a pair of bright headlights flashed in his face. The unknown driver beeped his horn and Mac relaxed, leaning against his car. He knew of only one car on Long Island with a horn that played the *Star Wars* movie theme.

"What the hell are you doing here?" he asked when Rick sauntered over.

Rick looked him up and down. A silly grin spread across his face. "Don't you remember, man? I told you I was diggin' Angie's sister Marie, so I asked her out. I'm here to pick her up for our date and saw your T-Bird," he replied, unaffected by his friend's surly tone.

Mac stepped closer to Rick, throwing him a challenging glare. "Then what are you laughing at?"

"*Moi?* I'm not laughing," he answered, remaining calm. "I'm as solemn as the Vulcan half of Mr. Spock."

"Well, it looks like his human side is showing, so wipe that smirk off your face."

"Sorry, man." Rick passed his hand across his lips.

Mac backed away.

"It's just that I'm not used to seeing you dressed like that," Rick told him. "And what's up with the flowers and fancy paper?"

"The flowers are for Angie." Mac's shoulders sagged. "Don't you remember? She dumped me last night."

"Oh yeah—right. Bummer, dude."

"I also wrote her a love letter." *And that's all he needs to know about that.* "I figure the flowers will get me in the door to see her, and the love letter will clinch the deal. Then we can make up and my life will return to normal. And by the way, I got your practical joke. So, if you don't mind, please remove the electronic laughing device from my office."

"Whoa, I'm not getting it, dude," said Rick with his hands up. "What are you talking about?"

Mac described what happened in his office earlier that day.

"Sounds like a cool gag. I wish I could take credit for it, man, but I'm innocent."

"C'mon, Rick, the joke's over. Only you and Angie have

keys to my house, and she won't even talk to me. It has to be you."

"Chill, bro, I'm tellin' you I didn't do it. Besides, I gave your key back last week."

Suddenly faced with the likelihood that he was losing his mind, or that the Spartan somehow played a part in the events of the afternoon, Mac admitted he remembered. It was a lie but preferable to the other two possibilities, especially the one about a haunted fountain pen. Haunted? Possessed? It was the first time he thought of it that way. Could the pen have helped him write the romantic words *and* the calligraphy? Normally a pragmatic man, Mac struggled to embrace the bizarre idea.

"Well, maybe I left the TV on," he said to Rick. "Forget I ever mentioned it."

"Sure thing, man. So, what do we do now?"

"Leave your truck parked here with my car and stay inside. Angie's not expecting me, and I'm counting on the element of surprise when she answers the door. If she sees your truck or my car, she might suspect something and bolt."

"Works for me. I'll stay here until you go into the house."

"Good. Then give me a few minutes alone with Angie before you pick up Marie."

Rick held his thumb up. "Affirmative, dude."

Mac smiled nervously and turned. Clutching the mysterious love letter and flowers, he strode up to Angie's front door, held his breath, and knocked.

"Well, look who's here," said Sal Russo, pulling the door open wide. "C'mon in."

Mac cringed when he felt Sal's heavy hand on his back. But instead of the pain he expected as punishment for breaking Angie's heart, one hand joined the other in a warm embrace.

"I guess you came to see Angie, but she's not home. I didn't know you two had a date tonight or I wouldn't have sent her out." Sal offered Mac a seat, smiling in obvious approval of the flowers.

The plastic-covered cushion seemed to exhale, echoing his own release of breath, when Mac sat on the sofa. *So he doesn't know. I get to live another day.* "But isn't that her car out front, Mr. Russo?"

"Yeah, that clunker wouldn't start so she took mine and went to St. Lucy's with her grandfather to play bingo."

"Her grandfather?" asked Mac, fidgeting with the flowers. "Angie told me that he lived at a retirement home."

Sal blew out a weary sigh. "He did, but it looks like he'll be with us for a while."

"Do you have any idea when she'll be back?"

"There's no telling what time they'll get home, especially if they're winning," replied Sal with a chuckle. "Why don't you go to the church and surprise her," he suggested." I never knew a woman who didn't love to get flowers."

Chapter Thirteen
It's Only Bingo

After a quick slice at Patsy's Pizzeria, Angie and Gramps stopped at a Speedy Mart for snacks before proceeding to St. Lucy's church. The large parish consisted of mostly Italians, Irish, and Polish women who made the best pierogies west of the Baltic Sea. They all attended bingo as faithfully as they attended Mass, so when Angie pulled into the parking lot, she circled it three times before finding a space in a well-lit area.

"Angelina, park over there." Gramps pointed to a spot under a broken lamp.

"Why, Gramps? It's safer here under the light."

"I know. Do it anyway," he told her with a furtive look over his shoulder.

"Oh, I get it," she said, easing the pink Caddy in the unlit space.

Angie shifted to "park" and switched off the engine. She grabbed her mother's bingo tote bag with the requisite daubers, deck of cards, tape, and lucky *Madonna* statue, slung her purse over her shoulder, and climbed out of the car. Gramps slammed the passenger door shut, clutching a Speedy Mart bag jammed with enough candy and soft drinks to put King Kong in a diabetic coma.

"They don't give us this stuff at the home," he said, checking its contents.

Angie sighed. "I'm not sure I should've either."

"Don't worry about me, I'll be okay," Gramps assured her, tearing into a super-sized candy bar.

Angie rolled her eyes.

"What?"

"Never mind."

Traditional foods were abandoned for the carnival-type fare served at bingo. And as Angie and Gramps crossed the parking lot, a grease-laden breeze from deep-fried corn dogs, nachos, and French fries floated by. Gramps inhaled deeply, savoring the aroma, and Angie wondered how his body will react to sudden, large amounts of fat and refined sugar.

They entered St. Lucy's vestibule, descending stairs leading to the large meeting room in the basement. Angie purchased two admission packets at the door. Handing one to Gramps, she said, "This should be enough to keep us busy for the night."

Long rows of folding tables stood like columns of troops across the floor arranged with military precision to accommodate as many players as possible. Most arrived early, catching up on a week's worth of gossip to pass the time until bingo started, while others separated, taped, daubed, marked, and arranged their cards in preparation. It was a mixed bunch, mostly seniors on their night out; and Gramps took full advantage, stopping to speak to just about every woman he encountered like a rock star greeting his fans. Angie couldn't risk losing him again and hung onto his arm as if he were a small child in a crowded shopping mall.

"C'mon Gramps. We came here to play bingo, not pick up women."

"But you don't understand, Angelina. That's exactly what I should be doing." His arm swept the expansive room. "You see all these ladies? This is speed dating for seniors!"

Angie closed her eyes and said a silent prayer for strength. After all, praying in church was like being in the express lane at the supermarket. You always got what you needed, just a little faster than usual. Okay, so they were in the church basement—close enough. The foreboding feeling in the pit of her stomach suggested that she was going to need all the help she could get.

"I don't think that's what they have in mind for tonight, Gramps. These women take bingo *very* seriously."

Gramps just shrugged. "So, where are we gonna sit, Angelina?" he asked with a mouthful of gummies.

"At Ma's table with her so-called friends," she said, tightening her grip on his arm. "Now stay with me."

Bingo players are superstitious *and* territorial. God forbid you should sit in their lucky seat or, worse yet, move a carefully-placed good luck charm. Angie understood bingo etiquette and kept a respectful distance as she directed Gramps past tables that were already occupied.

"Oh hello, Angela," said Mrs. Testa when she and Gramps arrived at her mother's usual table. "I didn't expect to see *you* here. And who's that?" she asked, squinting at Gramps above her dollar-store readers.

"Yes, Angela. Aren't you going to introduce us?" said Mrs. Kaminski as she taped her bingo cards to the table.

"This is my grandfather, Nick Russo. He's going to be staying with us for a while."

At that, Mrs. Carmella Lombardi looked up from her cards and gave Gramps an almost imperceptible nod. His jaw muscles tightened, but he remained silent. "So where is your mother tonight?" Carmella asked, turning her attention to Angie.

"Mom wasn't feeling well, so I thought I'd take Gramps to play in her place. But I can see I'm too late for that," she said, glaring at Mrs. Testa who had taken her mother's seat.

An elephant figurine and a blue-haired troll doll flanked Mrs. Lombardi's bingo cards. She positioned a St. Jude statue between them and said, "We have to get here early if we want our regular seats, Angela. They're lucky, you know."

Mrs. Kaminski wagged a finger in her friend's face. "I warned you not to sit there, Loretta."

Mrs. Testa continued to pre-daub her array of cards. "Well, Margaret always gets bingo when she sits here. When she didn't show, I thought why not? I could use a few wins."

Angie leaned across the table, casting an ominous shadow over Mrs. Testa. "Oh yeah? Would you jump in her grave as fast?" she snarled.

They all gasped. Angie knew she had gone too far. *There goes a friendly game of bingo.*

Mrs. Lombardi quickly changed the subject. "Tell me, Angela, how are the wedding plans going?"

Angie's head jerked to face her. "Fine, no problems at all," she replied as her eyelid began to twitch.

"Oh? I heard that you spoke to my Bianca at the country club today," she pressed, wearing a sinister smile. "Are you sure there's nothing wrong, dear?"

Angie's eyes narrowed. "Wrong? What could possibly be wrong?" she asked through gritted teeth.

"Nothing, of course. I was just..."

"Well, it was nice to meet you ladies. *Bona sera,*" said Gramps, suddenly taking hold of Angie's arm. She squirmed in his grasp as he led her away.

"What did you do that for, Gramps?" she demanded. "I

was just getting warmed up. That Mrs. Testa really ticked me off!"

"Take it easy, Angelina. It's only bingo."

"I never liked her, anyway," Angie said, elbowing her way between the tables as she ranted. "Wait till I tell Ma what she did. And that nosey Mrs. Lombardi is no better. The woman is pure evil. Man, I hate that family. Just because they own the biggest car dealership in town doesn't make them superior to the rest of us. Bianca works at the country club now, but she'll probably inherit it all someday. That's where I bought that piece of crap car I have. I bet she was in cahoots with the salesman to get even with me for the panty incident."

Gramps chuckled. "I remember that. It was a Monday, right?"

They had reached the opposite side of the crowded hall. Angie stopped short and spun around facing Gramps. "How do you know about that? I don't remember telling you."

"You didn't. I bribed your sister with a buck."

"We did a pinkie swear!" Angie cried, holding up her little finger. "I can't believe Marie broke her promise for a dollar."

"That was a lotta money back then, Angelina. Take it easy."

"Yeah, I guess you're right. Ma always says I get my hot temper from you. She blames the Russo red hair."

Gramps ran his fingers through his own shock of gray hair that once matched Angie's russet-colored tresses. "Bianca's grandfather, Mario Lombardi, said that about me, too."

Angie arched an eyebrow. "You knew Bianca's grandfather?"

"Yeah. I used to work for him."

"Doing what? I thought you worked in construction?"

"I did later. But times were tough when I first came over from the other side. I was just a teenager back then, and money was money, any way you could make it."

Angie folded her arms across her chest. "What's that supposed to mean?"

Gramps paused. His eyes shifted left, right, and left again. "Do you know how the Lombardi family got so rich?"

Angie shook her head.

Stepping closer to her, Gramps lowered his voice. "Mario Lombardi's father, Vincenzo, sold illegal booze during Prohibition."

"That figures. So when did you work for Bianca's grandfather?"

"After Prohibition. You see, by then Mario, Bianca's grandfather, was connected because of his father's bootlegging days. So when the Don had a beef with another boss, he let Mario muscle in on the other boss's territory. It was a small-time operation: gambling, numbers, protection. He offered me a job; I needed the money—end of story. Like I said, Angelina, times were tough. I went legit when your grandmother was expecting your father."

This was a part of her grandfather's life Angie never knew. It explained a lot but raised more questions as well. "Holy moly!" said Angie wide-eyed. "You were in the mob?"

"Don't look at me like that," said Gramps. "I wasn't no wiseguy. I just made pick-ups for the numbers racket."

"Well, what do you know? Stuck-up Bianca comes from a family of felons. Crime is probably in her genes. But that's no excuse for trying to steal my fiancé."

Gramps' eyes popped open. "What? That *buttana!* In my village, we'd shave her head and drag her through the streets!"

"Calm down, Gramps. Bianca didn't sleep with Mussolini. She just made a pass at Mac when we booked our wedding."

"No matter. Same thing in my village," he said, brushing her off. "So, what are we gonna do about it?"

"Nothing for now. But I can't let my guard down. Not even for a minute."

Meanwhile, Father Donovan appeared on stage, microphone in hand. As St. Lucy's newest and youngest pastor, he had earned the respect of his parishioners; but his slight frame and boyish, freckled face lacked the power to command their rapt attention. His baritone voice, however, compensated for the deficiencies in his physical appearance. "Ladies and gentlemen," he proclaimed like a circus ringmaster. "Please take your seats. Bingo will be starting shortly."

"Did you hear that, Angelina? What are we gonna do now? We can't play bingo standing up."

"I don't know. Every table is full. I swear they must pass these bingo seats down in their wills." Angie did a slow revolution. "Quick, Gramps," she said, tilting her head toward a table to their left. "Over there."

Gramps scurried after her, clutching his armful of snacks. "This is worse than getting a table at the early bird special," he said, puffing behind her.

Angie and Gramps scrambled over and flopped down at the vacant table like two thirsty travelers at an oasis, but their relief was short-lived. A rather large woman marched toward them dressed completely in black, her hair pulled back in a bun so tight she couldn't blink. One hand leaned on a cane, the other held a bag containing bingo supplies, knitting needles, and yarn. Angie recognized her immediately.

Thirty years ago, Mrs. Malafemina claimed her sanitation worker husband was killed, presumably ground to a pulp by the powerful blade of the garbage truck, when he slipped and fell into the hopper. His body—or parts of one—was never found. Not even a scrap of clothing. Talk around the neighborhood was that he just ran off and left her. Ever since then her face had only one expression—a scowl as dark and depressing as the widow's garb she wore every day.

"Get up! That's my seat!" she ordered Gramps in a voice so loud that they must have heard her in New Jersey. Everyone in the noisy church hall looked up.

"This one?" he asked, his eyes dancing with mischief.

"Yes, that one. I insist you let me have it now!"

A stunned silence gripped the crowd. All heads turned in unison. Startled eyes locked on the developing scene. No one moved a muscle as the tension became thicker than a muddy street in a spaghetti western shoot-out as every man, woman, and child waited to see who would draw first.

Mrs. Malafemina rapped the floor with her cane. "Are you deaf, old man?" she cried when Gramps didn't budge. "I *said* I want to sit in *that* chair, now!"

Angie was on her feet in an instant. Maybe it was an adrenaline rush at the sight of her grandfather being bullied, or maybe she was just fed up with being pushed around. Either way, she confronted the parish pariah, and two hundred people sucked in their breaths at once.

"Are you sure you want *that* one?" she asked, pointing to the chair Gramps occupied.

"Yes, I'm sure," Mrs. Malafemina replied, apparently satisfied she was getting her way.

Angie motioned to Gramps to rise. His knees cracked, and the sound echoed in the dramatic silence as he heaved himself up. Then Angie snatched the chair away and dragged it across the room.

"*There* is your seat," she said, returning to the flabbergasted old woman. "You're welcome to it!"

The room exploded into cheers and applause. No one had *ever* stood up to Mrs. Malafemina before.

"That's my granddaughter! That's my granddaughter!" shouted Gramps, beaming with pride.

"Well, I never!" The old woman shrieked, parting the crowd like the Red Sea as she stomped off to another table.

"That was great, Angelina!" Gramps said, hugging her. "I guess she really touched your buttons."

"What?"

"You know, flipped your switch."

"Oh, you mean she *pushed* my buttons."

"Yeah, that's what I said."

"Well, Gramps, it looks like Ma was right. I do take after you, red hair and all."

St. Lucy's parishioners enjoyed a little excitement as much as anybody, but the die-hard bingo players quickly settled down. Angie slid another chair over to the table for Gramps, sitting beside him in the only other seat vacated by Mrs. Malafemina.

"Ladies and Gentlemen, may I have your attention, please," said Father Donovan in his booming voice. "Our regular number caller had emergency hip replacement surgery yesterday and will not be with us tonight." There was some grumbling and murmurs of sympathy. "Is there anyone here willing to volunteer to call the bingo numbers?"

Gramps' hand was up like a shot. "I'll do it."

"Gramps no!" cried Angie, tugging on his arm. "It's not as easy as it looks."

He stood stiffly and shrugged. "What could be so hard about saying a few numbers?"

"You don't understand bingo players."

"Ah, you worry too much."

This has disaster written all over it, thought Angie as Gramps tramped up to the stage.

Left alone now, all Angie could do was play bingo while keeping an eye on Gramps. She knew the routine. Mark your cards for the different games and pre-daub the free space in the middle. When she was done, she opened a bag of chips and switched on her phone. "Holy Hannah!" There were over forty-five voicemail messages, all of them from Mac.

Angie had turned her phone off in the cab after leaving the restaurant the night before. Now her heart ached as she listened to Mac's voice begging her to call. *I feel so guilty putting him through this, but I know what I'm doing...I think.* Then Mac walked through the door.

"Omigod!" Angie slouched down low in her chair. From that vantage point, all she could see was the back of his head, but there was no doubt. It was Mac.

Angie knew every inch of his body. A warm tingle emanated from somewhere south of the border when her own body responded to thoughts of her favorite few inches. *That's it. I'm going straight to hell. How could I have such thoughts? And in church no less. Does it still count if you're in the base-ment?* But she couldn't restrain her desire any more than she could cease breathing...or eating chocolate.

Even though Angie had dumped Mac the night before, she still experienced an unexpected pang of jealousy when all of the women in the vast hall set their sights on him, unable to look away. *It's those bedroom eyes of his.*

Angie fought the urge to shout, he's mine! But when Mac did a sudden about-face, she vanished under the table faster than a roll of quarters in a Las Vegas slot machine. And when her heart beat returned to normal, she noticed the woman in the adjacent seat for the first time. With her hand at her throat, Angie gasped at a sight more terrifying than a yearbook picture on a bad hair day. More frightening than a pimple on prom night. *Miss Peacock?*

Angie's fourth-grade teacher, Miss Peacock, a/k/a Ol' Big Foot, had never been popular with the student body but was a dedicated teacher nonetheless. No child was ever left back under her strict tutelage. Angie also recalled her being two cheeseburgers short of obese with feet that bulged out of her pumps like over-stuffed sausages. Because of her ill-fitting shoes, Miss Peacock had an odd way of walking, with heavy steps that produced a *clip-clop* sound more ominous than the music from *Jaws*. Students scattered like frightened swimmers at the beach when they heard it.

Angie glanced up at a much thinner version of her former teacher. It seemed Miss Peacock's eyesight and memory had declined along with her weight because she returned Angie's gaze with a puzzled expression as if struggling to place the young woman beneath the table. But Angie couldn't risk drawing Mac's attention if Miss Peacock experienced a moment of mental clarity. She had to get rid of her, just in case.

"You're probably wondering what I'm doing down here?" she asked.

Miss Peacock just stared.

"You see, I dropped my lucky socks. I usually put them on the table right next to my bingo card."

Miss Peacock blinked as if she hadn't understood a word.

"I never actually wear them, though. That's probably a good thing because they haven't been washed in years and smell *really* bad," explained Angie in an attempt to gross her out and be left alone. "It's funny, but the more they stink, the more I win!"

Instead of reacting with shock or disgust, Miss Peacock replied, "Oh, I hear you, honey. I always bring my lucky bra and thong, but I *wear* mine."

"Omigod!" cried Angie, clapping both hands over her ears. But it was too late. She heard it. Miss Peacock in a push-up bra and a thong that may or may not be visible. Angie shuddered as she grappled with the disturbing image. Despite the fact that *Angie* had been grossed out instead, it seemed that Miss Peacock no longer posed a threat to reveal her presence. So, she gingerly peeked above the table, caught a glimpse of Mac, and sighed. He had a bouquet of flowers tucked under his arm and a white envelope in his hand.

The poor guy's probably carrying on with the wedding plans as if nothing happened. The envelope must be the church dona-tion, and those flowers better be for me. But I have no right to them now and wouldn't accept them even if he did find me. But how did he know I was here?

Angie's gaze lingered on Mac as several women approached him. They spoke briefly before he headed toward the exit. "Whew, that was close," she muttered, hoisting herself up from under the table. Only then did Angie realize that she had been holding her breath, and her hands were shaking.

The air in the church hall hummed with excitement now as fidgety players, heady with anticipation, shushed their neigh-bors to be quiet. Metal folding chairs scraped the floor. Bodies shifted in their seats. Bingo was about to begin, and hundreds of daubers drawn from tote bags like six-shooters were ready to stamp as many numbers as possible.

On stage, Gramps stood behind the microphone sand-wiched between the blower that mixed and dispensed the numbered balls and the electronic bingo board that displayed the numbers. All he had to do was remove a ball and speak into the microphone.

"B-2," called Gramps.

"Hey, Pops. Speak up!" piped a voice from the back of the room.

"B-2," he repeated.

"N-31."

"What did you say?" asked a man, cupping his ear with his hand. "I can't hear you."

"I *said* N-31. Turn up your hearing aid!" yelled Gramps into the mike. "If I say it any louder, my teeth will fall out!"

That got a laugh, but the tension in the hall simmered, threatening to bubble over as more players came close to winning the first big jackpot of the night.

"O-72."

"Shake it up, you old goat," a woman shouted when her number didn't come up.

"Yeah, this game is fixed!"

"Put on your glasses!"

"He must be blind! Where's your seeing-eye dog?"

Then the crowd really got ugly. They began to chant, "Change the caller! Change the caller! Change the caller!"

"Yeah, throw the bum out!"

For a few moments, Gramps looked askance at the sea of gray heads before him, his fists clenching and unclenching at his sides until an expression of unabashed defiance crept over his face. "Oh yeah? That's what *you* think. Nobody kicks Niccolo Russo around!" Shaking his fist above his head, Gramps thundered. "If I wasn't in church, I'd give you all a few choice words! You want louder? I'll give you louder!"

Taking a deep breath, Gramps screamed out the next number at the top of his lungs. Unfortunately, no one actually heard what he said because his dentures shot out of his mouth like a bullet. Pandemonium broke out as women screamed, bookies took bets, and children tried to catch them. Father Donovan clutched the crucifix around his neck and prayed, "Heaven help us."

They say when you're about to die, your life flashes before

your eyes. In times of extreme embarrassment or screw-ups (this was definitely in the screw-up category), time must stand still because Angie gaped in disbelief as Gramps' choppers seemed to defy the laws of gravity, floating in slow motion. In fact, it looked like they were still trying to call the winning bingo number before their inevitable descent onto Mrs. Malafemina's bingo card.

"Bingooooo!!" she yelled. It was the first time she smiled in thirty years.

Angie knew her neighbors well. They were good people who lived by three unwritten laws. Never discuss politics or religion and, for God's sake, don't ever mess with bingo. So, with that breach of unspoken etiquette, the assemblage of otherwise respectable citizens turned into something akin to an out-of-control audience at a wrestling match.

"You can't have bingo!" cried the outraged mob. "He didn't even call the number!"

Mrs. Malafemina brandished her cane like a weapon. "Oh yeah?" she screamed. "Says you and what army! The teeth said the number when they landed on my card. This is the first bingo I ever won, and I'm not giving it back now!"

Then all hell broke loose, or as Gramps liked to say, the pasta hit the fan.

Angie knew it was time to leave, especially with cries of "Get the cheater and get the teeth!" being hurled at Gramps.

Jumping from her seat, she dashed to the stage, leaping over tables and chairs like hurdles in a race. Gramps had managed to navigate the stage steps on his own and joined her just below the platform. They clung to each other while ducking flying Styrofoam cups, candy wrappers, and assorted good luck charms.

"What're we gonna do, Angelina?"

"Hide!" she shouted, dropping to the floor.

Chapter Fourteen
Cut Him Off at the Pass

Rick slouched in the front seat of his truck. Peering over the dash, his gaze fixed on Mac's lone figure on the Russo's front stoop. The porch light flicked on, and he watched as Mr. Russo opened the door and ushered Mac inside. Rick had agreed to wait in the truck before picking up Marie for their date so that Mac could have a private moment alone with Angie. After several minutes passed, he clicked on the dome light and checked his watch. "That should be enough time to make up."

Designed just like the communicators used on the Enterprise, Rick's cell phone chirped when he flipped it open before keying in Marie's number. In her room, Marie stood in front of the mirror above her dresser.

"Hello?" she said, swiping mascara on her stubby lashes.

"Hey, dudette. It's me, the Rickster."

Her hand froze mid-swipe. "Where the hell are you? I was beginning to think you stood me up."

"No way, man! I would have been there already, but Mac beat me to it. He told me to wait in my truck while he parleyed with Angie."

Marie's hand twitched, brushing her cheek with mascara. "You mean Mac is here?"

"Yeah. He walked in the front door a few minutes ago. Your old man let him in."

"Damn!"

"That's no reason to get bummed out," said Rick. "They're just gonna parley, ya know, talk like pirates."

Marie wiped the mascara from her face. "I know what parley means," she said testily.

"Then what's the problem?"

"I didn't think Mac would show up tonight, that's all. That changes everything."

"You mean *you're* standing *me* up?"

"No! We're still going out. First, though, we have to get Mac out of the house and quick!"

"You want to give me the 411?"

"I can't," Marie told him, stepping into her shoes. "I promised Angie I wouldn't tell."

Rick wasn't exactly sure, but he suspected it had something to do with Angie breaking off the engagement. He didn't let on that he knew. A promise is a promise, especially one invoked with the Vulcan Mind Meld. But why was Marie so upset that Mac was in the house with Angie and Mr. Russo? Once she sees Mac, they'd be all lovey-dovey again anyway. That's probably what was taking so long. "Then just tell your sister to hurry up so we can all go out tonight."

"You don't get it, Rick." Marie darted around her room, tossing things in her handbag. "My sister isn't home."

"You mean Mac is in there alone with your father?"

"Yeah. He has no idea Angie hasn't told my parents—uh—that thing I can't tell you about. And if Mac spills the beans about, ya know—about that thing, there's no telling what my father will do."

"He'll kill him!"

"No shit, Sherlock—wait a minute. How did you know my father would be mad?"

"Because I know Angie broke off the engagement, that's why," Rick blurted out. "Mac swore me to secrecy; but I'd rather have him alive, than dead with a secret. We've got to get him out of there!"

"Then get your Trekkie ass over here pronto!"

"I'll be there faster than a speeding bullet."

Two minutes later, Marie opened the door clutching her phone and handbag. She grabbed Rick by the front of his shirt and pulled him into the house. "We're too late. He's gone."

"No way."

"He must've taken off while we were on the phone."

"Diabolical," muttered Rick. "He made me park down the block. I bet he wanted to get rid of me."

"Then let's go," urged Marie, shoving Rick out the door. "If my father told Mac she's at bingo, we have to get there first and warn her!"

"Man, that was cool!" said Rick, breathless, as they careened into a parking space at St. Lucy's church. "I never drove that fast before in my life. It was just like warp speed on *Star Trek*."

Marie slid down from the passenger seat to the asphalt paved lot. "Yeah, Captain Kirk would be real proud of you," she said flatly.

Rick jumped out and beeped the doors locked. "Look. There's Mac's car," he said, pointing to the T-Bird.

"Damn! He beat us."

"You know, I still don't get it, Marie. What's with the 911?

If your parental unit didn't knock Mac off at the house, why are we sneaking around like ninjas?"

"Because Angie doesn't want to talk to him, that's why. It's my duty as her sister to tell her that Mac's here before she sees him first and freaks out. If Mac spots us now, that'll tip him off and spoil everything," she answered sharply. "Are you with me or not?"

"Oh, I'm in, man."

"Good." Marie hung her bag on her shoulder. "Then come with me."

Marie had been to bingo with her mother many times. She remembered it being a quiet, orderly, almost boring evening and was totally unprepared for the commotion they encountered when the double doors of the church basement flew open with a *"bang!"* forcing the pair to flatten themselves against the wall to avoid being trampled by the rioting throng that spilled out.

"Owwww!" cried Marie in pain. "Hey lady, you just stomped on my foot!"

"Sorry, honey," came a disingenuous apology from somewhere in the stampede of people.

"Oh yeah? Well, sorry's not gonna cut it!" she shouted back.

Already primed for a fight, the agitated woman lunged at Marie but was pushed along with the rest of the mob before she could reach her.

"Omigod!" cried Marie. "That was 'Ol' Big Foot."

Rick turned his head sideways to face her. "Big Foot? Like the hairy dude in the woods?"

"No, Miss Peacock, my fourth-grade teacher," she told him. "We just called her that because her feet popped out of her high-heeled pumps."

Rick raised his fists in a fighter's stance. "Did she hurt you? I'll take care of her."

"Forget it. She's gone," said Marie. "Funny thing is, it looked like the old broad was wearing a push-up bra."

Rick shot her a puzzled look.

"Never mind. We've got bigger fish to fry. Now I don't know what's going on in there, but it doesn't look good. Angie and Gramps could be in trouble. "C'mon," she said, tugging Rick's arm as they dropped to the floor. "We have to keep out of sight and find my sister before Mac does."

"Hey Marie, isn't that Angie over there under that table?"

Mac stepped into the noisy church basement, his eyes scouring the crowd for any sign of Angie in the unfamiliar setting. For a split second, he thought he spotted her red tresses among the mostly gray heads but was mistaken. On the contrary, he was the one who stood out in his formal clothes and bouquet of flowers.

"Hi there, good lookin'," flirted a saucy brunette. "Flowers for me?"

"Uh, no," mumbled Mac looking over her shoulder. "I'm sorry."

"Hey, aren't you that writer guy?" she asked, adjusting her bra strap.

"No. That's my cousin. We just look alike."

"Are you single?" an aggressive mother wanted to know. "I want you to meet my daughter."

"Yes—I mean no! Actually, I'm engaged."

The shameless parent shoved her daughter in Mac's face. "That's as good as single in my book."

"Ma, please," the timid girl protested.

"You're not married until there's a ring on your finger. Say hello to the nice man, Eleanor."

"Uh, no offense," said Mac, stepping back. "But I really have to find my fiancée."

"All right, mister. Have it your way. Good luck finding her in this place."

The woman has a point. It'll take me all night to find Angie in this mob. There are just too many tables, but...there's only one exit. If I wait there, I'll be able to catch her as she leaves. Just when Mac turned toward the exit, someone yelled, "Bingoooooo!" And, without warning, the room exploded into a barroom-like brawl amid screams of "Get the cheater!" and "Get the teeth!"

Get the teeth?

"Holy shit!"

Caught by surprise by the sudden storm of cups, candy wrappers, and bingo cards, Mac's head snapped back when something hit him right between the eyes. "Damn, I'm bleeding!" he squawked, touching his forehead. Even that didn't stop him, and Mac struggled to get back in the hall. *I've got to find Angie!* But the rush of the exiting mob carried him out through the open double doors.

"Hey, lady, you just stomped on my foot!"

"Marie, is that you?" cried Mac, riding the wave of humanity like a surfer.

Once outside, the raucous crowd calmed down, dispersing as soon as the cold, night air hit them. Left alone in the parking lot, feeling dazed and possibly bleeding, Mac's mind reeled with new suspicions.

That couldn't have been Marie's voice I heard. She and Rick are on a date. And if Angie was here, where the hell is the pink Cadillac? That car's impossible to hide.

"I bet she was home the whole time, and her father sent me

out just to get rid of me," he said, anger overtaking all sense of reason. "Dammit! I've got to get back to the house now!"

No longer intimidated, Mac jumped in his car, threw the engine in gear, and sped off, prepared for a showdown with Angie's father.

Twenty minutes later Sal Russo opened his front door. Smiling at first when he saw Mac, Sal's mood turned surly when he took in Mac's disheveled clothing and trampled flowers. "Where's my daughter?" he demanded.

"I don't know. Why don't *you* tell *me*?" Mac snapped, poking a finger in his chest.

Sal flicked Mac's hand aside. "I already *did*," he said through clenched teeth. "She went to bingo with her grandfather." He fixed an iron-like gaze on Mac, daring him to explain.

Whoa, this is getting serious, thought Mac. Mr. Russo had told him the truth after all. The last thing Mac wanted to do now was to make him mad. But it was almost too late for that. Mac could already see the veins bulging on his forehead.

I've got to come up with a good story or I'm toast.

Rather than make matters worse by describing the melee at the church, Mac came up with his version of what happened.

"Well, I did see her, Mr. Russo."

Sort of—for a second—maybe?

"But it was so crowded, we didn't have the chance to talk before bingo ended."

That was true, thanks to the mob that carried me out bodily.

"So, I came right over to meet her at home." *Not really, but it sounds good.*

"I guess I drove a little too fast and got here first." *Totally unintentional, but I can't stop now.*

Sal relaxed and backed off. So did the veins on his head.

"Yeah," he said slowly as if deciding whether to believe Mac's flimsy story. They probably stopped for ice cream on the way home."

Whew!

"Do you want to wait for her?" he asked, stepping aside.

"No. I'll just leave this here." Mac placed the ruined flowers on the coffee table. Then he reached in his jacket and pulled out the love letter. "But there is something you can do for me. Please give this to Angie. Hand it to her yourself. It's *very* important that she gets this."

"Did you two have a fight?" asked Sal, noticing the forlorn look in his eyes.

"No! I mean, nah," replied Mac with a casual wave. "Just make sure she gets this anyway. Okay?"

"I'll place it in her hands myself," Sal promised, assuring Mac that everything was under control, with the same authority that unnerved him before.

"Thank you, sir."

"One more thing, son. How'd you get that black ink on your forehead?"

Chapter Fifteen
What Would Captain Kirk Do?

"Ya know, if this were a *Star Trek* episode and Captain Kirk was playing bingo, right about now Scotty would beam him up to the Enterprise."

Angie knew that voice and whirled around. She and Gramps were still hiding under a table in the church hall while a few, but still potentially dangerous, parishioners clashed over Mrs. Malafemina's questionable bingo win. A relieved smile spread across her face as Rick and Marie crawled towards her.

"What are you two doing here?" Angie asked, forgetting her own absurd situation. "I thought you had a date?"

"We did, but Mac came to the house looking for you. He left after talking to Dad. I figured Dad told him you were here with Gramps, so we came to warn you."

"Good try, but you're too late," muttered Angie.

Marie rested on her heels. "You mean Mac saw you?"

"No. I saw him come in, but I was sort of under a table at the time."

"Don't tell me you've been here the whole night?"

"Of course not. Don't be ridiculous!" Angie crossed her

arms over her chest. "That was earlier. This is my second table."

"Nice move, sis."

"Well, I think this is way cool," said Rick. "It's like the fort I used to make with a blanket and my mom's dining room chairs, except for some sticky stuff I just sat in."

Marie narrowed her eyes at him.

"What?"

"So, how'd you end up down here?" asked Marie, turning to Angie. "And what got them all hot and bothered out there? I haven't seen this much action in church since the Pope said we could eat meat on Fridays."

"We experienced some technical difficulties during the game," Angie informed her.

"And why are they chanting, 'Get the cheater' and 'get the teeth'?"

"Technical difficulties," she repeated.

Marie switched positions to sit Indian-style beside Angie. "You mean, like with the PA system?"

"Not exactly," Angie said with a sideways glance aimed at Gramps.

"Then wha...?"

"Mawee, isth thss yaw boyfwend?" interrupted Gramps, speaking for the first time.

"Oh, yeah, sorry. Rick, this is my Grandpa Nick."

"Nith thoo meeth you," said Gramps.

Marie did a double-take. "Wait a minute! Why's he talking so funny?"

"It seems Gramps' teeth were a little anxious to get home tonight and tried to make the trip without him," Angie told her.

Nick smiled a toothless grin.

"What's that supposed to mean?" demanded Marie.

"It means his dentures flew out of his mouth while calling the bingo numbers."

"That was the technical difficulty?" asked Marie, wide-eyed.

Angie just shrugged.

"Awesome, senior dude," said Rick. He and Gramps bumped fists.

"How the hell did he do that? You were supposed to be watching him. Dad is gonna go ballistic! Do you know how much a new set of dentures costs?"

"It's a long story," sighed Angie. "I'll be more than happy to tell you later. Right now, all I want to do is go home, but we can't leave without Gramps' teeth."

"Okay. You stay here. Just tell me where they are, and I'll get them," said Marie, uncharacteristically taking charge.

Angie peeked out from under the table and directed her sister's gaze towards the apparent source of the riot. "I think his teeth are over there."

Marie's mouth fell open when she saw Mrs. Malafemina swiping the air, and anyone else in the vicinity, with her cane, including the floorwalker struggling to validate her numbers.

"Ooooh no," she said, retreating. "I know who that is. I'm not going anywhere near her. I think the old hag put a curse on me when I was in the second grade. That's probably why I can't lose weight."

Angie nudged her shoulder. "Come on, Ree. Ever since you were a kid, doughnuts were at the top of your own personal food pyramid. Don't blame it on her."

"Look who's talking?" she said, pushing back. "You always crossed the street rather than walk in front of her house."

"Hey, the world's a scary place when you're seven years old. I wasn't taking any chances."

"Are you two talking about the lady in the black dress?" asked Rick.

"That's the one," they said in unison.

"Leave her to me. I'll get your grandfather's pearly whites," said Rick, volunteering his services. "Just cover me."

"Cover you? Cover you with what?" asked Marie. "This isn't the OK Corral, you know? Although given our present situation, I could be wrong."

"I don't know. They say that in the movies. I always wanted to use that line. It's a classic. You know like, *"Stop the presses!"*

"Forget the movies! Just go before somebody calls the cops!" she ordered, pushing him out from under the table.

Rick was tall and lanky with the awkward gait of a teenager unaccustomed to his own body after a growth spurt, yet he moved with stealth-like accuracy, weaving his way through the mob unnoticed. But Mrs. Malafemina was surrounded, and he couldn't reach Gramps' teeth, innocently sitting on G-54. *What would Captain Kirk do?* A diversion always worked for the Enterprise landing party. So Rick stood on a chair and shouted, "Look, isn't that Tony Bennett over there?"

"Where? Where is he?" demanded the star-struck bingo players.

"Don't you see him? He's over there," said Rick, pointing toward the double doors.

All heads turned, straining to catch a glimpse of their beloved Italian singer. Rick swooped down, grabbed the dentures, and ran back to the band of fugitives under the table before anyone realized his ruse. "I got the goods, let's boogie!"

Angie took the dentures from Rick, passing them to Gramps. "Do you think you can run?" she asked him.

Gramps jammed them in his mouth and winked. "You'd be surprised what an old man can do when he's being chased by an angry mob."

They stayed low, moving as fast as the slightly plump Marie and Gramps' arthritic knees would allow past over-turned chairs, forgotten bingo cards, trash, and several decapitated troll dolls. Thankfully, the crowd was still more interested in a possible Tony Bennett sighting and Mrs. Malafemina's alleged bingo win than with the small group creeping across the floor. Once safely outside in the parking lot, Marie hooked her arm in Rick's and said, "You're on your own now, Ang. *I'm* on a date."

"Thanks, Ree. I owe you big time."

"Don't mention it," said Marie, brushing off the praise. "What are sisters for anyway?"

"It looks like you both rescued me tonight," she said, turning to Rick. "And you did it *just* like in the movies. Thanks." Angie rose up on her tiptoes and kissed him on the cheek.

Marie regarded Rick with a wistful look in her eyes. "Yeah, I have to admit that was pretty cool."

Rick shuffled his feet. "Aw, it was nothin'. I had a blast. And we can still make the movie if we hustle."

"Then let's boogie," said Marie, tugging Rick's arm. "Don't wait up, Ang," she added over her shoulder as they scrambled into his truck.

Angie sighed, hoping no one had noticed the tiny cracks in her usual self-confident façade under the scrutiny of the parking lot lights. Smoothing her hair nervously after her narrow escape, she wondered what had unnerved her more, the rioting mob or seeing Mac? Her brow creased when she extracted a crushed candy wrapper from the long-tangled strands.

"Well, it's just you and me again, Angelina," said Gramps. "What are we gonna do next?"

Angie swung around abruptly, taking hold of Gramps'

shoulders. "Next?" she exclaimed. There's no next. We're done for tonight."

"But I gotta make up for lost time," Gramps said earnestly.

Angie's arms fell to her sides. "Can't we just go home?"

"Sure, sure, Angelina," he agreed, patting her hand. "We'll go home. I gotta save my energy for tomorrow anyway."

"You have something planned for tomorrow?"

"No, but I'll be ready. At my age, I gotta make the most of any day above ground."

Too tired to argue, Angie's shoulders slumped. "Oookay," she said wearily, as they trudged across the parking lot.

"Ya know, you gotta admire that woman," mused Gramps when they neared the pink Caddy. "It took guts to stand up to those people."

"Yeah. I bet Mrs. Malafemina never thought she'd need that cane for more than walking," she agreed, as they climbed in.

"Maybe we should go back and help her," suggested Gramps.

Angie started the engine. "Won't have to. All she has to do is threaten to put a curse on them. They'll back off."

"I guess we won't tell your parents about this, right Angelina?"

"Are you kidding? News travels fast in this parish. They already know by now," Angie told him as she eased out of the parking space. "What the heck happened to you on that stage anyway?"

"I don't know, something just came over me," Gramps said with a shrug. "Do you think all them candy bars and sodas had something to do with it?"

"Probably. Either that or they just pushed your buttons," she said with a smile. "But you should have taken your own advice, Gramps. Remember? It's only bingo."

Chapter Sixteen
The First Love Letter

"Shhh. I don't want to wake Mom and Dad," Angie whispered to Gramps as they tiptoed into the dark house after returning from bingo. "I can't believe Ma's not waiting at the door. Someone must have called about the bingo riot by now."

"Who cares?" said Gramps, creeping through the living room behind her. "I haven't had that much fun in years."

"Well, don't get used to it."

Then the lights flashed on in the hall. Angie stifled a scream and dropped her handbag.

"*Mannaggia!*" Gramps cried, clutching his chest with both hands.

"Sorry about that, Pop," apologized Sal, stepping into the room. "I didn't mean to scare you."

"Don't worry, son. Now I can skip my next doctor's appointment. If I'm still breathing after *that*, my ticker's in pretty good shape."

When Angie's eyes adjusted to the light, she spotted the trampled bouquet on the coffee table. Wondering how they ended up in that condition at first, she winced at the memory of the bingo riot and figured Mac somehow got tangled up in it.

"I hope you weren't trying to call us tonight, Ang," began her father, "because I disconnected the phone so your mother could sleep undisturbed."

Thank you, God.

"Nope, we were too busy at bingo to make any calls. Right, Gramps?" Angie asked, poking him in the ribs.

"Ow! Yeah, right. We were *very* busy."

"And boy are we tired," she added for good measure. "So good night, Dad."

"Before you run off, there's something I want to talk to you about."

Gulp!

Angie turned slowly to face her father. "Sure, Dad, what is it?"

"Mac was here tonight and left those for you," he told her, pointing to what was left of the flowers.

"Thanks," she said, scooping them up, eager to get away. "Well, good night."

"Wait! I'm not finished."

Angie stopped dead in her tracks.

"I know it's none of my business, but did you two have a fight?"

Double gulp.

"Us? Fight?" sputtered Angie. "You mean me and Mac?"

Her father folded his arms across his chest. "No, you and the Easter Bunny. Yeah. You and Mac."

"No, of course not. I just told him that I had to take care of Gramps tonight." Angie aimed pleading eyes at Gramps, silently begging him to go along with her lie.

He nodded, giving her a conspiratorial wink.

Sal remained silent.

I may have to start going to church again if this keeps up.

Angie was thankful her father bought her story, although his dubious expression said otherwise. *I've seen that look before. Dad knows we're lying, but why isn't he saying anything? Who cares as long as I don't have to explain. Forget about going to church. I may have to become a nun. I wonder if the virgin rule is still in effect?*

"Mac also gave me this," said her father with an envelope in his hand. "He said it was *very* important. I promised I'd give it to you myself."

Angie hesitated.

"C'mon, Angie, it's late. Take this thing so I can go to bed already," urged Sal, obviously determined to keep his word.

When Angie saw Mac with an envelope earlier that evening at bingo, she thought it was the church deposit. Now she didn't know what to think. It looked like a harmless envelope. Just a folded piece of mashed and dried wood pulp—nothing to be afraid of. Then why *was* she afraid?

"What are you waiting for Angie?"

"Uh...nothing, Dad." But when her fingers touched the ivory paper, a spark cracked, and she took a step back.

"Oh, for chrissake—here!" Her father pressed the envelope in her hand.

"Uh, thanks, Dad." Feeling slightly unhinged from the experience, Angie hastily snatched her handbag from the floor. "Goodnight," She dashed to Marie's room before her father asked any more questions.

"What do you think that was all about?" Sal asked his father when she was gone.

Until that moment, Gramps had lived his life by a personal set of rules. One of his favorites, do unto others *before* they do unto you, came in real handy when he worked for Vincenzo Lombardi. Never admit to anything, were also words of wisdom that kept him out of trouble. Now he faced a dilemma. Tell his son the truth or break his promise to Angie. He'd never lied to Sal before (nodding didn't count). So, Gramps was forced to improvise on the spot with a new rule. It's not a lie if it's *partially* true.

"Probably just pre-wedding jitters," he told his son. "I wouldn't worry about it."

"Yeah, Pop, I guess you're right," said Sal with a shrug. "Anything I can get for you before I go to bed?"

Gramps plopped down in the recliner. "No, son. I think I'll just watch a little TV. You know, to unravel."

"You mean unwind."

Gramps pushed back on the arms of the chair and his feet popped up. "Yeah, that's what I said."

"Okay, Pop," said Sal with a smile. "Remember, the last one up turns off the lights."

"Sure, sure son. Goodnight."

Breathing a sigh of relief, Angie stumbled into Marie's bedroom. After dumping what was left of the flowers in the small trash can, Angie set her handbag on the dresser and closed the door. She had no idea that bingo, or Gramps for that matter, could be so exhausting. Thankfully, the evening was over—or was it?

Angie knew this might be her only opportunity to see what was in the curious envelope before Marie returned from her date with Rick. He was a nice guy, but from the way Mac talked about his friend, he still had some serious growing up to do. Although being more responsible was at the bottom of Rick's to-do list, he did rescue them tonight. His Tony Bennett diversion was a stroke of genius.

With the sealed envelope in her hand, Angie dragged herself over to the bed. There was a kind of aura surrounding the strange communication—not something you could see but a vibe that resonated throughout her body. She felt the unfamiliar sensation when she entered the house, not knowing the source, only to feel the spine-tingling energy intensify when she came in physical contact with the puzzling letter, if indeed it *was* a letter.

No one writes letters anymore, Angie thought, sitting cross-legged on the bedspread. Birthday, Valentine, or Christmas cards didn't count because someone else wrote the verse. All the sender did was sign their name. But this envelope bore no resemblance to an ordinary drug store greeting card. The paper looked expensive, there was no stamp or address; it simply said *Angelina,* and no one but Gramps called her Angelina. Mac may have delivered the note, but she was positive he didn't write it. His handwriting was as illegible as hieroglyphics, and the name on the envelope was written in calligraphy, definitely not his style at all. What's more, the paper, the handwriting— everything about the letter seemed out of place. It was as if it belonged somewhere in the past, and irrational fear gnawed at her insides again as she studied it. Terrified for no other reason than the unknown, she dared herself to break the seal. But fatigue trumped curiosity, and she drifted off into a deep sleep, still clinging to the unopened letter while she slumbered.

The first light of morning streamed through Angie's bedroom window, splashing bright patterns of light on the walls and across her face. As her eyes opened, she yawned and stretched like a pampered cat, smiling a lazy, languorous smile of contentment. Today was her wedding day.

Angie's enthusiastic bridesmaids had arrived at the house ahead of schedule to help her dress. They playfully roused her out of bed, and for once she didn't mind getting up early, as the house buzzed with the chaotic flutter of female activity.

"Where's my mascara?"

"I need more hairspray!"

"Damn! I got a run in my pantyhose. Who has clear nail polish?"

"Hey, girls," called Sal from the living room. "The photographer's here!"

"We'll be right there!" shouted Marie as she applied the finishing touches to Angie's make-up and hair. Twenty minutes later, the thumping of high heels rumbled down the hall as the bridal party assembled in the living room.

"Okay now, everybody say 'Zucchini'," coached the photographer.

In a slew of formal and candid shots, he captured the happy bride with her attendants before they all piled in a stretch limo for the short drive to St. Lucy's church.

There was standing room only in the beautifully decorated sanctuary, bursting with family and friends invited to witness the marriage of Angelina Russo and Conrad MacConnell. At the end of the long center aisle stood Angie with her father. He lowered her veil, squeezed her hand, and said, "Well, honey, this is it. Ready?"

"Yes, Dad," she said solemnly, hooking her arm in his, as Mrs. Kaminski began Wagner's *Bridal March* on the church organ.

Angie and her father moved slowly down the aisle on the long white runner, each step bringing her closer to the man she loved. Angie never took her eyes off Mac, and his gaze never left her face even as her father lifted her veil, kissed her on the cheek, and placed her hand in Mac's. It was the happiest day of her life. Suddenly, Mac's focus shifted somewhere over her shoulder and Angie turned violently, shocked to see his attention had strayed to none other than Bianca Lombardi.

Bianca wore a white gown, her body positioned like an athlete in a relay race directly behind Angie, ready to grab the baton and run with it. The baton, in this case, was Mac.

What the heck is she doing here?

Mac peeked around Angie's body, unfazed by Bianca's presence. In fact, a goofy grin spread across his face when another bride suddenly appeared, and another, and another until the entire aisle was full of happy brides. All that is, except Angie. A scream formed in her throat, but she was unable to make a sound.

Can't anybody see what's going on? He can't marry all of us. Nooooooo!

Tap-tap-tap. Tap-tap-tap.

Someone was rapping on a stained-glass window.

Tap-tap-tap. Tap-tap-tap.

It became louder and more urgent until...she woke up.

What the...?

Angie surfaced through the fuzzy layers of sleep before realizing she was in Marie's room at home. It was all a dream. No. A nightmare. But the rapping continued. Only now it was more like banging, and Angie's heart pounded against her chest when she saw a shadow at the window. Shaking hands leaped to her chest as if to contain the vital organ in her body.

"Open up, Ang!"

Marie?

"C'mon let me in. It's me, Ree!"

Angie scrambled to the window and wrenched it up. "Jeez Louise, sis. You scared the living crap out of me!"

Marie thrust her upper body through the open window. "Good. How the hell do you think I felt? For a minute there I thought I was at the wrong house. I'm just glad Mrs. Esposito's dog is in for the night."

Angie leaned on the sill. "You mean, Tiny? What are you worried about him for?"

"I don't know if you ever noticed, but that dog has a major attitude problem." Marie held her hands out. "Now pull me in."

"He may be a pain," agreed Angie, grabbing her hands, "but he'd never hurt anybody."

"That's your opinion. I don't like the way that mutt looks at me. I'm not in the habit of hurting animals, but that mangy dog will get a blast of pepper spray if he gets any ideas."

"Since when do you, *unh*, carry pepper spray?" asked Angie, tugging on Marie's arms.

"Since it came out in a cute little can with cool colors."

"That stuff scares me. Just be careful with it, okay, Ree?"

"Whatever you say. Just, *oof*, get me through this damn window."

"So, c'mon in already. What are you waiting for?"

"For you to pull me in."

"I *am* pulling."

"Shit! I'm stuck. How could this happen? I did this all the time when we were kids."

"Yeah, well, you were about twenty pounds lighter back then. I guess your *friends* stayed longer than expected, huh?"

"Very funny. I'll take in the welcome mat tomorrow."

"All right. Let's give it another shot."

"First take my bag." Marie pushed the designer knock-off from her shoulder and tossed it to Angie. She caught it with both hands like a medicine ball.

"What the heck's in this thing?" she asked, peeking inside. "It weighs more than a tray of Ma's lasagna."

"It's not that bad," said Marie. "Just my wallet, keys, pepper spray, hair gel, make-up, cell phone..."

"And Twinkies?" asked Angie, with a package of the cakes in her hand.

"You never know when your blood sugar might drop," said Marie.

"Yeah, well, that's not the only thing about to drop, so let's try this again." This time, Angie grabbed her around the waist. "On the count of three: one...two...threeeeee!"

Marie made an awful grunting sound as her buxom figure made it over the sill faster than Angie could manage. They both landed on the floor with a sickening *thud!*

"Thanks, *pant, pant,* Ang," said Marie, staring up at the ceiling.

Angie fell limply against the dresser. "Don't mention it. But why didn't you just come in through the front door like a normal person?"

"I forgot my key," Marie told her, rising on her elbows.

"I would have let you in."

"Do you have any idea what time it is?"

Angie half-turned to face Marie. "Yeah, it's about 10:00 p.m."

"Maybe in LA, but it's 1:00 a.m. in New York," she said, sitting up. "I didn't want to wake the whole house. When I saw your light on, I came to the window."

"So how was your date with Captain Kirk?" asked Angie with a smile.

Marie brought her knees up to her chest and wrapped her arms around her legs. "Great until I overheard a conversation from the next booth while we were having a pepperoni pie at Patsy's. They said Bianca Lombardi is spreading it all over town that you and Mac have broken up."

"I don't believe it! Ow!" exclaimed Angie when she banged her skull on a drawer knob. "I thought my nightmare ended when I woke up. I can't stand that family," she whined, rubbing the back of her head. "First, Mrs. Lombardi with her nosey, sarcastic remarks at bingo. Now, her stuck-up slut of a daughter's big mouth."

"So, that's what took you so long to come to the window. I didn't count on you being asleep. What was the nightmare about?"

"My wedding day."

Marie raised her eyebrows. "That's a nightmare?"

"Yes, because I wasn't the only bride in church. Every woman in America showed up to marry Mac—including Bianca, and that cheating snake didn't even look upset!" she cried, getting to her feet.

"Is that why you called off the wedding?" asked Marie, nonplussed. "You're worried Mac won't be faithful?"

Angie plopped down on the bed. "That might have something to do with it," she admitted "Ma always told me that trust was the most important thing in a marriage. I know Mac loves me, but lately, I'm having a little difficulty..."

Marie shot her a questioning glare.

"Okay, *a lot* of difficulty with trust issues," she said, resting her chin on her fists. "You don't know what it's like, Ree. Women practically trip over themselves to get a glimpse of Mac —that's bad enough. The fact that they want much more than a glimpse doesn't help."

Marie hoisted her bruised body from the floor. "They're just fans," she said to soothe her sister. "It's business. They mean nothing to Mac."

"I know that," Angie said, falling back on a pillow. "But he's a man, after all, and I know from past experience that it doesn't take much to arouse the male libido. My track record for having cheating boyfriends is a lot better than it should be. I guess it's taking longer than I expected for those emotional scars to heal. But my relationship with Mac is special. He loves me for who I am inside," said Angie, her hand over her heart. "He respects me as a person, one with a brain that he encourages me to use. When I'm with Mac, I know I can do anything. It scares me how much I love him, and it would just kill me if he cheated on me like all the others."

Marie joined her on the bed. "Oh, yeah, I could see that."

Angie sat up abruptly and clutched her by both arms. "You could? I knew it! I knew it!" she wailed. "He's been cheating on me, hasn't he? Tell me the truth, I can take it."

"Take it easy for God's sake. He's not cheating on you."

"But you just said..."

Marie pried Angie's fingers from her limbs. "I said I could see *why* you would dream that. Not that Mac would actually do such a thing."

"Oh. Why?"

"Because that's obviously been on your mind, and the dream was just your brain's way of telling you to cut that shit out. You want my opinion? I don't think you have anything to worry about."

"How can you be so sure?"

"Listen, Ang. I've seen the way that man looks at you. I also saw the look on his face when I returned the ring. Both looks add up to love in my book."

Angie sighed and unearthed the mysterious envelope from the folds in the rumpled bedspread. "I don't know, Ree. Maybe you're right. Dad said Mac asked him to give me this when he was here tonight."

"You mean Mac came back to the house after bingo?"

"Yeah, and I think Dad suspects something."

"What is it?" asked Marie, swiping the envelope from her hand.

Angie shrugged. "Some kind of letter I guess."

"You guess? Didn't you read it?

"Nope."

"Are you sure you're female?" cried Marie. "Aren't you dying with curiosity?"

"I can't explain it, Ree," replied Angie with a twinge of fear in her voice. "There's something about it that scares me. Don't you feel it?"

"Feel what?"

"Never mind," she said, shivering as if chilled.

"So, what are you waiting for?" asked Marie as she dropped the envelope in Angie's lap. "Open it."

Eerily drawn to the letter now, her fingers caressed the expensive vellum. And when she broke the seal, heat surged through her body, and her breath quickened. Angie wondered if Marie noticed, but she was powerless to stop, stirred by the almost visceral need to unfold the single sheet of paper. As she read the letter, her jaw dropped.

Marie reached over and lifted her chin. "Well? What does it say?"

Her hands trembling, Angie passed the note to Marie.

"Oh my God!" she cried, pressing the page against her body. "How freakin' romantic!"

"You know, I saw Mac at bingo with an envelope," began Angie slowly. "I thought he was still bringing the deposit to the church. He had flowers, too, but they didn't make it," she said, pointing to the trash. "Although I'm not convinced the letter is from Mac."

"Of course it is," said Marie. "Didn't Dad say Mac gave it to him?"

"Well, maybe he did," she conceded. "But I don't think he actually wrote it. Mac doesn't know how to write calligraphy. I bet he printed this out on his computer."

Marie held the ivory sheet up to Angie's nose. "I don't think so. Look closely. The spacing between the lines is uneven, and the size of the text isn't uniform either."

"So?"

"So?" said Marie, mocking her. "I can't believe you're being so stubborn. Don't you see? If this were a computer print-out, it would be perfect. This was definitely handwritten."

Angie pressed her lips together, snatching the letter from Marie. "Okay, then look at how he signed his name. I never call him Conrad, without laughing. If he wrote this, he would have signed it with Mac. And this," she continued, tapping the formal salutation, "since when am I Angelina? Gramps is the only one who calls me that. No, this isn't from Mac."

"Sure, it is," insisted Marie. "He probably wrote it that way because he wants you to know how serious he is."

Angie rose from the bed, the letter held tightly in her hand. She wanted to believe—actually it was more like she *needed* to believe—it was from Mac. "It is kind of nice."

"Are you going to answer it?"

Angie set the letter aside on the dresser. "No."

"Why the hell not?"

"You don't understand, Ree. Whether I like it or not, Mac is a celebrity. Wherever we go he attracts attention, especially from strange women. One of these days he's bound to slip up. If I give in now and marry him, I'll be setting myself up for a broken heart for life. Bianca only makes it worse because I know her."

Marie folded her arms across her chest. "Let me get this straight. You love Mac."

"Right," Angie said, tracing an invisible check in the air.

"You know Mac loves you."

"Right again," she said, making the check a second time.

"And because you're madly in love with Mac, you're

willing to let him go to avoid being hurt by something that will probably never happen?"

Angie's hands dropped to her sides. "That's about the size of it."

"Whatever happened to my fiery red-headed sister?" exclaimed Marie, jumping from the bed, standing nose-to-nose with Angie. "You never let anyone get you down before, especially Bianca. Remember the panty incident? Where's your self-confidence?"

Angie backed up. "Out the window I guess," she said with a shrug.

"That's bullshit and you know it!"

"Oh, don't worry about me, sis. I can take care of myself," insisted Angie, turning away.

"Of course you can, Ang. What I want to know is when the hell do you plan to start?"

Marie is right, of course. I was always confident, in control; no one ever got the best of me before. When did I become so insecure? But that doesn't matter anymore. Mac is my man and from now on, things will be different. "You're right!" she said, swinging around. "Who does Bianca think she is?"

"Now you're talking."

"Yeah. I'll straighten her man-stealing behind out," said Angie, her chin held high.

"Yeah. *We'll* show her who's boss."

"Wait a minute." Angie held her hand up. "There's no *we*. This is my problem. *I'll* do the showing alone."

"Oh, c'mon, Ang. It'll be fun. Just like when we were kids."

"Totally out of the question. I know you want to help, but please stay out of this.

Marie's shoulders slumped. "All right."

"I mean it, Ree—wait." Angie tilted her head. "Did you say, all right?"

"Yeah."

"Oh...Okay, then. Thanks," she said, bemused by the easy victory. "I knew you'd understand."

Marie clasped her hands behind her back, crossing her fingers, just like when they were kids. "If that's what you want, I'll do as you say."

Chapter Seventeen

Sunday Morning Will Never
Be the Same

Sunday was Mac's favorite day of the week. No alarm clocks, relaxing with the newspaper, a lazy cup of coffee, lounging in bed with Angie until noon. He liked to tease her awake with a kiss strategically planted on her warm body followed by the predictable results. His favorite move, in an area only he and the tech that did her bikini wax had access to, always got her full attention.

Not a moment passed when he wasn't aware of her beauty. Angie could be doing the laundry, taking out the trash, or weeding the garden. It didn't matter. It was all the same to him. And while she slept—oh God—while she slept her mouth formed a sensual little girl pout—a fact she always denied—that drove him crazy with desire. But his love was based on more than her physical appearance. Of course, that drew him to her initially; but as they grew closer, he became enamored by her fierce loyalty, sharp wit, and tender heart. Most of all, Mac admired her independent streak and determined refusal to let him spoil her. Angie wasn't in the relationship for the money or fame. Her feelings for him were strong and true, and Mac wanted all those feelings to last forever. He wanted forever, with Angie.

Cranky after a restless night, he woke in a passionate embrace with his pillow and the bewildering love letter on his mind. He wondered if Mr. Russo had given it to Angie. He also wondered how he actually wrote it. What's more, Mac didn't even know why Angie left him in the first place. Two days ago, his life followed a clear path to a blissful, contented future with the woman he loved. Now he felt lost, groping in the darkness for a way, any way, to lead him back on the road to her heart.

Mac had left his cell phone on the nightstand in case Angie returned his calls. Reaching for it, he checked his messages. Rick had texted that he'd be over with breakfast—surprisingly, good news. Still out of coffee, his refrigerator contained only a jar of olives and a wedge of cheese covered in colorful mold. No word from Angie.

After prying himself out of bed, Mac showered, dressed, and clipped his phone on his belt. The doorbell rang just as he began to shave. With the cordless shaver still in his hand, he tramped downstairs and opened the door. Rick breezed in, smiling, with breakfast, doughnuts, and two large coffees.

"Morning bro," he said cheerfully, heading to the kitchen. "It's a beautiful day in the neighborhood."

Mac followed half-shaven, lured by the aroma of bacon and eggs.

Rick spread their fast-food meal on the kitchen table. "Dig in, man," he said informally.

Mac sat across from Rick. "You look awfully chipper today," he observed, grabbing a container of coffee.

"Marie and I had a blast last night. I think this might be the beginning of a beautiful friendship."

Mac removed the lid from the paper cup. "Just a friendship?"

"Hell no, dude, but it's a great way to start."

"Well, at least one of us has a future," grumbled Mac after taking a sip.

Rick handed Mac a breakfast burrito and took one for himself. "Sorry man, I didn't mean to sound happy. You know, with *your* life in the crapper and all."

"My life is *not* in the crapper! Angie and I just hit a bump in the road, that's all."

"Sure, man, Whatever you say."

Mac set his coffee down, unwrapped the burrito, and lifted it to his mouth. "So where did you and Marie go last night? Dinner? A movie?"

"Well, after we left bingo at the church—" Rick stopped mid-sentence, with an audible gulp.

Mac dropped his breakfast before taking a bite. "Wait a minute. You were at bingo?"

"It wasn't my idea," sputtered Rick, with his hands up. "Honest."

"I thought I heard Marie's voice. And what was all that commotion about?"

"Angie said her grandfather started a riot. We had to sneak out like ninjas."

Mac slammed his fist on the table. "So, Angie *was* there! And she talked to you?"

"Hey, don't go postal on me, man. I had other plans. Marie said we had to go."

"Well, that's just great!" said Mac, slumping back in his chair. "Now the two of you are in cahoots, plotting against me."

Rick unwrapped another burrito. "No way. Marie dragged me there against my will. It was really cool, though, how she grabbed me by the collar and... Sorry dude, she can be very persuasive. By the way, what went down with Mr. Russo?

When he let you in the house, I wasn't sure if he was gonna hug you or kill you."

"Neither was I," said Mac, crossing his long legs. "Apparently, Angie is keeping our broken engagement a secret from her parents. Because if Mr. Russo knew, he would've let me have it as soon as I walked in the door. In fact, he told me where to find her. I thought he was just trying to get rid of me, but I guess he was telling the truth." Mac sipped his coffee, deep in thought. "So, her grandfather started the riot?"

"Yeah man," said Rick. "He's really cool, for an old dude."

"Mr. Russo told me the family was having problems with him."

"I don't know about that, but last night he had a problem keeping his teeth in his mouth."

Get the teeth! That had to be him.

"What happened to the letter you wrote to Angie?" Rick wanted to know.

"When I went back to the house after bingo, she still wasn't home. I had no choice but to leave it with her father."

Rick wiped his mouth with a paper napkin. "Do you think she read it?"

"I haven't heard from Angie, so I don't know what to think. I can't even be sure Mr. Russo gave it to her."

"Her old man's not so bad, I bet he did."

Mac picked a strip of bacon from his burrito, pointing it at Rick, as he spoke. "You thought he was going to kill me last night. Why the sudden change of heart?"

"I don't know—maybe because you're still breathing? That must count for something, doesn't it?"

Mac remembered how close he came to committing suicide by angry parent last night. "Yeah, I guess it does."

"You know, when Marie and I were in Patsy's having pizza, she overheard some talk about you and Angie from the next booth. They said someone named Bianca was blabbing to anyone who'll listen that you and Angie split up."

The mention of her name jolted Mac like a double espresso, and he dropped the bacon. "Bianca Lombardi?"

"Yeah, that's the one. You know her?"

"Wish I didn't."

Mac had forgotten about Bianca. She and Angie were always at each other's throats. Had been for years. He wasn't sure, but their acrimonious relationship might be the result of an incident in high school involving a pair of panties. Anyway, Bianca was always coming on to him. She even made a pass at him when they booked the wedding; probably figured it was her last chance before he was married. It would have been the last thing she *ever* did if he hadn't stopped Angie from choking her. Bianca never pulled a stunt like that again.

"Marie heard them say that Angie called Bianca at the country club and canceled the wedding," Rick informed him.

"My mother told me the same thing yesterday. But she made it clear to me that she re-booked for us."

"Maybe she made it up."

"My mother?"

"No, that Bianca chick."

Mac rubbed his chin. "Could be. From what I know of Bianca, she's capable of anything. Then again, Angie might have called her; she did return the ring. I just didn't think she'd be so quick about it. And if Bianca *did* make it up, that rumor could kill any chance I have of reconciliation with Angie. Whether I like it or not, I need to have a serious discussion with Miss Lombardi."

Mac jumped when his cell phone rang. "Maybe it's Angie!" He tore it off his belt and checked the number. "Damn, it's my mother."

"Want me to leave, man?" asked Rick.

"No, you might as well stay. We're all in this mess together now. Hello, mother," he said, lifting the phone to his ear.

"Conrad, I thought you were going to call me yesterday?"

"I was," he told her, rubbing the space between his brows, "but I got a little mobbed by my work."

Rick held his stomach, pretending to laugh. He leaned over too far and fell on the floor.

"What's that noise, Connie? Is everything all right?"

"It's nothing, Mother," he assured her. "A book just fell off the shelf. So what's up?"

"You still haven't explained to me why Angela canceled the wedding."

"I told you, it was probably just a misunderstanding. But if it makes you feel any better, I'm going over to the country club today to find out what happened."

"That's a good idea, Connie. Ask for the banquet coordinator. Oh, what's her name?"

"Bianca?"

"Yes, that's the one. She'll take care of everything."

She's taking care of everything all right. Just not the way you think.

"Okay. I'll call you in a few days."

"Promise?"

"Yes, Mother. I promise," he said and disconnected.

Rick gathered up the empty bags and paper cups. "So what's your game plan?"

Mac slipped the phone back on his belt. "I guess I have to see Bianca. But first I'm writing another letter to Angie."

"Do these letters you're writing have anything to do with that old pen you bought at the pawnshop?"

"Yes...No!" stammered Mac. "Oh hell, I don't know!"

"Hey, man, that's cool. There's a lot I don't remember either, like high school. That's still a blur." Rick stood and pushed in his chair. "Well, I gotta split. Call, if you need me to ride shotgun."

"Sure thing," said Mac, walking him to the door. "Thanks for breakfast."

Rick held up his hand, separated his middle and ring fingers, and said, "Live long and prosper, dude."

Mac finished shaving and shuffled back to his office. The Spartan lay on his desk just where he left it. Dropping into his leather chair, he thought about the love letter he wrote to Angie using the antique pen. *It was probably too short and didn't say enough. Maybe Angie didn't think I wrote it, or that it was from me? That's probably why she hasn't called. Hell, even I didn't think it was from me.*

Running his fingers through his thick, wavy hair, Mac blew out a sigh. "I have to keep trying if I want Angie back." With renewed determination, he extracted another sheet from the packet of paper on his desk and said, "Here we go."

The moment Mac's fingers touched the Spartan's sterling silver barrel, he felt the unearthly presence just like before. But instead of fear and resistance, he felt a calm acceptance, and he let the pen take over. Sometimes writing is like a volcano. It can be dormant for years, but when it erupts, there's no stopping the lava it spews. And with each stroke of the magical nib, tender prose flowed from Mac's heart, burning with the heat of passion like fiery lava, in another stirring love letter. His heart hammered, his pulse raced, but his hand remained steady as he wrote words he hadn't thought of. Words he wasn't aware of, with emotions he was powerless to control. Just when he thought he'd collapse from the strain, the pen stopped moving. The letter was complete. In that instant, his head cleared, and the pen slid from his grasp. Catching his breath, Mac gaped in wonder at another bewildering composition.

This letter was longer than the first, possessing the same appearance of a bygone era. And although the language and sprawling calligraphy were from another time, the message it conveyed was current and sincere. It was as if his heart, with each passionate beat, poured words out on the paper with his life's blood instead of inert, black ink.

A skeptic by nature, Mac usually scoffed at any suggestion of the supernatural, but there was no other way to account for the phenomenon he just experienced...again. He had entertained the frivolous, hypothetical theory of a haunted or possessed fountain pen after writing the first letter. Frankly, the thought scared the bejeezus out of him, but now he was willing to believe that the Spartan had some kind of power. Problem was, he couldn't figure out how or why.

"What the hell is happening to me?" he shouted into the empty room. "If there's someone, or something, here, can you please answer my question?"

Thankfully, there was silence. He probably would have wet himself if he got an answer, anyway.

Chapter Eighteen
Don't Break the Meatballs

On any given Sunday in America, the aroma of bacon and eggs awakens most families. Except at the Russo home. Instead of bacon and eggs, they wake to the savory scent of meatballs and sausage frying in olive oil to make a rich tomato sauce for their traditional family dinner later in the day. Another Sunday morning tradition was going to church.

When Angie and Marie were kids, their father roused them early to attend the nine o'clock Mass at St. Lucy's, though he never accompanied them.

"Why aren't you coming with us, Daddy?" the sleepy little girls would ask. "Why do we have to go to church and you don't?"

"Because I already went to Mass and came home while you were all still sleeping. See?" he'd reply, displaying a white bakery box. "I even stopped for doughnuts."

Despite any doubts the girls may have harbored, they forgave their father's harmless deception and went to church without him. It was as if the sugar-covered fried dough absolved him as sure as saying the Act of Contrition after confession. Although Marie didn't go to Mass anymore, she still got up early on Sunday. The aroma of sausage and meatballs was better than an alarm clock.

After throwing back the covers and climbing out of bed, Marie managed to pull a sweater, jeans, and ankle boots from her closet without waking Angie. She padded down the hall to the bathroom, showered, then stuffed her size fourteen body in the size twelve jeans. *Angie was right about the doughnuts*, she thought, as she wrestled with the zipper. Her head popped through the neck of her sweater, and she pulled it down quickly to hide the straining seams on her jeans. Then, with a few tugs of a brush through her damp hair, she stepped into her boots, grabbed her handbag, and headed to the kitchen.

Marie found her mother where she was every Sunday morning—cooking at the stove. The newest addition to the domestic scene, Gramps, was sitting at the kitchen table, and a contented smile spread across her face at the comforting sight of her family. It meant all was right with the world. Now, if she could only get Mac and Angie back together, all would be right with the universe.

"Mornin', Ma," she said and kissed her mother on the cheek.

Margaret lowered a meatball into the saucepot. "Good morning, dear," she replied.

Marie poured a cup of coffee and pulled a chair up next to her grandfather. "Mornin', Gramps."

No response. He just stared at his daughter-in-law, apparently mesmerized by the simmering tomato sauce.

"Gramps, I *said* good morning."

"Oh, good morning, Marie," he mumbled, his gaze locked on Margaret.

"Hey, Ma, what's the matter with him?" Marie asked, flipping through the Sunday paper.

Margaret tapped her wooden spoon on the rim of the pot

and turned. "I'm not sure. He hasn't taken his eyes off me since I told him we were having *lasagna* for dinner. Marie, please tell him to stop. He's making me uncomfortable."

"Hey Gramps, cut it out already. Here, read something." Marie slid the comics in front of him. "Ma won't be able to cook if you keep that up."

Gramps' eyes blinked into focus. "Oh, I'm sorry, Margaret. It's just that it's been so long since I had homemade *lasagna*."

"Didn't they serve it at the home?" she asked.

"That slop! I *skeeve* it! But that," said Gramps, indicating the pot on the stove. "That is manna from heaven, food of the gods...a masterpiece."

"It's only tomato sauce," said Marie.

"You don't understand. Your mother learned how to cook from your grandmother, may she rest in peace," he said while crossing himself. "It's like having her here with me again."

Gramps could be a pill at times, but Marie looked at her mother with tears in her eyes.

"I know, Gramps," she said as she squeezed his hand.

"I miss her, too," said Margaret, hugging him. "Mama taught me how to cook all of Sal's favorite foods when we were first married. I can still hear her voice. 'Be careful, don't break the meatballs when you stir the sauce'."

Bleepity-blop-blop.

The pot boiled suddenly like the La Brea Tar Pits. Exploding bubbles left red dots on the stovetop and floor. Margaret rushed over to wipe up the mess.

Gramps returned to his hypnotic food state. "Margaret, would you make me *Capuzzella?*" His question hung in the air like another bubble of sauce.

Marie remembered the dish her grandmother made for Easter. She wasn't exactly squeamish, but lamb's head on a platter wasn't her idea of a gourmet meal. The eyeballs didn't help either. All the men at the table fought for them like lions over a kill. Apparently eating the eye was some sort of Italian macho rite of passage.

"That stuff is *nasty,* Gramps," she told him, wrinkling her nose.

Gramps lifted his chin proudly. "Everyone in my village ate it."

"Well, they must have been *very* hungry," replied Marie with a shrug.

Margaret turned the sausage browning in a pan. "Pop, you know that's for Easter."

"Yeah, but I'm an old man. I might not last that long."

"We'll see. Let's get through today's dinner first before we plan a lifetime of menus, Okay?"

"Yeah, sure," he answered with a satisfied smile.

"Where's your sister this morning, Marie?" asked her mother.

"Still sleeping."

"Oh, that's right, "she said, adding the sausage to the savory ragu. "Your father told me you all went out last night. So how was your date, Marie? Pop, did anything interesting happen at bingo? Pop?"

Margaret turned. They were gone. "Ouch!" she cried when a bubble of sauce landed on her arm. "After all these years of cooking, I should know better than to turn my back on a pot of sauce, or my family, for that matter. At least, they could have said goodbye."

She continued to stir the pot, careful not to break the meatballs.

~

"Man, that was close," said Marie once she and Gramps were outside. She slung her handbag on her shoulder and sat on the front stoop. "We're getting pretty good at fast exits, aren't we, Gramps?"

"Too fast," he said, joining her on the top step. "I didn't have breakfast."

"That's because you were too busy undressing that pot of sauce with your eyes," she said with a playful jab to his shoulder. "Just be thankful we got out before Mom asked more questions. I don't know what I would have said."

"You? I gotta be good if I want any *lasagna*. Oh, I can see it now: *sasizza, ricotta, mozzarella*. What time's dinner?"

"We usually eat at three o'clock on Sundays."

"Good. I don't wanna be late," he said, rubbing his hands together. "So, did your sister read the letter from her boyfriend last night?"

"We both did. Hey, wait a minute," said Marie, narrowing her eyes at Gramps. "How do you know she got a letter?"

"I was there when your father gave it to her."

"Oh. So, I guess she told you about her broken engagement?"

"Yeah. I promised to mind my own business, too." Gramps admitted ruefully.

Marie rested her elbows on her knees. "I sort of promised the same thing. I just can't understand how Angie can be so stubborn. She won't see Mac or talk to him on the phone. She ignores his emails and voicemail messages and flat out refuses to answer the letter. All I know is if I ever got a romantic love letter like that, nothing could hold me back from the guy who wrote it. I wish there was a way to get them together. Once Angie sees Mac, I know it'll be impossible to keep them apart."

"Ah. That's how it was with your grandma and me," he

reminisced with a wistful smile. "Her parents didn't like me, but we were young and in love."

Marie turned to face her grandfather. "I've seen your wedding picture. You and Grandma had a big wedding. How did you get married if they didn't like you?"

Gramps leaned toward her. "Can you keep a secret?" he whispered.

"Cross my heart," she said, tracing an invisible X on her chest.

"We eloped," he said simply. "They were forced to accept me."

"No shit," said Marie, her interest piqued. "But why is that a secret?"

Gramps folded his hands and bowed his head. "Your Grandma, may she rest in peace, was embarrassed."

"About what? You got married, didn't you?"

"By a Justice of the Peace," Gramps told her. "But by the time her family found out we had eloped, your grandma was already expecting. We didn't tell anybody. Her parents still insisted we get married in church, and when your father was born, we said he was preapproved."

"Don't you mean premature?"

"Yeah. That's what I said."

Marie chuckled, then her eyes went wide. "You mean Grandma was pregnant with Dad in your wedding picture?"

"Yeah. And even though we were already married, your grandma felt ashamed that she was pregnant when she said her marriage vows to a priest before God."

Marie lowered her voice. "Does Dad know?"

Gramps shook his head. "We never told him. That's the only wedding picture we have and the only anniversary we ever celebrated."

"Wow, that's some skeleton in the Russo closet."

"Please, Marie, don't say anything, for your grandma's sake."

"Sure, Gramps. You can count on me," she promised, crossing her heart again.

"Nicky, Nicky!" Bernice Esposito had stepped out on her porch to retrieve the Sunday paper. "Nicky, Nicky. Is that you? Why don't you come over and visit for a while?"

"Go ahead, Gramps," said Marie, nudging him off the stoop. "I have to figure out a way to get Angie married without actually doing anything."

"Then come with me," he said with a mischievous glint in his eyes. "I got an idea."

"What kind of idea?" she asked cautiously.

"Your sister don't wanna see Mac, right?"

"Yeah..."

"Well, I know how to get Angelina and Mac together."

"No, Gramps!" she cried, leaping off the concrete stoop. "We promised Angie we'd stay out of her life, remember?"

Making that promise to Angelina seemed like a good thing to do at the time, thought Gramps. Now, it occurred to him that he might have been a little hasty in giving his word. But since when did a promise ever stop him from doing what he wanted to do? Never. Why should this time be any different? Because he made the promise to his granddaughter, that's why, not some chump who stiffed him in the numbers racket. Gramps could almost feel the rusty gears turning in his head as he struggled with this latest moral dilemma. Then the solution hit him like a shot of prune juice. It was time to update another rule.

Winking, Gramps caught Marie's eye. "Maybe I don't remember?"

"What's that supposed to mean?" she demanded, placing her hands on her hips.

"It means I'm an old man. I forget things sometimes," he

said with a self-satisfied smirk. "So I won't be breaking my promise to your sister, if I don't remember making it, right?"

"Oh, no, I don't like the sound of this one bit."

"Don't worry. I'll take care of everything...uh, what's your name again?" asked Gramps, scratching his head.

"Oh, cut that out," said Marie. "I get it. And what does Mrs. Esposito have to do with your idea?"

Gramps glanced at Bernice and waved. "You'll see," he said, turning back to Marie.

"All right," she agreed uneasily. "Just keep that overgrown hamster of hers away from me. He and I have a history of unresolved issues."

"You mean Tiny?"

"Humph," she grumbled, folding her arms across her chest. "There's nothing tiny about his nasty attitude."

"What's the matter, he don't like you?"

"That's about the size of it."

"Don't worry, Marie. I take care of the dog."

Bernice waited at the door while Gramps and Marie made their way across the street. Gramps shooed Tiny away before he could get hold of his leg as he ascended the porch steps. Tiny took one look at Marie and growled.

"See what I mean?"

"Don't worry about him. I gotta plan."

When they entered the house, Bernice took Gramp's arm. "Let's sit together on the love seat, Nicky," she suggested. "Won't that be nice?"

"Sure, sure, Bernice," he said, glancing over his shoulder. "You coming, Marie?"

She just rolled her eyes.

Once in the living room, Bernice squeezed next to Gramps on the loveseat. Tiny hopped up on the wide overstuffed arm beside her. Marie plopped down on the sofa, trying not to stare at the map of Italy on the older woman's forehead. *What the heck is Gramps up to?*

Bernice fluttered her stubby eyelashes, apparently moonstruck over every word Gramps said as they chatted.

Marie stifled a moan. *Whatever it is, I wish he'd hurry up. I can't take this anymore.*

"Nicky, would you like me to make some coffee?" offered Bernice.

"I'll do it," volunteered Marie, rising abruptly from the sofa.

Gramps leaped from the loveseat, blocking her path with his body. "No, I'll do it."

Marie tried to jostle past him. "No. *I'll* make the coffee," she said through clenched teeth.

"No. Please allow *me*," said Gramps, elbowing her aside. He scurried into the kitchen, leaving Marie alone with her neighbor.

She settled on the edge of the sofa and smiled at Mrs. Esposito. "Uh...nice weather we're having."

"Yes, dear. It has been nice," she agreed.

Now what? Keeping one eye on Tiny, Marie did a quick scan of her surroundings.

Mr. Esposito had smoked himself to death but earned a decent living doing it. And with the financial means to satisfy his wife's remodeling whims, built a front porch, expanded the living room, added a formal dining room and second-floor dormer with a full bath. The couple never had children, so the home's furnishings remained in pristine condition. Marie ran her hand over the brown, gold, and olive-green upholstered sofa, her foot tapping nervously, jumping at the sudden clatter of pots, pans, and cabinet doors slamming in the kitchen.

Bernice's brow furrowed with concern, and a section of northern Italy vanished in the folds of her skin.

"Do you need any help in there, Gramps?" yelled Marie.

He peeked around the kitchen doorway. "No, I'm fine."

Bernice gave him a cute little finger wave. Gramps smiled. Marie groaned, "God help me."

A couple of minutes later, Gramps appeared hefting a tray laden with pastries and coffee.

"How nice of you, Nicky," said Bernice, clearly impressed with his domestic skills. "There aren't many men who help in the kitchen anymore."

Gramps placed the tray on the coffee table. "Ah, it's nothin'." After filling their cups, he sat beside Marie on the sofa. "Tell me, Bernice, does your precious Tiny get much exercise?"

Marie shot him a suspicious frown.

"Not as much as he'd like. My arthritis makes it hard for me to walk," she replied, rubbing her knees. "I let him out in the backyard to do his business when I take my nap. That's the best I can do for my little sweetie."

"Would it help if Marie and I took Tiny out for a nice long walk today while you nap? We'll bring him back before you wake up."

"Oh, would you?" she said, clapping her hands together.

"Sure, we would. Right, Marie?" Gramps poked her in the ribs with his elbow.

Marie gave him a *have-you-lost-your-mind* look. "Oh yeah, we'd love to," she said flatly.

"Wonderful," said Bernice. "I'll get his leash."

"What the heck did you do that for?" Marie hissed under her breath when they were alone. "You know what a pain in the ass that animal is? Not to mention he's the dog from hell and will probably try to kill us the minute our backs are turned."

"Take it easy. Your grandpa will take care of everything."

"Well, I don't trust him." Marie pulled a small red cylinder resembling a tube of lipstick from her handbag. "It's a good thing I carry this."

Gramps' eyes widened. "You gonna put make-up on now?"

"No, it's pepper spray, just in case."

Mrs. Esposito returned with Tiny at her heels, handing his leash to Gramps. He attached it to the dog's collar while she patted his furry little head. "Be a good boy for Nicky. Mama's going to miss her baby."

Tiny ignored her completely. His eyes were glued on Gramps.

"So how is this nasty little creature part of your plan?" asked Marie as they ambled across the road.

"*Aspetta.* You'll see. Now we go to Mac's house."

"WHAT?" Marie stopped in her tracks, clutching Gramps' arm.

Tiny kept walking until his leash went taut. A low growl resonated from his throat despite almost choking on his collar.

"That's your idea?" she demanded.

"Uh-huh. I just wanna say hello."

"Doesn't sound like much of a plan to me. Besides, how are we going to get there? I returned Angie's keys. and I don't have a car."

Gramps reached in his pocket. "Will these help?" he asked, with a cluster of keys in his hand.

"Those are for Dad's car. How did you get hold of them?"

"Your sister dropped her handbag last night. I guess they fell out along with this." Gramps pulled Angie's cell phone out of his other pocket. "I was gonna give 'em back, honest."

"Yeah, that's what they all say."

"So, we're not gonna take the car?"

Marie commandeered the keys. "Of course, we are. You

might as well hold onto the phone for now. Angie's not using it anyway."

"Maybe you could show me how to work this thing?"

"We don't have time for that, Gramps. Let's just get in the car before I lose my nerve."

"Whatta you talkin' about? I gotta have nerve, too," he said, dropping the phone in his pocket.

"Why? Because Dad's car is pink?" she asked, giggling, as they walked up the driveway.

Gramps looked over his shoulder. "Yeah, I don't want Bernice to see me in that thing. I got an image, you know."

Marie opened the passenger door for Gramps, her brows rising in surprise as Tiny hopped in obediently after him. "How did you get him to do that?"

Gramps held up a plastic bag. "With this."

"Is that pepperoni?"

"Yeah, dogs love it." Gramps flipped a slice to Tiny. He caught it mid-air like a pop-up fly ball. "See?"

"You're full of surprises today, aren't you?" teased Marie. "Where'd you get it?"

"In Bernice's refrigerator. I could've used a few pastries, too. I missed breakfast, remember?"

"Well, hopefully, your plan won't take too long, and we'll be back in time for dinner."

Chapter Nineteen
Curb Your Dog

A half-hour later, Gramps and Marie turned the corner into Mac's neighborhood. She slowed the pink Caddy to a stop, parking at the curb across from his house. Gramps leaned forward for a better look through the windshield. "*Madonna mia.* Is that her boyfriend's house over there?"

"Pretty nice, huh?"

"What's the matter with your sister? She don't wanna live here?"

"You know Angie, it's not about the money. She wants to be able to trust him."

"So, what's the problem?"

Marie leaned back against the headrest. "Well, it all started in high school," she began, describing the situation with Bianca and Mac's fans.

"Angelina told me about the *buttana*," spat Gramps.

"Well, if you ask me, I don't think Angie has anything to worry about, even with Bianca," declared Marie, rolling down her window. "The important thing is that they get married and have kids while I'm still young enough to spoil my nieces and nephews."

"Don't worry, Marie, I take care of everything."

"You keep saying that, Gramps."

He wound Tiny's leash around his wrist. "I know. Just stay here," he told her, pushing the passenger side door open.

Marie jumped from the front seat and ran around the car. "Where do you think you're going?" she asked, facing him squarely.

"I'm just gonna walk the dog." Tiny wiggled his rear-end.

Marie leveled an annoyed glance at the dog. "You mean we drove here so Tiny could pee in a different neighborhood?"

"No," answered Gramps. "I'm gonna walk up and down the street until Mac comes outta the house."

"I still don't get what you're trying to do," she said with a doubtful look. "Besides, wouldn't it be easier to knock on his door?"

"Do you think I just got off the boat?" asked Gramps like she was a dim-witted child. "Anybody can do that. It has to look like we just happened to be here so we can say it was, you know, a coincidence."

Marie paused, then stepped aside. "Okay. Then what are you going to talk about?" she asked, giving in for the moment.

"I'm not sure," admitted Gramps. "Hey, you wanna bet on how long it takes for Mac to come out?"

"No!" she snapped. "You're in enough trouble with gambling already."

Gramps' shoulders slumped. "Oh. You heard about that?"

"Yeah. So, forget it."

Marie didn't know what Gramps had in mind, and he wasn't tipping his hand. But she'd gone this far already, so she might as well let him carry out his so-called plan. Besides, what could possibly happen with an eighty-year-old man and a small dog anyway?

"Okay. Walk the mangy mutt. But I'm going to keep an eye

on you in case something goes wrong," she said, checking her watch. "You've got fifteen minutes. If Mac doesn't show up, we're out of here."

"Nonga worry, Marie. I take care of everything."

She let out an exasperated sigh and trudged back to the car.

Tiny pranced up and down the block with Gramps, chasing bugs, sniffing the ground, lifting his stubby leg. The dog was Gramps' best friend thanks to the pepperoni, following him so close that if Gramps stopped short he'd have a furry tail. Tiny seemed to be enjoying the exercise though, taking the opportunity to do more than pee. Unfortunately, he squatted on a perfectly maintained lawn, and Marie watched in horror as the homeowner charged out of his house yelling like a pillaging Viking.

"That's what I was afraid of," she grumbled, hauling herself out of the car.

"What? Do I look like I'm *stunada?*" Gramps asked the outraged man as Marie arrived on the scene. "I'm not touching *that*," he said, shaking his finger at Tiny's steamy little mound of poop.

The man's eyes bulged out, like his red puffy cheeks, and would have seemed comical in his robe, slippers, and Shriners fez if he didn't look like he was about to have a stroke. "You bet your ass you are! *Your* dog just crapped on my property. *You* have to pick it up!"

"He's right, Gramps," said Marie. "It's the law. You have to do it."

"First of all, he's not my dog," explained Gramps. "Second, I tried to stop him, but it was too late. Don't I get credit for trying?"

The tassel from the angry homeowner's hat swung in front of his face like a pendulum. He swatted it in frustration over Gramps' slanted logic, knocking it off his bald head. "I wouldn't care if he belonged to the Queen of England!" he screamed. "Dog shit is still dog shit, and *you* have to get rid of it!"

Gramps waved his arm in the air. "*A fanabala.*"

"What did he say to me?"

Marie hiked her handbag on her shoulder. "I think he told you to have a nice day."

At this point in the argument, no one was paying attention to Tiny. He, on the other hand, never took his sharp eyes off Gramps, watching as though it was his responsibility to defend the nice human who gave him the tasty treats. And without warning, Tiny clamped onto the other human's leg like, well, like a dog in heat, and the furious man shook his leg violently. The little dog held on tighter until one last shake sent him airborne.

Mac's office faced the street, and he usually pulled the drapes closed to avoid outside distractions while he worked on his computer. But it was Sunday—the neighborhood was quiet —or should have been, and he had opened them wide to let in the sun, providing him with an unimpeded view of his street. Unfortunately, that view included an altercation taking place on his neighbor's front lawn.

"I wonder who Mr. Wilson is fighting with," he mused out loud. "That's funny. I didn't know he had a dog. Oh my God!" he cried suddenly. "Mr. Russo's pink Caddy! That's Angie's sister!" Mac bolted out the door, racing across the street in time to catch Tiny before he hit the sidewalk. "Ugh," he cried in disgust as the dog licked his face. "What the hell do you feed this animal? His breath stinks."

"I'll take him," Marie said, reluctantly, holding the squirming dog in her arms. Tiny growled and she almost dropped him.

Meanwhile, Mac jumped between the arguing men, trying to keep them apart at arm's length. Gramps swung his fist through the air. Mac ducked and pushed him back with a threatening glare. "Marie, what are you doing here with Mr. Wilson? Who is this man, and where did that dog come from?"

"Uh, uh," she stammered.

"You know these people, MacConnell?" asked Mr. Wilson, clearly surprised.

"Yes. This is my future sister-in-law and...."

"And my grandfather," Marie said, finishing the awkward introduction. "This is my Gramps, Nick Russo."

Mac lowered his arms. "It's a pleasure to meet you."

"Likewise I'm sure," replied Gramps.

They shook hands, sizing each other up in the process.

"You're pretty strong for a man your age," Mac told him.

"It's the Viagra."

They all backed up about a foot.

Gramps chuckled. "Only kidding."

Mac turned to Marie. "You still didn't answer my question. What are you doing here? Did Angie send you?"

"What? Who? Angie? No!" she floundered.

"Okay. So why *are* you here?"

"Well, it's like this," piped Gramps. "This here is Tiny. He belongs to Mrs. Esposito and ...uh... uh...he was having trouble doin' his business. We thought a change of scenery would help to, you know, loosen things up a bit. So we took him for a ride."

Marie gave him a *what-are-you-nuts?* look. Gramps just shrugged his shoulders.

"Well, apparently it worked," said Mr. Wilson. "On *my* front lawn."

"Is that what you two were fighting about?" asked Mac.

Mr. Wilson pointed an irate finger at Gramps. "*He* was walking the dog. *He* has to pick it up."

Gramps shook his clenched fist in the air. "Oh, yeah? Who's gonna make me?"

"*I'll* clean it up, okay?" Mac snapped, ending the scuffle. "Marie, please get me a plastic bag from the kitchen while I keep an eye on these two characters out here."

She passed Tiny's leash to Gramps. "Sure thing, Mac."

Marie knew the way to the kitchen where she pawed through cabinets and drawers until finding a suitable plastic bag. Although anxious to get back to Gramps, her legs suddenly felt inexplicably heavy and her pace slowed. She pressed on regardless, but instead of heading out the front door, she hobbled across the living room to Mac's office. Stopping in the doorway, her eyes were drawn to a curious beam of light hovering above his desk. *What the hell is that?*

As Marie entered Mac's office, she heard a low-pitched buzzing in her ears, and images of a fountain pen surfaced in her mind. The unexplained light shone brighter as she inched toward the shimmering beacon, entranced. Step by step, she approached the desk, drawing a sharp breath at what she found —a silver fountain pen that glowed like the aurora borealis. Beside the pen lay an envelope identical to the one Angie received the night before addressed to "*Angelina*" in the same calligraphy handwriting. A cold shiver ran through her. "Oh— my—God."

Call me crazy, but I think that pen wanted me to find this.

Marie touched the pen just to make sure it was real, extinguishing the light, instantly. The buzzing in her head ceased, replaced now by new revelations when she grasped the envelope.

This proves Mac wrote the letter that Dad gave Angie last night—and this one, too. I bet he even wrote them with that fountain pen. Now, all I have to do is convince Angie. If I take the letter and give it to her myself, she'll have to believe me. Though I should probably leave out the buzzing, the light, and the vision part. That'll just ruin my credibility.

"Damn! Why did I promise to mind my own business," she lamented while having an angel-and-devil-on-your-shoulder kind of moment.

"Don't touch it! Remember your promise," said the angel.

"Do it! Do it! Take the letter. You had your fingers crossed anyway," insisted the devil.

Marie went with the devil—she had to. Though instead of just sneaking out with the letter, she decided to tell Mac she took it and *offer* to deliver it to Angie. If he accepts, which is pretty much a sure thing, it won't be like she's butting in because she'll have his permission. She figured it would be a mission of mercy, like rescuing a drowning victim from certain death. And saving a life overrides any promises, especially ones made with your fingers crossed.

That decided, Marie stuffed the envelope in her handbag, ran across the street, and gave Mac the plastic bag. When he was done policing the area, a satisfied Mr. Wilson slapped the fez back on his head, tightened the belt on his robe, and strutted triumphantly home.

Mac's mouth opened and closed when Marie showed him the envelope, and a questionable glint flashed in his amber eyes. "How did...?"

"I didn't mean to snoop," she said quickly, "I thought a lamp was on in your office." *That's my story and I'm sticking to it.* "I went in to turn it off and saw this envelope on your desk. It's just like the one Angie got last night."

"So she did get the letter!" he cried, almost collapsing with relief. "I was afraid your father wouldn't give it to her."

"My dad can be a little tough at times, but he'll do anything for his family."

"Did she read it?" asked Mac, eager to know if the letter worked its magic.

"Yeah, but she doesn't believe you wrote it."

"Yeah—well, that makes two of us," he said, rubbing the back of his neck.

"What?"

Mac waved his hand. "Never mind."

"Sooo, would you mind if I delivered this one for you?" asked Marie.

"Mind? Hell no! I don't care as long as she understands how much I love her."

Marie put the letter back in her bag. "Don't worry, Mac. I'm on it!"

"Great, but before you go, could you get this horny animal off of me?" he asked, glaring at Tiny attached to his leg. "What the hell's the matter with him? Don't they have drugs for this kind of behavior?"

"Sorry about that," she said, tugging on his leash. "I'll put the little pain in the ass in the car."

When she returned minutes later, Mac and Gramps were smiling.

"What just happened here?" she asked suspiciously.

Gramps shrugged. "Nothin'." He winked at Mac.

"Oh—yeah right, nothing," Mac said, shaking Gramps' hand. "Well, thanks again, Nick."

"Ah, don't mention it."

"I won't forget this. I owe you one," Mac told him and turned, his steps a little lighter, as he ambled up the walk to his house.

Marie strolled back to the pink Caddy with Gramps and slid behind the wheel. Tiny hopped on Gramps' lap as soon as he buckled himself in.

"*Minga!* Your breath smells like *baccala*," he said, pushing the odoriferous dog in the back seat.

Marie turned the key in the ignition and revved the engine. "That's what you get for feeding him pepperoni."

"Speaking of food, let's go home already. I don't want to be late for dinner. I've been waiting a long time for that lasagna."

"Yeah, I guess you've earned it."

"I'm just glad I don't know nobody in this neighborhood," said Gramps, slouching down in his seat.

After merging into traffic, Marie glanced over at her grandfather, amazed that they had accomplished their mission...sort of. He had come pretty close to slugging Mr. Wilson, and it was a miracle he wasn't arrested for violating the "curb your dog" law or for attempted assault.

"You know, Gramps, I've got to hand it to you. Everything turned out alright today, though I can't figure out how. But I'm curious about something. Why did Mac thank you and tell you he owed you? You didn't do anything but cause trouble."

"Oh that?" said Gramps, looking out the window. "He thanked me because I invited him over to the house for Sunday dinner."

Screeeeetch!

Marie slammed on the brakes so hard, poor Tiny was thrown against the dash. He probably would have bitten her if his little eyes weren't rolling around in his head.

"You did *WHAT*?" Her hands tightened on the steering wheel rather than around her grandfather's neck.

"I invited Mac over for dinner."

Marie's head fell forward, resting on her white knuckles. "What did you do that for?" she whimpered.

"He's family—almost. Why shouldn't he eat with us?"

"Because I promised I'd stay out of my sister's life, that's why."

Gramps jabbed his finger in her face. "What about that letter? I heard you tell Mac you're going to give it to Angie."

Marie straightened. "That doesn't count. Mac *asked* me to give it to her."

"See? Then my plan worked, just like I said it would," he remarked proudly.

"Well, I wouldn't pat myself on the back so fast if I were you. A lot could happen over a meal at our house.

"Don't worry, I take ca..."

"I know, Gramps," she broke in, "you'll take care of everything."

Marie had serious doubts about the next part of Gramps' plan. The whole thing could blow up in her face. If it did, she'll have a lot of explaining to do. She was annoyed with him for plotting a strategy that put her in such an awkward position. She was even more annoyed with herself that she didn't think of it first.

Chapter Twenty
Trouble with a Capital "B"

Mac closed his front door, feeling guardedly optimistic. Unbeknownst to Marie, Nick had invited him over for dinner; said it was the next phase of his new plan. Whatever scheme the old gent had hatched, Mac hoped for the same result as the one he carried out that morning. However harebrained, his unorthodox method actually worked.

Trusting that the second love letter would have the desired effect, Mac grinned at the prospect of seeing Angie and patching things up with the woman he loved. And with Marie's help, Angie would have already read the second love letter by the time he arrived at her house. Mac had been so sure of their relationship, assuming Angie was as content as he, but he had been—and still was—totally clueless about something of such magnitude that she left him over it. Without her in his life, it was as if a part of his soul was missing, a part he never wanted to live without.

The clock on the fireplace mantel in the living room chimed ten. With several hours to go before dinner at the Russos, Mac wandered into his office to continue researching the Spartan pen. The screensaver on his computer monitor had popped up while he was conducting peace negotiations between Nick and Mr. Wilson, and seeing Angie's beautiful face on the screen stopped him cold. Her joy and love for him were evident in her eyes as he gazed at her laughing face through shimmering strands of windswept auburn hair. His heart twisted in his chest.

They had spent that morning in bed, a soft breeze caressing their skin as they lay, limbs contentedly entangled. Muffling a tortured cry, Mac recalled each nerve-tingling touch, blazing embrace, each tantalizing moment of pleasure. Later that afternoon, they enjoyed a picnic lunch on Asharoken Beach. Mac had been snapping pictures of Angie when a passing jogger offered to take one of them together. They posed with their arms around each other while the waters of Northport Bay lapped the rocky shore.

"One...two...three...smile," prompted the jogger.

Mac turned sideways, pulled Angie close, and kissed her cheek on "three," freezing the moment in time. He could still hear her giggle as she squirmed in his embrace, clearly enjoying the playful surprise.

"We were so happy then," he moaned, dropping into his leather desk chair when suddenly, Angie's image began to fade from view, one pixel at a time, like a foreboding omen. "No!" he cried, rejecting the negative thought, as she completely vanished from the screen. "No! That's not going to happen." Nick has a plan in motion. Marie was delivering the love letter. All he had to do was show up and claim his bride. What could possibly go wrong?

Getting back to his research, Mac clicked on a Spartan fountain pen website he had bookmarked earlier and read:

A pen manufacturing company located in New York City, founded in the early 1900s by Oliver Spartan, an insurance salesman. Although successful at first, the company survived only until 1908 after producing just 100 of the world's finest fountain pens.

Next, Mac looked up the cryptic markings that had piqued his interest the day before. He discovered that all Spartan pens had a unique series of letters and numbers to identify each feature. Following the basic system he found online, he was able to decipher the code: *19 F #100 M.*

19: Sterling silver
F: Filigree overlay
#100: Production number
M: Medium nib size

"Wow! Number 100," he said in awe. "I have the Spartan 100. The last one ever made. I wonder what happened to the other 99?"

This newfound knowledge, although interesting, did nothing to explain his mysterious letter-writing ability. However, even without any tangible evidence, Mac was now willing to accept that the Spartan enabled him to write the love letters. As far-fetched and crazy as that sounded, there was no other explanation. All he had to do was figure out how and why. Was the pen enchanted? Did a ghost or disembodied soul possess it? Or was there some other supernatural force involved?

The city and state inscribed on the pen's barrel prompted Mac to do another search. He Googled "Peabody, Massachusetts," looking for any clues to discover Edwin Alexander Sullivan's identity, but hit a dead end. Accustomed to tedious research for his books, Mac persisted, finding a link to the Peabody Historical Society. Although there was no reference to Sullivan on their web page, he sent an email anyway with a brief description of the pen and asking for whatever data they might have in their archives about an individual with that name who lived in the early 1900s. It was obvious that the man existed, and to own such a plush fountain pen meant Sullivan was no ordinary citizen, probably a businessman, and Mac hoped more information would be available because of that. Then, just to cover his bases, he logged onto a popular genealogy website where he found a thread referencing the Sullivan name and posted a request for any family history.

The mantle clock chimed again, reminding Mac of another task. Before going to Angie's for dinner, he had to have a serious talk with Bianca Lombardi. It was Sunday, but she worked weekends if a wedding was booked. He called the country club and the receptionist assured him she would be there.

The mansion that housed the Sound Harbor Country Club was built at the turn of the century by a former Robber Baron in the style of a French Chateau. With a foundation dug in the side of a craggy cliff, it was one of the few remaining palatial estates that denoted Long Island's north shore as the Gold Coast. The family lost the property in the 1929 stock market crash, and many years later, a group of New York City plastic surgeons saved the decaying manor house from the wrecking ball by going into the catering business. They installed a commercial kitchen, two swimming pools, restored the original tennis courts, and built several guest cottages and a nine-hole golf course on land that once occupied the formal gardens. When Mac cruised through the massive granite and wrought iron gates, he didn't notice the colorful mums that lined the winding gravel drive or the mature maple trees daintily iced with shades of orange and yellow. He remained focused straight ahead as he swung his T-Bird into a parking space at the far end of the lot, locked the car, and marched across the asphalt-covered surface. Carved mahogany doors opened automatically as he climbed the stone stairs at the main entrance.

Mac stepped into the lobby—the former drawing room and front parlor. Two huge marble fireplaces graced either end of the large open area, the only remnants of the original rooms after the walls were removed during the doctors' extensive renovations. Burning logs crackled merrily with welcoming warmth as Mac paused to take in the unimpeded view of Long Island Sound through ceiling-to-floor windows. The dignified space that had received high society was currently hosting half-drunk wedding guests milling about, oblivious to the spectacular view and architecture.

"What a waste," Mac grumbled, elbowing his way through the crowd.

Confrontations are unpleasant with anyone, Mac thought, hurrying down the corridor leading to Bianca's office. But a confrontation with Bianca Lombardi was different—more like approaching a pothole in the road. Your best bet to avoid damage to your car was to simply go around it. Sometimes that wasn't possible, and you were forced to drive over the damned thing. Unfortunately, there was no way to avoid this meeting, not if he wanted Angie back. This was a drive-over time for sure.

Coming to a halt outside of Bianca's office, Mac stared at her name on the door while the muffled sound of music from a wedding in the adjacent ballroom echoed the nervous *thump-*

thump in his chest. After taking several deep breaths in preparation for the inevitable damage, he closed his eyes and knocked.

"Conrad MacConnell!" squealed Bianca, flinging the door open. "What a pleasure to see you. Please, come in."

Said the spider to the fly, thought Mac as he entered, and closed the door behind him.

Bianca's office was decorated in a style that matched her personality: loud, gaudy, and expensive to maintain. Mac pitied the man foolish enough to marry her. There was no denying she was attractive, but unlike Angie, Bianca used her comely attributes like a finely-honed tool. She had a high-pitched, little girl voice that didn't exactly go with her long, shapely legs and intense, dark eyes that revealed nothing as if a curtain had been drawn across that window to her soul. Mac smiled, despite his nerves, picturing Bianca as a cross between Betty Boop and Cruella DeVille. Frightening, but effective.

"I'm sorry to bother you while you're working, Bianca," he began, "but something's come up recently that we really need to talk about before it gets out of hand."

"Of course, Connie," she said with a quick glance to his crotch.

Mac followed the direction of her gaze and groaned. Subtlety was not one of her best qualities. She was about as subtle as a land mine.

Bianca remained silent as she sashayed over to her desk. Standing behind the Louis XVI reproduction, she motioned for Mac to take a seat. He lowered himself tentatively onto an ornately upholstered sofa and crossed his legs. "You see, Bianca," he continued in a business-like tone. "It's come to my attention that you've been saying some things that aren't exactly...accurate."

"Connie, I don't understand what you mean."

Mac cleared his throat. "What I'm trying to tell you," he said pressing on, "is that people are repeating an...um...an *untruth* that they may have heard from you."

Bianca didn't blink.

Mac waited for a reaction.

She just stared. Her face could have been chiseled stone.

"Bianca?"

Silence.

Finally, she took an audible deep breath, and Mac watched apprehensively as her blank stare slowly morphed into a smug grin as she prowled around her desk like a feral cat. Alighting on the edge, Bianca pulled her pencil-thin skirt up and crossed her legs seductively. Mac's jaw dropped when she opened the two top buttons of her blouse, leaned forward—showing way too much cleavage—and said, "Connie, I'm sure I don't know what you're talking about."

What the...? Alarm bells went off in Mac's head. He expected denial, but not this. In an instant, Mac surged angrily to his feet. He couldn't believe Bianca was hitting on him again, and she was letting him have it with both barrels—in a manner of speaking.

"Listen, Bianca," he growled. "I know you've been spreading rumors that Angie and I have broken our engagement, but it's not true! I love Angie, and we're still getting married. So cut the crap and leave us alone!"

Bianca hopped off her desk, sprinting after Mac as he stomped towards the door. "Oh, Connie, what a terrible thing to say." Throwing herself at Mac, she wrapped her arms around him like a starving anaconda, and blubbered with phony sobs that would've made Scarlett O'Hara proud. "How could you think I would do such a thing? Angie and I are friends. I'd never do anything to hurt her. I know everyone hates me, but it's not my fault I'm so misunderstood."

Taken completely off guard, Mac just stood there as the hysterical Bianca clung to him.

Normally, Mac couldn't stand to see a woman cry, but this was no woman; this was Bianca Lombardi, and he peeled her off him like the skin of a rotten banana.

"This act won't work," he said in a menacing tone." I'm not falling for your fake tears. This is the last time I'm going to tell you. Stop spreading lies!"

Mac turned and stormed out without looking back. The office door was ajar, but he was too angry to notice. All he wanted to do was get the hell out of there.

Bianca let him go with an impassive expression that belied her true feelings. Dabbing her eyes with a tissue, she straightened her spine and said, "We'll just see about that."

Chapter Twenty-One
The Tarantella

The Sunday morning aroma of sausage and meatballs roused Angie from sleep. "Hey, Ree, time to get..." her words trailing off when she sat up and saw Marie's empty bed. "Probably out getting doughnuts," she muttered, falling back on the rumpled sheets.

Fully awake now, Angie thought of the vexing love letter her father delivered the night before. It occupied a small area on Marie's nearby dresser—and a large part of her mind. Turning in the bed, she reached for it. But when her fingers grasped the delicate paper, a searing rush of energy surged up her arm, straight to the very core of her soul. She bolted upright, stunned. *What the...?* Unaware that she was engulfed in the love letter's aura of magic, she rubbed her eyes and read the heart-wrenching note again. Although still puzzled by the old-fashioned language, the romantic message fueled her emotions nonetheless.

When did she become so insecure? How did she let her fears overcome her love for Mac? Angie couldn't believe what had happened to her. So what if he's rich and famous, and she's economically challenged. So what if women fawn over him.

That just meant she had to fight twice as hard to keep her man. But Mac said none of that mattered. Time and time again, he insisted the only thing that *did* matter was that they loved and trusted each other. Lately, she'd been having a bit of a problem in the trust department.

Then, there was Bianca. Her big mouth threatened to spoil everything. Angie shivered, pondering the reach of her poisonous gossip. "She has to be stopped!" Stoked now by a newfound sense of purpose, Angie threw back the covers and hopped out of bed. It was time to have a little chat with Bianca Lombardi.

Angie had to project a commanding presence for her meeting with Bianca. So, after a quick shower, she dressed in her favorite red power suit and matching kick-ass pumps. Further empowered with a few extra swipes of mascara, she grabbed her handbag and headed to the kitchen for coffee.

"Morning, Ma," she said, kissing her cheek.

Margaret tapped her wooden spoon on the edge of a simmering pot. "Good morning, dear."

An appetizing aroma billowed from the stove. "Smells delicious, Ma. What time's dinner?"

"The usual. About three o'clock."

"Good. That means I have time to run a few errands before we eat."

"Is that why you're in your work clothes?"

Angie poured a cup of coffee and took a sip. "Yeah," she lied, swallowing hard.

"Well, try not to be late, dear. I'm making *lasagna* for your grandfather. He's really looking forward to it."

"Where are Gramps and Marie, anyway?" Angie asked, leaning against the kitchen counter.

"I don't know. One minute we were talking, and then they were gone. It's like they...disappeared."

Angie's eyes lifted from her cup. "Oh yeah?"

"Yes. It was all very strange," said her mother, lowering the burner on the stove. "All I did was ask your grandfather about bingo and Marie about her date. By the way, did you have fun at bingo last night?

Margaret pivoted slowly. "Angela, I said, did you...?"

Angie was gone.

Margaret covered the pot with a lid. "Humph," she grumbled. "When will I ever learn?"

Once outside, Angie dug in her handbag for her father's car keys. She stopped after realizing the pink Caddy wasn't in the driveway.

"Crap! Marie got to it before me. But how'd she get the keys?" *I bet they fell out of my bag when I dropped it in the hall last night. Gramps probably swiped them after I went to bed. He may be old, but he sure is cagey.* "Now what do I do?"

Even though Angie's car all but died the day before, she had no choice now but to try and start it again. She stamped over to the Mustang parked in front of the house and wrenched the door open. Dropping into the front seat, she buckled her seatbelt and turned the key in the ignition. "Let's see what kind of mood you're in today."

The engine started on the first try but coughed and wheezed like a two-pack-a-day chain smoker. "Nice Mustang," she said, in a soothing voice. *If you run long enough to get me to the country club, you'll get a full tank of that nice hi-test gas. If you get me home again, I'll even throw in an oil change. Deal?"*

The motor squealed, rattled, and whirred as if thinking it over, then idled smoothly. Angie patted the dash affectionately. "I'll take that as a yes."

Traffic was heavier than usual on the Seaford-Oyster Bay Expressway. Speeding drivers whizzed by as Angie merged carefully into the northbound lanes. Cruising down the expressway, she deliberated over what to say to Bianca. Angie decided to catch her off guard at the country club and barge into her office. Besides, she couldn't think of anything else that wouldn't get her arrested for involuntary manslaughter.

Forty-five minutes later, Angie exited the expressway and drove along the pleasant stretch of road that led to the Sound Harbor Country Club. As she approached the stone gates, a gust of wind created a shower of autumn leaves covering the winding drive. The Mustang's tires crunched on the gravel beneath the red and orange carpet as she inched along. A minivan backed out of a space in the unusually full parking lot. Angie angled in. "Must be an Italian wedding," she muttered, getting out of the car.

Angie presented an indomitable figure in her red suit and matching shoes strutting across the lot. Ignoring the valet's whistles, she flipped her fiery red hair back over her shoulder defiantly and it practically sparked, threatening to ignite in the crisp, morning sun. Angie quickened her pace, making people step aside as if she were a powerful CEO as she charged up the stone steps. She almost fell forward when the double mahogany doors opened automatically.

Even the crowded lobby failed to hinder her progress. Oblivious to the music and laughter from a wedding in the main ballroom, Angie pushed through the guests, turning down the corridor that led to Bianca's office. The carpeted floors dampened the sound of her heels as she approached the closed door. Angie grasped the doorknob, ready to burst in and tell Bianca where she could stick her designer stiletto heels, but stopped, frozen in place. Inside, a woman wept hysterically.

When Angie was a teenager, she went to the latest horror movies to get scared out of her wits. Every movie had a suspenseful scene where the main character heard a noise in the basement or another equally creepy place. During those tense scenes, Angie often heard her inner voice shout, *Don't go in the basement!* knowing the killer, or another horrible fate waited in the darkness. She heard that voice now. But who listens to their inner voice? No one in the movies ever did and certainly not Angie. And what she saw after opening the door was worse than Freddy Krueger, Chucky, and Hannibal Lecter combined. It was Mac, *her Mac,* holding Bianca Lombardi so close in his arms she was practically in his back pocket.

Omigod!

Angie wanted to scream but clamped a trembling hand over her mouth.

Omigod! Omigod!

Her stomach lurched and the world spun uncontrollably. Angie clapped her other hand over her mouth, fighting the urge to throw up.

Omigod! Omigod! Omigod!

Her eyes filled with burning tears streaming down her face, blurring her vision. But it was too late. She saw them. In that one fleeting moment, Angie's fears were realized, and her heart was officially broken. *I'll never trust him again!*

Whirling around, Angie fled, her heart banging against her chest, barely able to breathe. She was running for her life, like being chased in a dream, but she was awake and living a nightmare. Somehow, she made it back to the lobby where she plowed into a wedding guest. "I'm so sorry," she apologized in a voice raspy from crying. "I have to get out of here!"

The man grasped Angie's hand, unruffled by the collision, pulling her into the ballroom. "*Ciao, bella. Venire con me, mio caro,*" he said with a smile.

Angie's knowledge of Italian consisted of wise guy slang and a few curse words she picked up as a kid when the adults thought she wasn't listening. She stared back at the man, uncomprehending.

"*Venire, venire*," he repeated.

"Listen, Guido, I don't know what you just said, but I gotta go."

"No, Guido," he said without freeing her. "*Mi chiamo Giuseppe.*"

"Okay, Guido, Giuseppe, whatever," she cried, nearing hysteria. "I have to go now!"

That's when Angie saw Mac stumble into the lobby.

"Holy macaroni!" she muttered under her breath. "He can't know I'm here."

Hoping to blend in with the crowd, she jumped behind Giuseppe. Another wedding guest grabbed her hand, and dragged her onto the dance floor. The band played the *Tarantella,* and the happy dancers twirled her around in a dizzying frenzy to the lively beat of the Italian folk dance. Into the center of the circle and out again, they danced, while she ducked behind anyone or anything to stay out of sight.

"Watch where you're going," said a woman when Angie tripped over her foot.

"Oops! Sorry about that."

"Hey lady, are you sure you're Italian?" asked a young man. "You can't do the *Tarantella* for shit."

"Hey! Watch your language. Does your mother know you talk like that?"

The dance would have gone on forever if it weren't time to give the newlyweds their wedding gifts. A line formed at the dais as the blushing bride stuffed envelopes in a white satin money bag with an expression that could only be described as "cha-ching." Thankfully, that just about cleared the dance floor, and the band gave up on the *Tarantella,* playing the hokey-pokey instead. Following the steps, Angie put her right foot in and out, catching another glimpse of Mac bursting out the door, as she turned herself around.

"Whew," she sighed, somewhat relieved. "That was close."

Still gasping for breath, Angie stumbled to the nearest table. She hung her purse on the back of a chair and flopped down. "Jeez, I've got to get more exercise," she muttered, with her hand at her chest.

That's when Giuseppe returned with a plate heaped with food.

"*Mangiamo,*" he said with an inviting smile.

She had to admit it looked pretty good, but this was no time to eat. So Angie did the worst mime act in history, patting her stomach with one hand and holding her other hand under her chin to indicate that she was full. Unfortunately, Giuseppe misunderstood. Without warning, he jerked Angie up from the chair, grabbed her from behind, and began the Heimlich maneuver.

"No! No! I'm not choking!" she cried, clawing at his arms.

Giuseppe squeezed even tighter.

"Stop that, for Pete's sake!" she shouted, stomping on his foot with one of her pumps. He let go, cursing in Italian. That, she understood. Grabbing her handbag, Angie bolted without looking back, like a caged animal released in the wild.

"*Arrivederci, Signorina,*" called Giuseppe, apparently thinking he had just saved her life.

Wiping the tears from her face with the back of her hand, Angie berated herself as she raced across the parking lot to her car.

How could I have been so stupid! Was this the first time he's cheated on me, or was I so blinded by love, that I didn't notice the others? I almost fell for that sappy, love letter crap, too!

Cramming herself behind the wheel, she fished her keys out of her bag and cranked the engine. The Mustang almost reared up, taking off at full throttle with the pistons pumping as if running the final stretch of the Kentucky Derby. An invigorating rush radiated through her body as she sped home on the expressway. She was beginning to feel like the old Angie again.

Get a grip! You can't give up. That's just what they want you to do. If I'm going down, I'll go down fighting, even if it means losing Mac, which pretty much seems to be the case anyway. One thing for sure, I can't let Bianca or Mac know I saw them together until I get even. They'll never know what hit them.

Chapter Twenty-Two
The Second Love Letter

Angie reined in the Mustang, screeching to a stop in front of her house. The pink Caddy was in the driveway—Gramps and Marie were home. She tumbled out of the car and rushed towards the front door hoping no one would see her arrive. Thankfully, it was open; and she scurried down the hall, locked herself in the bathroom, and splashed cold water on her tear-stained face and puffy eyes.

Marie had been staking out the street from her bedroom window ever since she and Gramps returned from Mac's. She peeked between the slats of the blinds when she heard Angie's car and hurried to the front door just as Angie ran in. Marie followed her down the hall to the only bathroom in the house just as the door slammed shut.

"Hey, Ang. Open up!"

"I'll be out in a minute," Angie told her, turning up the faucet.

Marie let out an exasperated breath. "I don't have to *go*. I just want to talk to you."

"Jeez Louise, can't it wait, Ree?"

"No." She twisted the doorknob. "Let me in."

The lock clicked open. Marie burst in, and leaned against the closed door.

Angie turned off the faucet and rested her hands on either side of the vanity. Hanging her head above the harvest gold sink, she waited for Marie to speak while water dripped from her face.

"Well, now that you're here, what is it?" she asked, pulling an olive-green towel off the rack.

Marie took one look at Angie's red eyes and gasped. "What the hell happened to you?"

"Nothing," she said, drying her face. "Now what was so important that I couldn't use the bathroom in peace?"

With Mac's letter in her hand, Marie said, "I wanted to give you this, so you'd have time to read it before dinner."

Angie winced, but managed to fight the tears that threatened to flow again when she beheld another envelope bearing her name. *There's that weird buzzing sound again.*

"What's the matter?" asked Marie, confused by her reaction. "It's another love letter from Mac. Here, take it."

Angie threw the towel on the vanity. "No!"

"But, Ang, I'm sure he wrote this one," insisted Marie, unaware of what had taken place at the country club. "Mac handed it to me himself—Oops!" One hand flew to her mouth. The other grasped the doorknob. "Gotta go."

Angie reached over her head, holding the door closed. "What do you mean he handed it to you himself? You went to see Mac? I thought I asked you to stay out of this."

"I did. It was all a big coincidence."

"A coincidence? I don't believe that for a minute."

"It was, I swear!"

Angie folded her arms across her chest. "Okay, I'm listening."

Leaning against the door in the small bathroom, Marie

began. "It all started when Gramps volunteered to walk Tiny for Mrs. Esposito. I couldn't let him go alone, so I tagged along."

"But Ree, you can't stand that dog."

"Trust me, the feeling is mutual. But the pepperoni Gramps fed him did wonders for the little fiend's behavior. Besides, I had my pepper spray if he turned on me."

"That must have been some walk."

"Oh, yeah, it was."

"But how did Gramps get peppero...? Never mind," Angie said, shaking her head. "Go on."

"Okay. Now Tiny was having bowel problems, and Gramps thought a change of scenery might help loosen things up, so we all took a ride in Dad's car."

Angie backed up and narrowed her eyes. "How did you get the keys to Dad's car?"

Marie exhaled. "Gramps found them in the hall."

"I *knew* it!"

"Then, *somehow*," continued Marie, sounding clueless as to how the next event actually occurred, "we ended up in Mac's neighborhood."

"Somehow?" exclaimed Angie. "That's the most ridiculous thing I ever heard."

"No, it's true. Though the guy with the funny hat that lives across the street from Mac wasn't exactly thrilled when Tiny crapped on his lawn."

Angie knew Mac's anal-retentive neighbor. "You mean Mr. Wilson?"

"Yeah, that's the one."

Angie lowered the cover on the commode. "I bet that went over big," she said, taking a seat.

"It did, depending on how you look at it," said Marie as she hopped up on the vanity. "Now, after Tiny relieved himself, Mr. Wilson expected Gramps to pick up the dog poop. Gramps wouldn't do it and said something to him in Italian. Well, the guy was in no mood to back down, and Gramps came pretty close to slugging him. That's when the pesky beast started humping Mr. Wilson's leg."

Angie laughed despite herself as she imagined the preposterous scene. "I know I'm going to hate myself for asking, but what happened next?"

"Now this is the coincidence part," answered Marie, getting caught up in her own narrative. "Tiny is a small dog and doesn't weigh more than the fur he's covered with. So when Mr. Wilson shook him off his leg, the little bugger almost went into orbit. Mac showed up just in time to catch him before he did a crash landing on the sidewalk."

Angie looked sideways at her sister. "Cut it out, Ree. Do you actually expect me to fall for that story?"

"I swear, that's exactly what happ—" Frantic knocking on the door cut Marie short.

"*Mannaggia.*" The doorknob jiggled. "Hurry up in there. I gotta go."

"Gramps, is that you?" asked Angie.

"Yeah, Angelina. It's me."

"Can you come back later, Gramps?" asked Marie.

The jiggling stopped. "Marie? What are you doing in there with Angelina?"

"Girl talk. What do you want?"

"What do I want?" he asked incredulously. "I gotta see a man about a horse. What do you think I want?"

"Okay," said Angie. "We'll be out in a minute."

"A minute's too long," he cried. "I'm old with a prostate the size of your grandmother's meatballs. It's either now or I pee in the hall and blame it on the dog."

The door opened. Gramps pushed the girls aside and hustled in. Thirty seconds later, he emerged.

"That was fast," said Marie.

Gramps just shrugged his shoulders. "Sometimes there's a will but not always a way." Sighing dejectedly, he shuffled into the living room.

Angie and Marie scrambled back into the bathroom. Angie checked her appearance in the vanity mirror. "How do I look?"

"A lot better than when you came in," Marie told her. "So are you going to tell me why you won't take this letter?" she demanded, waving the envelope in the air.

"No."

"No? That's it?"

"What part didn't you understand? The 'N' or the 'O'?" Angie asked over her shoulder as she breezed past her befuddled sister.

"But...but..." Marie checked her watch. It was two-thirty.

Angie stowed her handbag in Marie's room, kicked off her pumps, and changed into jeans, a pullover sweater, and ballet flats. She joined the family in the living room where her mother was arguing with Gramps. Nothing unusual about that except Tiny was the subject of the quarrel.

"I don't care!" Margaret cried. "That animal is *not* staying in this house a minute longer."

Gramps held Tiny at eye level. "Look at that face. How could you not love him?"

Tiny must have sensed he was on thin ice with the humans because he wagged his tail like a good dog. Margaret just wrinkled up her nose.

"Why can't you take him back to Bernice now?" she wanted to know.

"Because she's napping and won't answer the door," Gramps told her. "Probably doesn't have her hearing aids in."

Margaret pressed her lips together and exhaled slowly. "Okay. I give up. Just make sure he behaves because the minute that dog lifts his leg on my furniture, you're both out the door!"

"Don't worry about Tiny, Ma," assured Angie. "I'll keep an eye on him."

"Humph," she snorted, retreating into the kitchen.

"Thanks, Angelina," said Gramps. "I gotta stay on your mother's good side. I been waiting a long time for that lasagna."

"No problem, but it would help if you kept him on the leash anyway."

"Sure, sure."

With that crisis averted, Angie went to the dining room to help Marie set the table.

"I don't get it, Ang," whispered Marie as they folded napkins. "Why so glum? You should be happy. Mac wrote you another love letter. I bet it's even more romantic than the first."

Without warning, Angie burst into tears.

"What the hell?" Marie gripped Angie's arm, dragging her past their bewildered mother in the kitchen. Pushing the back door open, she didn't slow down until they were alone in the yard. "Jeez, Ang. *Now,* what are you crying about? Didn't you see Bianca and straighten her man-stealing ass out?"

"Ye...e...es," Angie stuttered between sniffles and gulps for air.

"Then what's the matter?"

"I was right," she sobbed. "I saw them with my own eyes."

"Who, honey? Who did you see?"

"Mac and Bianca Lombardi! He was holding her in his arms!" she wailed, collapsing on a weather-beaten picnic table bench, unable to go on.

Marie rushed to her side and patted her back. "I knew something was wrong when you came home looking like shit. Leave it to Bianca to screw things up." She gave Angie one of the napkins they had been folding. "Here, take this and tell me what happened."

Angie dried her eyes and blew her nose. "I went to the country club this morning to stand up for myself and tell Bianca off just like you said," she began. "And when I opened the door to her office, I saw them."

"Maybe it was someone else."

"Oh, it was Mac all right, Angie said, smoothing back her hair from her forehead. "I'm sure about Bianca, too. I'd recognize that oversexed hussy anywhere. They didn't hear me open the door to her office because Bianca was crying."

"Did they see you?"

"No. But I saw all *I* needed to see and took off."

Marie's expression turned grave when she checked her watch again. "Ang, remember yesterday when you said you owed me for returning the ring?"

Angie turned to face Marie. "Yeah," she said cautiously.

"Well, this is it. I'm calling in my marker."

"What the heck are you talking about?"

Marie whipped the letter out of her pocket. "It's time to return the favor. So, do me a favor already and read this."

"Do I have to?"

Marie slapped it into her hand. "You bet your ass you do."

Angie shuddered the instant the envelope touched her skin, and an infusion of heat flooded her body. She wondered if Marie noticed as the unnerving warmth traveled to the very center of her soul. When she extracted the letter from the envelope, it seemed to hum like a tuning fork, drowning out the sound of her heart pounding in her ears as she read the timeless message of love.

To Angelina, My Love,

It is beyond my comprehension how I continue to breathe, to function, to exist since I last held you close in my arms. If I were to draw you a picture of my heart, you would see that there is nary a space left in it for life-giving blood, being full already with my all-consuming love for you.

Imagine my love as the mighty redwood, strong and eternal with deep roots intertwined, joined with the trees of the surrounding forest. So vast are my feelings for you that if you were to wander through the woods and touch any tree, branch, or leaf, you would be able to feel my devotion there as sure as if you were here with me in my loving embrace.

I beg of you to return to my side, the way we were meant to be.

Your own,

Conrad

When she finished reading, an almost imperceptible breath of air brushed across her lips—a tender kiss.

Angie stared at the words without blinking, while tears welled in her eyes. One by one, the tiny droplets fell, forming miniature pools on the paper as she struggled to absorb the meaning of the amorous prose.

"Ang? Are you all right?" asked Marie.

She managed a slight nod.

"Then please say something—do something!" she begged, shaking Angie by the shoulders. "Talk to me."

Angie just passed the letter to her. "Read this," she said softly.

"Oh my God!" cried Marie, practically swooning. "I never

read anything so freakin' beautiful before in my life. Mac is really getting good at this love letter thing."

Angie had recovered enough to say, "He *is* a writer, you know."

"Yeah, but Mac writes murder mysteries, not romance novels," argued Marie. "This is totally out of his comfort zone."

"What does that prove?"

"It proves how much he loves you. C'mon, Ang. Wake up and smell the roses already."

"You mean the coffee."

"Whatever," said Marie. "My point is that Mac writes about murder, blood, and gore. If he can write something so completely opposite from the usual violence and mayhem—and do a pretty good job of it, too, I might add—it proves that he *really* loves you. Don't you get it? No one can fake this kind of writing."

"If Mac loves me so much, why was he with Bianca?"

"I don't have a clue, Ang. That's why you have to talk to him."

Angie let out a dejected sigh as her head dropped down on the picnic table.

"So what are you going to do?" prodded Marie.

Angie lifted her head wearily. "Nothing for now. I'm too confused."

"But Ang, this letter is proof that Mac loves you. Marry him, for cripes sake!"

"Listen, Ree, my heart's been squeezed through an emotional wringer today. I'm in no mood to make any spur-of-the-moment life-changing decisions. All I want to be concerned with right now is something simple—like how to keep Tiny from peeing on the furniture. Let's just go inside and eat. I always feel better after Ma's *lasagna* anyway."

Chapter Twenty-Three
Guess Who's Coming to Dinner

Mac drove up his driveway, staring into space as the garage door rose noisily on its tracks. He steered the T-Bird inside, shifted to "park" and turned off the engine.

The meeting with Bianca Lombardi was an abysmal failure. Mac left her office feeling sullied, craving a shower. No ordinary trickle of water would do either, hell, no. He imagined needing the high-powered blast you get after radiation exposure to remove the repugnant feeling of Bianca's desperate embrace. *I'd rather walk naked through Times Square on New Year's Eve than ever go through that again,* he thought as he climbed out of the car. What's more, two days had passed since Angie left him, and he still didn't have a clue—not even an inkling—as to why she broke off their engagement.

Once out of the garage, Mac keyed in the code, closing the door. Plodding up the walk, his mind became a jumble of potential explanations. Could it be that he was so caught up in his work that he forgot the little things that made a woman feel treasured and secure? It was even more difficult for him to admit that he might have taken Angie for granted—definitely, a major screw-up, he thought as he unlocked the front door and wandered into his office.

Mac tossed his keys on the desk and sank into his chair, blowing out a despondent sigh. He sat for a minute, brooding, before swiveling around and powering up the computer to check for messages. It was a long shot, but maybe Angie answered one of his emails. He found a short note from the Peabody Historical Society instead.

Dear Mr. MacConnell,

In response to your email, Alexander Sullivan was a prominent businessman at one time in Peabody during the early 1900s. Initially, he manufactured automobiles, then trucks and ambulances. The business was sold soon after the end of World War I.

Unfortunately, without more information, there is no way to be sure if he is the Edwin Alexander Sullivan from your pen since Sullivan was a common surname at that time. Thank you for your inquiry.

The Peabody Historical Society

Distracted for a moment from his troubled love life, Mac was somewhat heartened by that scrap of information. It confirmed his suspicion that Sullivan was, indeed, a businessman. Also, the time period from the email matched the copyright dates inscribed on the pen. Mac removed the Spartan from its case on his desk, wondering what life was like for Alexander Sullivan. With the puzzling writing instrument cradled in his hand, Mac closed his eyes, attempting to visualize the man who lived over a century ago.

Images of money crept into his mind first. That made sense. Countless contracts and business correspondences were probably composed and signed with the antique pen.

Thoughts of family followed, seeping into his subconscious, accompanied by feelings of great joy and even greater sorrow. It was almost too much to bear, and Mac dropped the pen, not quite sure what had occurred. Was there more to this mystery than just the letters? Was something or someone trying to communicate with him through the pen...like a medium?

The longer Mac thought about it, the more he believed it wasn't just about the letters or even the antique pen. The spirit of Edwin Alexander Sullivan was trying to tell him something. The joy Mac felt when holding the Spartan a few moments ago was how he felt when Angie accepted his marriage proposal. The sorrow, much like what he was experiencing without her. Maybe he and Mr. Sullivan have something in common.

Encouraged by the revelation, Mac clicked on the genealogy website he had registered with and let out a loud, "Woo hoo!" when he read the reply to his inquiry.

The Peabody Historical Society was right about Sullivan being a common name. His email request was answered with pages and pages of Sullivan family ancestors. It took a while to weed out the unrelated ones by date, gender, and location. And when Mac finally finished, Eddie Sullivan, Edwin Alexander Sullivan, Winifred Sullivan, and Bridget Sullivan from Gloucester, and Peabody, Massachusetts, remained.

Wanting to burrow deeper into the past lives of the Sullivan clan, Mac decided to hire a genealogist to compile an accurate family tree. He found one online that specialized in Irish immigration and ancestry. His cell phone buzzed just as he completed the application.

"Hey, man," said Rick when he picked up the phone.

"Hey yourself. What's up?"

"You're not gonna believe this," Rick bubbled excitedly. "Marie called and asked me out."

Mac rested his head against the back of his leather desk chair. "That's a good thing, isn't it?"

"Yeah, man, it's awesome! She invited me to her house for dinner today.

"Well, that makes two of us," said Mac.

"Cool! That means you and Angie are a couple again."

Mac rubbed his temple. "Not really," he said with a sigh. "Her grandfather extended the invitation, not Angie."

"Bummer, dude. What do you think is going on?"

"Nothing. Angie and her family have dinner every Sunday."

The meal was a weekly tradition and God help you—because no one else would—if you didn't show up. It was easier to get absolution from a priest than be excused from Sunday dinner. You'd have to be on the dark side of the moon with a note from NASA to justify your absence. In other words, attendance was mandatory.

"So how about it, dude?" asked Rick. "You want to ride over together? I'll drive." "

"Sure, but don't be late. I know from experience, that's the only thing worse than not going at all."

At exactly 2:59, Rick parked his truck in front of the Russo residence. The neighborhood kids crowded around it, begging him to honk the horn, and Marie peered through the living room drapes when she heard the *Star Wars* movie theme.

Up until this point, Marie was always the passive one, sort of letting life happen to her rather than taking charge of her own destiny. Now, as she watched Mac and Rick stroll leisurely up the front walk, she knew all that was about to change.

Her father and grandfather were on the sofa engrossed in a

football game. Her mother was in the kitchen putting the finishing touches on dinner. Angie helped her while keeping a watchful eye on Tiny. The stage was set for a family drama starring unsuspecting actors without a script.

"You're on," said Marie, waiting for her cue.

Chapter Twenty-Four
Mangiamo! Let's Eat

At exactly three o'clock, Mac stood on the Russo's front steps. Rick trailed behind him after locking his truck, arriving just as Mac rang the doorbell.

"I'll get it!" Marie shouted above the noisy TV. She took a deep breath and swung the door open.

"*Ciao*, dudette," said Rick, breezing in.

"Shhh," hissed Marie, her finger over pursed lips.

Mac sidled in beside Rick. "What's the matter?"

"Nothing yet," she told him. "Just keep your mouths shut during dinner. Let me do the talking, okay?"

"No problemo," said Rick, inhaling deeply. "Man, that smells good."

"Oh, it's going to be good all right," said Marie. "But I'm not talking about the food."

"What's that supposed to mean?" asked Mac.

Marie leaned closer to him. "Angie doesn't know you were invited."

"I know that," he told her with a dismissive wave. "Once she gets over the shock of seeing me, everything will be fine."

"I wouldn't count on that if I were you," she warned.

Mac placed his hands on her shoulders. "Why? You gave her the letter, right?"

"Calm down, Romeo. I gave it to her."

"Then, what's the problem?" he asked, dropping his arms to his sides. "Angie read it...didn't she?"

"Yeah, but something happened today and there's no time to explain," said Marie after glancing over her shoulder. "So fasten your seatbelts. It's going to be a bumpy night."

"Bette Davis, *All About Eve*, 1950," Rick cried like a game show contestant.

Marie rolled her eyes. "Can't you be serious for once?" she asked.

"You started it," answered Rick.

"Oh yeah? I can finish it, too," she fired back.

"Will you two knock it off?" said Mac. "Jeez, you act like you're married."

That brought their argument to an abrupt halt. Screeching chalk on a blackboard couldn't have done it any faster. Marie looked worried. Rick just smiled.

"Marieeee," called her mother from the kitchen. "Who's at the door?"

"Now what?" asked Mac. "Your mother knows we're here."

"Okay, here's the plan," said Marie urgently. "We all act like it's just another Sunday dinner. Don't say a word about the broken engagement. Act like it never happened."

"That's your plan?" asked Rick.

"Yeah. If you got a better one, feel free to jump in anytime."

"Here we go again," said Mac, exasperated. "Listen, Rick. I think Marie is trying to say that Angie still hasn't told her parents yet."

"Give that man a cigar," said Marie. "That's why it's such a good plan. You see, even though Angie might be a little shocked to see Mac, the last thing she wants right now is to have my parents find out she called off the wedding, especially with an audience. Angie may be uncomfortable, but I bet she'll do just about anything to keep her secret. She won't make a scene. After dinner, you two can kiss and make up. Just follow my lead. Hopefully, we'll get through this meal without anything more than a little *agida*."

"*Agida?* What's that?" asked Rick.

Mac smiled. "You'll find out if you hang around this family long enough."

In the kitchen, Angie was cutting mozzarella into cubes and shredding Parmesan cheese for the lasagna. She popped a piece in her mouth—a reward for the scraped knuckles she suffered from the sharp teeth of the grater. It was her own fault for not paying attention as she worked, wondering why her mother's catty friends hadn't blabbed about the bingo riot on Friday night. It didn't make sense. Those women lived for that kind of juicy gossip. Too bad it wasn't going to be as easy to conceal her broken engagement.

Maybe she'll tell her parents tomorrow, or the next day, or the next. Actually, it didn't matter when she told them. The repercussions will be worse than reliving puberty. Even that would be nothing compared to having witnessed Mac and Bianca nearly playing hide the pickle at the country club. Angie tried to block that horrible scene from her mind, but it was no use. She sniffled as hot tears pooled in her eyes. Tiny whimpered under the table as if sensing her distress.

"What's the matter, Angela?" asked her mother at the kitchen sink.

"Nothing, Ma. It's the onions," she said, wiping her eyes

with the back of her hand. "You know how they always make me cry."

Margaret dried her hands on a dishtowel. "But you chopped them twenty minutes a—" The doorbell rang, cutting her off. "Marieeee, who's at the door?"

Angie scurried to the bathroom for a tissue while her mother waited for an answer. Tiny followed, dragging his leash. He cocked his head sideways as if wondering what she was doing when she blew her nose. "It's okay, boy," Angie said, patting his head. "We humans do funny things sometimes. Now let's go see who came to visit." Tiny trotted behind Angie as she wandered into the living room. She skidded to a stop when Mac and Rick walked in.

Angie wasn't ready to see Mac. Not yet. Not now. And certainly *not* like this. Her heart beat wildly, banging in her chest. Sexual electricity crackled in the air. Angie inhaled sharply, gasping for breath, the strain to conceal her emotions unbearable as Mac swaggered toward her. The blood seemed to rush from her body, and the image of Gramps pouring a pair of cement shoes flickered in her mind when she couldn't move her feet. Closer, closer, he moved as invisible sparks arced between their bodies.

"Is this awkward or what?" Marie whispered to Rick.

"Negatory, dudette. It's beyond awkward. This is like in *Star Wars* when Luke Skywalker finds out his father is Darth Vader."

"No way," said Marie. "It's more like *Gone With The Wind* when India Wilkes finds Scarlett and Ashley together in the mill."

They were both right. To say this was just an awkward moment was like saying Niagara Falls is just a slow leak.

Angie wanted to run, but that would only arouse suspicion. So, she summoned the strength to act casual, which was nearly impossible being so physically close to Mac as her body reacted instantly to his warmth, the scent of his cologne, and his velvety smooth, fawn-colored eyes. In the thirty seconds they stood facing each other, he managed to reach into her heart, and Angie almost surrendered to him on the spot before using the image of Mac with Bianca as virtual smelling salts. Then, like a subject snapped awake by a hypnotist, she regained control. Glancing around the room, she didn't realize everyone was watching, confused by her actions, or lack thereof.

"Angelina, don't be shy. Go ahead, give your boyfriend a kiss," urged Gramps. "I remember when I was a young man. Your grandma, she couldn't keep her hands offa me. Ah, those were the days. The nights weren't bad either."

"Hey, Pop! That's my mother you're talking about," protested Sal.

"C'mon, you're a big boy now. Where do you think you came from anyway, the milkman?" Gramps burst into laughter at his own corny joke. His mirth was quickly replaced by a faraway look in his eyes, sitting soberly in the recliner, alone with his memories.

Gramps was right. Why didn't she look happy to see Mac or greet him with a kiss? And with her parents waiting expectantly, she had to do something. As far as they knew, Mac was still her fiancé. So Angie pasted a smile on her face, leaned toward him, and said in a strained whisper, "Make it snappy, then say you have to leave."

But instead of the quick peck she expected, Mac kissed her cheek slowly, his mouth and tongue lingering over the softness of her skin. Angie tried to back away, but Mac grasped her shoulders, pulling her close as he nuzzled her neck and thick russet hair. "I love you, Angie," he breathed softly in her ear while nibbling on its delicate lobe. "Just like I told you in the letters I wrote. Please, come back to me."

Holy moly macaroni!

Angie's knees felt weak, and she tingled all over because her libido skyrocketed to tear-each-other's-clothes-off-and-jump-into-bed-level. But even more shocking was the confirmation from Mac that he really did write the love letters.

Mac must have felt her body tremble under his touch because he loosened his grip and guided her to a plastic-covered armchair. Then, like every Sunday, he made himself comfortable on the sofa to watch the football game with her father. Rick joined them looking as uncomfortable as Captain Kirk surrounded by an army of Klingons, leaving Marie standing alone. Angie almost broke her neck motioning with her head for Marie to follow her outside.

Uh—uh—I gotta go," said Angie, rising from the chair.

"Where're you off to, Angie?" asked her father. "Mac just got here."

"Marie and I just remembered we have to water the garden," she sputtered as they dashed out of the living room, through the kitchen past their mother, and out the back door...again.

"I didn't know you had a garden, Mr. Russo," said Mac.

"We don't," he said without taking his eyes off the game, "but with three women in the house, you never know what to expect."

Seconds later, the kitchen door flew open, and Margaret strode into the living room. "Sal, since when do we have a garden?"

"Ree, how could you do this to me?" demanded Angie when they were in the backyard.

Marie held up her hands. "I didn't do anything. Gramps invited him."

"I should've known he couldn't keep a secret," she said ruefully.

"Actually, Gramps did keep his mouth shut. All he did was invite Mac over for dinner."

Angie spread her arms apart, palms up. "Then why didn't you stop him?"

"Hey, he almost went a few rounds with Mr. Wilson. Inviting Mac for dinner was nothing. You should be thankful that was *all* he did today."

Angie's arms flopped to her sides. "Well, this is just *great*," she said, her voice tinged with sarcasm. "I can't go back in there now."

"Sure, you can, sis. Just think of those incredible love letters. If a man wrote that romantic shit to me, I'd forgive him anything short of a sex-change operation."

"But Ree, I saw them with my own eyes. That image is seared in my brain. I can't forget it so easily."

"There has to be more to it," insisted Marie. "Why don't you give the guy a chance to explain? You owe him that much. If you don't like what you hear, *then* you haul his sorry ass out with the recyclables."

Angie plopped down wearily on the picnic table to ponder the current situation. The more she thought about Mac and Bianca, the more she had to admit Marie was probably right. Mac disliked Bianca almost as much as she did. Angie also knew Bianca was capable of anything short of murder. Although after what Gramps told her about the Lombardi family history, she had serious doubts about that. So she decided to contain her emotions long enough to give Mac the opportunity to explain after dinner. All she had to do now was save Tiny from a one-way trip to the dog pound. Her head jerked up at the thought.

"Tiny! Where's Tiny?"

"Don't look at me," said Marie. "You were the one who volunteered to dog-sit."

Angie did a quick scan of the yard. "Omigod! I forgot all about Tiny when I saw Mac. I have to find him! Mrs. Esposito will never forgive me if something happened to that dog."

"You mean like Ma beating the crap out of him with her wooden spoon for peeing on her rug?"

"Yeah, that would be kind of ugly."

"No uglier than that mole on her head."

Both girls shuddered.

"Well, I'm staying out here," announced Marie. "I can't handle the stress in there. All that sexual frustration is raising my blood pressure."

"Fine," said Angie. "But if anything happens to Tiny, *you* can break the news to Mrs. Esposito."

"Sure," said Marie with a shrug. "That onerous hound never liked me anyway."

Angie dashed into the house, heading straight to the living room. "Have you seen Tiny?" she asked her father.

"Yeah, the mutt wandered in here a few minutes ago, dragging his leash, so your grandfather took him out for a walk. I think he got him out just in time."

"Affirmative, dude." Rick raised his arm to bump fists with Angie's father.

Sal shot him an annoyed glance instead.

Rick shrugged and lowered his arm. "Totally on time," he said to Angie. "The little canine dude humped my leg a few times, then did some kind of funky rain dance. That's when Nick said he needed a little fresh air and took the pooch with him for company."

Angie heard Rick and her father speak—saw their lips move. But her brain and heart had turned to mush in Mac's presence, and she didn't understand a word they said. Mac remained silent—his eyes fixed on Angie as her father's gaze darted between them. Angie did a mental gulp when Sal furrowed his brow and rubbed his chin. *There's that look again.*

"You know, these two look like they could use a little privacy," Sal said, lifting Rick up from the sofa by his arm. "C'mon, I want to show you my new lawn mower."

Rick gave Mac a *"Help me"* look as Sal spirited him away.

Alone now for the first time in days, Mac and Angie just stared at each other. She stood facing him with her arms folded across her chest. "So?" she said, breaking the chilling silence first.

"So? Is that all you have to say to me?"

"What did you expect?" she retorted.

Mac leaned forward, resting his elbows on his knees. "I sort of thought you might tell me why you broke our engagement for starters."

"It doesn't matter anymore," replied Angie, slouching down in an armchair.

Mac rushed to her side, closing his fingers around her trembling hands. "Of course, it matters. *We* matter. Our future together matters," he said tenderly.

"The only thing that matters is that I was right," she exclaimed, jerking free. "And if you were any kind of a gentleman, you'd leave...now!" *So much for letting him explain.*

"The hell I am!" he exploded. "I'm not leaving this house until you tell me what you're talking about. This is my life, too, you know. If I'm being dumped, I deserve to know why!"

Whoa, this wasn't supposed to happen, thought Angie. But two days of pent-up emotions bubbled and hissed like a thermal geyser, and she leapt from her chair, hurling the accusation at him like a knife.

"You want to know why?" she cried. "I broke up with you because I always knew you'd cheat on me!"

Mac jumped back as if struck. "But I never cheated on you, Angie," he said, shaking his head. "I love you."

"I know you love me, but that has nothing to do with it," she snarled, crossing to the other side of the living room. "I've seen how women look at you. I knew it would only be a matter of time before your head was turned!"

"But, honey, baby," he continued following her. "I don't understand. If you know how much I love you, how could you think I'd ever do such a thing? You still love me, don't you?" he asked timidly.

Angie stopped short and spun around. "Of course, I do. I love you so much that I couldn't bear the thought of that ever happening. So I called the whole thing off—nipped it in the bud before my heart was broken."

"Oh my God, Ang. How could I have been so stupid? I'll make it up to you, I promise." But when Mac opened his arms to embrace her, he got the shock of his life.

"Is *that* what you did to Bianca at the country club this morning?" Angie screamed, on the verge of hysteria.

Mac flinched. His stunned expression spoke volumes.

"Yes, I saw you two together. I always had my fears, but I never dreamed it would happen so soon, and with that bimbo— how insulting. Tell me! Tell me how many other women have there been?" she demanded, covering her face with her hands, sobbing uncontrollably.

"I closed that door. How...? You must have arrived later and opened it just when Bianca threw herself at me. Oh, Ang, this is all a huge misunderstanding."

Mac started to explain, or at least give it his best shot, when

Margaret called out, "Dinner's ready. Everyone come to the table!"

The front door burst open. Gramps rushed in with Tiny. "It's about time. I didn't know how much longer I could stay out there before I froze to death."

Angie threw him a disapproving glare through her long, tear-spiked lashes.

"I mean, I was so hungry I didn't know how much longer I could *wait*," said Gramps, without missing a beat. "C'mon, *mangiamo*."

Marie set two more places while Rick and her father trooped in from the garage. Sal sat at the head of the table. Margaret's place was at the opposite end. Everyone else looked for a seat, but that simple act quickly turned into a wacky game of musical chairs.

Angie was determined to stay away from Mac. So, when he dropped down beside her, she sprang from her chair and scurried around the table. Rick looked puzzled when she shoved him aside, sliding into the empty seat between Gramps and Marie before he had the chance to sit. Unperturbed, Rick shuffled over to the vacated seat, but not before Marie motioned for Mac to trade places with her, next to Angie. When he did, Angie frowned and ran to her original seat, ousting Rick again. Mac had no choice but to sit beside Rick who was having trouble keeping up with the seating arrangements.

"Dude, is it like this every Sunday?" he wanted to know.

Marie gestured to him, jerking her hand across her throat. He got the message and clammed up. Tiny, on the other hand, was wired. His shaggy behind bobbed up and down like the humans in their chairs.

Sal observed the bizarre behavior, allowing it to go on for several minutes before banging his fist on the table. "That's it! I don't know what the hell is going on and frankly, I don't give a damn! I just want this nonsense to stop so I can have my dinner in peace. Now everybody *sit* down and *stay* down!"

When Sal spoke, everyone listened. Even the dog sat. Only Gramps seemed unaffected.

"Do you know how long it's been since I had home-cooked *lasagna*?" he asked rhetorically. "I can see it now. Thick sauce, meatballs, sausage." Gramps closed his eyes, drifting into what could only be described as a *lasagna* trance while the tension in the room thickened like the tomato sauce he envisioned. Even Marie was down to her last nerve, and Gramps was getting on it.

"For God's sake, Gramps. It's only food," she said sharply.

"Leave him alone," said Angie in his defense. "Gramps can dream about *lasagna* if he wants to!"

"That's not the only thing getting on someone's nerves in here, sweet pea," Mac snickered to Angie.

"Oh yeah?" she bristled, jumping up from her chair.

"Will you two cut it out!" bellowed Sal over their voices. "You're fighting like children."

Mac tilted his head toward Rick. "This is what I meant before by *agida*."

"*Agida*? You got *agida*?" Angie shrieked. "Well, if that's how you feel, why don't you just get out?" she commanded, pointing towards the door.

Obviously confused by her rude behavior, her father asked, "Angela, what the hell's the matter with you? That's the man you're going to marry!"

Hopelessly out of control now, Angie blew up like an ill-fated grade school science experiment. "Marry him?" she cried recklessly. "I'll never marry him! Not after what I saw today! The wedding is off!"

At that moment, the kitchen door swung open. Margaret entered, smiling proudly, with a bubbling tray of *lasagna*.

"What the hell are you talking about?" demanded Sal.

"The wedding is off!" Angie shouted again." If Mac were the last man on earth, I'd rather marry a monkey! At least the monkey won't cheat on me!"

Margaret's eyes widened and her face paled. "Jesus, Mary, and Joseph!" she gasped, then fainted, going down with a sickening thud. For a split second, the *lasagna* hovered in thin air then plummeted to the floor.

Gooey strings of melted cheese and bits of sausage and noodles splattered the table and dining room floor. Rivulets of sauce dripped down the walls like desperate fingers clinging for dear life. In true canine form, Tiny took advantage, helping himself to the human's dinner. Angie pushed him aside and began cleaning up the mess. Sal flew to Margaret's side, and Marie got the brandy. No one spoke—all shocked silent. Only the pitiful sound of sobbing reverberated like a single person clapping.

"Ang, are you okay?" asked Marie.

"Yeah, I'm fine," she answered, dry-eyed, too upset and angry to cry anymore.

"Well, if you're not crying, who is?"

Hunkered over the table was Gramps, his head in his hands, tears streaming down his face.

Angie went to him and draped a comforting arm around his shoulder. "Don't worry, Gramps. Everything's going to be alright."

"No, it won't," he wept.

"Sure, it will, Gramps. I'll just marry someone else."

"Oh, I know that, Angelina," he reassured her. "That's not why I'm crying."

"What is it then?"

"It's the *lasagna*," he wailed. "I could almost taste it!"

Chapter Twenty-Five
I Had a Secret

Mac and Rick left shortly after the main course did a swan dive. Gramps and Tiny went to bed early with their tails between their legs. Sal ordered Chinese takeout, and when he returned with the cartons of food, Margaret joined her family around the kitchen table while Gramps' snoring resonated throughout the house.

"How could this happen? How?" asked Margaret, wringing her hands. "I can't believe my daughters have been keeping secrets from me in my own house. Please pass the Lo Mein."

Angie slid the Chinese noodles over to her mother, too embarrassed to answer.

"I had a feeling something wasn't right with you two when Mac showed up alone after bingo," admitted Sal, reaching in a brown paper bag. "Damn, they forgot the Wonton soup. What the hell was in that envelope he gave me, anyway?"

Angie leaned one elbow on the table, resting her chin in her hand. "It was a love letter," she whispered.

"A love letter?" asked Margaret, her ire forgotten for the moment. "How romantic."

Sal rubbed the back of his neck, knitting his brows. "I don't get it. A man writes you a love letter, and you kick him out of your house? It was probably a lousy one if you treated him like that."

Marie looked up from her plate of fried rice. "No, Dad. It was beautiful."

"Angela. You showed the letter to your sister and not me?" Margaret asked, sounding hurt.

"I'm sorry, Ma. I wasn't sure that Mac actually wrote them."

Margaret twisted in her chair, facing Angie. "You mean there's more than one?"

"Yeah, Ma. I have two."

Margaret slapped the table with her palm. "I want to see them now!"

"All right. I'll get them," Angie mumbled, sliding her plate in front of her father. "Here, Dad, you can have my Egg Foo Young. I'm not hungry."

Angie retrieved the letters, placing them on the kitchen table in front of her mother. At first glance, Margaret appeared puzzled. "Don't you think it's strange that Mac addressed the notes to you as Angelina? Your grandfather's the only one who calls you that."

"I know," Angie said, sliding down in her chair. "That's why I had my doubts."

"But he handed the first letter to me, himself," insisted Sal.

"Someone else could have written it for him," Angie said, turning to him. "You know, like John Alden or Cyrano. That doesn't prove a thing."

Marie pointed to the flowing script. "Look, Ma. Did you notice the handwriting? Mac wrote in calligraphy."

"Yes, it's lovely," she observed. "When did Mac learn how to do this?"

"Never, as far as I know," Angie told her.

"So, what convinced you, Marie?" asked her mother. "Why are you so sure that Mac wrote these letters?"

"Because I saw *that* one on his desk today," she explained, pointing to the second envelope." I knew Angie would believe me if I told her Mac wrote the letter and I delivered it myself."

"I delivered one, too," said her father, taking offense. "You think I made all that up?"

"Of course not, Dad," Marie assured him. "But I saw something when I was in Mac's office that might make a difference."

Angie bolted upright. "Wait a minute, Ree. You didn't tell me you were *in* Mac's house. Just that you and Gramps were walking the dog across the street."

"And what were you and your grandfather doing at Mac's house?" asked her mother.

Marie gave them the condensed version of Gramps' plan and his encounter with Mr. Wilson. When she was done, Margaret resumed wringing her hands.

"You mean to tell me that your grandfather knew about your broken engagement *and* the letters?" she asked, almost in tears. "I can't believe I was the only one who was left in the dark."

"What about me?" asked Sal. "I live here, too."

"That's different, dear. Daughters always confide in their mothers, until now," she said, with a side-glance at Angie and Marie.

"So, Marie, what exactly did you see?" asked her father.

Marie hesitated, took a deep breath, and said, "Well, after I got the plastic bag for Tiny's poop, I walked past Mac's office and saw a light over his desk."

"Sounds to me like he left the lamp on."

"No, Dad. The drapes were wide open, and the room was

bright. Besides, I checked. All the lamps in the room were off. But this light was different." Marie moved her hands like a hula dancer. "It sort of floated in waves over a pen on his desk. I think it wanted me to see it."

"That's ridiculous," said her pragmatic father. "It was probably just a reflection."

"You might be right about the reflection, but the pen was no run-of-the-mill ballpoint. This was a fountain pen—a really old one, too. I even touched it, just to be sure it was real."

"Well, was it?" asked Angie.

"Oh, it was real all right. But as soon as I touched it, the light went out. I know, it still doesn't explain *how* Mac wrote in calligraphy, but it *is* possible that he wrote the letters with that fountain pen. I even saw ink stains on his hand. That proves something. Doesn't it?"

They all exchanged questioning looks, except for Margaret. She had been reading the letters during the discussion with a dreamy, faraway look in her eyes.

"You never wrote letters like this to me when we were going together," she said to her husband.

"I didn't have to. You were willing to marry me, remember?"

Margaret put the folded sheets of paper back in the envelopes. "Yes, but it would have been nice, anyway."

"Women," muttered Sal. "Can't live with them," then his voice changed to a sweet and loving tone, "and you sure as hell *never* want to live without them," he added with an affectionate squeeze to his wife's hand. She returned the squeeze as they gazed into each other's eyes.

Angie and Marie rose from the table. It was time to leave their parents alone.

"Angela, just one more question before you go," she said, handing the letters to Angie.

"Sure, Ma. What is it?"

"After reading these letters, it's obvious that Mac loves you very much. Why do you reject him?"

"You know, Ma, I'm not sure I even know anymore."

Chapter Twenty-Six
Where in the World is Niccolo Russo?

Men are like Monday mornings after a long weekend, thought Angie when the bedside clock jarred her awake at seven. They both arrive too soon, entering your life when you're not exactly ready. She hadn't been prepared for another relationship when she met Mac but welcomed him into her life, nonetheless. Now Angie wanted to avoid the harsh truth of Monday—life without Mac—and skip right over to Tuesday, a day that doesn't get the credit it deserves.

A Tuesday won't shock you back into the workweek, there are no holidays on a Tuesday, and there's never a deadline on that mundane day of the week. That's where Angie wanted to be—on a dull and boring Tuesday. But the alarm blaring on the nightstand reminded her that she wasn't there at all. Maybe Rick has the right idea using TV and movie fantasies as temporary mental vacations, she mused, still groggy from sleep. But she wasn't in a sitcom or a movie. She had top billing in the ultimate reality show.

Angie turned off the alarm, rolled over, and glanced at Marie in the adjacent bed. She could sleep through an F5 tornado, and Angie watched the blankets covering her sister rise and fall in perfect sync with her even breathing. Trying to be quiet anyway, Angie got out of bed and gathered her clothes. She hung them on the hook behind the bathroom door and headed to the kitchen before dressing for work.

The unofficial rule of the house was that the first one up makes the coffee, so Angie grabbed a filter, measured the grinds, and filled the reservoir in the drip pot. While it brewed, she sat at the kitchen table trying to figure out how to straighten the mess she had made of her life. The morning paper slamming against the front door interrupted her thoughts.

Angie padded through the living room for the free newspaper—the only perk from her job—and before opening the door to retrieve it, something got her undivided attention faster than a buy-one-get-one-free shoe sale at the mall. On the floor was an envelope addressed to "Angelina."

Could this be another letter from Mac? But how did it get here?

Although Angie still wasn't convinced of Mac's innocence or of his ability to write such romantic love letters, the power of the enchanted letter couldn't be denied. When Angie bent down to retrieve it, the envelope seemed to jump into her hand, sending electrifying tingles throughout her body. "I'll never get used to that," she muttered as it fell from her grasp.

Reaching for the envelope again, Angie tapped it several times with her finger as if testing for heat. *Nothing—no tingle.* Deciding it was safe to handle, she picked it up and shuffled to the kitchen to read the letter over her morning coffee, passing her room on the way.

Gramps should have been up by now, she thought, stopping at the door. Even if he were still sleeping, he snored loud enough to register on the Richter scale. But Angie didn't hear a thing.

"Gramps, time to get up," she said, and knocked.

No response.

"Gramps?" she said, a little louder this time. "Are you okay?"

Silence.

Omigod! He might have fallen. Maybe he had a stroke or a heart attack!

"Don't worry, Gramps! Angelina's coming!"

Alarm bells clanged in her head as she stormed in and scanned the room. The letter, now forgotten, fell from her grasp. Gramps and Tiny were gone.

Her first impulse was to grab her cell phone and call 911. It was gone, too, but that wasn't important now. Racing to her parents' room, she banged on their door. "Mom, Dad! Wake up! Gramps is missing!"

The family dressed quickly after Angie called 911 from the phone in the kitchen. Then Angie, Marie, and their mother perched nervously on the plastic-covered sofa while Sal paced around the living room. Officer Dominic Perini arrived fifteen minutes later.

Dominic was married to Angie's cousin, Evelyn, the daughter of Margaret's second cousin twice removed on her father's side, which made him practically a stranger. But the Russos valued familial bonds claiming relations, however distant, faster than a five-year-old adopts a stray puppy, and he was considered family. In high school, Dom had a head of thick, black curls and the physique of a Chippendale dancer. All that changed after he knocked up cousin Evie. A balding man with a belly shaped like the jelly doughnuts he ate every morning was all that remained of his former physique.

"When did you last see your father, Mr. Russo?" he asked while scribbling notes on his pad.

"About five o'clock last night," answered Sal. "And please, call me Sal. We're family."

"Sure, Sal," he said, nodding. "Do you remember what your father was wearing?"

"I don't know. Probably something polyester."

"Were there any problems in the family? Any fights or disagreements that might have given him reason to leave?"

"Well, he was pretty upset about the *lasagna*," Angie told him.

"Lasagna?" asked Dom with an arched brow.

"Never mind," she said.

"What's the missing person's name and age?" he continued.

"Nick Russo, eighty," replied Sal.

Dom's face broke into a wide grin.

"What's so funny?" demanded Sal. "A missing eighty-year-old man is nothing to laugh about!"

"You're right. This *is* a serious situation. I just smiled because I know him."

"You know my father-in-law?" asked Margaret, her voice tinged with shock and embarrassment. "When did you meet him? At cousin Rocco's wedding? At Aunt Bessie's funeral?"

"No, the Almost Heaven Retirement Home. We get calls from them all the time. Mostly 911 emergencies, but there have been several involving Nick." Dom turned aside to Marie. "Your grandfather's quite a guy."

"Yeah, he's a hoot all right," she replied vapidly.

"Why did they call the police on my father?" asked Sal.

"To put it delicately," began Dom, "he made numerous, indecent proposals to the female residents."

Sal rubbed his temples. "I know, I know. He was kicked out because of that. But to call the cops? He's an old man. They had to know he couldn't *do* anything."

"Sure, they did. But the management had to take some kind

of action when the women complained. They couldn't ignore it and risk a lawsuit."

"So what do we do now?" asked Angie.

"After I call in the missing person's report, I'll see if anyone's seen Nick wandering the neighborhood. You and the family can help by checking his regular hangouts."

"My father just moved in with us. He doesn't have any hangouts that I know of."

"He went over to Mrs. Esposito's a lot," said Angie.

"You mean the lady across the street with that nasty mole on her head?" asked Dom.

"Yeah, that's the one," she answered. They all shuddered in unison.

"Okay," said Dom. "Let's see if he's there before reporting him missing."

"I'll start the car while you check across the street," said Sal, dipping in his pockets. "Hey, where are my car keys?"

Marie dug in her handbag. "Sorry, Dad," They dangled in her hand like bait.

Sal narrowed his eyes, snatching them from her grasp. "I'll be waiting in the car."

Angie and Marie pulled on their jackets. Margaret slipped into her coat. "I'll lock up and meet you all outside."

Margaret went through the house, closing doors, and locking windows. In Angie's room, she spotted an ivory envelope on the floor. It was just like the other two—addressed to "Angelina" in flowing calligraphy. She heard Sal honk the horn and hesitated. Margaret knew it was wrong but stuffed the letter in her purse anyway. *I'll light a candle and pray for forgiveness later.* Then she locked the front door and hurried to the Caddy.

"What took you so long?" asked Sal, as she slid beside him.

"I couldn't find my keys." *Better make that two candles.*

Angie, Marie, and Dom gathered on Mrs. Esposito's porch as Angie read a note taped to her door.

Dear Nicky,

My sister in New Jersey had a heart attack and needs me to take care of her. There was no time to call, and I knew you'd take good care of Tiny until I return.

Bernice

"Well, at least we know Gramps was here and that he's okay," she said, passing the note to Dom.

"How can you say that? There still could've been foul play. Look, I think that's blood!" he cried, shoving the red-stained slip of paper in Angie's face. "I should get this to the lab right away."

"Don't bother," she said, pushing it aside.

"Don't bother? What the hell are you talking about?"

"Relax, Colombo," said Marie. "Take another look at that note."

"Why should I waste time doing that? I have all the evidence I need to..."

"Read it again," said Marie, cutting him off. "But this time, hold it up to your nose and take a whiff."

"You want me to smell it?"

"Just do it."

Letting out a resigning sigh, Dom slowly lifted the note to his nose. "Is that... pepperoni?"

Angie and Marie exchanged knowing glances. "Yeah, it's pepperoni," said Marie. "Gramps has been giving it to Tiny so he'll behave. That proves he's been here and that he's okay."

"So, it's pepperoni and not blood," Dom said, resuming

command. "He's still a missing person. I'll make out the report and meet you by your father's car."

Dom slipped the grease-stained note between the pages of his notepad and trotted over to the Nassau County patrol car parked at the curb. He wedged himself behind the wheel, keyed in Gramps' information on his laptop, and walked back to the Russos' car. Marie lowered the window as he approached and held out a slip of paper. "Here's my cell phone number just in case you have news."

"Sure thing," he said. "And don't worry, Mr. Russo, I mean, Sal. We'll have your father home in no time."

"Give my regards to Evelyn and the children," called Margaret as he strode back to his patrol car.

"Well, I guess we'll start with Patsy's," muttered Sal, pulling from the curb. "Angie took him there for pizza before going to bingo Friday night. Maybe he got hungry after he went to bed and snuck out for something to eat."

"I wish I hadn't been so hard on him," lamented Margaret during the ride to Patsy's. I should've been more understanding. He and Mom were married for a long time. He was probably acting up because he was lonely."

"Don't be so hard on yourself, Ma," said Angie, trying to comfort her." Ree and I aren't exactly innocent bystanders. We had something to do with Gramps running away, too."

"I should've let him smoke his damn cigar," said Sal. "What's the harm of a little smoke in the house anyway? He's my father. I should just be happy he's still with us," he added as he coasted to a stop in front of the restaurant. "Well, here we are."

"I'll go in," volunteered Marie and hopped out of the car.

"Gramps isn't here!" shouted Marie, running towards the Caddy. "They haven't seen him since he came in with Angie on Friday night," she said as she yanked open the door and climbed in.

"Then we have to keep looking," said Margaret. "He couldn't have gone too far with his arthritis."

"Don't worry about Gramps, Ma," said Marie, slamming the door shut. "He's tougher than you think. We'll find him."

"Marie's right," agreed Sal as he eased into traffic. "Just keep your eyes peeled for an old man with a scrawny little dog."

They searched every street, avenue, boulevard, and cul-de-sac in the neighborhood. One hour later, there was still no sign of Gramps.

"Ree, why don't you call Rick," suggested Angie as her father turned down the next block. "Maybe he can help us find Gramps."

"Duh! Why didn't *I* think of that?" Marie pawed through her handbag, pulled out her cell phone, and keyed in his number. "I'll tell him where we are."

"Speaking of making calls, Ang," said Marie after talking to Rick, "What about your job? Shouldn't you call your boss before he reports *you* as a missing person, too?"

"Omigod!" Angie cried in a sudden panic. "I completely forgot about work! Quick! Give me your phone." Angie snatched the phone from Marie and punched in her work number.

"Yeah, hi. It's me...I know, I know," she said, slouching dejectedly in the back seat. "But...But...I'm *sorry*...But my Gramps is missing...Uh huh...Uh huh. Okay. It won't happen again...thanks. Bye."

"Did he fire you?" asked Marie.

"No, but he wasn't very happy either," said Angie, handing the phone to Marie. "My boss is a decent guy, though. The newspaper has a police scanner. He said he'd call me if he hears anything about Gramps."

"That's about all we can do for now," said Sal. "We might as well go home and let the police do their job."

The family was quiet, their nerves on edge, while on the way home. Lost in their own thoughts, everyone jumped, startled back to the present crisis when Marie's phone rang ten minutes later.

"Hello?" Oh, hi...Yeah...really? Okay...fine. Bye. Stop the car!" cried Marie after disconnecting. "That was Gramps. I know where he is."

"So are you going to keep it to yourself?" demanded Sal as he pulled over to the curb.

"Well, this is one of those good news, bad news kind of things," began Marie. "The good news is that Gramps is alive and not in jail."

"Then what's the bad news?" asked her mother.

"The bad news is that he's at Mac's house."

Angie bolted upright and faced Marie. "Mac's? What the heck is he doing over there?"

"I don't know, sis. He didn't take time to chat. He just told me he answered your phone a minute ago and freaked out when somebody said the police were still looking for Nick Russo. Your boss must have heard that on the scanner and called your phone. I guess Gramps didn't count on anybody discovering he flew the coop so soon."

My phone? He doesn't know how to use a cell phone," said Angie. "Even if he did, how did he get it?"

"He might have found it the other night with Dad's car keys," said Marie, looking guilty. "He *was* going to give it back, honest."

Angie narrowed her eyes at Marie. "Oh, yeah? When?"

"Eventually, but that's not important now."

"Your sister is right," said Sal. "Marie, you better call Dominic. Tell him we found your grandfather."

"Yeah, let's get this over with and take Gramps home," said Angie. *At least I'll get my phone back. I'm not so sure about Mac.*

Sal shifted gears and steered onto the road.

"Dad, stop the car!" Marie cried again.

"That's the second time you told me to stop!" said Sal, sounding irritated. "What's the matter *now*?"

Marie turned and looked out the rear window. "Nothing. I just heard the *Star Trek* theme. That's Rick's truck."

"I thought his horn played *Star Wars*?" asked Angie.

"It did, but he was in the mood for a change."

Sal blew out a dejected sigh and pulled the Caddy over. Rick slowed his truck to a stop and parked behind them. Marie lowered the back seat window as he sauntered over to the car.

"I've been driving all over town. Any news yet?" he asked Marie, peering in.

"Yeah, Gramps just called. We've been looking in the wrong neighborhood."

"Awesome!" he said, bumping fists with Marie. "Where is he?"

"At Mac's house," she told him. "Why don't you meet us there?"

Glancing down at his feet, Rick asked, "Are you sure about that? Isn't this between you and the parental units?"

"Of course we want you to come. We're all in this together now."

His face broke into a wide grin. "Totally righteous, man—I mean, dudette."

Chapter Twenty-Seven
Two's Company, Three's a Crowd

Gramps lay awake in Angie's room for several hours after dinner—unable to sleep, afraid to dream. Tiny, on the other hand, was curled up on the floor next to the bed, his little paws twitching as he slept.

"*Madonna,*" moaned Gramps as he remembered the look on his daughter-in-law's face just before she dropped the lasagna. That image and the ruined meal will haunt him for some time. He accepted that as God's way of punishing him for interfering. What he couldn't accept was that he unwittingly thwarted any possibility of reconciliation between Angie and Mac.

Angie should've been home instead of with him at bingo. If he hadn't eaten all that candy and junk food like he was *morte di fame*, he wouldn't have caused the riot. And if he hadn't invited Mac for dinner, they wouldn't have argued. Gramps knew he spoiled everything by moving in with his son. It was a huge mistake. The whole family would be better off without him, and there was only one way to make things right. He had to leave. Making that decision was easy. *How* to leave was more of a problem. In the faint glow of the nightlight, he mulled over his options while packing his few belongings.

I could pretend to have a heart attack. The ambulance will take me out, no questions asked. But that will only make things worse when they find out I faked it. Or I could climb out the window. Nah, I'll probably break a hip and be more trouble than before. I know, I'll throw Tiny out the window, say he ran away, and go out to look for him. Realizing none of his ideas would work, Gramps' shoulders drooped, and when he shoved his hands in his pockets, he felt something cold and smooth. *What's this?* It was Angie's cell phone—that sparked an idea. And like a Grandmaster chess player, he sat on the edge of the bed to formulate his next move.

Gramps pretended to snore until certain the family was asleep, then he snuck in the kitchen where he plucked the plastic bag of pepperoni from the fridge, grabbed a phone book, and tiptoed back to Angie's room. Tiny whimpered as soon as he smelled the spicy meat, and Gramps tossed him a slice to keep him quiet. He begged for more after swallowing it in one gulp.

"Shhh," whispered Gramps. "There's more where that came from if you keep your little trap shut." Tiny seemed to understand what was at stake because he sat immediately and licked his chops.

Next, Gramps flipped through the phone book, ripping out a page and stuffing it into his pocket. Then the unlikely pair of fugitives skulked through the living room and out the front door. Gramps stopped at Bernice's house to drop Tiny off but found a note on the door.

"Well, it looks like I'm stuck with you for a while," Gramps said to his floppy-eared friend. Tiny just wagged his tail and, *brrrurppp*, farted a stinky pepperoni fart.

"*Mannaggia!* I guess I deserved that, too."

Now, all he had to do was call a cab from the list on the

page he'd torn out of the phone book. Gramps still had a few bucks stashed away from his last gambling win and could afford the fare back to the Almost Heaven Retirement Home. He figured they'd have to take him in if he showed up late at night. Then, in the morning, he could beg for forgiveness and promise to behave. That's when it dawned on him that he didn't know how to use a cell phone.

"*Mamma mia!* What are all these little pictures?" he muttered and proceeded to tap the screen indiscriminately with his stiff arthritic fingers.

A photo of Angie popped up, but it was upside down. Gramps flipped the phone trying to right it and heard a *click*. Now *his* picture was on the screen. *Not bad looking for an old man.* He tried tapping the screen a few more times before spotting a symbol that looked like a telephone handset. Mac's picture appeared when Gramps touched it and dialed his number automatically.

"Angie?" asked Mac, sounding groggy when he picked up. "Oh, honey, is that really you?"

"No, it's Nick."

"Who?"

"Nick. You know, Angelina's grandpa."

"Oh right—sorry."

"Did I wake you?" asked Gramps. He knew he did, but he was just being polite.

"No, I must have dozed off on the couch," said Mac. "I'm sorry I didn't recognize your voice, Nick. It's just that you're calling from Angie's phone, and I thought it might be her. What are you doing with it anyway?"

"She...um...let me borrow it," he lied. "But forget about that. I need a favor." Then, like his rules, Gramps made a quick modification to his escape plan. "I took Tiny out for a walk and locked myself outta the house. They're all asleep, and I don't wanna wake them. Do you think I could come over to your place for the night?"

Mac didn't answer right away. He just let out a heavy sigh.

"You owe me a favor, remember?" *When all else fails, play the guilt card.*

Mac let out another sigh. "Yeah. C'mon over."

"Could you do one more little thing for me?"

"Sure, Nick. What is it?"

"How 'bout calling me a cab? I got lucky with your number, but I can't work this phone thing for nothin'!"

A yellow cab swerved towards the curb in front of Mac's house. "Get out, both of you! shouted the driver, stopping the car with a jerk when he slammed on the brakes. "And don't you *ever* bring that miserable mutt in my cab again!" he added as Gramps and Tiny piled out.

"*A fanabala!*" yelled Gramps as the driver hit the gas, spinning his wheels, and took off in the dark.

Mac opened the door when he heard the screeching tires. "What was that all about?" he asked as Gramps and Tiny ambled in.

"I guess the guy don't like dogs," replied Gramps with a shrug and dropped his suitcase on the floor.

"What's with the luggage, Nick? I thought you were just walking the dog?"

"Oh, that?" said Gramps, kicking the suitcase behind him. "Uh...uh...I have extra-large poop bags in there. Yeah, that's it," he continued, proud of his latest fib. "The little dog has been having, ya know, issues lately; and I need to carry a lot of the big ones when I walk him."

A few seconds ticked by as Mac considered Gramp's lame explanation. Although anything was possible with Nick, even a dog with irritable bowels, Mac knew he was lying. Problem was, he didn't know if he should let him stay the night or put him back in a cab and send him home. But it was late and he was too tired to argue. Besides, one night with him was better than waking up the whole Russo house. He'd actually be doing them a favor. "Okay, fine," he finally said, running his fingers through his hair. "It's been a long day. Why don't you get some rest."

"So, it's gonna be just us two bachelors, eh?"

"Yeah, for one night only. So don't get too comfortable," said Mac, closing the door. "I'm in enough trouble with the Russos already. I don't need to add kidnapping to my list of insurrections against the family."

"No. No. I just stay for tonight."

"Suit yourself." Mac directed Gramps toward the den. "The TV is in there, the remote is on the coffee table. You can sleep in the upstairs guest room."

"Sure, sure. *Grazie.* I won't be no trouble. You won't even know I'm in the house."

Mac arched a questioning brow. He wasn't so sure about that.

"Looks like I gotta do one more thing before I turn in," said Gramps when Tiny whimpered at the door.

"Well, don't lock yourself out again, okay?"

"What? Oh, yeah," said Gramps and shrugged. "What a *stunada,* right?"

Mac just sighed, rubbed the space between his brows, and turned. "I'll be working in my office," he said with a worried glance over his shoulder.

Tiny bolted as soon as Gramps opened the door, lifting his leg on the first blade of grass he found. Then he scurried back into the house and up the stairs. Plodding behind his furry partner in crime with his suitcase, Gramps addressed himself as well as the dog. "And try to behave while we're here. We can't afford to get kicked out again. There's no place else to go."

Thinking he was alone for the night, Mac began another love letter. He had just written "Dear Angelina" with the Spartan when Gramps sidled into his office and coughed to get his attention.

"What are you still doing up?" asked Mac as he wadded the unfinished letter into a ball. "I thought you'd be in bed by now."

"I'm not tired," replied Gramps as he shuffled over to Mac's desk. "Hey, that's a nice pen you got there."

Mac looked up at Gramps and smiled. "That pen is older than you."

"Not many things that old still work. Me? I'm good for nothin'."

"That's not true, Nick."

Gramps lowered himself into an overstuffed chair. "Sure, it's true. Don't you remember what happened today?"

"Well, that wasn't entirely your fault. You were only trying to help. Everything would've worked out fine if Angie hadn't seen me with Bianca. But there is something else you can do for me."

"Wait a minute." Gramps glared at him with narrowed eyes. "Before I help, what about you and the *buttana*?"

"*Buttana*?" Mac furrowed his brow. "Ohhh, you mean, Bianca."

"Yeah, that's the one."

Mac swiveled in his chair to face Gramps. "I never got the chance to explain about that."

"So, what are you waiting for? I'm all ears."

"It all began when I found out Bianca Lombardi was

spreading rumors that Angie and I broke our engagement," explained Mac. "Well, Angie did, but I wasn't going to let that happen. I went to see Bianca at the country club to straighten her out, and she denied everything—acted like she didn't know what I was talking about. Frankly, I expected that. I told her to leave us alone anyway. I also made it clear to her that I loved Angie and that we were still getting married."

"Keep going."

"Then I tried to leave, but before I reached the door, Bianca jumped in my arms and stuck to me like we were covered in Velcro. I didn't know until today that Angie saw us. I guess by the time I pulled away from Bianca, Angie had already gone."

"Sounds good enough to me," said Gramps, staring into space. "I remember fighting off a few women in my time. It could happen to anyone. So, what is this thing you want me to do?"

"Well, as you can see," said Mac, indicating the pen and bottle of ink on his desk, "I was about to write another love letter to Angie. All you have to do is watch me write it."

Gramps brows knitted together. "Watch you? Like a witness?"

Mac's eyes lit up. "Yes, Nick. I need you to be my witness."

"Okay." Gramps held up his index finger. "First, I gotta change another rule."

Mac leaned forward. "Another what?"

"A rule." Gramps rubbed his chin as he explained. "You see, I got these rules. One of them is about making promises."

Mac cocked his head to the side. "What does that have to do with watching me write a letter?"

"A lot. Don't you see? I promised to stay out of Angelina's life. And we all know that promise didn't take. I can't break it again."

"I'm sorry, Nick. I understand if you can't—"

"Oh, I'll do it," he said, cutting Mac off. "I just have to tweak things a little."

Mac rested his elbows on the arms of his chair. "How do you do that?"

"Just listen." Gramps shifted in his seat. "Now, if I watch you, I wouldn't really be doing anything, right?"

"Right," said Mac, crossing his legs.

"If I'm not doing anything, I'm not butting in."

"Right again."

"And If I'm not butting in, then I'm not breaking my promise to Angelina, right?"

Mac chuckled and said, "Makes sense to me."

"So, what's wrong with watching?"

"Absolutely nothing."

"That's right, nothing," said Gramps. "Let's get started. Us bachelors gotta stick together."

"Great! Now hand me that fountain pen. If this works out, I won't be a bachelor much longer."

Certain now that Alexander Sullivan's restless spirit was behind his letter-writing ability, Mac took several deep breaths in preparation for another supernatural experience. Though still baffled why Sullivan's ghost chose to meddle in his love life, he also had the uneasy feeling that this was his last chance to convince Angie of his love for her. It was time to pull out all the stops and bare his very soul in this final letter. *She already thinks I'm an insensitive idiot. After the dinner fiasco, she's convinced I'm an insensitive idiot and a cheater. I have nothing to lose.*

Mac spread a clean sheet of paper on his desk. Gramps rose from his chair, passing the Spartan to Mac with the solemnity of a priest offering the sacrament of communion. Then, like a venerable scrivener of a bygone time, Mac poured out his deepest, innermost feelings with the Spartan in an elegant Victorian script. Gramps' mouth fell open, his eyes glued to the nib that gently stroked the paper as Mac—with Alexander Sullivan's help—composed another enthralling love letter sure to melt Angie's heart.

"*Madonna mia.* How'd you do that?"

"Do what?" asked Mac, unsure of how much to tell him.

"All the fancy writin'."

Mac paused. "Would you believe me if I told you a friendly ghost did it for me?"

"I'm not so sure."

"You know, Nick, forget what I just said. There's no ghost. I was only kidding," said Mac, noticing Gramps' doubtful expression. "Truth is, I'm not exactly sure how I wrote this letter or the others. I know this will sound crazy, but the only explanation I can come up with is that the fountain pen might have some kind of power."

"You know, you remind me of a man from my village, Massimo Gandhi."

"Massimo? Don't you mean *Mahatma* Gandhi?"

"Nah, it's Massimo. He looked normal, just like you, until his mind snapped when his wife ran away with a waiter on a cruise ship. After that, he had all his hair cut off and walked the streets wearing nothing but a diaper."

"Are you telling me you think I'm crazy?"

"Not yet," Gramps told him. "Even Massimo took a few days to find a barber."

Mac slumped back in his chair. "I guess I can't blame you for thinking I'm insane after what I just told you."

"Well, actually, you still look okay; but the minute I see you with a box of Depends, I'm outta here."

"Thanks for the vote of confidence," said Mac, pulling a blank envelope from the desk drawer.

"What are you gonna do now?" asked Gramps.

"I'm going to address this letter to Angie."

But before the Spartan came anywhere near the envelope, "*Angelina*" slowly materialized one letter at a time, like a phantom stenographer taking silent dictation. Mac rolled back in his chair like he was pushed. "Holy shit! Did you see that?"

Gramps bobbed his head up and down, making a hasty sign of the cross. "I thought you said the *pen* had power?" he asked, wide-eyed.

"That was a hypothetical statement," said Mac.

"Hypo what?"

Mac rubbed his face with his hand. "That means I wasn't really sure."

"Well, hypo-shmypo," said Gramps. "That pen didn't even touch the paper. How do you explain that?"

"I can't. Hell, I can't explain any of it."

"Maybe that old lady at bingo put a curse on me," said Gramps, backing away. "Now I'm seeing things."

"You didn't imagine it, Nick. I saw it, too."

"Great. Now they'll say we're both ready for the loony bin."

"Does that mean you'll back me up on this to convince Angie I wrote the letters?"

"Sure, sure," said Gramps. "And you can forget what I said about Massimo, too."

Mac inched his chair cautiously toward the desk. He folded the letter gingerly, placing it in the envelope. "Thanks, Nick. I'm going to deliver this letter to Angie tonight. It can't wait until tomorrow."

"Okay, I was gonna turn in anyway," replied Gramps, yawning. "That was enough excitement for an old coot like me."

"Wait a minute. Before you go, we need to talk."

"I'm sorry, Mac," sputtered Gramps. "I don't know how your electric razor fell in the toilet."

"What?" asked Mac, rising.

"Isn't that what you wanted to talk about?"

"No, it isn't."

"Oh. Okay, then you can forget about that, too," said Gramps.

Mac just rolled his eyes. "Actually, I wanted to thank you again for all you tried to do today," he said, extending his hand.

Gramps embraced him in a bear hug instead. "Aw, it was nothin'. And don't worry, *figlio*. Everything's gonna be okay. We're all gonna be family soon."

"Good. Then *you* can pay for the plumber."

It was after midnight by the time Mac turned the corner to Angie's block. He killed the headlights, cut the engine, and rolled to a stop in front of her house. His hand touched the letter in his jacket pocket, close to his heart. Then he crept up the walk and slid the last love letter under the door.

"Edwin Alexander Sullivan, whoever you are," he whispered almost in prayer. "I hope your efforts have not been in vain."

Mac woke early the next morning to the unfamiliar sound of Tiny scratching the door. No use ignoring him, he knew the consequences. Throwing on his robe, he slid his bare feet into sneakers and walked Tiny at the curb until the finicky mutt found just the right spot to do his business. When he was done, Mac pulled a plastic bag from his pocket and performed his civic duty. Back in the house, he gave his four-legged house-guest a bowl of water.

Even from the kitchen, Mac could hear Gramps snoring like a lumberjack. So, after dressing in khaki slacks and a navy blue shirt, he slipped on a jacket and went out to get breakfast for his unexpected company. He returned with coffee, bacon, and eggs, and almost stepped in a puddle: a gift from Tiny.

That's what I get for giving him water.

"It's a good thing you didn't do that in Mrs. Russo's house yesterday, or you'd be in dog heaven by now," he said in a firm tone as he cleaned the soiled floor.

Tiny only wagged his tail while sniffing the air. Apparently, bacon was his next favorite food after pepperoni.

Mac dropped the bags of food on the kitchen counter. Hanging his jacket over the back of a chair, he sat at the table eating breakfast with Tiny positioned strategically beside him. A shaggy paw nudged Mac's leg, and pleading puppy dog eyes stared up at him as if to say, *I'm here. Remember me?* Mac tried to ignore him but finally caved in, giving the little beggar what was left of his meal. He'd lost his appetite anyway. All he could think about was Angie and the letter.

The clock over the mantle chimed nine. Upstairs, a phone rang, and two minutes later Gramps burst into the kitchen, visibly shaken. "Mac, I got a problem."

Please, God, I hope Tiny is the only one I have to clean up after today. "What kind of problem, Nick? What's the matter?"

"Some guy called on Angelina's phone to tell her that the police are still looking for her grandfather. Mac, that's me!"

"I *knew* you weren't telling me the truth last night," Mac said, shaking his finger in Gramp's face. "Did you really think I'd buy that extra-large poop bag story?"

"I know, I know. Give an old man a break. It was the best I could come up with. I think I'm losing my touch. But *what* am I gonna do *now?*

"Take it easy, Nick," said Mac with a consoling hand on his shoulder. "What exactly did you tell him?"

"Nothin'. I said he had the wrong number and hung up.

Madonna mia. I didn't think my family would find out I left so soon. Mac, I gotta call them now!"

Chapter Twenty-Eight
The Usual Suspects

Elizabeth and Walter MacConnell were seated at the breakfast table, not speaking as usual. In the habit of reading the morning paper with his coffee, Walter held the publication up so he could see through the bottom of his bifocals. Most mornings it was just a newspaper, nothing more. Today he used it as a shield, a wall, anything, as long as it served as a barrier between him and his wife.

Their son Conrad had displeased Elizabeth. According to her, it was entirely Walter's fault. Accustomed to taking the blame for just about anything, Walter usually shouldered the burden with stoic acceptance. But today his wife was being unreasonable. He could almost feel the heat from her angry gaze through the newsprint like a bug under a magnifying glass.

"I'm sure there's a very good reason why Conrad hasn't called," Walter finally said from the safety of his tabloid sanctuary.

Elizabeth poured herself a cup of coffee from the pot on the kitchen counter. "You don't understand. I know he's hiding something."

"Oh, he's probably just busy working on another book," he said, turning a page.

"There you go again, making excuses for him. That's probably why he's been lying to me, too."

Walter lowered the newspaper. "What the hell are you talking about?"

Elizabeth pulled up a chair. Leaning close to her husband she said, "Connie has been avoiding me ever since we talked on the phone Saturday morning. He won't return my calls and gives me flimsy excuses when I ask why."

"What makes you so sure he's lying to you? Sounds to me like he just wants some privacy."

"I'm his mother," she told him, folding her arms across her chest. "I can feel it."

"Okay, okay. I give up. Whatever he's doing, it's all *my* fault. *Now,* can I finish my paper?"

"No. Get dressed," she said, jumping up from her chair. "We're going over there right now."

Walter raised his eyebrows. "Where? There? You mean to his house?" he sputtered.

"Yes. That's exactly what I mean."

The paper crumpled in his lap. "Liz, why don't you calm down before storming over? In the mood you're in, you're likely to say something you'll live to regret. And if you do, I'll have to live with it, too."

"It can't wait. We have to resolve this today."

"All right, all right, I'll go," he agreed, "but under protest, you understand."

"Makes no difference to me," she said with a wave. "I just need a few minutes to get dressed." Having the last word, she spun around, leaving the kitchen with a triumphant spring to her step.

Walter had been married to Elizabeth long enough to know that a few minutes was more like an hour. After smoothing out the wrinkled pages, he continued to read what was just an ordinary newspaper once more.

The Monday morning weather report predicted climate conditions typical for Long Island—rain accompanied by a sky as gray as an unfired lump of clay. Despite the gloomy conditions, Mac was guardedly optimistic that Angie would return to him after reading his, or Alexander Sullivan's, final letter. His last shot at happiness. In the living room, Mac lit some kindling in the fireplace. The doorbell rang just as the fire caught, warming the room with its burning split oak logs. "Hey, Nick! Could you get that?"

"Yeah, sure, Mac. I'll get it," shouted Nick from the foyer.

Gramps had been pacing, waiting for his family to come and take him home. "Well, I guess it's time to take my medicine for running away." He squared his shoulders and opened the door, prepared for his son's disapproving glare. A cold gust of air swirled around him when Elizabeth MacConnell barged in.

"Who are you?" she asked brusquely.

"I'm Niccolo Russo," replied Gramps, proudly. "Who are you?"

Elizabeth ignored his question. "Since when does the gardener answer the door?" she snorted, making a quick assessment of his unkempt clothing.

"Gardener? I'm no—"

"Oh, never mind. Just get out of my way," she ordered, pushing him aside.

Walter trailed in reluctantly behind her. "If I were you, I'd consider myself lucky that was all she said."

Seconds later Mac wandered into the foyer. He found Gramps standing alone looking somewhat perplexed.

"Who was at the door, Nick?"

"Don't know," he replied with a helpless shrug.

Mac arched a questioning brow. "You don't know? Well, what did they look like?"

"One was a mean-looking woman with skin the color of week-old *mozzarella* and a face that looked like she just ate some bad *scungili*. The other was a man who followed her the way a street sweeper follows the animals in a parade. Glad to have a job but afraid he'd have to take some crap along the way."

Mac laughed at the unflattering, yet accurate, description of his parents. "Oh, that's my mom and dad."

"*Madonna,*" said Gramps, smacking his head. "I'm sorry, Mac. Me and my big mouth."

"No problem, Nick. Where'd they go?"

Gramps pointed towards his office. "I think they went in there."

At the open doorway to his office, Mac cleared his throat. "Hello, Mother," he said, ambling in.

Elizabeth spun around, startled. She had been rifling through the papers on his desk. "Connie, my darling! Come here, my boy." With all the drama of a diva, she rushed over to Mac and kissed him on both cheeks.

"She insisted we come over, son," said his father as they shook hands. "I told her to respect your privacy, but you know your mother."

"I understand, Dad. Don't worry about it. I'm actually glad you came over."

Walter raised his eyebrows. "You are?"

Mac let out a heavy sigh. "Yes," he said, running his fingers through his hair. "I have some bad news. You might want to sit for this."

Mac's parents settled in the two armchairs in his office. He leaned against his desk facing them. "Angie and I have been having problems lately," he began. "I thought I could patch things up with her in a day or two and you'd never find out, but—"

"Ahem."

Glancing up, Mac spied Gramps standing in the doorway.

"Oh, I'm sorry. Mother, Dad, this is Nick Russo, Angie's grandfather."

Walter rose from his chair, strode over to Nick, and gave him a warm handshake. Elizabeth didn't move a muscle.

"It's a pleasure to meet you," she said to Gramps as if each syllable caused her physical pain.

Gramps' jaw tightened. "Nice to meet you, too."

"What's he doing here?" Elizabeth hissed, turning to Mac.

"He needed a place to stay last night."

"So why here?"

"Because Nick did me a huge favor yesterday. I couldn't turn him down when he asked me for help."

She tossed a disparaging glance in Gramps' direction. He returned her scathing gaze.

Noticing the acrid exchange, Mac aimed a worried glance at his father. Walter tilted his head toward the door. Mac understood—better to keep these two separated. "Uh, Nick. Would you mind leaving us for a while?"

"Sure, sure. I know when I'm not wanted," replied Gramps, narrowing his eyes at Elizabeth. "Call if you need me."

Mac's mother shifted in her seat, apparently pleased with herself for ousting him. "See, Walter. Didn't I tell you he was hiding something from me? Now, Connie, tell me what's going on between you and Angela. Your father said to leave you alone —that you were probably busy working on another book. But I knew better."

"Well, Dad's partially right. I was working—but not on a

book." Staring down at the floor with his hands in his pockets, Mac continued. "I was writing letters to Angie with this," he said, indicating the Spartan pen.

"That's a fine-looking fountain pen, son," commented Walter, stepping over to his desk.

"I bought it at a pawn shop, Dad. You should've seen the big guy who owned the place. What a character."

Elizabeth's eyes widened. Her hand fluttered to her chest. "A pawn shop! Did anyone we know see you there?"

Mac chuckled. "Don't worry, Mother. I don't think your bridge partners frequent that neighborhood."

"But what on earth were you doing," she lowered her voice to a whisper, "at a pawn shop?"

"I had a flat right in front of the place and went inside to kill time until the auto club changed the tire. You know, I'm still not sure why, but while I was there, I bought this fountain pen."

Elizabeth shot to her feet. "I want to see that thing," she muttered. And when she lifted the pen from Mac's desk, she let out a blood-curdling scream and dropped it like it was a white-hot branding iron.

"Look at my hand! It's burned!"

Sure enough, a red impression matching the silver filigree pattern on the pen's barrel was emblazoned on her palm.

"I'm branded! Scarred for life!" she shrieked and bolted to the bathroom.

Mac lifted the pen from the floor. It was cool in his hand. "That's funny. I've been writing with this for two days. Even Nick handled it yesterday. Neither one of us had that kind of reaction."

"Your mother's probably having another one of her hot flashes, son," his father reassured him. "I'd better go to her."

Walter scurried down the hall, stopping at the closed bathroom door. "Liz, are you alright in there?"

The door opened a crack. "What do you want?"

"I came to see if you were okay. Excuse me for being concerned."

Reaching through the small opening, she said, "I'm fine. Just give me your phone and go away."

"My phone? Who the hell are you calling at a time like this?" sputtered Walter. "I thought you were hurt."

"I have to call my hairdresser to change an appointment."

"For that, you had to run to the bathroom? What about your hand?"

Elizabeth grabbed the phone from her bewildered husband then looked down at the place where the pen had singed her skin. "It's gone," she said slowly, in disbelief. "The burn is gone."

"How could it be gone? You ran out of the room screaming like your hair was on fire."

"I have no idea. Now leave me alone," she barked. "I'll be out in a minute." The door slammed in his face.

"Well?" asked Mac when his father returned. "How's Mother?"

"Oh, she's fine. Just like I thought—a hot flash." Walter scratched his head. "Still, I never heard her scream like that before. Menopause does strange things to a woman."

"Do you think she'll be more comfortable in the living room, Dad? You know how she loves a cozy fire?"

"It's worth a try, son. Right now, I'd do just anything to put her in a good mood."

Mac and his father withdrew to the living room. Walter slouched in the loveseat while Mac stirred the logs in the hearth. Elizabeth strolled in several minutes later in much better spirits than when she left.

"Glad to see you're feeling better, Mother," said Mac.

"Thank you, Connie," she said, smoothing her hair.

"See what I mean?" joked Walter in an aside to Mac. "*Mentalpause.*"

"I heard that!" snapped Elizabeth, dropping down beside her husband. "I can't explain what happened either. All I know is that your pen is dangerous!"

Dangerous wasn't the first word that came to mind when Mac thought about the Spartan or Alexander Sullivan, for that matter. But there was definitely something else going on besides love letters. Now he was sure of it.

"So, Connie," his mother prodded, invading his thoughts. "Finish telling me about the problems you and Angela are having. I knew something was wrong when she canceled the country club."

Mac put the fireplace poker in its stand and plopped down in an overstuffed armchair. Burning wood crackled in the hearth as flickering shadows from the dancing flames smoothed the taut muscles in his face, softening the anguish in his troubled amber eyes as he mused over what to say. Mac hated telling his mother she was right. She enjoyed it way too much. But with no word yet from Angie, it was no use trying to hide anything from her now. After heaving a mournful sigh, he recounted the events that had occurred since Friday night when Angie ran out of the restaurant and his life.

"So," he finally said to his parents. "I guess it's over between us."

Sal Russo motored down the quiet residential street past a brick and stucco sign identifying the sub-division as North Shore Estates.

"Turn here, Dad," directed Angie.

Sal whistled. "So this is where Mac lives?" he asked, obviously impressed with the upscale development.

"His books are very popular," Angie told him.

"Now I know where you've been going for all those business trips," said Margaret facetiously.

Angie's eyebrows shot up then knitted together. With an accusing stare, she glowered at Marie.

"Don't look at me like that," she said. "I didn't tell her."

Leaning forward, she asked her mother, "You mean you knew all along that I was spending the weekends at Mac's?"

"Of course, I did." Margaret turned to face Angie. "I may not have a college education, but I'm not stupid."

"But why didn't you ever say anything?"

"Because you were engaged and in love. Besides, your father and I trusted Mac. We knew how much he loved you and that he'd never hurt you."

"Too bad I couldn't be so sure of that," she mumbled, falling back in her seat.

"Great," said her father. "Now that that's all out in the open, do you think you can tell me which house is Mac's?"

Angie pointed to the two-story Dutch colonial. "That's it over there."

"Nice house," said Sal as he eased to a stop at the curb. Everyone spilled out of the car except Angie. "I'll wait here."

"Oh, no you're not," said Margaret, pulling her arm. "You're going to have to see Mac sooner or later. If this is what you truly want, if you really don't want to marry him, it shouldn't bother you to be in his presence for a few minutes."

"All right, all right," she grumbled as she climbed out.

Rick's truck cruised down the street moments later. He tumbled out after parking behind the pink Caddy. "Greetings, family unit," he said, ambling over.

"Greetings yourself," said Marie, slinging her handbag on her shoulder. "What took you so long to get here?"

"A couple of kids on skateboards stopped me—wanted to hear my horn. I told them I couldn't because I was on a mission," he said proudly.

"Okay. Now that we're all here, including Rick, let's get your grandfather and go home," grumbled Sal leading the entourage up Mac's front walk. Margaret hung onto Angie's arm, plodding behind him. Marie and Rick brought up the rear.

Meanwhile inside, Gramps paced around Mac's foyer waiting for his family to arrive. "I guess I'll have to eat crow when my son gets here," he muttered then stopped short. "Or... I could talk my way out of this if I play my cards right," he schemed, when the doorbell rang, interrupting his thoughts. "*Mannaggia!*" Clutching his chest with his hand, Gramps opened the door. Before he could say a word, Angie pushed everyone inside ahead of her.

"I think I'll stay out here for a while," she said, slamming it shut behind them. Mac wasn't the only one she couldn't face. His parents' car was in the driveway.

"Pop, what the hell happened?" demanded Sal. "Why'd you leave? We were worried sick."

"I'm sorry, son," he said, sounding penitent. "It's just that I made so much trouble for everybody. I thought you'd be better off without me."

"What the hell are you talkin' about?"

"Ever since I moved in with you, there's been nothin' but trouble. I brought shame to your house. It's all my fault. I never should have come."

"That's not true," said Margaret. "We're family. We belong together."

"Margaret's right," agreed Sal. "Where else can you go

anyway? No other home will accept you after what you pulled at Almost Heaven."

"Oh, that's right. Then I'll get my own place."

"Oh yeah? How're you going to pay for it? Remember, you gambled your pension away online?"

"Then I'll get a job bagging groceries. Maybe I'll get an employee discount so I can afford to buy food."

"Pop, no one will give you a job. You're too old."

"I can get a job if I want to!" roared Gramps, shaking his fist in the air. "I might be 80 years old, but I'm still strong *come un leone!*"

"Calm down, you two," said Marie. "You're making a scene."

"Nick, is that you?" shouted Mac from the living room. "What's going on out there?"

"Oh, it's nothing," he yelled back. "I'm just talking to my son."

"See?" said Marie, nudging Gramps' shoulder.

"All right," he conceded reluctantly. "I'll stop if he stops."

Sal helped Margaret off with her coat. She draped it over her arm and took his hand. "What the hell," he said, calming down. "Let's go in and get this over with."

"Where's Angelina?" asked Gramps, scanning the foyer.

Marie jutted her jaw toward the door. "Outside."

"What's she doing there? Her future mother-in-law is here."

"Oh. That's why she wouldn't come in," said Margaret as they ambled towards the living room.

"I don't blame her," said Gramps. "That woman could give the Pope *agida.*"

～

Bianca skidded her car to a stop in front of her mother's stately home. She jumped out without bothering to lock it. Using her key, she dashed into the house, her spiked heels clicking excitedly on the polished wood floors. "Ma! Ma! Where are you?"

"In here having breakfast," replied Carmella Lombardi from the formal dining room.

Bianca scurried in looking flushed.

"I didn't expect to see you today," she said, swallowing a mouthful of eggs. "Why aren't you at work?"

Bianca remained silent as she strolled to the buffet and poured a cup of coffee. After taking a long leisurely sip, she turned slowly to face her mother—a sinister smile spreading across her face. "Is that any way to speak to the future Mrs. Conrad MacConnell?" she asked triumphantly.

Carmella set her fork on the edge of her plate and dabbed her pale, thin lips with a cloth napkin. "You mean...?"

"Yes, it's time."

"Are you sure?"

Leaving her half-empty cup on the buffet, Bianca pulled a high-backed chair from under the dining room table and sat beside her mother. The wild look in her eyes spoke volumes. "Yes, mother. It's *finally* time."

Carmella shoved her half-eaten meal aside, her face contorting into a maniacal expression with a gargoyle-like grin. "Didn't I tell you we'd get our revenge if we were patient? Aren't you glad you listened to your mother?"

Bianca picked up a slice of toast from her mother's discarded plate. "Yeah, Ma. You were right," she said, taking a bite. "Those holier-than-thou Russos always snubbed us because of Great Grandpa's bootlegging days. Now, after all these years, we'll get even with the whole damn family."

"Your grandfather, Mario, even gave that ungrateful Nick Russo a job when he didn't have a pot to piss in and couldn't speak a word of English. And how did they repay us? With insults," spat Carmella, throwing her napkin on the table.

"That's right," agreed Bianca. "Even when Daddy took Grandpa's money and opened the dealership, a legitimate business, our family never got the respect we deserved."

Carmella leaned against the back of her chair, her hands folded contentedly in her lap as she reminisced. "I was so happy when you paid that salesman to con Angie into buying the Mustang," she said proudly. "It felt good to see her suffer with that lemon. But even that wasn't enough satisfaction."

"No, Ma. That's small potatoes because soon I'll be Mrs. Conrad MacConnell—living in the big house with all his money instead of that low-class Angela Russo who wouldn't know a shrimp fork from a pitchfork. This will ruin her life."

"I have to admit I was tempted to call Margaret after the bingo riot. I wanted to see her shamed and embarrassed. I'm glad you convinced me to wait. The Russos think they know our family secrets. Well, they have no idea we know theirs. *This* is the moment we've been waiting for."

"Great minds think alike, don't they, Ma? Now our plans will finally pay off to avenge our good name. In one fell swoop, the entire Russo family will be punished, and Conrad MacConnell will be my prize."

Chapter Twenty-Nine
The Final Showdown

Angie huddled under the covered stoop of Mac's house beneath a darkening sky, chilled to the bone. She shoved her hands in her jacket pockets and wondered how long she could hold out before succumbing to pneumonia, which wasn't a bad idea. Being in the hospital would be a good excuse to avoid facing Mac for a month at least.

Then it began to rain.

"Well, that's just great!" she griped, pulling up her collar. "Can it get any worse?"

Of course, it could, she realized minutes later when Bianca and her mother drove up. That's when Angie knew she had been right all along. She couldn't trust Mac. Bianca had won.

I guess it's time to face the truth. Mac and I are history. Why else would Bianca be here? But I'm not about to hand him over to her on a silver platter either, especially in front of my family. I'll make her fight for him. Angie charged into the house before Bianca was out of her car.

Tiny greeted her at the door, wagging his tail as she shrugged off her jacket. His shrill yapping brought Mac to the foyer.

"Who is it now—? Oh, Angie," he cried, rushing toward her. "I knew you'd come. I'm so glad you're here so we can—"

"Stay away from me, you—you low-down-dirty-dog," she spat, cutting him off. "I'm only here because of my family. After today, I never want to see you again!"

Marie came up behind Mac, sidled over to Angie, and took her arm. "Take it easy, sis," she said calmly. "You two can talk this over later after we take Gramps home."

"But didn't you read my letter?" cried Mac.

"I read them both," she growled as Marie led her away. "What a fool I was to trust you and fall for all that mushy Victorian romance crap. I actually believed that you loved me."

"But I wrote three letters!" he groaned mournfully as they shuffled down the hall. "There were three!"

The two families had assembled in the living room, separated by furniture and space. Walter and Elizabeth MacConnell were ensconced on the love seat. Gramps, Angie, and her parents converged on the sofa. Rick and Marie occupied the two armchairs. Looking miserable, Mac staggered in with Tiny trotting at his heels. He stood beside the fireplace while the mantle clock ticked away the uncomfortable minutes.

The tableau resembled a scene from Mac's latest book, *Intrigue at the Inn*, when the clever detective rounds up the usual suspects to reveal the murderer. The only difference between the present situation and his book: no one had been murdered—yet. Outside, a sudden gust of wind howled, almost drowning out the doorbell when it rang.

Gramps jumped from the sofa. "I'll get it," he volunteered, scuttling to the foyer.

Sinister clouds churned above, and thunder rumbled in the distance when Gramps opened the door. His mouth went slack-jawed at the sight of Carmella and Bianca Lombardi.

"*Madonna mia.*" Gramps crossed himself then quickly shut the door.

Bianca overpowered him, forcing it open with her body.

Carmella swaggered in. "Not so tough anymore are you, old man?" she said, hurling a withering glare at Gramps. He crossed himself again as Bianca and her mother marched into the house like a conquering army.

"Bianca, what the hell are *you* doing here?" demanded Mac when they barged in the living room.

She pointed her long, red acrylic fingernail at Angie like the grim reaper. "What the hell is *she* doing here?"

"Is that the *buttana?*" Gramps wanted to know.

"What did he say?" asked Mac's mother.

"Nothing," answered Carmella, ignoring the insult.

Even if Bianca heard the offensive slur, she didn't flinch. Every fiber of her being was focused on Mac like a raptor diving towards its prey. The look on Angie's face must have confirmed Mac was hers for the taking; and with talons poised, she closed the distance between them.

"Conrad, dear," she said, slithering beside him. "Why are you so surprised to see me? After our meeting at the country club, I assumed you'd be expecting me so we could make our announcement together."

Angie's red tresses almost sparked into flames. Her brown eyes, molten from the heat of her anger, darted between Bianca and Mac. Margaret grasped her hand.

"What the hell are you talking about, Bianca?" demanded Mac as he recoiled from her.

"You know, Conrad, our wedding plans. You proposed to me yesterday. Don't you remember?"

No one moved, blinked, or said a word. All action stopped cold as if the pause button had been pressed on a remote. Bianca's lip curled in a malicious sneer, obviously enjoying the result of the bomb she just dropped, until a flash of lightning and a crack of thunder jolted everyone to their senses.

Mac's hands balled into fists at his sides. "Dammit, Bianca! I did no such thing! As I recall, I told you to take a hike—to hit the road. Hell, I did everything but get a restraining order! I know what I said. I made it clear to you that I loved Angie and that we were getting married!"

"No Conrad, it's *me* you want to marry," she said, her voice wickedly sweet. "I understand why you can't admit it now with *her* here. I'll just see Angela to the door so you can tell the truth."

"Big mistake," said Marie.

"Totally," agreed Rick.

"Don't listen to her, Angie. She's lying!" said Mac, rushing to her side. "The door to Bianca's office was open when I left. I didn't realize it at the time, but now I know you were there. You saw Bianca throw herself at me, but you left before I told her to leave us alone." Mac knelt at her feet. "You left before you could hear me tell her that I loved *you*, Angie. Please, you have to believe me."

"Poor Conrad," said Bianca, unruffled by his remarks. "I'm sure you may have felt that way before. But when Angela called me to cancel the wedding date, I knew you were destined to be mine. It was perfectly natural for you to turn to me after being dumped, and I was there for you." Tossing an insinuating side-glance at the stunned group, she added, "*if* you know what I mean. Oh, and by the way, I accept your proposal."

"*Mamma mia*," Gramps said to Marie. "Now the pasta's gonna hit the fan."

Then, without warning, Angie sprang to her feet, lunging at Bianca.

"Angie, no!" cried her mother. "Sal, do something!"

Before Angie's father could react, Mac grabbed Angie around the waist.

"Let me go!" She yelled, kicking and screaming. "I swear I'll kill her!"

Bianca scrambled in her four-inch heels. "If she lays a finger on me, I'll have her arrested!" she cried at a safe distance, standing beside her mother in the living room doorway.

"Don't do it, Ang! She's not worth it," cried Mac, still struggling to control his fiery wildcat.

"Do it, Angelina! Do it," yelled Gramps.

"Holy shit! Holy shit!" Cried Marie as she burrowed in her handbag for her pepper spray.

Tiny bared his teeth and growled.

Then Angie suddenly went limp in Mac's arms. "Wait a minute! Wait a minute!" Turning slowly to face him, she said, "I didn't cancel the wedding."

"What did you say?" asked Mac, releasing her.

"I didn't cancel the wedding."

"Of course, you did, dear," said Elizabeth MacConnell, speaking for the first time. "You know how emotional you get. You're just a little confused, that's all."

"Me confused? No way. Not about that," said Angie boldly. "I called the club to speak to Bianca but not to cancel the wedding. I called to ask if we could re-book another date without losing our deposit."

Mac placed Angie on her feet and held her by her shoulders. "Then why did you tell me that the wedding was off?" he pleaded. "Why wouldn't you talk to me?"

"Because I was afraid," she replied, her voice quivering. "Because for the first time in my life I knew what it felt like to really be in love."

"I still don't get it," said Mac. "That's why you *should* marry me."

Angie turned her back to Mac, folding her arms across her chest. "Well, yeah, if you were just an average guy with an ordinary job, but you're a famous writer, a celebrity. Every female on the planet wants to hop into bed with you, and they aren't shy about it either."

"But I've told you a hundred times that I don't care about them," he said, spinning her around to face him. "I love *you,* Angie. *Only* you."

"Don't you see?" she said, arms spread apart. "I've been hurt so many times before by men who said they loved me. I believed them, too, until they cheated on me when the next pretty face came along."

Mac held her trembling hands in his. "But honey, I never cheated on you. Never!"

"Well, I wasn't so sure about that at the time," Angie told him, staring down at the floor.

"What did I ever do to make you think I was cheating?" he asked, lifting her chin.

Angie's shining dark brown eyes swiveled up, meeting his questioning gaze. "Nothing. You didn't do a thing," she replied, shaking her head. "I was just afraid to trust you—afraid to open my heart to another man again and set myself up for a heartbreak that I'd never recover from. Even though I loved you and wanted to marry you, I didn't think I could live with the possibility of being hurt hanging over my head day after day. I didn't think I could ever be happy wondering when your resistance would eventually crumble, and you'd cheat on me like the others. I figured it was better to give you up rather than suffer the pain and humiliation if you had an affair."

"I'm so sorry, Angie," said Mac tenderly, gathering her in his arms. "I never knew you felt that way."

"And I didn't want you to know, so I tried to ignore the leering looks and lewd proposals you got from your so-called fans," she said, resting her head against his muscled chest. "I pretended it didn't bother me, but then I started to doubt that you or any man could withstand that kind of constant temptation. And as the wedding date got closer, I panicked." Angie raised her head, blinking back tears. "I didn't know what to do so I told you I called it off. I needed time alone to think, and I couldn't do that with you around."

"Don't feel so bad, Mac," said Margaret from the sofa. "You weren't the only one who didn't know."

"Hey, what am I, chopped liver?" Sal said, turning to his wife. "She didn't tell me either."

"Sorry, Mom, Dad. I had to work this one out for myself."

"So why did you go to see Bianca?" asked Mac.

"After I read your second letter, I began to see that I was wrong not to trust you. Then Marie told me she heard Bianca spreading rumors that we split up. I knew Bianca was lying and decided to tell her off. That's when I saw you with her at the country club."

"But if you didn't cancel the wedding..." Mac's voice trailed off. Then his attention shifted from Angie to his mother. "You lied to me, Mother. *You* told me Angie canceled the wedding."

Elizabeth MacConnell just sat there, speechless for the first time in her life.

Struggling to control his anger, Mac glared at his mother. "I love Angie. How could you betray me? Why would you sabotage my happiness?"

Elizabeth leveled her icy gaze at Bianca. "It was all *her* idea."

Another bolt of lightning blazed across the sky. The lights flickered, and a deafening clap of thunder rattled the walls. Elizabeth attempted to rise from the sofa, but Walter seized her arm, forcing her to sit. "Let's see you talk yourself out of this one, Liz," he said. "Go on. Explain yourself."

Elizabeth MacConnell stared at the floor and cleared her throat. "You know we always had our parties at the country club, Connie," she began, her voice monotone and flat. "What I didn't tell you was that Bianca always helped me, and we had formed a friendship of sorts over the years. I guess it might have slipped out once or twice how I felt about Angela while in her company."

"Keep going," urged Walter.

"When Angela called the club about changing the wedding date, Bianca knew something was wrong between you two. She called me and said it was the perfect opportunity for both of us to get what we wanted, and we made a deal. The plan was to tell you that Angela canceled the wedding so you'd think she didn't want to marry you. Bianca said she'd handle the rest. All I had to do was wait."

"So when I told you today that Angie and I were having problems..."

"I called Bianca. She said I got what I wanted. Now her family could finally have their revenge and get even with the Russos."

"Revenge?" asked Margaret. "Revenge for what?"

"For the way you disrespected our family," replied Carmella, still in the doorway. "You Russos always thought you were better than us. You always looked down on us because of the Lombardi family business," she sneered, inching closer to Sal with every word. "Well, we may have been bootleggers and small-time thugs, but so was your father. You had no right to snub us because Nick worked for the family, too."

"I know all about that," said Sal, rising from the sofa to meet her, "but my pop turned his back on that way of life. Your father-in-law made a career out of it and didn't quit until he died clinging to his dirty money!"

Standing before Sal now, Carmella lifted her chin defiantly. "That's not the whole story," she said in an ominous tone. "Do you know *why* your father suddenly quit?"

"Yeah, because he got married and wanted to make an honest living."

"Oh, he got married all right, by a justice of the peace, and kept it a secret because your mother's family didn't approve of him," she ranted, unable to stop her emotional tirade. "When they discovered their precious daughter had eloped, the family pretended it never happened and insisted on a church wedding. Even then, she begged your father to stop working for my father-in-law, but Nick wanted to stay because he was making good money. It wasn't until your mother was expecting *you* that he quit."

"What the hell does that prove?" Sal shot back.

"The only thing it proves is that you're my son," said Gramps, stepping between them.

"Oh, he's your son all right," snarled Carmella. "Your *bastard* son!"

Margaret sucked in her breath. "Carmella Lombardi. How *dare* you say such a thing?"

"Pop, what the hell is she talking about?"

"Nothin', son," said Gramps, quickly steering him from Carmella. "Don't listen to her. She's crazy!"

Carmella held her ground. "No, Nick! *You're* the crazy one thinking you could hide the truth forever," she fumed in a deranged frenzy. "You told everyone Sal was born premature, but I know the truth. Your wife confided in me, and I've waited all these years for the right moment to expose your secret and punish your family!" Then, looking directly at Sal, a haughty set to her jaw, Carmella announced, "Your sainted mother walked down the aisle in church wearing a white wedding gown already knocked up!"

"Oh, my God." Sal slumped on the sofa with a dazed look on his face.

Margaret rushed to his side. "Angie, does Mac have any brandy in the house?"

"But Mother," asked Mac, sounding hurt and confused. "I thought you liked Angie? How could you get involved in this crazy vendetta?"

"I do like Angela, but that had nothing to do with it. I knew she wasn't good enough for you. I wanted you to see that she was low-class and not worthy to be your wife. You're a successful writer with a brilliant career. Angela would only drag you down. Don't you see?" she pleaded. "I did it *all* for you."

"But why Bianca?"

"Her family has money," answered Elizabeth tersely. "Bianca understands society. She'd be an asset to you socially and professionally. She's the perfect wife for you and will rear your children properly."

"Children? Have you lost your mind?" cried Bianca. "I never said I'd have children. That was not part of the deal. No! Children are totally out of the question."

Stunned, Elizabeth MacConnell's face turned a deadly shade of white. "You harlot! You trollop. You conniving hussy, you..."

"*Buttana?*" suggested Gramps.

"You *buttana!*" she shrieked. "You tricked me. You said you'd love to have Mac's babies and give me grandchildren."

"Of course, I lied, you old bag. I knew how you felt about Angie so I played you like a two-bit harmonica. How else could I become a celebrity's wife and get Mac and all his money, too?"

"But I want grandchildren," she wailed like a spoiled child.

"Cry all you want, but there's no way in hell I'm having any snotty-nosed brats. I've spent way too much time and money on this body to ruin it with sagging boobs and stretch marks. Do you think I was born with these?" asked Bianca, jutting out her chest. "This is what a $5,000 boob job looks like. See? They're perfect!" she said proudly, ripping open her blouse to show off her remanufactured breasts.

"Holy shit," sputtered Mac.

"I knew they weren't real," said Angie. "Look, Ree. They don't even move."

"All I can say is she *definitely* got her money's worth."

Sal sneaked a peek. Margaret hit him with her purse. "Hey, I'm retired, not dead."

"Do something," she told him. "She's old enough to be your daughter."

"Okay. Okay," he said, throwing his jacket to Bianca. "Jeez, cover yourself up, for chrissake."

"This is so cool," said Rick. It's just like in the movies."

Gramps stared without blinking.

Meanwhile, the thunderstorm showed no signs of abating like the tempers in the house as lightning slashed the sky in brilliant, ragged arcs. No one noticed the lights flickering when another bolt cracked hitting a nearby power line. Then everything went black.

"Don't move!" Mac ordered, taking charge. "I'll get a flashlight and check the fuse box. Dad, come with me. Everybody else, stay where you are. And for God's sake, don't panic!"

The women panicked anyway, screaming in terror, and bolted for the door.

Smack!

"Ow! Somebody hit me," whined Mac's mother.

Whump!

"Hey, who pushed me?" cried Carmella.

Grrrr!

"Will somebody get this damn dog off my leg!" shouted Sal.

"Cut that out," squawked Bianca, slapping away groping hands blindly in the dark. "Hey! Somebody just grabbed my tits!"

"Omigod! It's a home invasion! I'll save you," Marie cried with her pepper spray aimed in the direction of Bianca's screams. She was ready to open fire when the lights flicked on, stunned silent at the sight of Carmella crawling towards the door, her mother about to whack Elizabeth with her shoe, and Bianca's arms flailing.

"Get him! Get the old coot away from me!"

"Gramps?"

"Stop him! He's molesting me!" Bianca hollered.

Marie hesitated.

Tiny, however, remained fixated on the small red can in Marie's hand. It must have looked a lot like pepperoni because before anyone could stop him, he jumped in the air, ricocheted off the sofa, and grabbed it in his mouth, spraying Bianca in the face.

"Help! They're trying to kill me!" she screamed, tearing out of the room as if a swarm of killer bees was chasing her. Tiny spat out the can, apparently disappointed that it didn't taste anything like pepperoni.

Sal bounded over to his father. "Pop, what the hell's the matter with you?"

"Yeah, Gramps. How could you do that to Bianca?" echoed Angie, scurrying to his side.

He shrugged his shoulders. "I don't know. I never felt fake ones before. At my age, who knows if I'll get another chance?"

Sal threw his hands up, exasperated. "I give up. You're all crazy."

Angie had to admit Gramps had a point. "So, what did you think?"

"I'm not so sure," he told her, scrunching up his nose. "It was like squeezing a soggy *cannoli*."

"But if you didn't like the way they felt, why are you still smiling?"

"Because I like *cannoli* anyway I can get them."

Chapter Thirty
La Famiglia

The sweet taste of revenge Bianca and her mother so desperately craved had suddenly turned sour and unpalatable. Bianca's plan was foiled. Her vengeful tide had receded. All was fair and calm—for now.

Marie and Rick went to the bakery for Italian pastries while Walter trudged outside with Gramps to assess the damage to the power pole. In the bathroom, Bianca washed the stinging pepper spray and black streaks of make-up from her face. Buttoned up and presentable again, she joined Margaret, Elizabeth, Sal, and her mother in the kitchen.

Thin shafts of light poked through the thinning storm clouds. Angie stood pensively in front of the living room window gazing at the mist hovering above the pavement as if lava had flowed and cooled instead of rain. Mac crept in behind her, placing his hands on her shoulders.

"I'm so sorry for not trusting you, Mac," Angie said, staring straight ahead into the distance. "I really made a mess of things, didn't I?"

"Don't ever be sorry, honey," he said, turning her body to face him. "If I weren't so self-absorbed in my work, I would have noticed that you were unhappy. I'll never take your love for granted again."

"I wasn't unhappy," she said, lifting her eyes to meet his, "just afraid of what might happen."

"Nothing ever did, did it?"

"No, but it sure looked that way. I just can't believe Carmella and Bianca held a grudge against my family for so long."

"Well, it's over now. We're together again, right, angel face?"

"Forever," she answered, melting into his arms.

"But you haven't mentioned the love letters," Mac said, nuzzling her neck. "I wrote them because you wouldn't see me or answer my calls or emails. It was the only way I knew to tell you how much I loved you. Did you like them?"

Angie stepped back. "Oh, the letters were awesome, but they confused me more than anything. It was like someone else wrote them—someone from a faraway place and time. Though in my heart, I always knew they were from you."

Mac took her hand. "Well, you had a funny way of showing it at dinner on Sunday," he said, leading her to the love seat by the fire.

"Bianca took care of that," she replied as she curled up beside him. "I thought seeing her with you at the country club was proof that my suspicions were correct. Until then, all I had were irrational fears. What I want to know is how did you write those letters? Calligraphy is *so* not your style."

Mac pulled Angie close and told her about the flat tire in front of the pawnshop. She giggled when he described O.B. Pickett—listened intently when he shared what he knew of Edwin Alexander Sullivan and the Spartan fountain pen.

"I didn't have a clue about the pen until I used it to write the first letter," he began. "The calligraphy and the old-fashioned style of writing—none of it seemed possible. Even though it scared the hell out of me, I had no choice but to suspect that something supernatural was afoot. After I researched Mr. Sullivan, it all started to make sense, sort of."

"Do you really think his spirit helped you write those letters?"

"It had to be him," said Mac. "I just can't figure out why. And I don't even care anymore now that you've come back to me," he hugged her tightly and kissed the top of her head.

"You know, I asked my family to stay out of my life. I'm glad they didn't listen to me. I'm also grateful that Mr. Sullivan, whoever he was, didn't either."

Margaret cleared her throat, startling them. She had slipped into the room unnoticed. "In all the excitement, I forgot to give you this," she said with the third love letter in her hand.

"Oh my God!" Angie cried, sitting upright. "That was under the door this morning. I forgot all about it when Gramps went missing."

Margaret lowered her eyes. "I found it on the floor in your room," she said sheepishly. "I hope you're not mad at me for taking it."

"No, of course not, Mom, but..."

"I know, I know. I should've minded my own business. But if I did, I'd have been the only one. "Now, Mac," she said, placing the ivory envelope in his hand, "you can deliver this yourself."

Gramps wandered into the living room. "And I saw him write every word. I swear on a stack of bibles."

Mac accepted the letter from his future mother-in-law with head bowed like a nobleman being dubbed a knight. Turning to Angie, he gazed deeply into her misty eyes. "This is for you, Angela Russo. Take it without reservations. Read it and know how much I love you."

Margaret sighed, pressing her hand to her heart. "Let's go," she whispered to Gramps.

Angie paused briefly, pondering the whirlwind of events that lead to this defining moment. Ghosts? She never believed in such things before. Yet, although they were alone, she had a peculiar awareness of a third person in the room.

Sensing her hesitation, Mac asked, "What is it, honey?"

"He's here, isn't he? Alex Sullivan's spirit."

"You feel it, too?"

Angie wrapped her arms around herself as if chilled. "Yes, and I hear a low humming in my head. That happened every time I touched one of the letters."

"I got dizzy when I wrote them—like I was outside of my body," admitted Mac. "I was afraid to tell anybody."

Angie reached for Mac's hands. "It frightened me at first, but I'm not afraid anymore," she said, holding them tightly. "Do you think Mr. Sullivan is happy?"

"Yes," answered Mac. "I know I am, too."

A warm gust of wind suddenly rushed down the chimney whipping the pile of smoldering embers in the fireplace back to life. Mac and Angie jumped when the orange flames crackled suddenly like a dying patient returning from the brink of death. Another gentler breeze followed, sweeping away all thoughts and distractions, allowing the reunited lovers to focus on this last love letter together. Then, with a steady hand, Angie broke the seal.

Halfway through the letter, Angie's dark brown eyes welled up, blurring her vision. Glints of gold sparkled through her tears—a reflection of the flames dancing in the hearth like glimmering moonlight on the water. She passed the folded sheet of paper to Mac. "Read it to me," she said softly. "Please."

To My Angel, Angelina,

I surrender. I have been defeated. The battle of love has been lost, and you, my dearest, are the victor. Now I offer my heart and soul to you as the spoils of war. Come, come to me, and claim your prize. I wait for you with passionate anticipation. I will not resist you, ever.

If you demand a kiss, I will give it but only one because the kiss I offer you will last a lifetime. If you command me to hold you in my arms I will reach for you but a single time because once I have you in my loving embrace I will never let you go. If ordered to face death for you, I would gladly die the martyr providing the last vision my eyes beheld would be of your beautiful face.

Do not attempt to comprehend the fathomless capacity of my love. Just allow yourself to be consumed by it, my darling, and be cherished always as my beloved wife.

Yours alone forever,
Conrad

Although having written the letter, Mac read slowly, adjusting to the old-fashioned meter and phrasing. Gaining confidence, he picked up speed, assuming the proper cadence of the Edwardian-style language. Angie noticed an odd inflection in his voice, a nuance she never heard before—something else from the past? No matter. Nothing mattered anymore as long as they were together.

When Mac finished reading, Angie went pliant in his open arms, feeling safe and secure, embraced again in his love. Pulling back slightly, his mouth sought hers in a crushing kiss with a hunger that had been building for days. Angie clung to him as if they shared one heart, one breath.

"Does this mean you'll marry me?" Mac asked when they parted.

"Yes, Mac," Angie answered breathlessly. "I'm yours alone forever."

"Then I think this belongs to you," he said, as he took Angie's hand and slipped her engagement ring onto her finger.

Mac kissed her again, long and hard, running his hands up her back, through her luminous copper mane as if erasing the memory of their separation. With their bodies pressed together, Angie felt Mac's heartbeat in sync with her own, inhaled his scent, drew strength from the impassioned heat of his chest. She smiled contentedly knowing he was hers once more.

Marie and Rick burst into the foyer moments later, their arms laden with white bakery boxes. Tiny danced at their feet.

"Hey, Ma!" shouted Marie, "We're baaack."

"Did you get the coffee?" asked Margaret as they breezed into the kitchen. "I can't believe there's no food in this house."

Angie and Mac ambled in behind them. "That's sort of my fault," Angie told her mother.

"All that's going to change now," Mac said, beaming.

"Well, c'mon on, everybody," urged Margaret. "We can start with the pastries until the coffee is ready."

Marie handed her mother a stack of plates and mismatched coffee cups from the cupboard. Rick arranged the assorted Italian cakes on a platter after dropping an American Parcel envelope on the table.

"What's that you got there?" asked Mac.

"I don't know, man," he said, licking a dollop of sweet ricotta cream from his finger. "Some dude in a brown van left it by your door just as we got here."

Angie poured the freshly brewed coffee. "It's addressed to you, Mac," she said, glancing at the shipping label.

"For me? I wonder what—?" Mac's bedroom eyes widened, startled awake when he ripped it open. "Oh my God! These are the results of my genealogy search. It's Edwin Alexander Sullivan's family tree!"

Bianca pushed her chair closer to the table. "Who's that?" she asked, reaching for a cannoli.

"It's the original owner of the antique fountain pen Mac used to write love letters to me," Angie told her.

Elizabeth stirred her coffee. "The one that burned me?"

"Yes, Mother," said Mac, "and now I know why."

"Humph," she grumbled, folding her arms across her chest.

Mac thumbed through the documents while everyone took his or her seats at the kitchen table. It was an odd gathering: friends, family, and former bitter enemies from different social backgrounds, nationalities, and cultures. And despite all that had transpired, they shared in the excitement of Mac's research.

"Mother, didn't you do our family tree a few years ago?" asked Mac.

"Yes. I tried to do it myself with one of those new computer programs. For some reason, I could only get as far back as your great grandmother VanDorn." Elizabeth held her head at a haughty angle. "You remember, Connie, the VanDorns of Philadelphia? I always told you we came from a prominent family."

"Look at her," Angie whispered to Marie. "After everything that happened, she still has her nose up in the air. I swear if she ever got caught in the rain, she'd drown."

"Why'd you stop there?" Mac wanted to know.

"Because I couldn't find any records before her birth. It was as if someone cut off that branch of our family tree."

"What was her name again?" he asked.

"Eugenia. Eugenia VanDorn."

"That's old news, son," said his father. "Tell us about Mr. Sullivan."

"Sure Dad." Mac cleared his throat. "Edwin Alexander Sullivan was born in 1888 in Gloucester, Massachusetts, the son of Irish immigrants, Eddie and Bridget Sullivan, nee Lenehan. He later settled in Peabody, Massachusetts, and formed a business partnership with Jonathan Cromwell."

"Is that all?" asked Angie. "That doesn't explain why his spirit is hanging around with you and the pen."

"Spirit? Like a ghost?" asked Carmella, sounding frightened.

"Yes," said Bianca, glancing sideways at her mother. "It's Edwin Alexander Sullivan's ghost. Pay attention."

"Shhh," said Margaret. "Let him read."

Carmella nodded nervously, making a gesture under the table to ward off evil spirits just in case.

Mac flipped ahead a few pages. "That's odd," he said, frowning.

"What? What's odd?" asked Elizabeth, drawn into the story now.

"The man was born Edwin Alexander Sullivan, but his name changes to just Alexander Sullivan when he lives in Peabody."

"Sullivan's a pretty common name. I wonder if it's even the same person?" Sal mused, setting his coffee cup down. "If not, that whole report is garbage."

"Let me finish reading before we give up, okay?" said Mac.

"Then read already," urged Marie. "I can't take the suspense."

Mac arranged the report, tapping it lightly on the table to neaten the stack of papers. He took a deep breath then indicated a section on the top page with his index finger. "Here it shows Alexander married Winifred Cornelia Armstrong in Peabody in 1915. They had one daughter; Victoria Bridget Sullivan born in 1918."

Angie shook his arm. "Then what happened?"

"Oh my God!" said Mac.

"What? What?" asked Marie excitedly.

"I think I know why Mr. Sullivan's spirit worked through the pen to write the love letters."

"Whatta you waitin' for?" asked Gramps, leaning forward in his chair. "I'm an old man, remember? Hurry up!"

"It says Sullivan's wife died in 1918, a victim of the Spanish flu epidemic. After her death, he volunteered for the Red Cross Ambulance Corps during World War I and was sent overseas. Shortly after arriving in Italy, he died in a mortar explosion while delivering medical supplies to a field hospital."

"Oh, that's so sad," said Margaret.

"Yeah, but what does all that have to do with you?" asked Angie.

"Don't you see? Alexander Sullivan lost his wife during the epidemic. I bet she was the love of his life. That's probably why he went overseas. Without her, he had nothing else to live for."

"So you think he wrote those love letters because you were about to lose the love of your life, right?" concluded Angie.

"That has to be it."

Angie snuggled next to Mac. "Well, his plan worked."

"The mystery of the Spartan pen has been solved," announced Mac. "I think we should frame these documents so we'll never forget Alexander Sullivan and how close Angie and I came to losing each other. Who wants another biscotti?" he asked cheerfully as he stuffed the report back in the envelope.

"Look, Mac, you dropped one," said Angie, lifting the page from the floor with little more than a cursory glance, then froze, staring wide-eyed at Mac.

"Angie, honey," he said, shaking her. "What is it? Say something."

"We were wrong," she said slowly.

Mac slapped the table with the palm of his hand. "I knew it! Now I'll have to start over."

"No! Alexander Sullivan is the right guy."

"Then what's the problem?"

"There's no problem," she told him. "But he didn't help you just because he lost his wife."

"Why did he then?"

"He helped you, Mac, because Edwin Alexander Sullivan, son of poor Irish immigrants, is your great-great-grandfather!"

This time Elizabeth MacConnell fainted.

"That's impossible!" insisted Elizabeth when she came to. "My son and I are not descendants of ordinary shanty Irish immigrants. No! I won't accept that. I have proof."

"Get down off your high horse, Liz. The proof is right there in the family tree," said Walter. "Go ahead, Angela, tell us what it says."

Mac handed the shipping envelope to Angie. She removed the report, putting the loose page back in place. After glancing at the eager faces around Mac's kitchen table, she shifted in her seat and began reading.

"Just like Mac already told us, Mr. Sullivan volunteered for the Red Cross Ambulance Corps after Winifred's death. He shipped out to Italy leaving his infant daughter in the care of her maternal grandparents. Sadly, they died of the flu about the same time Alexander was killed overseas. That's when Victoria became a ward of the state."

"But didn't the first report say that Sullivan had a business?" asked her father. "The little girl would have inherited his money, right?"

Angie looked up and tucked an errant lock of hair behind her ear. "You'd think," she agreed, "but it seems Mr. Sullivan had invested heavily during the war and had some serious debt. After his estate was settled, there was nothing left for his daughter."

"Then what happened?" asked Margaret.

"At that point, the genealogist Mac hired had hit a dead end just like his mother. Only he didn't give up and discovered why. It was because all the documents stored in the Peabody Town Hall were destroyed in a fire."

"You mean like deeds and wills?" asked Marie.

"Yeah. And birth certificates."

"I still don't get it," said Marie.

"Then listen up because this will explain everything," Angie said, waving the report in the air. "Victoria was one of many children orphaned by the flu without papers or identity because of the fire. Childless couples traveled to Peabody eager to adopt them. And when new birth certificates were issued, the adoptive parents' names were recorded as the birth parents. One of those couples was Philip and Julia VanDorn."

"That has to be a coincidence," insisted Elizabeth. "How can anyone be sure? You just said the original documents were destroyed."

"They were," said Angie, turning to Mac's mother. "At the Town Hall. However, the professional genealogist knew his way around the Family History Library archives in Salt Lake City. That's where he found the Sullivans along with Victoria's original birth record, the amended birth certificate, and adoption papers."

"But my grandmother's name was Eugenia, not Victoria," insisted Mac's mother.

"It doesn't matter," replied Angie. "The paper trail clearly shows the name change when Victoria was adopted. The VanDorns raised her as Eugenia, and she lived out her life in Philadelphia, never knowing she was adopted. That's why you couldn't find your ancestors. You were researching the wrong name. Eugenia VanDorn is really Victoria Sullivan."

"No! That can't be true," she cried. "Those documents must be forged."

"I don't think so. Here, see for yourself." Angie slid the report over to Elizabeth. "The new family tree continues with Eugenia, I mean Victoria, getting married, having children of her own, and their descendants, right down to you, Mac. There's no doubt that Alexander Sullivan is your great-great-grandfather."

Elizabeth MacConnell, nee VanDorn—or Sullivan, blanched, stunned to the core. The world as she knew it had just collapsed around her.

"So you're not an aristocrat after all," said Walter smugly. "How does it feel to know that your ancestors were really poor immigrants like the Russos and Lombardis?"

"Not so good," she admitted in a humble whisper.

"So we're just a bunch of ordinary people, right?" asked Walter soberly.

"Yeah! Isn't that great!" cried Gramps, rising from his chair. "And I'm so happy that my granddaughter's getting married and my family is together again," he said and began to dance the *Tarantella*.

Everyone joined in except Elizabeth MacConnell who was busy trying to pull Tiny off her leg.

∾

The past three days had been mentally, emotionally, and physically draining for the reunited couple. Later that evening, they relaxed on Mac's living room sofa, exhausted, but finally happy.

"What you need is a vacation," he said to Angie while massaging her shoulders.

"You don't have to tell me twice," she agreed, her tense muscles yielding to the firm yet gentle kneading. "How about another cruise?"

Mac nuzzled her neck. "I'll book it tomorrow," he promised, playfully nibbling her ear.

Turning suddenly, Angie said, "But there's still something we have to do."

"Now what? Haven't we been through enough already?"

"Just one more thing, honey. You forgot about O.B. We have to go to the pawnshop and thank him. If O.B. hadn't convinced you to buy the Spartan pen, we wouldn't be together again."

"You're right," agreed Mac. "We owe it all to him."

Chapter Thirty-One
Howdy, Pardner

The next morning, Angie and Mac rolled to a stop in front of the Take It or Leave It Pawnshop. "Well, here it is," he announced, shifting to park.

Angie peered through the passenger side window. "Are you sure about that?"

"Sure, I'm sure." Mac directed her gaze to the street signs. "See? Future and Des Tiny Roads, just like I told you."

"So then why does that banner over the door say Grand Re-Opening?"

"Beats the hell out of me," admitted Mac as he climbed out of his SUV. "It certainly wasn't there last week. In fact, the only sign I saw was a small cardboard one that flipped over from *closed* to *open* just before I walked in."

Angie stepped out of the car onto the sidewalk and slung her handbag over her shoulder. "Well, there's only one way to find out."

After beeping the SUV locked, Mac sauntered over to the pawnshop entrance. He grasped the brass knob, turned it, and pushed. The bells on the door jingled happily as it swung open. Angie blinked in the dim light, then gaped openly when she entered.

"Oh my God, Mac. It's exactly like you described." Revolving slowly in place, Angie seemed to drink in the atmosphere, reveling in the mysterious shop. "Look, Mac!" she cried, taking off suddenly. "A Cabbage Patch Kid! I always wanted one of those."

"You'll have plenty of time to shop later," he said, reeling her in by her arm. "First let's tell O.B. that we'll name our first child after him."

"O.B. MacConnell?" she asked, snapped out of her nostalgic euphoria. "Jeez, Mac, that's as bad as Conrad."

"Okay. So maybe it's not such a good idea," he agreed, taking her hand. "Now come with me. I'll show you where I bought the Spartan."

Mac led Angie to the back of the store. He tapped a bell sitting atop the glass showcase beside the cash register. A dwarfish-looking clerk appeared within seconds, hobbling out of what Mac remembered as O.B.'s office.

"That doesn't look like the man you described," Angie whispered to him.

"No. That's definitely not him."

A green visor shaded the little man's buggy eyes that squinted through wire-rimmed lenses as thick as the glass counter. "May I help you?" he inquired.

"I'm looking for someone that works here," said Mac.

"That would be me. My name's Phil."

"No, not you. I was here three days ago—on a Saturday to be exact. I bought an antique pen from another employee."

Phil furrowed his brow. "I'm sorry, sir, but I think you have confused this shop with another store."

"No, this was the place," insisted Mac. "I remember every-thing...but you."

"Then you must be crazy because we were closed Saturday."

"But...but, that's not possible."

Angie took Mac's hand. "C'mon, honey. We'll come back another time."

He pushed her hand away. "No, Angie. I'm sure I was here." Mac pointed to the empty space beneath the glass. "See? The pen was right there. O.B. handed it to me on this very spot."

Phil's eyebrows shot up and his supersized eyeballs threatened to pop out of his head. "Wait a minute. Did you say O.B.?"

"Yes," replied Mac. "Otis Bean Pickett."

"Now I *know* you're crazy!" he growled in a voice disproportionate to his size. Directing Mac towards the exit with a stubby finger he roared, "Get the hell out of here before I call the cops!"

"What the...?" sputtered Mac. "Why can't I talk to O.B.? Please, we have something important to tell him."

The agitated clerk calmed down, and his lined face took on a forlorn look. A light fixture directly above illuminated Phil's head and visor, giving his complexion a green, frog-like pallor. Sharp eyes darted between Mac and Angie. Phil rolled up his sleeves as if ruminating over what he should do in the eerie silence that followed. "All right," he finally said. "If you really want to know."

"Yes. Yes! I do." insisted Mac.

Phil blew out a heavy sigh. "You can't see him because O.B. Pickett is dead."

Mac felt an icy chill down his spine. He shivered as the hairs stood up on the nape of his neck. "Did you say d...dead?"

"You heard me. Dead."

Angie put her arm around Mac's shoulder. "Are you sure?" she asked Phil. "My fiancée is not prone to lying. If he said O.B. Pickett was here, I believe him."

"I should know," Phil told her. "O.B. was my friend. I went to his funeral."

"But how can that be?" asked Mac, his mind reeling from the unbelievable news.

"Got a minute?" asked Phil. "It's quite a story."

"Yes," said Angie. "We need to know what happened."

Phil dragged three rickety folding chairs from behind the counter, stirring up a cloud of dust. Mac and Angie lowered themselves into two of them. Phil occupied the third, his feet dangling above the worn wooden floor. He sighed as he removed his glasses, cleaning them with the tail of his grimy shirt. It didn't help. They were still dirty, but the simple act seemed to calm him.

"O.B. loved this store," he began slowly. "Problem was he just didn't fit in. O.B. stuck out in this neighborhood like buck teeth before braces."

Despite the gravity of the moment, Mac smiled at the thought of the Texas giant.

"Now there's a rough bunch of kids that hang out in the streets, and those hoodlums picked on O.B. daily. He might've been big, but he was a gentle soul and always turned the other cheek." Resting his glasses on his nose, Phil paused.

Mac could see the sorrow in his eyes magnified by the thick lenses. "Go on," he urged gently.

"One night they showed up with a gun, pretending to rob the place, but their shenanigans got out of hand. The gun went off. O.B. took a bullet in his chest. The police are still looking for his killers and the weapon."

"Oh my God, how awful," said Angie.

Mac leaned forward. "But that still doesn't explain how I met O.B."

"And I can't explain it either," said Phil, sliding down from his chair. "Now O.B. had no other family so he left the shop to me. Today's the first day it's been open since his death." The squat man all but disappeared when he bent down behind the glass cabinet and extracted a long roll of paper. "I was just about to hang this in the front window when you two walked in."

Mac and Angie sidled up to the counter as Phil smoothed a large poster over the glass. A picture of O.B. wearing a ten-gallon hat stared back at them—a number to call with information pertaining to his murder emblazoned below his face.

"That's him," said Mac, tapping the poster excitedly. "That's the man who sold me the pen. I'd never forget that face. I even remember thinking he needed a ten-gallon hat, but he wasn't wearing one when I saw him."

"That's funny," mused Phil. "O.B. told me that hat belonged to his daddy. He never took it off." Phil shrugged and rolled up the poster. "So, I've told you everything. I don't know where you were or who you talked to, but it certainly wasn't O.B. Pickett."

"Well, Conrad MacConnell," said Angie, using his given name in a playful, reproaching tone. "How are you going to explain *this* to our grandchildren?"

Mac wrapped his arm around her shoulder. "I don't know, Ang," he said, hugging her to him. "Some things defy explanation. Like Alexander Sullivan and the Spartan pen, they just have to be accepted."

"Wait a minute, young lady," piped Phil. "Did you say Conrad MacConnell?"

Angie rolled her eyes. "Here we go."

"Of course! I thought you looked familiar," said Phil, adjusting his visor. "I love your books. I just finished *Intrigue at the Inn*. What an ending. I never saw it coming."

"Thank you," said Mac with forced enthusiasm. "I'm so glad you enjoyed it."

"Would you mind signing my book? It's right here," asked Phil, pulling a copy of Mac's novel from a nearby shelf.

"Sure," said Mac. "Anything special you want me to write?"

Phil dug a felt-tip pen out of his vest pocket. "Just write: To my friend, Phileas Blogg."

Mac arched an eyebrow. "Phileas Blogg?"

"Yes, that's spelled, P-H-I-L-E-A-S," he explained. "I go by Phil in social situations."

Mac shrugged and scribbled his name.

"Thanks," said Phil, obviously pleased with his auto-graphed book. "What a coincidence you came in today. A package was delivered for you this morning."

"Here? For me?" asked Mac, his voice an octave higher than usual.

Phil retrieved a plain brown box from his office and placed it on the counter. "Yeah, it confused the hell out of me, too. I was going to take it to the post office later today."

Mac stepped cautiously toward it. "That's my name all right," he said, scratching his head.

"I thought it was a mistake, but I guess someone was expecting you."

"Well, aren't you going to open it?" asked Angie, turning to Mac.

He shoved the carton aside. "I'm not really sure I want to."

"Then I'll do it."

Mac stepped back while Angie tore impatiently at the wrapping.

"Take it easy, Ang. It could be a bomb or anthrax!" he cried as she ripped it open.

Angie chuckled. "This isn't a scene from one of your novels," she said, then sucked in her breath when she gazed inside. "Holy cannoli!"

"What's the matter, Ang? What's in it? Is it empty?" asked Mac, inching closer.

"Oh, there's something in it all right." Angie slid the package in front of him. "Here. See for yourself."

A cold shiver raked Mac's body as he peered over the side and whistled. "I don't freakin' believe it."

Phil slid a step stool over. "What is it? Let me see," he said, hopping up on the stool.

Mac and Angie held their breaths as he peeked in the box.

Phil blanched. "Great Merlin's ghost!" he cried, lifting O.B.'s ten-gallon hat into the light. "Impossible! O.B. was buried with this hat. I placed it in the casket myself."

Inclining her head towards Phil, Angie caught Mac's eye and tapped her temple with her index finger. "There has to be some other explanation—a clue of some kind." She began rummaging through the box. "I knew it! See? There's a note. It's addressed to you, Mac."

Mac swallowed hard, his expression wary as he reached for the mysterious note. At that exact moment, the bells on the door jingled, but no one entered the shop.

"Cripes, this place is spooky," Angie said to him. "Just read that thing so we can get the heck out of here."

After nodding slightly to Angie, Mac took a deep breath and unfolded the yellowed sheet of paper. It quivered in his hand, emitting an eerie glow over his face as he read.

Didn't I say you'd never forget me?
Happy trails, pardner.
Otis Bean Pickett

Epilogue

The young man seated at the desk was dressed in a rented tuxedo. Although he pulled at his collar, uncomfortable in the formal suit, he'd never been happier. Before him, a blank sheet of stationery waited to be transformed into yet another love letter. And within seconds of grasping the Spartan, he began to write.

To My Dearest,

I never thought this wonderful day would come. My heart is full to bursting with joy. You are a precious gift I truly don't deserve but will gladly accept on our wedding day. I promise to love and cherish you forever.

Your Adoring Husband-to-Be

After reviewing the composition, he capped the pen and folded the sheet of paper. The pitter-patter of footsteps approaching from behind caused him to twist suddenly in his chair as he tucked the note in his pocket.

"There you are, O.B.," he said sweetly. "Don't be shy. Come here to your Uncle Rick."

Little O.B. jumped obediently in his lap.

Rick ruffled O.B.'s fur and scratched behind the dog's ears. "Hey, boy, where's your old man?"

"Who are you calling an old man?" asked Mac as he and Angie ambled into his office.

"Hey, dude and dudette!" cried Rick with a grin. "I'm glad you're here. I wanted to thank you for the use of your house and for letting me write a letter to Marie with the Spartan before saying, "I do.""

"You don't have to thank me," said Mac with a playful jab to his shoulder. "We're family now. It just seemed right."

"Well, the pen didn't burn my hand, so I guess Alexander Sullivan approves, too," said Rick, handing it to Mac. "You might say he gave me the Spirit Seal of Approval."

"Come here, O.B.," called Angie. "Don't get Uncle Ricky's good clothes full of dog hair."

"Oh, that's all right," said Rick. "He's an angel compared to his daddy. Who would have thought a dog as homely and nasty as Tiny could produce such a sweet-tempered offspring?"

"I guess like you and me," said Mac with an adoring look at Angie, "he picked the perfect mate."

"Too bad you didn't have a church wedding," Rick said to Angie as she straightened his tie. "Your mother was a little bummed out that you eloped."

"More like *way* bummed out," she said, stepping back, satisfied with his appearance. "But she got over it real quick when I told her Father Donovan performed the ceremony in the chapel."

"So when are you two going to have a little dude so Marie and I can be aunt and uncle to a human? No offense," he said to O.B. as he patted his head.

"Funny you should ask," said Mac, wrapping his arm around Angie's shoulders. "We have something else to celebrate today besides your wedding. Congratulations! You're going to be an uncle!"

"Awesome, dudes!" Rick cried happily. He hugged Angie and Mac until they begged him to stop.

"Now you and Marie better get busy so our kids can grow up together," said Mac, smoothing his rumpled tux.

"No problemo, *kimo sabe*. We'll get right on it ASAP!"

"That must be the limo," said Angie when a horn honked outside. "You guys get going. I'll see you later at the church."

"Yeah, man," Mac to Rick. "Your bachelor days are over."

"All I can say to them is goodbye and good riddance."

Irish and Italian families tend to be large so there was standing room only in St. Lucy's church for the marriage of Marie Russo and Carrick DiNapoli. Mrs. Kaminski sang "Oh Promise Me" as she accompanied herself on the church organ while the guests took their seats. She sang the enduring song at every wedding. And like a priest, no one got married at St. Lucy's without her. Margaret Russo—escorted by cousin Dom—was seated in the front pew. She joined Gramps and Bernice who wore a large-brimmed hat to hide the bandage on her forehead where the unsightly mole used to be.

Leading the bridal procession during the opening verse, Angie glided over the white runner followed by her cousin Evelyn and her two children who served as flower girl and ring bearer. Then Mrs. Kaminski played the first majestic bars to Wagner's *Bridal March* and everyone stood, eager to catch a glimpse of the bride. But instead of continuing with the traditional piece, Marie and her father bopped down the aisle as the Dixie Cups belted out "Chapel of Love."

Angie was stunning as usual, but Marie almost glowed,

looking positively radiant in her mother's wedding gown, outshining her sister that day. It almost took an intervention, but she managed to shed a few pounds, and the vintage gown fit perfectly. The antique lace veil Marie wore belonged to her grandmother, Angelina. A gift from Gramps.

Rick and Mac stood proudly with Father Donovan, and Rick's jaw dropped as his beautiful bride approached the altar. When Marie and her father reached the end of the aisle, Sal lifted her veil, kissed her, and faced Rick. "You better take good care of my little girl."

"That's exactly what I intend to do," he replied with utmost conviction.

Sal placed Marie's hand in Rick's then turned to take his place beside Margaret in the first pew.

"Well, now both our daughters are married to good men," she said to him once he was seated.

"And we did a damn good job raising our girls, too," he said with a shy smile as he pulled an envelope from the pocket of his tux. "Now it's time for us."

"What's that?" asked Margaret.

"You always wanted one, so I figured now was a good time to start writing you love letters."

"To My Dearest Domenica" was inscribed on the outside of the envelope. Margaret blotted a tear with a lace-trimmed handkerchief and hugged the letter close to her heart. "Oh, Sal, how sweet. You even used my Italian name."

"You know, I'm not sure if I did that or if Alexander Sullivan made the decision for me," he confessed with a wink.

"In the name of the Father and of the Son and of the Holy Spirit," intoned Father Donovan. Everyone snapped to attention as he began the nuptial mass.

Father Donovan prayed with his arms open wide like a loving father embracing his family, giving Mac pause.

When he was growing up, he didn't think about anything besides how much homework he had, his next birthday, or what he wanted for Christmas. But today, after all that happened over the past year, Mac finally realized something that most people take for granted. Something that isn't appreciated until it's gone—your family—his, Angie's, Rick's, even Bianca's. They were all connected by blood, marriage, or a shared history that drew them together. By choice or by chance, it was a history that created the sequences in the unbroken chain of life. From their earliest ancestors to the present, it was a history linked together by love.

Alex Sullivan certainly knew the power of that love when he reached out to Mac through the Spartan pen as *The Love Letter Ghost.*

Glossary
Italian Words and Phrases

Gramps' Italian vocabulary is a mixture of Italian American slang and wise guy-slang with a little Sicilian and Neapolitan thrown in for good measure. After many online searches for the correct spellings and translations, I decided to use the expressions and words that I'm most familiar with. So don't go calling the language police on me because they're all correct. It just depends on what part of Italy or Sicily your family came from, how long they've been in the U.S., and the neighborhood they settled in once they arrived. *"Mamma mia!"* Just have fun with it. I'm sure that's what Gramps would want you to do.

a fanabala: go to Naples, go to Hell.

agida, agita: aggravation, heartburn

arrivederci, Signorina: goodbye, Miss.

aspett, aspetta: wait, hold on

baccala: dried fish

bona sera: good evening.

buttana: slut, whore

cannoli: Italian pastry filled with sweetened *ricotta* cheese.

capisce: understand, get it?

capuzzella: marinated lamb's head made traditionally for Easter.

ciao bella, venire con me, mio caro: hello beautiful, come with me, my dear

come un leone: like a lion.

figlio: son

gavone: dummy, idiot

grazie: thank you.

la famiglia: the family.

lasagna: Italian dish made in layers of wide noodles, sauce, meat, and cheese.

Madonna, Madonna mia: My Madonna. Oh my God.

Mamma mia: oh my mother.

mangiamo: let's eat.

mannaggia: darn

minga: darn, damn

mozzarella: A mild, white Italian cheese.

paesano: pal, buddy

parmesan: A hard, sharp, dry Italian cheese

ricotta: a soft Italian cheese.

sasizza: sausage

scungili: a shellfish, conch

skeeve, shkeeve: with disgust

stunada: acting crazy, ditzy or not thinking

tarantella: Italian folk dance.

venire, venire: come, come.

mi chiamo: my name is.

morte di fame: dying from starvation.

And just in case you were wondering, Mrs. Malafemina's name means "evil woman."

Author's Notes

Writing *The Love Letter Ghost* took an enormous amount of time and effort yet brought equal amounts of joy and personal satisfaction. Oddly enough, the research, especially for Alexander Sullivan, gave me the most pleasure. Alex lived through tumultuous times in history, and I used my author's poetic license to change names and dates of actual events to fit the timeline and plot of my story. These and other references will be explained in the order they appear in the book.

Although there is no direct reference to Angie's neighborhood as Levittown, some readers may recognize the similarity to their hometown of New York's Long Island. The demographics made it a perfect fit for Angie and her middle-class, Italian American family so I chose to model her home in many ways after the groundbreaking community.

I created The Massachusetts Hurricane of 1915 in Chapter Nine after discovering the New England Hurricane of 1938 (or The Long Island Express) during my research. On September 21, 1938, the actual hurricane made landfall on Long Island as a Category 3 and tracked north, affecting most of New England and southwestern Quebec, killing anywhere from 682 to 800 people. I needed a catastrophic event to occur involving Alex's mother in Gloucester, so I renamed the storm and moved the date up a few years. Wikipedia.org described the hurricane with enough detail to enable me to conjure up my own storm for *The Love Letter Ghost.* .

During 1905-06, Hamilton S. Corwin founded The Gas-au-Lec Machine Company. What follows is an excerpt from an article titled, "Yesterday's Technology, Ready for the Future," by Jim Motavalli, published in the New York Times on November 19, 2000.

Another curiosity was the Gas-au-Lec, produced in 1905-06 by the Vaughn Machine Company of Peabody, Mass. The company's ambitious president, Hamilton S. Corwin, thought that the public would flock to buy what his advertisements called "the simplest gasoline car in the world." The 4-cylinder, 45-horsepower car boasted an auxiliary electric motor (connected to the drive shaft) that started the car without a crank and offered extra power for reverse gear and hill climbing. Despite these innovations, the Gas-au-Lec was a failure, with no more than four cars produced.

This article was my inspiration for creating the character of Alex Sullivan's friend and business partner, Jonathan Cromwell, the Cromwell Machine Company and the Power Automobile.

Like Mac, I too found a plethora of websites when researching fountain pens. So, not to bog down the story with too much information, I made up the name of the pen and the identifying code. Any resemblance to an actual fountain pen name and code is purely coincidental. The filling instructions could be used for any fountain pen of that era. I extracted this information from richardspens.com, rosspens.com, and vintagepens.com.

Sadly, World War I has been reduced to little more than a footnote in American history. The Great War that began in 1914 introduced trench warfare and planes for combat that, combined with the Spanish Flu, affected millions before ending in late 1918. All names, dates, and events regarding that conflict are true and accurate, although I adjusted my characters' lives to fit into history. Again, Wikipedia.org proved to be a tremendous source of information.

In the conversation between Alex and Winnie's father in Chapter Eight, Mr. Armstrong mentions having met Samuel Clemens, aka Mark Twain. If Mr. Armstrong had existed, he certainly would have been invited to the dinner that was held on March 17, 1909, at The Lotus Club in New York City. Andrew Carnegie was the guest of honor with Mark Twain in attendance, paying tribute to Mr. Carnegie as a citizen and for his generosity as a philanthropist. This information was extracted from a *New York Times* article printed on March 18, 1909, found on twainquotes.com.

The Spanish Flu Pandemic of 1918 was a true occurrence in world history. Most of the details included in my story were gleaned from Wikipedia.org, PBS.org, and virus.stanford.edu websites. Although I did my best to adhere to the historical facts, there were variations between the websites. However, I did modify some dates and sequences of events to fit the timeline of the story.

Although Ernest Hemingway did serve overseas during WWI, the meeting between him and Alex on the battlefield is pure fiction. According to Wikipedia.org, Hemingway was wounded in Italy and received the Silver Medal of Military

Valor from the Italian government for dragging a wounded Italian soldier to safety despite his own injuries. To fit that incident into the timeline of *The Love Letter Ghost*, the date of that incident was changed from July 8, 1918, to sometime in October of 1918.

Acknowledgments

How I was able to author a novel is still a mystery to me. The fact that I completed a manuscript and published it is nothing short of a miracle. So, it is obvious that I didn't do it alone, and I would like to express my sincere gratitude to all those who helped to make that possible.

I'd like to thank the members of the Freedom Library Writers Group for their encouragement and guidance. Group leaders, Carol Jones and Lyn Hill were instrumental in taking this fledgling writer by the hand, helping me to nip, tuck and polish my words into a draft to be proud of. Although I had the story idea, I couldn't have achieved what I did without the group's gentle critiques and advice.

I have much love and appreciation for my friends and family. Thanks to; Kaye Viscosi and Kathy Warren who offered to read my early drafts. To my sister, Jen Cuilwik for her unwavering support and for introducing me to the late Minna Seligson, Associate Professor of Liberal Arts and Science at Briarcliffe College, who read my manuscript and offered insightful comments on the plot and characterization that improved my work. To Kathy Dobronyi, author of *Under the Wings of a Good Luck Phoenix,* and Kathy Rothenberger, editor extraordinaire, who did an excellent job of editing my manuscript. And to Jay and Lesly Ginsburg for their friendship and support. All their expert and honest opinions led to many revisions that improved *The Love Letter Ghost*. Special thanks to my brother Joe, and to my brother Pete and sister-in-law Diane for their love and valued input especially when selecting the cover design, and for their support during the years it took to bring this book to fruition. And to everyone else who ever asked me "how's the book?" Then stopped asking when life took an unfortunate turn, and writing was set aside.

High praise to Stephanie Larkin, president of Red Penguin Books, along with the rest of her professional staff who did all the heavy lifting to make this book possible. I can't thank them enough for such a positive experience. Thanks to Valentina Janek, author of *From Fired to Freedom* and the host of the *Long Island Breakfast Club Show* for introducing me to Stephanie Larkin and Red Penguin Books.

I will always be grateful to the memory of my late husband, Bob who missed me during my writing sessions behind closed doors, ate fewer home cooked meals than he preferred, but supported me in my writing endeavor nonetheless, every step of the way.

Not only is this book a miracle, but I've also experienced another, and I thank God for sending my wonderful husband, Carmine into my life. His love, guidance and encouragement were major factors in moving forward again with my manuscript to make this book a reality.

About the Author

M.E. Saladino is a free-lance writer and columnist for *Ocala's Good Life* magazine. A native New Yorker, she and her husband live in North Central Florida.